ALWAYS

RIVERHEAD BOOKS

a member of Penguin Group (USA) Inc.

New York

2007

ALWAYS

NICOLA GRIFFITH

RIVERHEAD BOOKS
Published by the Penguin Group
Penguin Group (USA) Inc., 375 Hudson Street, New York, New York 10014, USA · Penguin Group (Canada), 90 Eglinton Avenue East, Suite 700, Toronto, Ontario M4P 2Y3, Canada (a division of Pearson Penguin Canada Inc.) · Penguin Books Ltd, 80 Strand, London WC2R 0RL, England · Penguin Ireland, 25 St Stephen's Green, Dublin 2, Ireland (a division of Penguin Books Ltd) · Penguin Group (Australia), 250 Camberwell Road, Camberwell, Victoria 3124, Australia (a division of Pearson Australia Group Pty Ltd) · Penguin Books India Pvt Ltd, 11 Community Centre, Panchsheel Park, New Delhi–110 017, India · Penguin Group (NZ), 67 Apollo Drive, Rosedale, North Shore 0745, Auckland, New Zealand (a division of Pearson New Zealand Ltd) Penguin Books (South Africa) (Pty) Ltd, 24 Sturdee Avenue, Rosebank, Johannesburg 2196, South Africa

Penguin Books Ltd, Registered Offices: 80 Strand, London WC2R 0RL, England

Library of Congress Cataloging-in-Publication Data

Griffith, Nicola.
    Always / Nicola Griffith.
       p.   cm.
    ISBN 978-1-59448-935-8
       1. Torvingen, Aud (Fictitious character)—Fiction.   2. Ex-police officers—Fiction.
    3. Lesbians—Fiction.   4. Self-defense for women—Fiction.   5. Real estate investment—
    Fiction.   6. Fraud investigation—Fiction.   7. Atlanta (Ga.)—Fiction.   8. Seattle (Wash.)—
    Fiction.   I. Title.
    PS3557.R48935A49   2007   2007000908
    813'.54—dc22

Printed in the United States of America
10   9   8   7   6   5   4   3   2   1

This is a work of fiction. Names, characters, places, and incidents either are the product of the author's imagination or are used fictitiously, and any resemblance to actual persons, living or dead, businesses, companies, events, or locales is entirely coincidental.

While the author has made every effort to provide accurate telephone numbers and Internet addresses at the time of publication, neither the publisher nor the author assumes any responsibility for errors, or for changes that occur after publication. Further, the publisher does not have any control over and does not assume any responsibility for author or third-party websites or their content.

For Kelley, my queen

ALWAYS

ONE

IF YOU WALK INTO A BAR AND THERE'S A MAN WITH A KNIFE, WHAT DO YOU DO? WALK out again. If you can. In Atlanta it had been a kitchen, and a woman, and I couldn't.

It's a five-hour nonstop flight from Atlanta to Seattle. I had slept the first three hours, but I didn't want to sleep anymore. If you don't sleep, you don't dream. I pressed my forehead against the vibrating cabin window and stared down at the Rockies, visible only as winks of snow in the setting sun.

Next to me, Dornan stirred and put his guidebook facedown on his lap. He peered over my shoulder at the scenery below. His T-shirt was still very white and his eyes very blue, but his hair, just long enough to hint at waviness, was flat at the back. "Looks like Mars," he said.

I nodded. There were places there where no one had walked. Perhaps one day I would go exploring.

Dornan leaned back. "You missed dinner." It was unclear from his tone whether he thought that was good or bad.

"I can eat when we get there."

"I don't know," he said, and tapped the book on his lap. "I've been reading the tourist guide. The good restaurants mostly seem to shut at ten." Right around when we'd be landing. "There's always room service."

You can't learn much about a city from a hotel room, and I needed to hit the ground running. My mother would arrive in two days. "Let's talk about it when we get there."

Books were all well and good—I'd already read several histories, maps, and guides to Seattle since deciding on the trip—but I preferred somatic information to extra-somatic. I would know what I wanted to do when I smelled the air and tasted the water.

"So," Dornan said. "You haven't told me much about the new bloke."

I didn't say anything.

"Your new stepdad."

I looked at him.

"Well, he is, technically. So what's the story? You haven't even told me his name."

I opened my bag—once again I resented the nasty ripping sound of the Velcro flap, and missed the bag I'd given away—and pulled out the report.

"Eric Loedessoel," Dornan said, reading over my shoulder. "Wait." He pulled back. "You researched your stepdad?"

"It wasn't difficult."

"That's not . . ." He shook his head.

I leafed through the list of sources: medical bills, brokerage accounts, limousine service, phone records, grocery bills, restaurant bills, and so on. Then the data itself. There was a photograph of Loedessoel taken last year in Washington, D.C., and a photo of his new wife, dated two months ago.

She was wearing a hacking jacket and turtleneck, a riding hat tucked under her left arm. I wondered what the photo opportunity had been, and why she looked happy. She hated horses. Her hair was dark honey streaked with grey, and cut in a soft, chin-length bob. It looked all wrong; my mother had had long hair for as long as I could remember. She had gained a few pounds. She looked younger and softer.

"Thumbnail sketch," I said. "Male Caucasian, mid-fifties, five feet eleven, hundred and seventy-eight pounds, grey hair, grey-blue eyes. Born in Bergen to Norwegian parents; two sisters, one brother. Parents deceased. First year of medical school in Oslo, where he married a Danish woman, and the remaining years in Seattle, at the University of Washington. Graduated in the top third of his class. Never practiced, though." No hint as to why. "Divorced the Danish wife a few months after graduation."

"Children?"

"No."

"Thank heaven for small mercies."

My stomach squeezed. The possibility of step-siblings hadn't occurred to me. "Job in Washington, D.C., with the Norwegian trade delegation. Climbed the ladder. Directorships in several pharmaceutical and biotech companies. Financially stable. Current residence in London." Chelsea. I wondered if and when he would move into my mother's official ambassador's residence. I wondered if she still actually lived there.

I read some more. Dornan returned to staring out the window.

Loedessoel's net worth was nearly four million dollars. Well matched with my mother's assets. It would have seemed a lot to me four years ago. I started skimming. Clothes, hair, and manicure spending about what you'd expect for someone in his position. Cars: many purchases and resales. In the last three years, a Porsche Carrera, a Jaguar S-type, a Maserati, a vintage Bentley—that one had been sold after numerous high bills for replacement parts.

"He likes cars," I said.

"Lots of men do."

I skimmed the list of affiliations, memberships, and subscriptions: Mystery Guild Book of the Month Club, local wine society, the American Museum of Natural History, chamber of commerce, the local Gilbert and Sullivan Society. "He likes operetta."

"That's not exactly sinister."

"Well, no."

"But you're frowning."

"I'm trying to imagine my mother beaming fondly at a man dressed as the lord high executioner."

"Giggling behind a fan."

I stared at him.

The seat belt light went on. "Look at that," he said, and busied himself with the tray table and footrest.

WE WALKED past the tired people in baggage claim and to the man holding a sign saying Torvingen.

"I'm Aud Torvingen," I said.

He didn't bat an eye at the Norwegian pronunciation but said, "Jeff," and led us to the town car.

I fastened my seat belt and opened my window, and we pulled smoothly past the hordes waiting for taxis.

"Maybe you aren't potty after all," Dornan said, leaning back on the grey leather. He'd thought I had lost my mind when I'd first suggested FedEx-ing the luggage. Then I'd offered to pay, and suddenly it hadn't been such a bad idea.

Traffic was light. The cool air, heavy at first with jet fumes, then the scents of late cherry blossom and second-growth conifer, reminded me of Oslo last year. It had been May then, too.

The engine hummed. I'd never driven a Lincoln, but I suspected it would handle like a squashy pillow. The interior wood trim, black bird's-eye maple, was so heavily varnished it looked like plastic.

If I'd done my research correctly we were on Highway 99, which ran north and west into the city along the waterfront. I could sense the empty horizon stretching to my left, but I couldn't see or smell it; there was a steady offshore breeze and the moon was hidden behind dense cloud. In Atlanta it would be twenty degrees warmer. In Oslo, twelve degrees closer to the Arctic Circle, the sky would still be light. There would not be so many cars on the road. My mother and new stepfather would be in the United States by now, in New York, or possibly Vancouver.

From a distance the Edgewater Hotel looked like a warehouse building, but as we approached, it became clear that what had seemed to be corrugated iron was in fact massive vertical timbers. Fir, I thought. Very Scandinavian. It was just after ten-thirty when we pulled into the parking lot. "Wait," I told Jeff. "We'll be out in ten minutes."

The lobby was all exposed wood—definitely fir—and polished slate. I handed my Total Enterprises credit card to the woman behind the desk. She handed me two keys.

"They're not next to each other. I'm sorry."

"Not a problem," I said, and gave one to Dornan. "Don't unpack if it will take you longer than ten minutes."

In my room were two faxes, and a large FedEx box. I put everything on the bed and opened the window, which was less than eight feet above the water. I listened a moment; all I heard was the slap and slip of Puget Sound against the pilings driven deep into the muck of Elliott Bay. I closed the window. Being so close to the water was less than optimal, in terms of security. I took a dime from my wallet and balanced it against the glass. There were a dozen portable in-truder alerts on the market, but low-tech worked well enough.

One of my credit cards wasn't plastic but specially sharpened ceramic. I extracted it from my wallet and slit the tape on the FedEx box. The clothes were still on their hangers. I hung them in the wardrobe, and my toiletries bag above the mirror in the bathroom. I set up my laptop but didn't connect to the local network—security precautions took time—and glanced at the faxes, one from Laurence, one from Bette, both of which could wait. After a quick visual check of the room I shut the door, rattled it to make sure it was locked, and headed for the lobby.

Dornan was four minutes late. He had changed his T-shirt and put a sapphire in his right earlobe.

"Belltown," he said. "That's the only place we'll be able to get anything to eat at this time. Belltown," he said again to Jeff as we got in the car. "Somewhere called the Queen City Grill?"

"On First," Jeff said, and turned left out of the parking lot.

"First and what?" I tried to visualize the city plan, which was a confused mix of the original diagonal and later north-south grids. If you could believe the maps there was even a spot, north of here, where "First" intersected with "First."

"First and Blanchard."

Blanchard. Between Bell and Lenora. A little north and east of downtown, a little south and west of here. "Why are we heading north?" Northwest.

"If I take you south there's no cross street for a while."

"Thank you."

We turned right, heading northeast, and then right again, finally moving south and east.

"After all these years I still can't believe how early Americans eat their dinner," Dornan said, as we passed dark storefronts. "Look at that. Can you imagine a U.K. city the size of Seattle shutting down at ten?"

"No."

"It makes no sense."

It did to me. The city was full of Norwegians and Swedes who had formed the backbone of the fishing and shipping industry and a large part of the paper and lumber industry, and then settled back to work hard, live quietly, and grow. They would write back to relatives dug into their *fjell*-side *seter*s, or boiling and freezing in sod houses in the Midwest, and tell them about the good life, the teeming salmon and the miles of trees, and how it hardly ever snowed. Inevitably, the children of the brothers and sisters left behind would come for a month in summer to visit. And here I was.

AT THE Queen City Grill we were shown to one of the dozen or so booths running alongside the bar, a huge expanse of mahogany that looked as though it had been there a hundred years. It was enhanced by a double handful of the young urban gorgeous. One woman with long glossy hair and skin the color of toasted flax smiled and tipped her head back to laugh. Her companions laughed, too. She sipped her martini, and when she leaned forward, the cream silk of her dress pulled tight across her hips. Her lips left a red print on the rim of her glass.

"See anything you fancy?" Dornan said, studying the menu, which was very short and specialized in steaks and seafood with an Asian tang.

"Crab cakes look good."

The wine list turned out to be heavy on Washington and Oregon vineyards I'd encountered only in travel guides. I put it down. The woman at the bar laughed again, and the server appeared.

"What do you have on draft?"

I settled on something called Hefeweizen, Dornan ordered a kamikaze, and we asked for oysters to start. The Hefeweizen came with a wedge of lemon in it, and looked like cloudy lager. It tasted better than it looked. The oysters were cool and slippery and tasted like the beach at low tide. We focused on the food for a while.

The woman at the bar slid from her stool and stood, gathering purse and wrap.

"It's good to see your appetite returning," Dornan said. He was concentrating on squeezing the last drop from his lemon onto the oyster on his plate. I let him tip it into his mouth and swallow, then nodded at the last remaining half-shell.

"How's your appetite?"

"Let me put it this way, Torvingen. For once, I think I'd be prepared to fight you for it."

We ordered another dozen.

Two intense twenty-nothings took a seat at the bar and started arguing about whether cyberpunk owed its attitude more to Materialist philosophy or to a misguided interpretation of Descartes' interpretation of Aristotle.

"So," he said. "How are you?"

"How do you mean?"

"You know what I mean. It's been nearly a year. And then the incident with your self-defense student. And now your mother is coming. Talk to me. Tell me how you feel, what you think."

I thought Mr. Materialism was about to get lucky: Ms. Cartesian Dualism was leaning forward in the kind of unnatural pose that had been practiced in front of the mirror because someone once told her it made her throat look delicious, and holding her hand palm up while she talked, tilted towards him in a way that could be interpreted only as *Touch me.* And indeed, Mr. Materialism was beginning to stumble over the bigger words as his subconscious figured out what was going on and diverted blood from his brain to more important organs. Although Dornan's degree from Trinity was in philosophy, I doubted that's what he meant. I shook my head.

He drank off his kamikaze, sighed with pleasure while he refilled his glass from the cocktail shaker, and nodded over at the debating couple. "Did you ever argue philosophy with a girl in a bar?"

"There are easier ways."

He nodded. "Buying her a drink always worked for me. So have you tried any interesting approaches lately?"

I looked at him.

"You could at least reassure me that since, ah, well . . ." He hated to mention Julia's death. "I just don't think it's natural to be so— Look, I know how you are, what you're like. You shouldn't deprive yourself . . ."

"I haven't."

He sat back and looked expectant.

"Her name was Reece."

His expectant look didn't waver. Ever since I had let him help with the cabin in North Carolina last year he seemed to believe he deserved a window into my life. I had not yet worked out how to shut him out, or whether I wanted to.

"When I went back to the cabin last month Tammy had a party. She introduced me to Reece. We had a conversation that ended up in bed. She's a very pleasant woman. It was a very pleasant evening. I doubt I'll ever see her again."

I had needed the animal warmth of the sex, had welcomed the familiar building heat of skin on skin, the harsh breath, the shudder that starts in your bones. The terrible urge afterwards to weep until I howled had been new.

"That Tammy. Isn't she something?" It had been three months since she'd returned his ring, but his voice still throbbed with pride.

"She is." She was a piece of work. He was better off without her.

SOMEONE HAD turned on the fire in the corner of my room. The dime was undisturbed. I turned off the fire, put the dime in my pocket, and opened the window.

I read the faxes. Details from Laurence about how my Seattle real estate revenues had fallen against local benchmarks, the addresses of my local real estate manager and my cross-shipping warehouse, and a list of lease-holders of that property in the last eighteen months—far too many. Bette's fax was a detailed, itemized list of OSHA and EPA complaints leveled by person or persons unknown against either me, as the property owner, or various lessees, along with pages of definitions of various regulations, and the names of relevant people at both regulatory offices to deal with the complaints.

I turned to my laptop. The fan hummed and the hard drive chuckled as it ran its anonymizer software and automatically cleaned itself of anything but the most basic programs: no documents, no cookies, no automatic updates downloaded from the Web, no e-mails, no address book, nothing. Just an operating system unencumbered by experience or past history, lean and sure, memory constantly scoured and reset for instant, optimum efficiency. Stupid, to be jealous of a computer.

I set every firewall I could, then hunted for and matched the hotel network. I logged in to my e-mail account. Nothing.

I logged out, wiped all the cookies again, just in case, and checked my antivirus software. All my personal data was safe on the flash drive on my key ring.

It was late, according to my body clock. Nearly four in the morning.

I tapped the faxes into a neat pile and put them next to the phone on the cherry-veneered desk by the window. I'd study them carefully in the morning. On top of the pile I put my maps and two books about Seattle. Tomorrow I'd start learning this city the way I liked best, by moving through it.

I undressed and carefully laid my clothes over the back of the desk chair, easily to hand in case of emergency.

I stood naked by the open window. The water was black. Kuroshio, the Black Current, the vast ocean stream that poured past Japan and arced north, keeping the inlets of the Pacific Northwest from freezing. I could lower myself into the lightless water and slide beneath the surface, leave it all behind. Give it all away and never look back. I wish my father had left all his holdings to my mother instead. I wouldn't have to be in Seattle to deal with a real estate manager stealing me blind. I wouldn't have to meet my mother and brand-new stepfather. I wouldn't have been at leisure to teach a self-defense class.

The room felt as warm and moist as the womb. I got dressed.

ON FOOT, I could head south. I walked through the night, swinging my arms, glad that there was nothing to my right but Elliott Bay. I could feel the open water, taste salt on the breeze. I walked up and down artificially graded hillocks of grass, avoided a tree. When I ran out of park I turned left, under the Alaskan Way viaduct; I saw traces of the homeless—a burnt-out trash can, a slashed sleeping bag—but the streets and train tracks were silent.

In Atlanta at one o'clock on Thursday morning I would have had downtown to myself, but Seattle's center flickered with flashes of restless, contradictory life. As I walked down First, south of Queen City, I could have been looking at two different boulevards. On my left, the fifty-foot-tall sculpture of *The Hammering Man* banged away silently in cultural ecstasy outside the Seattle Art Museum. On my right, a man and a woman stepped into the street from the Lusty Lady, whose pink neon sign flashed cheerily, its letter board declaring VENI, VIDI, VENI. Peep shows for the classically educated.

Pioneer Square wasn't really a square but a triangle, partially cobbled, with a totem pole and a drinking fountain. The buildings were old brick and wrought ironwork, painted to match the blue-and-rust paintwork on the Tlingit totem. There had been more trees in the guidebook photos, plane trees. I couldn't think of any diseases specific to plane trees, and wondered why they been taken down. It was still a picture-perfect vision of the heart of an established city whose industrious citizens slept well—or would have been without the thump of club music, and the homeless who lay on benches or leaned against the wall in knots of two or three, not unlike the hipsters at the bar earlier. Some of them were young and some smoked, but none wore white and none of them laughed; most had more tattoos than teeth. They stopped talking as I neared. I nodded. They smelled of tobacco and old wine, like old people in hot countries, which is not how the homeless in Atlanta smell.

Guidebooks never told you everything. Seattle was another country.

SELF-DEFENSE IS NOT JUST A SKILL, IT'S A WORLDVIEW. LIKE THE SCIENTIFIC METHOD—
or religion, or motherhood, for that matter—once you accept its precepts you
see things differently. I didn't intend to tell my students this. Just as you don't
try to interest six-year-olds in natural history by discussing physiology and
adaptive evolution—but take them, instead, to a pond to watch tadpoles turn
into frogs—on the first day of class you don't tell grown women to change their
lives. You show them how to punch a bag.

I parked outside Crystal Gaze, under the only streetlight. It was a long way
from the side door. I turned off the Saab's heater and got out. 5:56 on the second Tuesday of February. My breath hung in a cloud as I zipped my jacket. The
sky was the heavy grey of unpolished pewter, shading to iron in the east. The
still dark reminded me of Mørketiden, the days of Norwegian winter when you
don't see the sun.

Crystal Gaze is Atlanta's alternative bookshop and personal wellness center,
more comfortable with chakras than choke holds. My class, the advisory board
had decided, could go ahead as long as it was in the basement space. It was a
very nice space, they said, even without a window: newly painted, new carpet,
and a room air-conditioner; big and bare, eminently suitable for physical activity. It also had its own convenient side entrance. In other words, sweaty women
reeking of the body would not trample through the main floor and disturb patrons who were browsing their way to the next level of spiritual enlightenment.
They agreed I could bring in four big mats and a punch bag and leave them for
the duration of the course.

The stairwell smelled of concrete dust. My boots echoed. There were damp
footprints on each tread, including one set of those pointy-toed, needle-heeled

shoes that look as though they would leave the wearer utterly crippled. I peered more closely. Two sets of pointy toes. Or—no, one set whose owner had walked down, then turned and taken a couple of steps back, then decided to head back down and go through with it.

Americans rarely have the same appreciation of punctuality as Norwegians, so when I opened the basement door at precisely six o'clock I was mildly surprised to find nine women already sitting on the corded blue carpet. Nine pairs of shoes were lined up neatly under the bench. Second from the right were the pointy-toed spike heels: brown fake-alligator ankle boots. Several of the women could have owned them—lots of lower-tier business clothes and careful makeup—though I'd bet on the white woman with the curly hair in a powder blue blouse with a wide silver stripe. At least she was wearing trousers, unlike the woman in the brilliant green skirt and matching jacket.

"We will begin with the closed fist," I said. "Please stand."

They gaped at me, then a stout woman with wiry grey hair and sensible workout clothes stirred, said, "Don't need names for that, I guess," and hauled herself to her feet. One woman who had been sitting in full lotus position with her palms up stood with the ease of a dancer, or perhaps a yoga practitioner, though the muscles around her eyes were tight. Another—matte black dye job, who had sat with legs spread and weight tipped back on her many-ringed hands—rose with the awkwardness of a day-old foal, just a bit too quickly to match the boredom she was trying to project. There were several obvious cases of nervous tension, including Blue Blouse; one openmouthed possible breathing difficulty, which I hoped wouldn't develop into asthma due to poor air quality; and one set of tilted shoulders that looked to be more the result of habitual bad posture than a structural deficit. On first assessment, the only possible powder keg was a white woman who jerked to her feet and kept her chin down; who didn't lift her eyes from the floor, even when the door banged open behind me.

"Oh," said the latecomer. Softball muscles played in her forearm as she shifted her gym bag from right hand to left, and through her warm-ups her quads bulged like those of a soccer player. "Sorry I'm late."

I wheeled the punch bag and frame away from the painted breeze-block wall and into the center of the room. The heavy bag swayed. I dropped the stabilizer on each leg and slapped it into place.

"This bag is filled with sand. You can't hurt it." It couldn't hurt them, either, because I'd had it fitted with a custom cover of latex over foam to protect their beginner's hands. I nodded at the middle-aged woman with the wiry hair. "Come and give it a try."

"Me?"

Basic rule of animal behavior: control the leader of the herd. For a group of women who had been together less than ten minutes, that meant the cheerful motherly one. "Stand here. Make a fist. No. Keep your thumb out of the way."

I found their ignorance difficult to believe. Dornan had tried to warn me. He had watched me thumbtack my poster to the public board in one of his cafés and shaken his head. *I don't think you know what you're letting yourself in for. Anyone could show up. Southern women with big hair, big teeth, big nails. Women with husbands and babies.*

"The thumb always goes on the outside of the fingers," I said, and raised my hand to show them. They all nodded and flexed experimental fists. I got behind the bag and steadied it against my body. "Now hit it."

The stout older woman glanced around, but didn't seem to find any hints, so she stepped up to the bag, and gave it a tentative tap. Self-consciousness, the curse of Western womanhood.

"Again, only this time, say 'Blam!'"

"Blam?"

"Like a cartoon. Pretend you're in a Saturday-morning animation: Blam! Pow! Zap! You're an invincible superhero. It's not really you hitting this bag, it's the character you're playing."

She pulled a face at her audience, moved half a pace closer to the bag, said "Blam!" like a ten-year-old boy waving a homemade lightsaber, and thumped it. The difference was audible. "Cool!"

Everyone grinned. I nodded at her to go again.

"Whap!" she said. "Zammo! Bam bam bam!" Her face got red and her hair stuck out.

"Okay. Good. Next!"

They lined up. The newcomer assaulted the bag with a flurry of ferocious punches, added a couple of elbow smashes, and finished with a "Whomp, whomp, you asshole!"

"Next."

The yoga woman, light but competent, followed by Dye Job who shrieked "Fuck!" when her fingers got mashed between bag and ring metal, a lesson she wouldn't forget in a hurry. Blue Blouse and Green Skirt surreptitiously removed rings and pocketed them. Blue Blouse was clearly embarrassed but hit the bag anyway, after a fashion. Then, because it was her turn and it was expected of her, Carpet Starer came to the bag, managed "Bang, bang," in a tight whisper, and poked it with her knuckles. I nodded and called "Next!" because I had seen so many women like her—in shelters, in hospital emergency rooms, bleeding bravely in their homes—and it was important not to let her know I was paying attention. Next was Green Skirt, who unselfconsciously hitched up her skirt, brushed back her bangs, and flipped her hair over her shoulders before beginning. Then Sloping Shoulders, then Breathing Difficulty.

Now that everyone had had a go, I made the line hustle.

"Run!" I said. "Faster. Hit it three times. And again. Experiment: stand closer, try the other hand, point the other leg forward. Shout when you hit it. Hit it five times. Don't think. Do. And run. And again." The air began to hum, and muscles plump, and just before the room kindled I clapped my hands and said, "Enough. Please sit." They did, in an obliging circle, some smiling, and Blue Blouse scooted to her left with an ingratiating bob of her head—teacher's pet—to make a space. I took it.

"I am Aud Torvingen. Aud, rhymes with crowd." They waited for more, but I wasn't interested in proving I was qualified to teach them, and the name of the class, Introduction to Women's Self-Defense, was self-explanatory. I nodded to Blue Blouse that it was her turn. She told us she was Jennifer, and we went round the circle briskly: Pauletta, with the green skirt and a gold cross. Suze, the latecomer. Katherine, the bad posture. Sandra, the carpet starer. Kim, with long red nails. Therese, the yoga woman. Christie, the dye job. Tonya, the breathing difficulty with carefully straightened hair. Janine, the middle-aged woman, "Or Nina, I don't mind which."

"Pick one," I said.

"Nina, then."

"Fine." I waited a moment. "Self-defense has only one goal: to survive."

"And kick butt!" said Nina.

"No." They blinked. "One goal, to survive."

"Wait a second," Suze said, "just hold on." She leaned forward. "You're saying we can't fight?"

"I'm saying that from a self-defense perspective, the only goal is to survive. Fighting is neither here nor there." Wrinkled brows. The flick-flick-flick of Kim's long red nails, one by one, against her thumb. "Of course, once you've ensured your survival, kicking someone to death is an option."

Therese lifted her shoulders, momentarily losing that Zen poise as nasty reality intruded on her nice, clean middle-class understanding.

Suze was still frowning. "So are you saying we should or shouldn't fight?"

"You're grown-ups. Make your own choices. My job is to show you the basic tools and techniques of self-defense: how to stay out of trouble, how to recognize it if it finds you anyway, how to deal with it using what's available—whether that means words, or body weapons like elbows and teeth, or found objects."

Therese probably thought of found objects as sea-etched glass and drift-wood from Jekyll Island. For Kim it might be a lottery ticket. Sandra, now, she would understand the concept: the heavy-buckled belt he pulls from his pants, the quart bottle of Gatorade he's drinking from when she foolishly mentions she forgot to buy the mushrooms, the broom handle brandished like a quarter-staff when he sees a footprint on the kitchen floor.

"What you do with those tools is up to you. I can tell you what I might do in any given situation, or at least give you my best guess, but that doesn't mean you should do the same."

Pauletta touched her crucifix lightly. "So, okay, what would you do if you walk into a bar and there's a guy with a knife?"

"Walk out again."

"That's it?"

"It's one option. Prevention is better than cure."

"But what if he's threatening someone?" Suze asked.

"This isn't Bodyguarding for Beginners or Heroism 101."

"So you'd let him cut some girl, just walk out and leave her?" Pauletta.

"Depends." It always depends.

"On what?" Suze, leaning forward again.

"Everything. How I'm feeling that day, what city I'm in—even what part of town in that city. What the assailant looks like, and the potential victim. The number of exits. The general mood of the bar." They were not getting it. *Women with babies...* "Anyone here have kids?" Nods from Therese, Nina, Sandra, and Kim. "What would you do if your child came home from school crying?"

"Oh," said Therese after a moment.

"Right," said Kim, nodding, "it depends."

"I don't get it," Suze said.

Therese said, "If my twins come home at the end of the day it means one thing, if it's at eleven in the morning it means something else—"

"If Carlotta's crying because some girl stuck gum in her hair I have to do different things than if it's because her teacher died in a car crash," Kim said.

"But you always comfort them, first," Nina said. "You make sure they're safe—"

"And that they feel safe," Kim said.

"Yes," said Therese. "And you always try to find out what happened, make sure it doesn't happen again."

"Basic principles," Nina said. They smiled at each other, pleased.

Suze frowned and opened her mouth. I forestalled her. "Basic principles. That's what I can give you. Any mother will tell you that if you take a favorite toy from a two-year-old he will scream. I can tell you that if you kick the leg with enough force at a particular angle you will detach the kneecap."

Suze brightened. "So are you going to show us that kneecap thing now or what?"

I studied her a moment. I nodded at her quads. "You already know how to kick things. That's not why you're here. One of the things you need to learn is who to kick, and when." I looked around the circle: different ages, races, classes. Different ways of looking at the world. "When do you hit someone?"

"Depends," Nina said. Fast learner.

"Yes. On what?"

They all looked hard at the carpet, like teenagers desperate not to be called on in class.

"Everything?" Christie said.

I smiled. "Yes. Let's go back to what Pauletta said earlier. Walking into a bar . . ."

Every student learns at school how to fake attention. I watched it start to happen now.

"Or a supermarket at night. Or an empty church." Most of them came back. "How do you approach it? What do you do? What do you look for?"

"I walk in like, Don't fuck with me!" Suze said.

No one said anything.

"Not looking like a victim is a good first step. But it takes a lot of effort to project aggression all the time." I paused, trying to think of a metaphor that might mean something to all of them, something American. "You've all seen old westerns. The gunslinger steps through the saloon doors and stops." Nods. "That is exactly what not to do."

If gunslingers really had paused in the saloon doorway, conveniently backlit by the noonday sun and blind in the sudden interior gloom, their days would have been short. The unassuming ones would have lived longest, the ones who slipped through the swinging doors behind someone else, slid along a side wall, and looked over the room before ghosting up to the bar and ordering what everyone else was drinking. By the time the bad guys in the black hats at the card table had realized he was there, he would have known who was the ringer with the derringer in his pocket, where the exits were, and whether the gang leader might be delayed on his draw by the necessity of first dumping the pretty saloon girl from his lap.

"Imagine you're walking into—Tonya, pick a place."

"Kroger."

"What time, what day?"

"A weeknight, after work, but late, maybe nine o'clock."

"So it's dark outside and bright inside. First thing: park near the entrance, under a light. Don't unlock your door until you've looked around. Keep your eyes open and your hands free. If you have to turn a corner on the way to the door, take it wide."

"Why?" Therese said.

It took me a moment to realize she was serious, she really didn't know why. I had planned this lesson meticulously: an orderly progression of building blocks. We had already wandered off the road, out of necessity, and it was clear that sticking to the plan would be like digging a foundation in sand. I let it go. "Because then you'll see anyone on the other side before they see you." Therese nodded thoughtfully, filing away the information for further reflection. Suze said, "Huh," but quietly. Jennifer looked worried. "So now you walk into the supermarket. It's bright. What do you do?"

"Wait for your eyes to adjust," Kim said confidently.

Like a sun-struck calf waiting for the hammer. "It would be best to keep moving. Head towards the grocery carts or baskets, and as you do, sweep the place visually. See them before they see you. You'll grasp things instantly that you don't consciously know you know. Your subconscious works a lot faster than your conscious mind. So let it do the preliminary work. Swing your gaze slowly from one side of the aisles to the other. If something or someone snags your attention, you can hang a mental tag on it to come back to later. That sweep should take no more than three or four seconds. Whatever you see, don't stop." No point spotting a guy in a black hat minding his own business at the other end of the bar if there's some grinning idiot right next to you swinging an axe. "The trick is to not draw anyone's attention until you've completed the sweep."

"So what if there is a dangerous person?" Jennifer, for whom Kroger was suddenly looking like a jungle.

"Hey, I know the answer to that one," Nina said. "Leave, right?"

I nodded.

Jennifer was not convinced. "But what if they follow you?"

"Then you get in your close-by, well-lit car and drive away."

"But what if you trip or something and he catches you first?"

Suze stirred restlessly. "Then you fucking hit him."

"Right," I said to the group as a whole. "So let's go back to the fist." I stood and motioned for them to do likewise.

I lined them up, facing me, and held my right hand up, showing them how to make a fist again while I walked along the line, rearranging fingers and thumbs. "Think of your fist as the point of a spear. The forearm is the spear shaft. It has to be strong and straight, no weakness at the wrist. The wrist is where you want all your tension. Good. There are seven basic points to remember when hitting or kicking." There could just as easily have been six or eight, but human brains find sevens and threes significant. "One, strike from a firm base. The firmer the better, because, two, most of your power comes from the torque generated by your hips. Stand with both feet firmly planted and swivel your hips as you punch—throw that spear forward, don't push it. You can't get good movement from a bad base. Three, strike on the out breath, preferably with a good loud yell."

"Blam?" said Nina.

"Whatever you like."

"What do you yell?"

"Probably depends," Suze said to Christie, who giggled.

"Four, strike hard and fast. Power comes more from speed than weight." More strictly, the greater the mass and acceleration, the greater the force. "Five, strike right through the target. There's no point stopping on the surface. Six, you almost always need to be closer to the target than you think. Seven, be prepared to strike more than once. Let's try it. Suze, hold the bag. Jennifer, you're up."

It was tempting, watching them flail at the bag one by one, to stop them, to show them how it's really done, but although I would have enjoyed the whip of power, the hard ram of bone on compact sand, it wouldn't help. They would try to imitate my stance, my noise, my expression; they would try to learn the lessons I had learnt, not their own.

They watched each other, subconsciously took note of what seemed to work: when Suze took her weight on her back leg, Jennifer, who was holding the bag, moved back a good inch; when Suze stepped into the punch, Jennifer moved five inches. When Nina tapped the bag, then moved closer by half a step and walloped it, they noticed. Gradually, they adjusted their stances, their speed, their noise, feeling out what worked for them and what didn't. I wanted them to learn something unique to them, that came from them, not an artificial overlay that would evaporate in the first flash of fear adrenaline if they were ever threatened.

"Kim," I said, the second time she hit the bag, "you can hit it harder than that."

"I can't." She unfolded her fingers and held out her hand, showing me the four perfect crescent-moons on her palm.

"You'll have a hard time with some of the finger strikes, too."

"What can I do?"

"Cut your nails."

"I been growing them two years!"

"Your choice."

She wasn't the only one who gave me the withering look so many southern women—of any age, or race, or social standing—learn before puberty: a combination of scorn and the deep existential fear of being the one to stand out in a crowd and risk being pecked to pieces. They seemed surprised when I didn't wilt.

By now, Suze—and Christie, copying her—were whaling satisfactorily on the bag. Therese had become efficient, and Pauletta and Nina were encouraging each other with whoops and catcalls. In a pinch, all five of them might throw a punch. The other half of the class—Katherine and Tonya, for whom the idea of punching anything induced agonizing embarrassment, or at least blushes and giggles, Jennifer, who looked away whenever she sidled up to the bag to hit it, and Sandra, who could not seem to make a sound—would probably never hit anyone with their fist even if their lives depended upon it.

I clapped my hands. "Some of you will find punching easy—fun, even. Practice when you can: at home, at work, in the garden. Some of you will find that punching doesn't suit you; don't worry about it; we'll find something that will. Punching a person, though, isn't the same as hitting a bag. Suze, where would you punch an attacker?"

"Right in the fucking nose."

I nodded. "Noses are full of nerve endings; even a comparatively weak blow will cause pain and tearing. A stronger blow will break the nose. One problem, though."

"Yeah?"

"Step in front of me. Imagine you're going to hit me in the nose." Suze was about five-seven, five inches shorter than me. "You need to be closer." Clearly she had never hit anyone before.

She moved in another six inches. We were standing almost belly to belly.

"Now, in slow motion, throw the punch." As her fist neared my nose I said, "Freeze there." She stopped with her arm fully extended, at an upward angle of about forty degrees. I turned to the rest of the class. "She has to hit up as well as out, which reduces both power and accuracy. A fist strike to the nose of a standing opponent is not efficient when they're taller than you."

"What about his chin?" Jennifer said.

"Nearly as high up, and very hard on the knuckles. Never hit bone with bone unless you have to." How did people survive long enough to reach adulthood without knowing these things?

"So knock him to his knees, then hit him," Nina said, looking around for laughs.

"Fine. But how? Suze, you can put your arm down."

"Solar plexus," Therese said. Not *gut* or *belly* but *solar plexus.* Lots of time with a massage therapist, personal trainer, or individual yoga instruction.

"Good. Come out here and show me. Slow motion, like Suze." She threw a slow, tidy punch targeted one inch below my xiphoid process. "Freeze it there." I turned to the rest of the class. "See how she's thrown the punch beyond the skin so that the fist would end up buried to the wrist? Assuming your assailant doesn't have abs of steel, that would put them down for at least a minute."

"One minute?" Pauletta said. "You mean like sixty seconds? That's it?"

"Kick him in the nuts," Tonya said, then blushed. Half the class hooted.

"Tonya's on the right track. If you want a downed opponent to stay down, a kick's probably the best choice. All right, a volunteer to pretend to be the attacker Therese has just put on the ground and Tonya's about to kick to death."

I wasn't a bit surprised when Tonya looked at Katherine, who stepped forward. Always easier to kick the one you know, however slightly.

"On the floor. Curl up as though you've just been hit in the stomach—no, tighter. Where would your hands be? Right, curled around yourself. Now, think: you can't breathe, so what would you be trying to do?" She struggled in mock weakness to sit up. "Good." And it was. In my rookie police classes, the women had always been better at role-playing than the men. I made another mental note, to exploit that. "Good," I said again. "Okay. Stay like that." I turned to Tonya. "What could you kick?"

Tonya circled the reclining figure dubiously.

"Huh," Pauletta said, "she's sitting on her balls."

A few sniggers at that. "Tonya?"

More circling.

Suze couldn't stand it anymore. "In the face, right in the fucking face!"

"That would work," I said. Tonya was no more likely to be able to kick a person in the face than punch them. "Anything else?"

"Lower ribs," Therese said.

"Good, yes. The floating ribs are easily detached, from front, back or side. Anything else?"

"His spine," Nina said unexpectedly. "Circle round and get his spine."

"Or the back of his head," Kim added.

"Or you could try a combination of spine and head: kick the place where the back of the neck meets the skull."

Tonya liked that idea much better: he wouldn't be watching her kick him. She stopped behind Katherine and took a deep breath.

"Slow motion," I reminded her.

She tried. She would have missed by a couple of inches, she nearly fell over, and she blushed afterwards, but that didn't matter: she did it, and she didn't giggle.

"You can get up now," I said to Katherine. In the next class I'd show them how to break someone's spine even with bare feet, but right now I didn't want them getting locked into one type of body weapon. Beginnings are delicate times. "Now we'll move on to the fingertip."

"Pretty anticlimactic," Nina said.

"It's certainly a different kind of tool," I said. "Its target—its job, if you like—is different, too. Smaller, more vulnerable, like the fingertip itself. Think of the soft places: the eye, the hollow of the throat, the mouth."

"The mouth?"

"Are you willing to be a guinea pig?" She lifted her hands, as if to say, How bad could it be? I crossed to her side in one stride, hooked two fingers into her mouth along the cheek, and stepped past her so that she arched back on her heels and my hand was on my shoulder as though carrying a sack.

"Jesus," someone said.

Nina was wide-eyed and struggling and would have fallen, helpless, if I wasn't supporting her against my back. "I won't let you fall," I said. "Are you all right with this?" She swallowed—her whole face moved—but nodded gamely. "From here I can throw her sideways, backwards, or rip half her face off. Not everything is about hitting." I turned, eased her upright, and took my fingers out. "Thank you." I walked to the bench and removed a packet of handiwipes from my jacket pocket.

She flexed her face a few times while I cleaned my hand. "That was . . . It felt so wrong."

It was an important lesson: shock, the breaking of the social compact, was as difficult to deal with as being hit in the face with a shovel. But we'd go back to that another day.

"You could've bit her," Pauletta said to Nina.

"I could not, not the place she had her fingers. Here, open your mouth—"

"Nah-ah."

"Do it your own self, then," Nina said, and for the next thirty seconds they all hooked their mouths with their fingers, like suicidal fish, all except Jennifer, who said loudly, "That's disgusting!" and Therese, who, when she saw me noting her lack of participation, merely raised her eyebrows and held her hands out as if to say *Not unless I wash them first*, and shook her head. I nodded. I wouldn't put my hands in my mouth without washing them, either.

"What else?" said Suze. "How do you get the eyes?"

"Like this," Christie said, "ha!" and did an uncoordinated imitation of Bruce Lee doing *bui tze,* the shooting fingers.

"You could," I said, "but it's hard to be accurate with that move." And if she missed, she'd break her fingers. "There's an easier way. All of you: point your index finger at me."

"Left or right?" Katherine.

"Whichever you'd use to point at something. Now bend it down a little. Tuck the tip of your thumb underneath your index finger's middle joint. Keep your finger and thumb joined together like that and pretend to tap on someone's window with it. Put some play in the wrist, whip it back and forth—like Jennifer—so your hand looks a bit like a chicken pecking at something."

They all had it.

"Now peck the center of your palm. Go gently."

They did, over and over.

"Now imagine what that would do to an eyeball."

"Like popping gum," Kim said admiringly.

"Eeeuw." Jennifer flung both hands away from her. "I couldn't do that!"

"Anyone else?"

"I'm not sure," Therese said, troubled.

"I could do it, no problem," said Suze. "Yeah."

I considered them. "Self-defense isn't magic," I said. "In any kind of real fight, unless you cold-cock someone from behind with a pipe, you will get hurt. No matter how good you are, things go wrong. Adjust to that now: nothing goes to plan, ever. You'll get hurt, and you'll have to hurt them. But you mend. And what happens to them isn't your problem."

All rather disingenuous, of course, given the demographics of attacks against women, but at the beginning it's important to keep things simple and not scare them to death.

"In the next class we're going to role-play a little. We'll learn how attackers think and what they look for, and what you can do about that. Meanwhile, I'd like you to do something for me before the next class. Make a list of all the reasons you wanted to learn self-defense in the first place. All the things you or your mother or your friends worry about. Put them in a column. In the column next to them put what you'd be willing to do to your attacker to stop it.

So, for example, decide if you would rather be raped than feel the rapist's eyeball burst all over your hand. Decide if you would rather blow someone's head off with a twelve-gauge shotgun rather than let them pinch your backside. Decide whether you'd be willing to let a teenager torture your cat instead of dislocating her shoulder, whatever. It won't be easy. But think about it as clearly and fully as possible, and decide."

T W O

I WOKE EARLY, STILL ON ATLANTA TIME, SHOWERED, REREAD BETTE'S FAX, SAW HER note at the end, and called. I was shunted straight to her voice mail, which surprised me. Bette was almost always at work. It's how I imagine her: behind her big teak desk, lizard brown and stick thin, chin wattles hidden by pearls, her Prada and Chanel suits always two years out of date. Seven years ago she had looked sixty-five; she still did. I dialed her home number and she picked up on the first ring.

"Aud? Well, hell, somebody call Ripley's. You did as I asked for a change." Her incongruously lush, Lauren Bacall voice was always startling. "You signed those papers I gave you last week?"

"No."

"Why not?"

"I haven't decided."

"I spent a hell of a lot of your money making those adoption papers watertight. Sign or not, you're getting a bill."

I ignored that. Laurence had probably paid her already.

"Well, you talked to OSHA yet?"

"I haven't even had breakfast yet."

Silence, one of her go-for-broke silences. I knew what was coming.

"So. When you going to get around to telling me about that envelope from Norway?"

"Bette . . ."

"Now don't 'Bette' me, not this time. I didn't trouble you with it last year because your friend just died. I didn't trouble you with it when you came in for your year-end taxes because you still looked thin and peaky. I didn't even trouble you with it last month, when you were here to talk about your will and power-of-this and power-of-that, because of that mess with your student. But, look, sweetie, it's been a year—"

"Not quite." Not until the seventeenth.

"—you're looking good again, and I need to know just what it is I'm holding in my safe. It smells bad, for one thing."

The day I had written that letter, had bled all over the envelope, Julia had still been alive. Twelve hours earlier she had sat on my lap in her blue dress . . . Or had it been grey? And I couldn't remember how she'd worn her hair.

I heard the faint tick-tick that meant Bette was fiddling with her big clasp earrings, which also meant she was frowning.

"It was a kind of insurance. I don't need it anymore." Most of the people named in the letter were now dead.

DORNAN AND I ate breakfast in the hotel's huge dining room cantilevered out over Elliott Bay. There wasn't much to see; the bay was draped in low cloud and fine rain like mist. I ate bacon and eggs and sausage. Dornan, tourist book on one side and maps on the other, crunched happily on toast. His fireplace, he said, had a remote control, and someone had thoughtfully provided a teddy bear. "Of course, I didn't find it until I crawled under the covers, when I got the fright of my life." I added a little salt to my eggs. "Do you have a bear?"

"I have little rubber ducks in my shower."

"I went for a walk this morning. It's been a while since I've seen a proper morning. Bless the time difference. Did you know there's a nice park near here? And dozens upon dozens of little espresso carts selling latte and Frappuccino—Frappuccino in this weather."

It would be in the high sixties today, about twenty degrees cooler than in Atlanta. I ate some more sausage.

"What do you want to do? It's not the sort of day to play tourist in the outdoors," he said.

He had lived most of his life in summers like this, in Dublin, and I had grown up in Norway and England. But I'd been in Atlanta since I was eighteen, and Dornan only a few years less. Sometimes the body acclimatizes so thoroughly that we forget things have ever been different.

"I have some business. We could meet for dinner. You?"

"I consulted the very nice concierge, who tells me that once you're downtown you can ride the buses for free." Free was a magic word for Dornan. "I thought that if I might persuade you to drop me somewhere I'd spend the day doing my research: eating and drinking and absorbing whatever it is that makes Seattle . . . well, whatever it is."

The name of the very nice concierge turned out to be Pascalle, and after breakfast she told me that, yes, the Audi A8L Quattro I had ordered had arrived twenty minutes earlier, and here were the keys.

THE AUDI felt like a banker's car: beautifully machined, competent but not compassionate, giving the driver a sense of admiration but not involvement. The six-speed transmission had very sensitive shift-mapping, matching revs on the downshifts, moving for an instant to neutral and selecting the lowest gear. It was almost as seamless as a manual transmission. I switched briefly to the hybrid manu-matic, then switched back. Too fussy. So was the MMI, the multimedia interface. I turned off the navigation and turned on the radio. Rain spattered the windshield and was automatically wiped away. I rolled up all the windows except the one on the driver's side.

THE OCCUPATIONAL Safety and Health Administration deals mainly with employers, the leaseholders rather than owners of any particular piece of real estate. The offices of Region Ten, OSHA, were on Third Avenue. The lobby was the kind one would expect of an office building in any big city, hard floors, steel-doored elevators, people carrying briefcases. But every other person walking across the echoing space carried a go cup, and business attire was casual, Eddie Bauer slacks speckled with rain. Many, I guessed, had used public transport and then walked. In my Armani suit I cut through the crowd like a hammerhead among trout.

The OSHA suite was on the seventh floor. I lied to a perfectly nice man called Michael Zhao, expressing extreme concern for my cross-shipping facility on Diagonal Avenue South, in the Duwamish district, professing an overwhelming affinity for statistics, and asked for CFR citation and OMB control numbers regarding intermodal containers, confined and enclosed spaces, conveyors, docks and loading docks. I smiled winsomely and asked if he'd be willing to let me take a peek at the records for my place, and had he any experience himself of walk-through inspections? He talked happily for two hours.

The EPA, on Sixth, was another matter. It was a much bigger operation, for one thing. The woman I eventually found my way to was about fifty with faded red hair and shoulders that slumped more from weariness than habitual bad posture. Her nameplate read Antonia Merrill. I nodded sympathetically at the empty cubicles around her and said, "It looks as though this year's budget cuts are hitting you hard. I'm hoping I can help you with at least part of your workload."

KARENNA BEAUCHAMPS CORNING, my local property manager, had an office suite on the twenty-third floor of Two Union Square. The door to Corning's suite was frosted glass, the handle substantial. The young man at the front desk looked up when I walked in.

"Good morning?" he said, not sounding too sure. Perhaps it was because I wasn't carrying a briefcase. He glanced at his appointment book.

"Which is Ms. Corning's office?"

"It's the first on the l— That is, is she expecting you?"

"No, but I doubt I'll take more than an hour of her time. If she has any other appointments, it would be best to cancel them. I take my coffee with cream, no sugar." He paled before he flushed.

The door to Corning's office was solid-framed oak. She looked up from her keyboard, and then past me. "Where's Gary?"

"At the front desk." I shut the door and took a seat opposite. She frowned. "Is he all right?"

"My name is Aud Torvingen. Of Total Enterprises."

Her frown flickered, then deliberately eased into a smile that was just a touch quizzical. It was nicely done. "Ms. Torvingen. I'm surprised, of course, but . . ."

She waited for me to apologize for the inconvenience. "Diagonal Avenue South," I said. "Revenue from my property there is sixty percent below that of comparable properties."

She smiled. "It does sound bad, doesn't it? But Seattle has been hit harder than many cities by the recent slowdowns. The last two years have been hard on the import and export of goods in particular, which will of course have a great impact on cross-shipping facilities." My silence seemed to encourage her. "In addition, I'm afraid your property has suffered by comparison with the recent upgrades undertaken by most of your competitors. You may recall that I recommended we follow suit some time ago. As it is, we had to let it on a short-term lease to a movie production company."

She held her up her hand, as though I were about to interrupt her.

"But, you're probably thinking, there's been no shortage of tenants. And that's true. But while it was certainly the case ten years ago that a company that signed a lease would have been a sure thing, times change. Productivity is the key in this business, as in many others, of course, and companies will spend a great deal to abandon a seemingly profitable position if they can increase their long-term productivity by breaking a lease and moving to new premises. Particularly if there's been trouble with regulatory agencies." She smiled and picked up the phone. "Would you like some coffee?"

"Does that usually work?"

She stopped, finger an inch above the intercom button. "Excuse me?"

"The smile and the patter, does it usually work?" There was a tap at the door and Gary came in. The spoon on the saucer rattled a little as he put the coffee on the desk. He left without saying a word and I realized I hadn't thanked him.

"I'm sorry?" Corning said, staring at the gently steaming cup.

"I'm not particularly interested in an apology. You're fired. I have already instructed my attorney to that effect." I stirred and sipped. Just the right amount of cream. "However, I would like to know why you have let one of your valued clients lose money hand over fist for more than eighteen months. Or perhaps I'm not the only one?"

Her eyelids swelled slightly. "It is not within my power to control calls to OSHA and the EPA."

"You've been in this business for a long time and know everyone in the relevant local bureaucracies—city, county, state, and federal. It is within your power to mediate with those agencies. It is within your power to apprise me of developments. It is within your power to negotiate with the leaseholders towards a satisfactory outcome."

"The regulations—"

"Don't matter much, as you know. If they did, the relevant agencies would have prevented you from leasing the facility anew each time and taking your percentage."

"If you're suggesting—"

"What I want from you is a full and frank explanation of the situation and I'd like it by Monday. Do you think that's possible?"

"The situation is extremely—"

"Do you think that's possible?"

"I don't know."

"I can of course find out for myself, though in trying to duplicate what you already know I might inadvertently dig up all kinds of information you would rather keep private, and which I would have no compunction in turning over to the authorities. Take a minute to think it over while I finish this excellent coffee." I sipped while she wrestled with whatever conscience she had left.

"It's possible."

"I'm delighted to hear it." I stood. "Monday. Nine o'clock sharp."

Walking down Third Avenue to the car, I passed a chocolate boutique. I stopped and ordered a dozen truffles which I sent, along with an apology for my rudeness and thanks for the coffee, to Gary.

NEXT ON my list was the Fairmont Olympic Hotel, where my mother and her new husband would be staying. The hotel was set back a good twenty yards from the street behind a U-shaped driveway. Even on a sunny day the huge building would keep the doorway in shade.

The events manager was in his early twenties and a zealot. He declared he would show me around personally, and proceeded to do so, leaving no function room unturned, beginning with the ballroom, "which, should you choose to celebrate your special day with us, is as you see more than adequate to accommodate a wedding party of up to three hundred." From there we admired the "sweeping staircase, perfect for those unforgettable moments." He actually clasped his hands to his chest. He regurgitated the publicity brochures while I noted guest and staff exits, elevator and stair distance, and window placement. He did pause in his flow when I insisted on sitting at four different tables in the formal Georgian Room, "just to get the feel of the place." I found two tables that gave a view of all entrances and exits. The tiny private dining area, "The Petite, for more intimate dining," gave me a few concerns, but Shuckers, the pub-like oyster bar, was easy enough to parse. Then it was on to the lounges, the Terrace, and the Garden, "winner for three years in a row of the Seattle Best Martini Award, a light and airy atrium featuring innovative finger foods, an assortment of cocktails, and jazz from nine till one a.m." Perhaps in the evening, with the right lighting and a band to disguise the echo, it would feel less like a grandiose greenhouse.

When he had finished his tour he gave me a dazzling smile and asked if I wanted to step into his office to look over rates and sample menus. I nodded vaguely and said I'd think about it and, oh, was that the time?

I had no idea why my mother had chosen such a place to stay. The rooms themselves were gracefully proportioned, with high ceilings and huge windows, but the fussy chandeliers and potted plants, the ornate balustrades and striped-silk upholstery would have led to lifted eyebrows and a comment about elegance and simplicity from the Else Torvingen I had grown up with. The idea of her playing Yum-Yum began to seem not so far-fetched.

BY MIDAFTERNOON, as I drove south on the curving Alaskan Way viaduct towards my warehouse, the low grey overcast and misty rain had been replaced by blue sky and puffy white clouds. The city was laid out on my left: the post-pomo industrial skeleton of Safeco Field, glittering office towers, stepped condominiums with rooftop gardens, and a massive neon goddess sign that turned out to be the Starbucks logo, serene under the light, luscious air. On my right, Puget Sound glittered in the sunshine, making even the container ships and huge orange cranes along the wharves look mischievous and elfin, a good-humored joke that lay lightly on the earth. The traffic was heavy but astonishingly well behaved; vehicles stayed in their lanes and signaled when they turned, and the drivers kept their free hands on their oversize go cups rather than their horns. I listened to KUOW, the local NPR station, with half my attention, and looked for the right exit.

Two miles south of the city center Highway 99 returned to ground level and the view was of oil-streaked concrete aprons and rusting shipping containers. My exit led through a series of yards and warehouses and rail spurs, the clanging heart of a working port. The streets were named after states and Native American peoples: Colorado Avenue, Duwamish, South Nevada, Snoqualmie.

I parked outside a corrugated steel warehouse. At some point it had been painted pale blue, but now it was mostly grey and rusty orange. The docking gates down the side were shuttered. Instead of semis in the parking lot, there were two trailers with Hippoworks Productions blazoned on the sides, a couple of vans, and an assortment of SUVs, all sparkling with sunlit raindrops. This was all mine, even the puddles on the worn asphalt, gleaming with oil rainbows, but it didn't feel like mine, and I didn't really want it. I'd never wanted it. Once I'd sorted out the problems, I'd sell.

NO ONE checked my ID, no one even noticed as I stepped through the open rolling doors of my warehouse. I stood for a moment in the shadows by the right-hand wall.

I had thought that stepping onto a film set would be like being dropped inside a manic depressive's head: periods of frantic activity punctuated by stressful, motionless silence as cameras rolled, followed by people rushing around setting up the next scene, with perhaps the occasional diva- or director-style tantrum to relieve the tedium. Here, the atmosphere reminded me of watching a road crew set up in an arena on the sixtieth stop in a world tour, or riggers raising the traveling circus's big top: purposeful and brisk, with just the hint of a swagger, experts saying with their bodies and their competence, This is our world.

Forty or so people did not come close to filling the space, which was bigger than I'd expected, and more than fifty feet high in the center. In the far left corner, carpenters sawed and hammered; in another, two middle-aged men with paint-spattered clothes said something to a woman in a white coat at a makeshift counter, who was brushing back her mid-blond hair with her wrist. I hung a tag on the woman. A man and woman were walking with loaded plates over to a woman who presided over what looked like piles of Goodwill clothes. One man jumped off a platform about fifteen feet high onto an inflated bag that made a gassy whoosh, and then rolled off and started climbing back up to the platform while air compressors thumped. At the far end, in a blaze of lights, about two dozen people crouched behind cameras and cranes and dollies—they seemed to have adapted some of the decades-old rail tracks inset in the floor—or paced out marks, while a worried-looking man with glasses checked and rechecked snaking cables and a control board. Two men were lifting something from a box and onto the pile of old clothes. I hung a tag on them, too. There were monitor screens everywhere, even by the entrance and food counter; people glanced at them reflexively every so often. Something squawked over my head: a speaker on a makeshift shelf nailed to a joist. No one yelled Lights! or Camera! or Action!

I went back to the two men. One of them, slim and cocky as a flamenco dancer, had turned to say something to a woman dismantling an arc light, but the other was looking in my direction, and it was immediately clear why my subconscious had told me he didn't fit. He had dark hair and a bony face—the kind of face teenage boys develop during their first major growth spurt. I doubted he was even sixteen, far too young to be on a film set. An anomaly, but not a danger.

The woman in the white coat was the caterer. She said something to the two men with the paint-spattered clothes that made them laugh, then pointed with a big knife to a platter of sandwiches, and went back to chopping. Perhaps it was the big knife that had flagged my attention. It shouldn't have. My subconscious should have put the knife and the coat and the food together and given me the green light. I watched a little longer, but she just kept chopping, and she chopped like a caterer. No threat there.

Now people began to glance at me: quick flicking looks. Perhaps it was the suit. But they were obviously used to strangers. No one came over to find out who I was.

After a while, a pattern emerged: the woman with the heap of clothes was sorting through them, hanging some on the racks behind her, laying some on the table, dropping others in a series of cardboard boxes. The costumer. The worried man with the glasses was some kind of technical coordinator. I couldn't tell who was the director or the producer or cinematographer, but every now and again someone would walk over to a man who sat to one side of the soundstage with a clipboard and pen that glinted gold. He also wore glasses, and the self-conscious frown I'd seen people adopt when they feel uncertain but want to look authoritative. In half a dozen places there were easels with placards that declared: FERAL: A FINKEL AND RUSEN PRODUCTION. Underneath, in hand lettering: LADYHAWKE MEETS DARK ANGEL! Everyone wore jeans or khakis or cutoffs. Several were very young, too young to drink, but only the one I'd tagged earlier was still obviously school age. No one looked remotely like a star.

Judging by the body language on the soundstage—moments of stillness, tightened jaws, short nods—it looked as though there were two sets of opinion about something. Before it could be resolved, a large truck pulled up outside, followed by another. There was a slamming of cab doors and the rattle of a tailgate, then the beep-beep-beep of a large vehicle backing up slowly.

A handful of people detached themselves from their tasks and headed my way, just as three people came in, two men and a woman with short, glossy hair, each pushing and pulling two loaded wardrobe rails, and laughing. Someone on the soundstage started shouting names, and half a dozen more people left what they were doing and made for the exit. Three or four more took the opportunity to head for the food counter and get some coffee. I wandered a little closer.

A few more of those flicking glances but they didn't interrupt their conversation. There was a massive coffee urn and a commercial espresso maker. Most people seemed to prefer the urn.

The caterer was handing a plate to one of the carpenters. ". . . to Rusen. Tell him I know he's busy. Tell him I said to eat." He ambled off, plate in one hand, coffee in the other, towards the soundstage.

I examined the food: roast chicken breasts in rosemary, bread, rice salad, pasta salad, potato salad, skewers, two piles of roast beef sandwiches and tuna salad sandwiches, ready-cut pizza, and fruit on shaved ice. While I watched, the caterer lifted out the half-empty fruit platter and replaced it with halved strawberries and melons still oozing from the knife. Her hands were gloved, small for her height—she was five six or seven—and her movements as clean as a poem. I was surprised and not sure why. She felt my gaze and looked up. Greyblue eyes, soft as dove feathers.

A crew member trundled a cart of shrubbery between us. Two others waddled by with potted palms. Most of them were heading towards the soundstage, where a woman halfway up a ladder was pointing and ordering this here and that there in a seemingly endless series of commands. Midstream she yelled, "Joel. Joel!" The man at the control panel pushed up his glasses and frowned. "Cut the stage lights." Joel pointed at his watch and shook his head. "There won't be any shoot at all if you keep those . . . Ah, hell with it—" She jumped down from her perch and strode over. She waved her arms. A moment later the arc lights went down with a thunk. The activity onstage seemed to increase. The man with the pen sat by himself, but now there was a plate of chicken on the floor by his foot. Rusen. I walked over. Up close the fineness of his sandy hair and his smooth skin told me he was in his late twenties or very early thirties, much younger than his clothing style or attitude. He looked rather forlorn, like an eight-year-old in a suit who has just lost his first chess championship.

"Busy time?" I said.

He looked up, mouth pursed, then leapt to his feet. "I'm so very glad you could—" He realized his hands were full, and turned and dropped the clipboard on his chair. He held out his hand again. I shook it and smiled gravely, wondering who he thought I was. "They'll be at this for a while longer, but, please, come this way. We"—he remembered the food, and picked it up—"I have to— Bri?" The boy at the props table, the one with the bony face, looked up. "Bring me a coffee, would you, and—no, no, never mind, Ms. Felter and I will get our own."

Ms. Felter? The boy, Bri, at least, didn't seem surprised by Rusen's mental U-turns. The man I'd seen Bri with earlier—also young, but not a teenager— joined him. Rusen and I walked to the counter, where the carpenters were taking advantage of the temporary chaos to get another cup of coffee. The caterer was chatting, standing wide-legged and easy, knife moving idly this way and that as she talked, taking up her space a little too aggressively, the way women who have been raised with a lot of brothers tend to do in a group of men. It was clear she had never considered using the knife for anything but food preparation; there was no awareness of its edge and balance as it related to the soft skin of the men around her.

She saw Rusen. "Hold it," she said, to her audience and to Rusen, who stopped guiltily and waited while she filled a cup from the urn, added a pretty swirl of cream and a sprinkle of sugar, and handed it over. He looked apologetically at me before he took it, which made her frown. She studied me, and after a moment she picked up her knife and hefted it. Perhaps the body language was unconscious, but the message was clear: if you hurt him, I'll hurt you. I smiled. After a measuring moment, she nodded. Something about the way her head moved made me realize she was very tired. She turned back to Rusen, looked at the plate, raised her eyebrows. "Yes," he said. "I will."

Rusen led me outside to one of the trailers, which was crammed with a heavy-duty digital editing suite at one end and a miniature office set up at the other. I sat on an office chair, a brand that costs almost a thousand dollars. He put his coffee and his plate down carefully.

"Now I appreciate that we're several days behind schedule, Ms. Felter, but I hope the fact that CAA has sent you all the way up to our humble set bodes well, despite the, ah, the various delays."

Felter. CAA. An accounting firm? It didn't matter. I wouldn't correct him. I would learn more and, if it seemed desirable, would take advantage of his confusion. "Go on."

"The cancellation from Fox was very disappointing but I have high hopes, very high hopes, that our unique brand of televisual entertainment will find its niche."

"Niche?"

"Niche, did I say niche?" He chuckled, but it didn't sit well on his boyish face and he kept glancing over my right shoulder. "What I meant to say was demographic. I am still convinced that we have an untapped market in the fifteen- to twenty-four-year-old male and female urban viewership."

"Still?"

"Yes, yes, it's true we've been trying for eighteen months now to secure a network deal, but they seem to lack vision, they're not willing to get behind a new concept, to take a glorious risk!"

"Risk?"

His blink rate rose and he started to tap his pen on his thigh. "Not that this project's risky. No, not at all. Not in the sense of perhaps failing. No, no, it's sure to succeed, practically guaranteed."

I said nothing, having no idea what he was talking about.

"I'm sorry," he said, and sighed, and smoothed his face with his left hand. "Using that word was foolish. I know there are no guarantees in show business. Let me begin again. I believe in this project; I believe we have a good product. The delays are not our fault. We have a good crew who are willing to work, and we can be back on schedule by the beginning of next week. I'd be willing to give your agency a very substantial part of the back end in exchange for . . ." He stopped. Sighed again. "I'm doing this all wrong, aren't I? Oh, jeezy petes, I wish Finkel was here. He's good at this."

Finkel and Rusen. Producers. "Mr. Rusen, I'm not from CAA. I own this property."

"You're the landlord?"

"Yes."

"You got my letter? I was beginning to think Ms. Corning hadn't forwarded it. I was getting desperate."

"You sent me a letter?"

"Yes. About the EPA stuff? They wouldn't talk to me, and Corning said it would all have to go through you. She said— Ah, jeepers. You didn't get it, did you. You're going to kick us out."

"No."

"You're not going to break the lease?"

"It's in both our interests for you to be able to stay and do your work." The place may as well be earning until I decided what to do with it. "Let me be sure I understand you. You tried to talk to the EPA?"

He nodded. "But they said I wasn't the owner and it would have to go through whoever had the legal authority to make decisions. I looked at the lease, and I thought that would be Corning, but she said, no, it was you. She suggested I write a letter explaining things. She said she'd forward it. That was seven weeks ago."

"And OSHA?"

"They're talking to me. At least they were. I thought I was getting somewhere, but then the guy I was dealing with got transferred or something, and the new guy, Zhao, said we'd have to start over. And I was beginning to despair, because with Finkel away, there's just too much stuff to do. And he's better at this kind of negotiation than me."

"Where is he?"

"He had a family emergency." He made a vague gesture with his pen.

"When will he be back?"

"I don't know."

"When will you know?"

"Not sure about that, either."

I breathed slowly and evenly. "If you had to guess, when do you think it might be?"

"A week? His boy's sick. Real sick."

"It might be better not to wait." He looked nervous, more like that child chess player than ever. "I've already talked to Zhao at OSHA, and to EPA. Informally. Most of the write-ups are minor infractions: they only investigated because they had to, it's the law, but if you make suitable apologies and promises, they'll let you off with a stern letter and a proposed inspection schedule."

"Yeah, that's what the first guy said."

"We can persuade Zhao to agree, but you'll have to make the approach, as a representative of the employer, and it'll have to be cap in hand." I frowned. I had no idea why I was offering to help. Perhaps it was because he so clearly needed it. "Do you have any of their correspondence here?"

He blinked, then nodded, then scooted his chair to a keyboard and tapped a few keys. "What do you need?"

I remembered one of the OSHA sheets. "They have complaints about severely limited natural ventilation, potential to accumulate or contain a hazardous atmosphere, and other things relating to a definition of a confined space. Which this warehouse clearly isn't. That would be a place to begin."

"Confined space," he said, and touched four keys. The printer began spitting.

"That was fast."

"New software," he said. "My design. It works like a spreadsheet, so you can organize by category, but virtually—you don't have to designate the category beforehand. The tricky part was the search engine. I came up with a sweet algorithm . . ." He leaned forward and stopped tapping, and as he talked about each problem he had solved he started to look less like a precocious child than a confident MBA. When it was time to lead the conversation back to OSHA all his vagueness was gone.

"Two more things. Are there any minors on the set?"

"Minors? Children?"

"The laws are slightly different for anyone under sixteen. You'd have to be careful. Also, you might want to consider getting security at the door. You have a lot of valuable equipment here."

"We have access cards. And when we're shooting we have a person on the door, but there's always someone around—" His pocket tweedled. "Excuse me." He answered the phone. "Rusen. Boy, already?" He looked at his watch. "You're right. Okay. One minute." He folded the phone away. "Sorry about that, hadn't realized how late it's getting. They're ready to run tape on a stunt shot we've been trying to set up for hours. Want to watch?"

IN THE warehouse everyone—props and catering and wardrobe and grips—was standing close to a monitor and checking obsessively. Rusen walked to his place by the soundstage, which now looked like a messy jungle with a vinyl floor. The heavy scent of lilies was overpowering. My throat itched.

Two of the people who had brought the extra costumes earlier now stood with the caterer, juice cartons in hand. She had wide shoulders, a tight waist flaring into rounded hips, and muscles on her fingers and forearms and neck. I guessed her back was also finely muscled, and her legs. It was muscle that comes with intensive training from an early age, the kind a trapeze artist or free climber or high diver develops. Not something acquired behind a food counter.

She was drinking water from a bottle labeled Rain City while the wardrobe assistant woman talked.

". . . so I said, No shit? And he said, 'Do I look like I'm kidding, ma'am?' So John and me"—the assistant nodded at the man next to her—"got out of the car and they opened up the van and made us show receipts for, like, half the shit we bought this afternoon until they decided to believe we hadn't stolen it. I thought Kathy was gonna punch my lights out for being so late. But if—"

A klaxon hooted, lights flashed red. Everyone instantly shut up and turned to the monitor, and then it was so quiet I could hear John breathing through his mouth. When I looked at the monitor I saw that through the eye of the camera the soundstage now looked like a huge florist's wholesalers. I looked up at the stage and the image disappeared, back at the monitor and it reappeared. All about perspective.

"Roll sound," a man with a self-important goatee and one heavy gold earring said loudly. "Roll camera. And . . . action!"

The diver, now dressed in the kind of tight black gear Hollywood thinks elite law-enforcement units wear, ran along his platform, looked behind him, and took a dive onto his air bag.

"Cut!"

Some thin applause from the direction of the soundstage. The caterer said to no one in particular, "Waste of film."

"C'mon, John," the wardrobe woman said. "Kathy'll be having shit fits." They left. I stayed. The caterer tipped her head back and finished her water. Her throat moved strongly as she swallowed, but she moved just a fraction more slowly than I expected. She watched me as she crushed her bottle—she wasn't wearing gloves now; her fingers were short and powerful—then picked up the large triangular knife and turned back to her chopping board. I couldn't tell what she was cutting. Sometime in the last half an hour she had retied her hair.

"What did you mean, that it was a waste of film?" I said.

Her chopping didn't miss a beat. "They'll have to reshoot."

"Why?"

Chop, chop, chop. "You could see his face."

"It looked good to me."

Now she turned around. "It wasn't good. I should know. I did that job for six years."

"But not anymore?"

She gestured at her counter and chopping board with her knife. "What does it look like?"

It looked like tomatoes. I smiled. "I'm Aud Torvingen."

"Well, good for you."

I kept smiling. She was busy. I was a stranger. Perhaps she thought I was here to hurt Rusen in some way. "I don't know your name."

She pointed the knife at a Plexiglas sign that said Film Food and held a small tray of business cards. I picked one up. "Victoria K. Kuiper."

"But no one calls me that," she said, with a certain satisfaction, and started to turn away, but the klaxon hooted again, and the red light flashed, and we turned obediently to the monitor.

The director shouted, the camera whirred, the stunt actor dived onto the bag.

"Better," the caterer said to herself, nodding.

"It looked exactly the same to me."

"Nope. He tucked his chin more: not so much face." She was studying me again, and now that she was still I could see the vast fatigue moving below the surface. "So, Aud Torvingen. You didn't say why you were here, but I can guess. And my answers are the same as they were last week: I have no clue about and no interest in finding out just how fast this company will crash and burn. My business is food, not reporting bad management."

"Bad management?"

"Gone deaf?"

I shrugged. It didn't work on everyone. "Tell me why you think the set's badly managed."

"Why?"

"Because I want to know."

"Now that I believe: you want something so you expect you'll get it. You people are all the same. I don't know what song and dance you sold Rusen in his trailer but I've been around film half my life"—she must have started barely in her teens—"and I'm not in the market for bullshit. Oh, and anything you take from this table, you pay for."

"I'm not selling anything."

"Walking in here in Armani like a CAA toad, and Rusen going all gooey-faced, like you've just offered him prime time for his useless pilot?" She pointed the knife at me. "Sure you are."

Her grey eyes were red-rimmed, and the shadow under them almost matched her irises. She had been up a very long time. She clearly wasn't happy. Let her keep her knife, then. "I'd really like to talk to you about your thoughts on the management of this set."

She picked up a cloth and wiped the blade. "I don't need people like you getting in my way. Stunt work wraps after this and the crew'll want coffee before hair and makeup arrive to do the actors and we have to start all over again."

"What about tomorrow?"

"With any luck at all I'll be sleeping all day tomorrow."

"Tomorrow night?"

She turned her back to me and started chopping. She swayed very slightly. I wondered how many hours she'd been up. There was a smear of tomato between her pocket and her lower ribs where she might have leaned against a counter. It would stain if she didn't put it to soak soon, but that would be the last thing she would want to do when she got home, exhausted. Maybe she had someone to do that for her.

IT WAS six-thirty by the time I got back to the hotel. Pascalle gave me several suggestions for places to eat in typical Seattle neighborhoods. I scanned the list. One had the same prefix—547—as Kuiper's business number. The Jitterbug, in

Wallingford. It seemed as good a place as any. I got directions, then collected Dornan from his room.

We drove north on I-5 and exited on North 45th. After a mile or so I took a random left and drove slowly down a quiet, tree-lined street. Craftsman bungalows mainly, with gardens tending towards the English country cottage perennial, but the well-lit front rooms were affluent and urban: paintings and sculpture, books, exposed brickwork and oiled wainscoting, brushed-steel audio-visual equipment, good lighting, sophisticated interior color.

"These people have got to be Scandinavian," Dornan said. "Look at the cars."

Most houses had two cars to a driveway, one an old favorite such as a dull red Saab from the late eighties, or a mustard yellow Volvo of the same era, the other something new and imported: a Lexus RX, a Subaru, an Audi. Maybe I should have rented a Ford. "They're good cars."

"And so very practical."

Dornan mused aloud on the Norwegian nature of the city: a hotel on the edge of the water called Edgewater, a wine bar in a bungalow called the Bungalow, a bakery called the Bakery. "The Boulangerie doesn't count," I said. "It's in French."

I got back onto 45th and in the Jitterbug we were seated in a booth in the cozy back bar.

Dornan, after a lengthy conference with the server about the pros and cons of triple sec (sweet) and Cointreau (less so), ordered another kamikaze, and I chose a pilsner. The calamari we shared as an appetizer was fresh and tender.

I told Dornan about my visit to OSHA and EPA, and Corning.

"So you think she'll actually tell you what's going on on Monday?"

I shrugged. "She'll tell me or I'll find out on my own. It's not rocket science. Like any other investigation, you just follow the money. But why do the work if I can get her to admit her part?" This way I wouldn't have to bother bringing charges or being a witness.

"I thought you were just going to sell and walk away."

"I am." Probably.

"Then this is about you wanting to win first?"

"Something like that."

"You could just kick her round the block a few times."

"This is less effort."

He gave me the look that said he knew there was more to it, something to do with what had happened with my self-defense class, but said only, "What do you suppose rockfish is?"

We asked, and were told that Europeans called it mullet, which set me thinking about red mullet and how the Romans had prized them. I ordered the Thai steamed rockfish, he took the oven-roasted chicken.

"The drive to the warehouse was nice," I said as we ate, and told him about it. "But the site had no security. I just walked right onto the set. I tried to talk to the producer but he— What?"

"Set? A film set?"

"A company called Hippoworks is filming a TV pilot."

"What kind of pilot?"

I thought about it. "It's called *Feral*."

"Who's starring?"

I shrugged.

"Christ, Torvingen, it could have been someone famous. You could have had lunch."

"Do you want to go?"

"It's a film set."

I took that as a yes. "I'm going back tomorrow. You can come if you want. I have to talk to one of the producers. And maybe this most annoying woman, who seems to have some opinions." I dug out her card. "She runs a catering company, oh, excuse me, craft services. Film Food."

He looked at the card, gave it back, grinned. "Is she Norwegian?"

"You can't say things like that when you meet my mother."

"I don't intend to say anything to your mother except 'please' and 'thank you.' Are you picking her up from the airport?"

"The consulate will see to that." She would be taken off the plane and ushered through the VIP courtesies and probably be at the Fairmont before the economy passengers were clearing the gate—if she was flying. For all I knew, she could be arriving by train or car. However she traveled, at some point she would be standing in her suite at the Fairmont, and then she would phone me.

"When was the last time you saw her?"

"Let's talk about something else."

"Fine. How's your fish?"

"Delicious. But it's not mullet." I made a note to look up "rockfish" later.

IN THE car, I said, "Do you know what CAA is?"

"In what context?"

"The Film Food woman said I looked like a quote CAA toad unquote in my Armani suit."

"Ah. That would be Creative Artists, a big Hollywood agency. I believe they do all wear Armani. Apparently they also move together in groups, like killer whales."

"How do you know all this stuff?"

"I read *Entertainment Weekly*."

Which just reminded me of Loedessoel.

Dornan was grinning again. "Did she really call you a toad?"

IN THE hotel, I had a phone message from my lawyer, Bette: "I faxed those papers, but let's talk before you sign 'em." It was one o'clock in Atlanta; it could wait until tomorrow. I checked the fax: twenty-two pages of poor-resolution printing. I wished Bette would join the twenty-first century and use e-mail like everyone else.

I booted my laptop. An e-mail from Laurence, my banker, with estimates of the worth of my property should I choose to sell. *Let me emphasize once again, though, the importance of local expertise. I'll send you a list of eminent local real estate agents tomorrow.* I sent him a quick acknowledgment, then opened a search box.

Rockfish turned out to be a kind of bass, not mullet at all. Rusen, it seemed, had graduated from UCLA film school just a few months ago. Before that he had been some kind of software wunderkind. His small company had been bought out by a local behemoth. He was probably bankrolling his own production.

My eyes felt dry and gritty. I closed the laptop.

I emptied my pockets onto the dresser, pondered the Film Food card. Victoria K. Kuiper. Sounded Dutch. *But no one calls me that.*

Someone had turned the covers back. I found the teddy bear and dropped it on the floor. Found the remote for the fire and turned it off.

Vicky? Definitely not. Vic wasn't right, either, nor Tory. Those muscles on her arms. Kory? Kuiper? Per? Stupid woman, waving that knife around. Film Food. Very Norwegian. My mother . . .

LESSON 2

THE HEATING DUCT HISSED AND FILLED THE BASEMENT WITH THE SMELL OF BURNT dust but not much warmth. I made a mental note to talk to the Crystal Gaze advisory board about that. At some point in the last week someone had left a whiteboard balanced on the stacked chairs by the bench, and a grey pegboard against the far wall. Suze was there on time. They all were, which surprised me. I'd expected two or three dropouts. Today no rings glinted, no earrings dangled, no chains apart from the crucifix around Pauletta's neck. But there were two pairs of wicked heels under the bench. Everyone wore pants and a tank top or a short-sleeved T-shirt, except Sandra. It wouldn't surprise me to find she had a lot of long-sleeved shirts in her wardrobe. Kim's fingernails were maroon today, and still long.

"Did everyone do their lists?" General nodding, a few movements towards bags or coats. "No. I don't want to see them. I want you to remember, during this class, what you wrote down."

Suze stirred slightly. I gestured for her to speak.

"You ever write one of those lists?"

"No."

"So how do you know what you're willing to do, when it comes right down to it?"

I could point to the bullet scar on my arm and the thin white seam under my ribs, I could tell her about the man I had put in a coma at the end of last year, or the gunman I had killed with a flashlight when I was eighteen. But she wasn't really asking about me. "We can never know. Not really. Every situation is different."

She frowned.

They know nothing, I reminded myself. "Are you willing to be a guinea pig?" I said.

"Sure," said Suze.

I stepped to the center of the room, beckoned for her to join me, and the instant she began to move I lunged at her, fist raised. She flinched and stepped back and turned away, hands going up to protect her head. Most of the others—but not Sandra—shot backwards like iron filings suddenly attracted to the wall. After a moment Suze looked up to find me standing two feet away, arms at my sides.

She started to uncurl. "What the fuck was—"

I lunged again, and again she flinched and stepped back, but this time she didn't turn aside, her eyes stayed on me, and her hands went only halfway up. Everyone else was pressed flat against the wall.

"One more time," I said, and lunged, and once again she flinched, but her step back was small, her hands were in fists, and her chin pointed up. Therese looked as though she was about to protest.

I raised both palms and stepped back two paces. "Thank you. I won't do it again—to you or anyone else—without warning." It took Suze a moment to decide to believe me, then she lowered her fists, but not her chin, and rejoined the others who were stepping cautiously away from the wall.

"So," I said, "what did we learn from that?"

"Never volunteer." Pauletta, and she sounded put out.

"Besides that." No one said anything. "All right. What did Suze's first response look like to you?"

"Like you scared the shit out of her for no good reason," Nina said.

"And what about her second response?"

"The same, but less."

"I was not scared." Several of them nodded sympathetically, even though every single one of them knew this wasn't true. Christie patted her on the arm.

"And the third time?"

"Like she was about to run but changed her mind."

"She was going to fight," Christie said. More nods.

"She did flinch," Pauletta said, sounding as though she were trying very hard to be fair, even though I didn't deserve it.

"Yes. Almost everyone will flinch. Suze did very well." Christie smiled. Therese looked slightly mollified. I wondered whether to file flattery under useful teaching technique or craven behavior. "So, the same apparent situation, three different responses. They were different responses because Suze interpreted each of my attacks differently. She gained experience. She extrapolated. By the third time she knew I wasn't going to hit her. She'd also had practice at responding. In other words, each situation was different. Even though what I did was exactly the same, Suze's experience level had changed, so it was a different situation."

Which is why Sandra had moved only after she saw that everyone else had and might notice if she didn't.

"One way to get some experience without being in real danger is to do a little role play. Has any of you ever done any acting?"

They all studied the carpet very carefully.

"Not since fourth grade," Nina said eventually. "The nativity play."

"Yeah?" said Pauletta. "Who did you play, the donkey?"

"Pauletta, Nina, you're our first volunteers. Pauletta, stand over here. It's night. You're waiting at a MARTA station. You're the only one on the platform, and the train's late. Imagine that. Pretend you're doing it."

Most women learned very young how to play the roles expected of them. Girls' games were built on the notion: play Mom, play nurse, play teacher. They played and played and played until they learnt to inhabit the roles.

Pauletta started looking up and down the imaginary train line, rising onto her toes, then rocking back onto her heels. She put her hands on her hips, sighed in exasperation. The picture of a tired, irritated commuter.

"Nina, over there. You're male, about thirty, you've had a couple of shots of Jack Daniel's, you feel like a big man. Imagine how that feels. You walk onto the platform and see this sweet young thing waiting at the other end. You realize that if you wanted to, you could have some fun."

Women observed male behavior closely, learnt to parse every nuance. Like antelope with lions, their safety sometimes depended on it.

Nina leered and sauntered forward, head relaxed, gaze moving here and there, taking in the fact that they were the only people, slowing as she approached the woman on the platform. Pauletta turned her shoulders slightly away from the man and put her hands in her pockets.

"You can speak, if you like."

"Um-*um*," said Nina, appraisal vibrating in every syllable. "Hello, *darl*in'."

Pauletta looked away. Perfect.

"Okay. Freeze frame." I turned to the rest of the class. "What do you see?"

"She's frightened," Jennifer said.

Nods.

"She's hoping he'll just go away," Tonya said. More nods.

"Do you think he will?"

"Fuck no," said Suze.

"How do you know that?"

"Look at him. He's gonna play with her. He knows she's not gonna stop him."

"So what do you think will happen next? Therese?"

"I'm not sure," she said. The delicate muscles at the top of her shoulders flexed as she folded her arms. "It depends on what she does."

Sandra was watching the imaginary platform intently. I said, "Does anyone think Pauletta could stop him at this point? Sandra?"

When she heard her name her belly tightened—the waistband of her sweatpants moved a good inch—and she didn't look at me, but nodded.

"Why do you think that?"

She looked at me sideways. "Because he doesn't really want to hurt her."

Pauletta broke her pose and turned round. "What—"

"Nina, stay exactly as you are. Everyone, look at Nina. Look carefully. Remember what you see. Nina, tell us what you were imagining your character to be thinking. You can move now if you want."

She turned round. "I was thinking, Hey, I feel good, she looks good, wonder if she wants to chat. When she turned away, I thought, Uptight bitch, and got ticked off. She messed with my mood, you know?" I could almost hear a voice from her teenage years: *Smile, foxy lady, I'm feeling so mellow. . . .*

"Who are you calling an uptight bitch?" Pauletta said.

The two of them clearly trusted each other reasonably well. I wouldn't do what came next with Sandra or Jennifer or Katherine. "Pauletta, if you'd go back to how you were before you saw the man come onto the platform, that's right, turned this way, hands out of pockets to begin with. Nina, I want you to imagine that this time you mean business. You were out drinking because you just got fired. You don't feel good, and you want this woman to not feel good, either. You want to hurt her. Think about it, get a clear picture in your head of how you're going to hurt her. No, start back here again. Good. Go."

The difference was obvious. This time there was no swagger. Her head did not turn, because she already knew they were on their own. Her gaze was focused on Pauletta, chin slightly down. One hand came forward, the other stayed in her pocket, but tense. Unease rippled through the women behind me.

"Okay. Stop. Thank you. Take a moment to stretch." More to shed the role than anything. I turned to the rest of the group. "Did you see the difference?"

Everyone nodded. "It was creepy," said Christie. "He—she—had a gun in his pocket."

"Nina?"

"A knife," she said. "Short and wicked."

"Man, you had me convinced," Pauletta said. "You are scary for a little round white person."

"So," I said. "We all knew before he even opened his mouth that it was different, that this time he was starting out serious and the first time he wasn't. It could have become serious, but it didn't start that way, and right at the beginning Pauletta could have stopped him without laying a finger on him."

"No touching?" Pauletta said.

"The force is with you, Luke," Nina said.

Everyone smiled very hard.

"You can think about it that way if you like. I see it more as taking up space. Imagine I'm the woman on the platform. I'm looking for the train. The man, the first man, enters. Now, instead of turning away, putting my hands in my pockets—which is basically taking up less space, pretending to be invisible and hoping he'll just go away—I turn towards him, look him in the eye, and nod calmly. I'm saying, I see you, we're alike, you and I: two people waiting for a train. Equals going about our business."

"Yeah, but you're six feet tall," Kim said. Lots of nods.

"It's not about how tall you are."

"Right."

"I was Atlanta PD. I've met carjackers and muggers and psychopaths. They all go for someone who looks like a victim: who doesn't take up space, who apologizes, who doesn't want to appear rude, who tries to pretend nothing's happening. All of them go for the low-hanging fruit."

"Fruit?" Pauletta said.

"Wait, wait." Therese. "Clarify your statement for me, please. Are you saying we have to act the way you do, marching about like some, some . . ." She searched for the right word, couldn't find it. "That we have to deny our femininity?"

"No."

"Then what are you saying?"

"Yeah," Kim said. "Why should we have to cut our fingernails, then cut our hair even shorter?"

"No shoulds from me. Only information to help you make choices. For example, Kim, do you cut your nails and have a wider arsenal of possible responses to attack or do you choose to keep them long and either spend a bit more time learning palm strikes or accept the fact that one day something could happen where having shorter nails might have made the difference?"

"They're my nails!"

"Yes."

"I don't see why I should cut them."

"Then don't." I wasn't seeing the problem.

"What about short hair, and always wearing pants?" Therese said.

"Not everyone could wear it like that," Jennifer said, with an ingratiating smile in my direction, "but it does look super nice on you. And there's nothing wrong with pants as a personal choice."

They all shifted, reminded that it wasn't nice for southern women to insult another's appearance.

"And, hey," Nina said, "maybe she doesn't wear pants when she's not in class." She looked at Kim. "You sure stopped wearing skirts quick enough."

"No point flashing booty just for sisters."

"Only makes sense," Pauletta said.

She and Kim and Nina eyed each other, then nodded, allies.

"Besides, short hair is very attractive in its own way," Nina said, stroking her own carefully shaped grey cut.

"Totally," Christie said. "I think about cutting mine all the time."

"Oh, don't do that," Tonya said. "It's lovely. So long and straight."

"No one has to cut their hair, no one has to wear pants, no one has to trim her nails. It is in your best interests to know what all your choices mean. Looking as if you're afraid means you're more likely to be attacked. Statistically."

"Cite your sources," Therese said.

"My own personal experience as a police officer. The Women Against Rape survey published in London in 1985. Ongoing U.S. Department of Justice statistics." The WAR survey had held up remarkably despite the intervening twenty years and four thousand miles.

"She was a cop," Pauletta said.

"She's our teacher," Jennifer said, nodding.

"Trust or don't trust, just don't question?" Therese put her hands on her hips.

"What is your problem?" Suze said.

"I'm curious about what she's trying to teach us here, exactly."

"Why don't you ask her?"

"I think that's what she's trying to do," I said, and gestured for Therese to go ahead.

She struggled for a moment. I could guess what her essential problem was, but it took her a while to get there. "It's not fair."

"No," I said.

"We shouldn't have to act differently, just to not be attacked in the street. It's not fair."

"No. But that doesn't matter."

She looked puzzled.

"What matters is what happens. The strong attack the weak." I wasn't sure how I could make it more plain. "Big countries invade little countries, the alpha hippo savages the beta hippo, the jock beats the nerd. Why? Because they can. Because they believe they don't have a lot to lose but a great deal to gain. In economist-speak, they have strong incentives."

Tonya looked interested. "So what we're doing is learning to disincentivize them?"

"Yes."

"But we shouldn't have to," Therese said.

"No. But shoulds and shouldn'ts don't matter."

The corners of Therese's eyes and mouth pulled away from the center and her head moved back half an inch, as though someone had shoved a bucket of raw tripe in front of her and suggested she eat it. It was the way of the world. There was nothing I could do to change it. The only way to help her was to continue with the lesson.

"Now, where were we with the role play?"

"Not looking like a victim," Tonya said. "Disincentivizing."

"Pretending we're six feet tall," Pauletta said.

"Yeah, you do it with mirrors," Nina said. Everyone except Katherine smiled, relieved that we were all on the same side again. I raised my eyebrows at her.

"It's okay for everyone to make jokes," she said. "But what if you're really not six feet tall? What do you do if a man at the MARTA station starts talking to you?"

"Would you want him to talk to you?"

"No!"

"Then say so."

"Say so?"

"Clearly and simply: I won't talk to you."

"Isn't that kind of rude?"

Rude. To a man who had invaded her personal space, made her afraid, and was testing to see what kind of victim she'd make.

"It's neutral. A statement of fact."

"Wouldn't it provoke him?" Jennifer.

"Nina, would it have provoked you?"

"No-o," she said. "No, I don't think so. It would've made me shrug, maybe, and think, Bitch. Maybe I would've said that to her face." Jennifer flinched.

"Something to add to your list: would you rather be called a bitch or put up with an hour's harassment by a drunk at a MARTA station who may or may not be working himself up to jump you? Bear in mind that if you do tell him to go away, you need to also make sure your body is saying the same thing as your words: everything in line, no ambiguity."

"But if he's drunk he won't listen," Jennifer said.

"He certainly won't if you don't say anything. No one is a mind reader."

Blank looks. There were times when I felt that although we had arrived in the same room, we had traveled through different dimensions.

"You have to say the words out loud. Again, fair play doesn't matter. What you want, or what you think he should already know, doesn't matter. What matters is what you actually say—with your body and your words. No one can read your mind. If you say, 'I don't want to talk to you. I don't want you anywhere near me. If you so much as touch me with the tip of your finger, I'll call the police and have you charged with assault,' he'll understand." He wouldn't necessarily listen, but he would understand.

"That seems a little excessive," Therese said.

"If that's the first thing you do, maybe. If you've already made it plain with body language, and already told him verbally you don't want to talk, then no."

Enough chitchat.

"Let's practice. Pair up. No, Tonya, you go with Nina, Katherine with Pauletta." Time to do a little mix-and-match. "Therese, I want you over here with Sandra." Therese was physically and emotionally contained and wouldn't intimidate Sandra. "Suze with Kim." Perhaps the nail issue would get sorted there. "Christie, you're with Jennifer. Nina, Pauletta, Therese, Suze, and Christie, come and get two chairs each, put them wherever you like, just make sure they're next to each other, like a bench. Sit down. You're on a bench in Piedmont Park, on your lunch break. It's a lovely day. You're by the lake. All the other benches are empty but there are people playing Frisbee in the distance. Then someone—that's your partner," I said to the women still standing, "some stranger comes along and sits on your bench."

"Man or woman?" said Pauletta.

"That's up to you."

"Is he—or she—a creep?" Christie.

"Anyone who sits next to you when all the other benches are empty is a fucking creep," said Suze.

"Point," said Nina.

"He could be blind," said Katherine.

Or an alien or a secret agent. "He'd have a white cane," I said. "There again, perhaps it's simply a woman who admires your shoes and wants to know where you got them. You decide. Get as loud as you want, but nothing physical, not at this stage. You have two minutes, then swap places. Begin."

I stood by Nina and Tonya but focused my attention on Therese and Sandra. Role play could bring up powerful emotions, and if I was right about Sandra, she was a walking time bomb.

I could tell by her open shoulders and legs that Sandra had chosen to play a man, which didn't surprise me: it was a way to feel powerful. When s/he sat, he gave Therese a quick, uncertain smile and opened his hands and widened his eyes. I didn't hear what he said but Therese leaned forward.

By this time Nina had already laughed in Tonya's face, and they had switched roles. Christie and Jennifer seemed to be in a stilted conversation about hairstylists.

Sandra/the young man edged closer to Therese, who backed up a little, and it was clear from the expression on the young man's face and the way he almost reached out to touch Therese's sleeve, then dropped his hand suddenly and put it in his lap that he was saying something like, No, wait, please, I'm sorry, I know this must seem weird, but you're the only one who can help me. And Therese looked around, the way we do when we wish help would arrive in the form of a loud-voiced acquaintance with whom we can leave without appearing discourteous, and the young man chose that moment to put his face in his hands. Therese hesitated.

On the other side of the room, Katherine was backing off as Pauletta said, "This is my bench, asshole. Go find your own." Kim was sitting fairly close to Suze, smiling into her face, touching her hand, and Suze was blushing.

Sandra's young man hitched himself just a little closer—very natural-looking, and with a pleading expression—and Therese still hesitated, and then it was too late: he had fixed her gaze with his and she was deep in the well-bred woman's trap.

I stepped in. "Are you two all right?"

Sandra, still as a young man, said, "Fine, Officer, just fine. It's . . . well, my dog, Earl, died, and this was the place he liked best. We used to come out here—but you don't want to know that. I was out walking just one more time, only—it was just that I imagined I saw him, leaping up for that Frisbee, and I got this lump, and I just had to sit, and this kind lady . . . well, it's embarrassing, but we're just fine now, thank you."

We. He'd taken the reins and made it impossible for polite, appropriate Therese to say anything without looking rude or stupid.

"You do that very well," I said. No doubt because she'd been living with an expert. Sandra—because, just like that, she was Sandra again—laughed, and her laughter was low and self-mocking and shot through with bitterness. To the class in general I said, "Switch roles if you haven't already," and sank to my heels by Therese, who was sitting very upright.

"I fell for it," she said. "I can't believe I fell for it."

"A lot of people do. That's how Bundy worked: put his arm in a sling and got his victims to feel sorry for him. Women are trained to take care of people. It's a habit, a dangerous one. Take a moment, then let's see you swap roles."

Elsewhere in the room, the pairs were becoming partners, Christie saying to Jennifer, *That was awesome. I mean, I totally didn't want to sit on your bench. But what if I tried . . .* and Kim to Suze, who was still blushing, *So, what, you'd let any female who told you you had pretty hands get up close and personal? You don't think a girl might be more interested in that wallet in your back pocket than your flustered ass?*

Sandra settled herself on the imaginary bench and looked off into an imaginary distance. Therese took two deep breaths; her face smoothed and her shoulders dropped. She sat down on the bench. Sandra looked up at her/him—Therese's body language was so neutral it was hard to tell—and said, "I am so very, very tired and I want to be alone. Please leave my bench." Therese started to get up—as any reasonable person would—but then, mindful of her recent embarrassment, sat down again. Sandra said indifferently, "I'm going to stand and walk over to another bench. I can't stop you following me, but if you're hoping I'll run or scream or faint in terror, you'll be disappointed. I just don't care."

An intuitive leap, an apparently inexplicable impulse, can save your life or someone else's, but it's rare to find a person who can trust their instincts to that degree. You have to be able to get out of your own way. It's always fascinating to watch. Therese looked up at Sandra, momentarily blank, then understanding swarmed over her face and she said in an ordinary voice, "I don't believe that's true. You do care. That's why you're here."

They faced each other, perfectly still.

I stepped back. "Time's up, people." I waited until I had their attention. "Okay. Things we've learnt. That an assailant will use your sense of politeness and good behavior against you. He or she may flatter and flirt. Flattery is an enormously useful tool." Kim nodded significantly at Suze, who scowled. Christie looked from one to the other, puzzled. "He or she will try to affiliate, to persuade you that you are in some way a team. She may ask to come in and use your phone; he may say he has had an accident. Remember, you owe strangers nothing: no explanation, no apology, no thanks, no smile, no assistance."

"But . . ." Katherine. She shut her mouth, frowning.

"Go on."

"It's . . ." She shook her head in frustration.

"It's hard," Therese said. Everyone turned. "We're supposed to be nice. It's at the heart of everything we do. I hadn't realized that. But then I was playing at sitting on the bench, and this young man comes and sits next to me. He starts talking to me, and I'm thinking, *Why's he doing this?* because, as Suze says, you *know* anyone who sits on your bench without even asking is weird or wants something, no matter what they say, but he talks and I don't do or say a thing. Even when a police officer comes along, I say nothing. He had me. I'm smart, I'm educated, and he *had* me. It was as though he'd tied me up and stuffed my mouth with a rag. All he did was hint I was stupid to think he was any threat—just hint, not even say it out loud. I didn't want him to think I was foolish. So I did nothing. I knew he wasn't right but I still did nothing. And I don't understand."

"Embarrassment," I said. "Self-consciousness."

"Yes," she said, "but *why?*" She practically vibrated.

"Define for me the words *feminine* and *ladylike* and *womanly.*"

Silence. Then, "Pretty," Nina said.

"Soft," said Suze.

"Kind," said Jennifer.

"Sexy."

"Nice. Well behaved."

"Weak—" said Therese.

"Nurturing," and "Motherly!" Pauletta and Tonya said together.

"—emotional, hysterical, and irrational." Therese was breathing hard.

"Vulnerable," said Christie, and looked it.

THREE

DORNAN AND I SAT OPPOSITE EACH OTHER AT A SMALL WOODEN TABLE BY THE WINDOW
of Tully's coffee shop in a neighborhood called Greenwood, sipping and watching the world go by as the sun sailed out from behind clouds, then hid again. The chairs were plain pine with a clear, polyvinyl varnish, a marvel of modern design and construction: cheap, comfortable for just long enough to drink a cup of coffee, easy to pick up and put down, durable, washable. Quite unlike the Wiram art chair I'd seen in Atlanta before I left.

"What's the use of a chair you don't want to sit in?" I said.

"To get your guests to leave early?" He wasn't really paying attention. He was watching the growing queue at the counter, studying the customers, how the throughput worked. It's how I'd persuaded him to come with me to Seattle in the first place: to discover the secret to coffeehouse empires. His café chain, Borealis, had seven outlets. He wanted more. We had already had latte and espresso and Americano and green tea at separate Tully's in Capitol Hill, Wallingford, and the University District. I was now drinking something called Safari Tea, because it was caffeine free, and trying not to think about meeting my mother.

"I like the Tully's layout," I said. "I can sit almost anywhere and have a view of the door, and if I have to have my back to it, there are enough windows to see moving reflections if trouble heads my way. There are no hidden corners, no blind spots. No shadowed places by the entrance to deter customers."

"Deter customers?" Now he was paying attention.

"I've told you this," I said. "People are more comfortable if they can sit with their back towards a solid wall, even if they don't know why."

"I thought you were talking about design nonsense, about feng shui."

"No."

We were quiet for a while. I mused some more on the Wiram chair.

A man with a bad hairpiece came in, stood in line for thirty seconds, saw it wasn't moving, and left.

"Jonie wouldn't have let that happen."

"No." Jonie, his favorite barista, was always watching. I had seen her bring him a fresh Americano, just as the thought was forming in his mind.

"I wonder how she's managing."

"Fine," I said.

"I'm having to pay her more," he said.

"She deserves it." I didn't know why she stayed. We were quiet a minute, watching the young Tully's barista begin to slowly fall apart. Dornan stirred; I could tell he wanted to go help.

But the Seattle customers remained unfazed. Someone said something that made everyone smile, even the barista, and Dornan relaxed. I wished I could. My mother might be in Seattle by now.

"Feng shui does, in fact, mention solid walls," I said. "Good design is good for a reason. Did I tell you about the chair I saw in Atlanta just before we left? It was an art furniture exhibit at the Lowe Museum . . ."

The first item in the exhibit had been a two-drawered nightstand. From a distance its dark red wood looked top-heavy and unstable, as improbable as the skeleton of a T. rex. The catalogue told me it was a cubist-constructivist side table, and talked about its construction of sixty perpendicularly aligned rods, two hundred forty sides, and seventy-eight joints, all perfectly machined to within three one-thousandths of an inch—aerospace tolerances. It talked about Wiram's early modern influences, about Fibonacci numbers, negative space, and Euclid's harmonic proportions. It did not tell me what kind of tree the wood was cut from.

". . . I looked at this furniture, and I thought what a cold life the maker had led, and how I could have ended up like that."

"If you hadn't met, well . . ."

"Julia. Yes. And it made me think about Luz."

"I don't know anyone else who thinks of a ten-year-old girl when she sees furniture."

"She's happy with the Carpenters—"

"Carpenters, ha, I get it."

I stopped. Carpenters. Luz's stepfamily. Their name had never really registered before. "Not that," I said. "She's happy there, or she was a few weeks ago, and they love her. But they've got no money, and they don't know how to fight the kinds of things she'll have to deal with. It would be easy to say, Oh, I don't know anything about kids, here's a big fat check every month, but I'm responsible. I should legally adopt her. I intend to legally adopt her. But what does that mean? Adoption is like marriage, it should mean something, it shouldn't just be a piece of paper."

"Okay."

"But there's no order in a child's life, no clear goal. You can't orchestrate the experience, things just happen. And when I was looking at this furniture, I knew, as clearly as I know this tea is disgusting, that no child ever ran into that man's workshop at a critical juncture and made his chisel slip a hair and cut the ball of his thumb, spill the blood in a Rorschach spatter that pissed him off, but then made him go, Oh!, and gave him an idea. No. Here was a man who might notice a bloody and magnificent sunset over the city but not really see it, because he couldn't see something like that unless he was on vacation, wearing shorts and sandals and with a glass of pinot noir in his hand. Am I making sense?"

"Well, no, not really."

"It's the difference between cold-blooded and taken-on-the-volley decisions. If you get your arm caught in a bear trap and then you see a hungry grizzly thundering down the trail, you have a choice: cut off your arm or die, right there. No time to think. Boom, you do it. But if you get caught in a trap and then nothing happens for a day you have to deliberately consider what it means to cut your own arm off. You have to worry about whether or not you've made the right decision. Even when you pick up your Swiss Army knife you wonder if you're doing the right thing. When you lay the blade against your skin you wonder. Even when you've cut through the skin and fat and muscle, severed the first tendon, are unfolding the saw for the bone, you think, It's not too late to stop."

"I do wish you wouldn't talk about things like that." His head had pulled back, the way a cat's does when you peel an orange. "And I don't understand how adopting a child is like . . ." He flapped his hand squeamishly.

"It's not about having kids. It's about everything. It's about the fact that with rescuing Luz, it was the bear trap and the bear, but with my mother, with adoption, it's a deliberate choice."

"Ah. Your mother."

I moved my tea to one side.

"Love isn't like losing an arm," he said.

"Yes, it is. Except it's your autonomy, not your arm."

"It's not the same. Look"—he tapped the table until I did, literally, look at him—"you talk about control and order and structure, but that's not really who you are. No, let me finish. You do plan and prepare and practice, and you do like your life to be orderly, but— Okay. Think of it this way. You're standing on a deserted road in Arkansas with a small child and suddenly a woman pulls a gun. You're in someone's house and the intruder turns out to have a knife. You're driving down the street and the car in front of you hits black ice. What do you do?"

"Whatever it takes." Fast and free and fluid.

"You improvise. Exactly. That's what life is, one big improv session."

"Improvisation is not . . . reliable."

"No. But that's the way it is—"

Shoulds don't matter.

"—life is about doing the best you can. Living with ambiguity. Risking failure. Letting go of the notion of perfection."

We reflected on our shoes for a while.

"So tell me more about this furniture you hated so much."

"I didn't hate it," I said, surprised. "It was fascinating. Some of the pieces looked as impossible as the flight of a jumbo jet." Yet they had cried out to be touched. For the drawer to be pulled in and out, sliding with the extravagant precision of a luxury handgun. For flesh and bone to trace the intersection of one plane with another, follow the distribution of tension across space, weigh the amazement of an empty fulcrum—a false one, a joke, if you like—until you figure out the real center. Yet it had all felt like lies. "You know what it was? It wouldn't just stand there and be. It tried to hide behind its own cleverness. It wasn't brave."

"Furniture as philosophy?"

"You'd think so, from the catalogue." I related snippets of the catalogue blurb, quoting liberally from the artists' statements.

"They said it was what?" he said.

"A chair taken seriously as such," I repeated. "A chair truly interrogated, a chair raised to the level of a question."

"Is that right," he said, and shook his head, and we both laughed.

———

ON THE drive to the Tully's in Ballard, the sun came out and stayed out, and the car began to smell comfortably of Dornan's new leather jacket and the bag of unground beans he'd bought on Capitol Hill. The red brick of the side streets glowed and for a moment the city looked almost European.

I'd let him pick the radio station. He chose jazz. I listened and tried to understand why people liked it. It reminded me of the Wiram furniture: afraid to stand still and be known.

"About my mother," I said. "She sent e-mail from the plane last night. She's arriving this afternoon and will call my room at the Edgewater." Only Dornan, Luz, and Bette had my cell phone number. "They'll be jet-lagged, so I'll meet her for an early cocktail in her suite, their suite, and spend more time with her tomorrow—which is when you can meet her, if you like."

He nodded. "We're still on for visiting your film set this evening?"

"Yes." I slowed behind a pickup truck that seemed to think twenty-five miles an hour was degenerate and risky. "After lunch, do you want to go to the museum?"

"Shouldn't you be getting back in case your mum calls?"

"I spent too many years as a child sitting and waiting for a phone call." I accelerated past the truck.

"I think we could slow down a little."

"Sorry." I eased back on the accelerator.

"It'll be fine," he said. "You'll be fine."

I nodded.

"Have you considered taking her a gift of something, a present? Flowers, maybe."

"Flowers?"

"I always take my mum flowers."

He liked his mother.

AFTER LUNCH I went to the Pike Place market and bought calla lilies, and then walked along Western to buy a Loetz glass vase—art nouveau, in iridescent blue-green and silver—to put them in. When I got back to my dim hotel room,

I filled the vase and trimmed the flowers and wondered how I would get the full vase and loose flowers to the Fairmont. So I put the stems in two tooth mugs— I had to prop the flowers against the bathroom mirror—poured the water out of the vase, and dried it with a towel, which left lint all over it. And then the lilies, which were too long to stay in the tooth mugs, fell out and smeared the mirror with pollen, which, when I wiped it away with a hand towel, stained the white cotton deep orange. I started to feel the way I had when I was five and had tried, for Mother's Day—which in England is in March—to make a collage of spring flowers poking through the snow from sugar paper and glue and Rice Crispies, and ended up ruining the granite counter in the kitchen. The smell of the lilies was thick and cloying, and the center of the flowers, with their deep, speckled pink throats and thrusting yellow stamen tongues, looked diseased. I threw them in the bin.

The room was too hot and smelled heavy and sweet, like rotting jungle. My scalp itched with sweat. My heart rate was high, close to ninety, my breathing shallow, my muscles trembling very slightly. Dornan and his stupid caffeine.

I called room service and ordered chamomile tea, and then opened the armoire, sat on the bed, and surveyed my wardrobe.

My mother was used to the high fashion of London, and if we had been meeting in a chic restaurant in, say, Atlanta, the occasion would have demanded the Vera Wang dress or the Armani or Max Mara suit, but this was Seattle, and I was her daughter, and the meeting would be private.

The first time I remembered my mother talking about clothes was when I was ten years old and we went shopping together. Normally, I would go with my father, when he was in town, or one of my mother's smooth-faced assistants. I picked whatever I liked, without consultation, and they paid. Sometimes, if I was in Yorkshire, I went with my friend, Christie Horley, the Honourable Miss Christie, whose purse was held by her nanny, or, on rare occasions, her older sister. At those times Christie and I picked things for each other, commented rudely on each other's choices, laughed, tried on something else. On the day I went with my mother to the designer boutique of a London department store to find a jacket, I wasn't sure who was supposed to choose. I would lift a hanger from the rail, hold the jacket against myself, and look at my mother. She would nod in her noncommittal diplomat's way: I acknowledge the jacket. I got more and more restless; I was doing something wrong, but I didn't know what, or what to do about it. Looking back, she probably had no more idea of how to go mother-daughter shopping than I did, and neither of us was capable of simply asking the other for opinions or suggestions: asking made one vulnerable. Eventually, after about fifteen jackets, clumsy with self-consciousness and embarrassment, I tried to jam the hanger back on the wrong rail, which was full, and the jacket fell on the floor. I wanted her to hold out her arms, I wanted to run away and cry, I wanted to kill something. "This is a stupid shop and I don't want a stupid jacket!" She nodded, picked up her purse, and said, *With clothes, err on the side of elegance: rich but simple, in color, cut, and cloth.* I nodded as though I understood, and she stood, and we left. We went to a tea shop and drank coffee. *What we wear sends a message,* she said, as though we'd been having a continuous discussion on the matter. *It broadcasts our confidence, our means, our taste. You can insult a host by underdressing, and hurt a friend by overdressing. If in doubt, choose simple style and top-quality cloth. Casual elegance.*

It was useful advice, but I had gone home that day without a jacket, and I never went shopping with my mother again.

I wondered, as I pulled on a sleek, forest green silk-and-cashmere turtleneck, beautifully cut lamb's wool skirt, and four-hundred-dollar boots, if my mother had any friends. It was difficult to picture her at a party other than a polished diplomatic function. No nightclubs, or walking tours of the Mediterranean, or weekends in wine country. I couldn't imagine where she had met Eric. I remembered the photo of her, laughing. Perhaps a charity hacking event. Did they shop together? For what kind of clothes?

I popped loose a button taking off the skirt. She'd married a man who liked fast cars and Gilbert and Sullivan; the suede trousers would be more suitable.

On the way out, I put the lily-laden wastebasket in the corridor to be emptied. The smell made me want to retch. I put the Loetz vase on the backseat of the car where I would see it tomorrow and remember to return it. I opened all four windows.

Halfway down Second Avenue, I changed my mind, and instead of continuing to University Street, turned right on Stewart and drove to Pike Place. The market was closing and stank of fish-slimed tile and discarded ice. All the flower stalls but one were shut tight, and that was in the process of closing.

"Wait," I said, "I need some flowers."

"Not much left, but take pick," the tiny Korean woman said.

There were no roses or orchids, no lilies or carnations, nothing left but the kind of raggedy garden flowers that were one step up from weeds: snapdragons and gerbera daisies and freesias. They smelled light and lovely, and their colors were bright and cheerful. The exact opposite of elegance. I bought a handful of each, and gave her an extra twenty dollars for the plastic bucket of water to stand them in until I got to the hotel.

BETWEEN THE valet parking station and the reception desk in the lobby of the Fairmont, two bellboys offered to carry my sloshing bucket and little vase. When I gave my name at the desk, the receptionist summoned the special elevator, then asked if I'd need any help getting to the Presidential Suite. If she had said, *Ma'am, that bucket is ugly, please let one of the staff take it up via the service elevator so our guests won't have to see it,* I might have accepted. Instead I took a perverse delight in pretending to misunderstand. "Oh, it's not heavy, but thank you." She nodded in that *You are of course crazy, but you're the customer and, hey, it takes all kinds* Seattle way, and appeared unperturbed when I changed my mind and told her I'd take the flowers and leave the bucket with her, and did she have any spare tissue paper to wrap the vase?

THE PRESIDENTIAL SUITE had double doors and a bell push. My first surprise was that my mother answered the door herself. The second was that her hair was almost wholly grey. I was still staring at it when she plucked the vase and flowers from me, put them on a table, and took both my hands in hers. They felt smaller than they should have, and very cool.

"Aud," she said, and we stood there without speaking, and then she ran her thumbs over the backs of my knuckles. It had been twenty-five years since she'd done that, but my body remembered, and it was telling me I should be half my mother's height, while my eyes told me I was, in fact, an inch taller. She smiled, squeezed, and let go. My hands sank to my sides, though in some alternate reality they reached out. "Aud, I would like you to meet my husband, Eric Loedessoel. Eric, this is my daughter, Aud."

A man stepped forward from nowhere, and the world snapped back to its proper dimensions. I held out my hand, he grasped it in his, and shook vigorously.

"Aud, I am so very, very pleased to meet you." A mid-Atlantic accent. We were speaking English, then. I looked at his hand, and he let go. He smiled. The dental work was not visible. "My apologies," he said. "It's just that I've wanted to meet you for so long."

"The flowers," I said. "They need to be in water." I looked around for the usual efficient assistant.

"Come and sit," my mother said, and picked up the vase and flowers and moved through the double doors to the sitting room. She even moved differently, as though she had been unbound in some way. Eric and I followed.

There were flowers everywhere, huge formal arrangements in stately vases. A purple petal fell off one of the snapdragons and settled forlornly on the red carpet. She pointed to a sofa upholstered in cream-striped beige silk.

"I won't be a moment." She stepped into the guest bathroom and ran water. Now that I couldn't see her I realized I had no idea what she was wearing. Something green?

"Aud?" I looked up. Eric gestured at a wet bar, and a row of bottles and glasses. "Something to drink?"

"A kamikaze," I said, just to see how he'd handle it.

"Ah. Well, a kamikaze just happens to be one of the hundreds of cocktails I have no idea how to make." His shoulders were loose and relaxed. "If you have your heart set on one, we could figure it out between us. Failing that, we can get the bar to send one up, or I could promise you I'll learn how to make it for next time, and meanwhile make you something I'm more familiar with."

I said nothing.

His pause was very brief. "I understand gin and French pretty well, but admittedly only straight up and on the dry side. I understand a good malt whiskey and fine bourbon. Your mother made sure we have akevit—though I tell you frankly I don't know good from bad—and of course we have a variety of beer. Or we could simply try the wine the hotel sommelier recommended to match the food."

On the table, not at all hidden by the flowers, were three beading bottles of white wine, two decanters of red, and an ice bucket with champagne. In the center was an artful arrangement of silver salvers: seafood, antipasti, salad, and glistening caviar with the old-fashioned accompaniments of toast points and minced onion and chopped egg.

"I know," he said, nodding. "I'd hoped for turkey on rye or tuna salad, but the chef's pride seems to have been at stake."

I'd forgotten he'd spent a lot of time in Washington, D.C. He was wearing a white turtleneck in knitted silk and casual trousers in grey. His shoes and belt were thick and polished. His hair was also thick, with a natural-looking wave. He looked like a cross between a gay soap opera star and a member of the Senate.

"There," said my mother, and put the Loetz vase and flowers on a side table. "Lovely. The perfect antidote." She waved at the heavy vases, the stiff drapes, the gleaming silver, and glistening fish eggs, and her whole body swayed, like that of younger woman. Though her waistband was a little larger than it had been. "You always did have a good eye."

Waistband. Jeans. She was wearing jeans.

"Aud?" I dragged my gaze away from the little rivets on her hip pocket. Both of them were looking at me. "A glass of wine?"

"Good," I said. "Yes. Please."

My mother in jeans, married to a man wearing Polo. The glass in my hand was reassuringly cold. I kept sipping until it was empty.

"An Oregon pinot gris," Eric said as he refilled it. "I'm glad you like it."

"Yes," I said, and they talked some more, some polite chitchat about Vancouver and flights and food while I gathered my wits.

After a while my mother noticed I was beginning to understand what they were saying. She put her wineglass down. "How are you, Aud?"

"I'm . . . well."

"When did you arrive in Seattle?"

"We've been here since Wednesday."

"We?"

"Dornan. He's . . ." He drinks coffee. I kill the people who mess with his girl-friends. "He's a friend."

Like Eric's, my mother's pause was barely noticeable. "I'm so sorry not to have invited him. We must meet tomorrow. For dinner, perhaps. Yes. Dinner. Tomorrow." It had been a while since I had seen my mother surprised enough to repeat herself.

"What do you think of the city?" Eric said.

"I like it. An interesting blend of American and Scandinavian. And you— how long will you be staying?"

"A week, perhaps ten days."

"I hear you have family here."

"I do, but due to an unfortunate accident of timing, they are halfway through a six-week visit to India."

"We want to spend much of our time with you," my mother said. "I want to hear about your life. Do you have pictures?"

"Pictures?"

"The filthy American habit," Eric said, but in a tone that meant he approved. "Photos in your wallet, pictures of your house, your children, your dog, your corner office."

"One of many habits Eric learnt in this country," she said, and laid a hand on his arm. They smiled at each other. She looked at me. "For the first time I think I appreciate the sentiment. I, for example, will be very pleased to see a picture of your daughter."

We were still speaking English but she was beginning not to make sense again.

"The little girl," she said. "The one who was in such difficulties last year."

"You want to see a picture of Luz?"

She nodded. Perhaps she wondered if I had had brain surgery in the years since we'd last seen each other. "Eric tells me that when you live in America and have a child, it is expected."

"I don't know if I do have a child, exactly."

"Then you need to make up your mind." While I tried to parse that one she turned to the hors d'oeuvres and with quick, economical movements dabbed caviar on a toast point, which she put on a plate and handed to me. Her hands were slender and much bigger than Kuiper's.

My mother made a toast point for Eric, and one for herself, took a sip of wine, and again laid her free hand on Eric's arm. The look she gave me was full of meaning, but I had no idea what it was. "I can't tell you what is right," she said, "but I can tell you what is expected—by others, and by this child. It doesn't matter what she calls you, Mor or Tante or Aud, if legally you are her mother, somewhere inside she will one day expect you to behave as one. It doesn't matter if this is likely, or even possible, it is what she will expect. One day."

Her fingers were white at the tips. Eric would have a bruise tomorrow. I ate my toast point.

I **WAS AT** the Edgewater bar, halfway down my second pale green cocktail, when Dornan joined me.

"Is that a kamikaze?"

"I thought I'd try it." I pushed the glass aside. Too much lime. "Ready for that film set?"

"You saw your mum?"

"I did." I dropped cash on the bar and stood. "She wants to invite you for dinner tomorrow."

"Tomorrow?"

I nodded. He reached past me for the kamikaze and drained it in one swallow.

THE PARKING lot was full, and the air trembled below audible range with generators and the subtle pheromones of stress and excitement. The light slicing from the partially open warehouse door was blue-white against the inky sky, and the air was stiff and charged, as though before a storm. I felt every bone snug in its socket, and Dornan's eyes shone.

Inside the warehouse, the noise and heat and light were intense. He paused on the threshold, trying to take it all in, then made a beeline for one of the Hippoworks posters.

Kuiper and another woman at the food services table were shoveling food onto plates that were snatched out of their hands by a seemingly endless stream of actors, grips, sound technicians, and extras in street-kid clothes.

"*Killer Squirrels,*" Dornan said.

"What?"

"Anton Brian Finkel." He tapped the notice. "He made a film in the eighties about squirrels who eat alien nuts or something and go rogue. Great film to watch when wrecked, all these tiny squirrels flying about, trying to look menacing. It's got to be the same man."

"I don't know." From here Kuiper looked very busy.

He saw that I wasn't really paying attention, and followed my gaze. "You going to introduce me?"

"Maybe when she isn't so busy. I'll take you to Finkel's partner, Stan Rusen."

We headed through the streams of eating extras to where the lights and cameras were clustered, but the one giving orders was the bad-tempered Goatee Boy, who today wore his earring in the other ear, not Rusen.

I led Dornan back outside, to the Hippoworks trailer, the one with the lights on. I banged on the door. I was just about to bang again when it was yanked open by a woman talking over her shoulder to whoever was at the other end of the trailer.

". . . can't tell you how pissed off I get when he does that. Oh. Well, who the hell are you?" It was the woman who had been ordering everyone about on the soundstage last time I was here. The set dresser.

"Good evening," I said, and gestured for Dornan to follow me inside.

"Hey," she said as I brushed past her. "I said, who the hell are you?"

"She probably heard you the first time," a man near the door said. I recognized him, too: the technical coordinator she had been arguing with yesterday.

"Joel," I said, remembering. He shifted in surprise, and that's when I saw Rusen, who was sitting at his keyboard looking overwhelmed. When he saw me, he jumped up.

"Aud, hey, glad you came. Peg, Joel, I'm sorry but we'll have to do this later. Boy," he said when they'd gone, "all those two do is squabble: I can't do my job when he does this, I can't get any work done when she does that. This is not like film school." He rubbed the back of his ear. "I'm worrying if I can afford to pay anyone next week and they're carrying on like a couple of kids."

I introduced Dornan. They exchanged pleased-to-meet-yous. "So can you? Pay them next week?"

"Maybe. I'm hoping Anton will be able to figure out a way to sweet-talk the bank."

"Know when he's due back?"

He shook his head, then forced a smile. "Say, I probably sound as bad as Peg and Joel. You didn't come here to listen to me complain. What can I do for you?"

I nearly said: Have you eaten? Kuiper would no doubt be nicer to me if I could tell her he had. "I need some information."

He sat back at his keyboard. "Okay."

"To begin with, general details on everyone who works here: names, résumés, references, date of hire. Anything you think might be useful background information. Former workers, too, please."

"Not a problem." He started tapping.

"Also any documentation you have with regard to meetings or correspondence with EPA and OSHA."

"Easy enough."

"Yesterday, someone on the set mentioned that she thought this production might crash and burn. Any idea what she might have meant by that?"

He dragged his eyes away from the screen and rubbed behind his ear again. "Well, the OSHA thing is killing us."

"Apart from that."

"There have been some delays. Annoying things. Little things."

"Such as?"

"The lighting tech spending five hours getting the set lit right, and then coming back from break to find someone's messed it all up. Hours of night footage lost on the way to the lab. When we reshoot during the day using day-for-night exposures, we find it's all screwy, though the camera guy swears it was set up right. Not so little, that one."

"Write it all down. E-mail it to me." I gave him the address. I couldn't spend every minute with my mother. It would give me something to do while I waited for Monday. And unlike Atlanta, this time I'd be helping people to help themselves. "I'd also be happy to take a look at your accounts, see if I can see a way out of this mess, but I'd understand if you felt uncomfortable with that."

If he didn't give it to me, I'd just take it, but there was no harm in playing nicely, especially when it saved time and effort.

"I'll have to talk to Finkel about that," he said. "Anything else? Did you read the promo material?"

"Not yet, no."

"Oh," he said.

"But my friend Dornan here is a big fan and would no doubt love to hear all about it. He was just telling me about *Killer Squirrels*."

"Oh, jeepers. You saw that? What did you think?"

Dornan paused, then shrugged. "Well, it's a fine film if you're twenty and out of your head and it's two in the morning and there's nothing else on the telly."

Rusen laughed. "Boy, it's awful, all right. It was way before my time but even Anton admits it. *Feral*, now . . . Oh, this one's sweet, real sweet. It's about this girl—young woman, I guess—who wakes in an alley completely naked, and it's night, and she's in a strange city. There's all this—"

"I'll be on the set," I said, and they both nodded.

". . . with shots of steam, strategically placed to keep it PG-thirteen, but it's not cheesy, not even a bit, it's ambience, and then there's this noise . . ."

I shut the door on their strategic wisps of steam. The second woman from the craft-services table was lugging a stack of crates out to the Film Food van. Inside, the food line was down to four people: the bony-faced Bri and his friend, one of the carpenters in overalls, and the assistant wardrobe woman. I watched while Kuiper served them what looked like Thai food, shook her head at something the last one said, and picked up her huge knife again, this time to divide a big, squashy-looking cake. *"Gallia est omnis divisa in partes tres,"* she said, and no one got it. She seemed used to it. She wiped down the counter, those muscles around her wrists sliding over each other like the reins of a stage-coach, controlling everything precisely, checked the coffee urn, added coffee and water, and then turned to the pile of fruit waiting on her chopping board. She pretended she didn't see me. I let her chop for a while. Her hair was twisted up into a knot, and as the knife thunked rhythmically on the board, a loose swatch hanging by the side of her neck shook. Sometimes it looked blond, sometimes light brown. Her earlobe was as pink as a baby's tongue.

"Good evening," I said. If I hadn't been paying attention I would have missed the fractional hesitation between chopping. "Has Rusen eaten anything yet?"

"He's carrying a lot of weight on this picture. He needs to eat." She sounded defensive.

"What about the director?"

She snorted and kept chopping.

"I found out what CAA is."

"You must be thrilled," she said. Then she sighed. "Rusen told me who you are." It was an apology, I think.

I filled one of the cups with a stream of pungent coffee. I felt her watching but took my time, adding just the right amount of cream. Didn't stir. Sipped. Even more assertive than it smelled. "So," I said, and when I looked up, she was chopping again. "Unusual to find a caterer who knows Caesar's commentary."

"You really know how to endear yourself to a girl."

"I expressed it badly."

"No, you didn't. I could quote you more: *quarum unam incolunt Belgae, aliam Aquitani, tertiam qui* . . . But your eyebrows are already in your hair, proving my point. You couldn't be more surprised if I were a trained hamster singing 'Happy Days.'"

No, I wanted to say, let's not do it this way. Let's talk Latin. Do you know Petronius? Ovid? The *Aeneid*? But her look could have drilled granite. "Tell me about this production."

"Not my place. I'm a caterer." Chop, chop.

"But clearly Rusen talks to you. Why is that?"

She didn't say anything. I swallowed more coffee, noticing for the first time in months the slight tightness on the right-hand side of my throat where a razor had opened the skin like silk. That had been a rusty blade. Kuiper's knife would cut bone deep without effort. "All right. Let's talk about catering. If I said I was planning a wedding at the Fairmont and wanted you to cater for three hundred guests, what kind of menu would you suggest?"

"You're not planning a wedding."

"I'm just—"

"Bullshitting me. I don't know why." The knife thunked energetically on her board. She'd take her fingers off if she wasn't careful.

In this light, her hair was the color of sandstone. She was like sandstone: a spire of rock rising from an otherwise featureless desert. No toeholds. I thought about toes for a minute, wiggled mine in their boots. Sipped at my coffee. Now that it was cooler it was beginning to taste almost smoky, not at all like that stuff from Tully's. "So," I said, "Rusen talks to you."

"It's not a crime."

"But as you've pointed out, you're a caterer."

She turned around. "And that, of course, makes me not worth talking to."

It was interesting, the basic dichotomy between her behavior and her face. She sounded and acted as though she were angry, or perhaps very sad, but the set of her facial muscles and the few, faint lines told a story of laughter and enthusiasm and occasional stubbornness. That was the woman I wanted to talk to.

"I've never been on a film set before in my life. I have no idea how it works. I own this warehouse. It's in my best interest to see that the production is profitable and keeps paying rent."

"So you're just here to help."

"Well, yes." Isn't that what I just said? "I'm trying to understand how things operate. It might help everyone. So, please, tell me how sets like this work."

"There aren't any other sets like this one. There are a lot of raw people. Finkel's an old hand, but he's not here, and Rusen's carrying everything. And it's his first film. He was a software architect." An image of someone building a skyscraper from Dalí-like drooping girders popped into my head. "He's smart, but this isn't film school. This might be my first craft-services job, but at least I've been on movie sets before."

"So he talks to you." Does he like it when you talk Latin?

"He hired me. You could say we're learning our jobs together."

A job. "So he asks your advice on things? When there are problems. And there have been problems. You said so." Just a job. Very good. "More than there should have been?"

"Like I say, there are a lot of beginners. Two of the camera operators. The sound guy. But there are a lot of old hands, too. Grips, carpenters, technical—"

"Joel," I said, looking at her small hand with its big knife.

"Joel. Peg. Kathy in costume."

"Which is why I'm wondering if there's been some deliberate sabotage."

I was also starting to wonder how to describe her hair. Sandstone wasn't quite right. Not blond, exactly. Not brown, either. All sorts of different snakes of color in this light, and shiny.

"Why are you giving me that weird look?"

"Weird as a beard," I said, and gave her my best smile. Beards were weird, when you thought about it. Always a different color to head hair. Animals didn't have different color hair on their heads and bodies, did they? Birds did, chickadees and woodpeckers. And badgers, too, come to think of it. Did they even have badgers in this country? Probably not. Hogs, though, they had hogs. "Gif me a hog!" I said in a bad German accent, and flung my arms wide. Now that I'd thought of it, it sounded like a lovely idea, luscious woman, luscious hair, but the woman stepped back and put a tray of stuffed mushrooms between us. Mushrooms. Not as good as truffles. Truffles. They used to use hogs to find them, get the hogs to snuff under the trees in the forest. "Snuffle my truffle," I said, grinning. Truffles, food of princes. Princes ate hummingbirds, too—hummingbirds with long, long tongues. Hummingbirds baked in honey, eaten in a palace. "Tongue palace," I explained, and the woman behind the mushrooms reddened. I reached for her, wanting to take her perfect pink earlobe in my mouth, but my stomach rippled.

"Oh," I said.

She said something, with a question on her face, but someone had turned the sound off.

I put my hand on my stomach. "It's like a heartbeat, but too low down."

She put her big shiny knife on the counter and started to come around to my side. This time my stomach pulsed. I frowned. "Where's the bathroom?" She pointed. "'Bye," I said.

The bathroom was cavernous and the toilets very small and a long way down. I vomited on target. Very satisfactory. Mouth tasted bad, though. And why was the stall door so far away?

I lurched at the sinks but once I had my hand wrapped around the tap they steadied down. I rinsed my mouth. The water felt like chrome in my mouth: hard and brilliant. Very odd. Everything was odd. I couldn't quite work out why.

I frowned, and the sink zoomed away and back again, like a fast-focus pull. And it was very shiny. Definitely not right. Maybe someone could explain what was going on. But that cook person, that Kuiper, I didn't want to look silly in front of her, no, and I couldn't remember where I'd put Dornan.

Fresh air. That might be useful. I knew where that was.

The night air was spicy and soft and quite delicious. I breathed it, in and out, in and out, and my stomach stopped rippling and I felt as light as meringue. By the time I reached the car I felt like a god.

Driving was marvelous. The wheel felt so good under my hands that I jigged it this way and that, and loved the way the tires bit into the road and the car seemed to be climbing a path to the stars, up and up and up, gliding over water that sparkled in the city light like fairy dust. The city was a wonderland. On one side, by the water, a herd of orange brontosaurus nosed at the stacks of little boxes saying Hanjin piled at their feet. I watched carefully but they seemed to be frozen in a line. Floating on the other side of the road in its own glow was the head of a vast green goddess. Lovely.

I jigged the car again, this time on a tight curve, and lights flared red around me. It was like being in a hunting print: mounts with red-coated riders, and the sound of horns. I tooted merrily. The road wound on, and then somehow I wasn't on it, but had been deposited in an open place. I stopped and got out. Funny-looking benches. I wandered over to one—I checked every few steps to make sure my feet were still there—and found that on the bench someone had left a pile of coats and old newspaper.

"Oh," I said, and the lump jerked and sat up, scattering coverings. "I know this place." A square, a triangle. "You must be a pioneer." The pioneer hopped off the bench and scuttled over to some of his friends.

"You dropped this," I told the group of pioneers as I advanced, holding the paper. None of them reached for it. I put it carefully on the end of the bench. Their eyes were very round. "I'm Aud," I said, "I love you all!"

I folded cross-legged to the grass, only it wasn't grass but gritty concrete, and started to tell them about the beauties of the night.

Now I saw that there were others crossing the square, and they were young and smooth and golden, and the music came from a doorway with a woman standing in front of it.

"Dance with me," I said to a young woman in a soft leather jacket, and held out my hand, but her eyes rounded, too, and she hunched up, like an anemone poked with a pencil. Strange and delicate thing. I laughed, spun on my heels. I danced for a while, with myself.

Soon there were many people watching, but none of them would dance with me. I would go find someone who would.

I wandered up and down the street, looking for my Saab, and felt enormously pleased when I remembered it was in Atlanta and I wasn't. "An Audi," I said to myself, and then there it was. Lovely.

Somewhere to my left, the night sparkled blue-white, blue-white, and people moved aside.

Key. I smiled and pulled the key from my pocket. I dropped it. The world swooped a little when I picked it up again. I dropped it again.

Two police officers appeared—where had they come from?—but I was more concerned with my key. Someone had made it very slippery. One of the police officers said something. I finally managed to grasp the key firmly. The other police officer said something, quite loudly, and approached, hand on his belt. I bowled him aside and pushed the little button on my key.

"Boop!" I said, like the car, delighted. It was magic: lights and everything. I pushed it again. Boop! Flash! Boop!

One of the officers was shouting now, and pointing something at me.

"That's dangerous," I told her. "That's a weapon."

"Yes, ma'am. Please step away from the vehicle."

"It's my vehicle," I said.

"Yes. Step away, ma'am. Now."

"No, it's *mine*." You had to be very patient with stupid people.

"You are intoxicated, ma'am."

"No, I'm not. I'm . . ." I almost said *I'm Norwegian* but I wasn't really sure that was true anymore. Not like my mother, anyway. "I'm from Atlantis." That wasn't quite right, either. I shrugged. Close enough. I put my hand on the car door.

"Step away from the vehicle!"

No *Please*, no *Thank you*, no *Ma'am*. Just plain rude. And couldn't she see that I had to leave, I had to leave right now?

"Put your hands in the air and step away from the vehicle!"

Oh, now she was making me cross. And who were all those people, and what were they staring at, and why was the other officer hiding behind his car door? Everything started to hop about. I frowned.

"Oh, shit, Henry, you better get that backup down here *now!*"

They ought to shut up and stop swaying. The officer crouching behind his cruiser stood and aimed at my torso. He had to steady something on the car roof. The flashing blue-white, blue-white of the lights gleamed on the sweat at his forehead. I felt sorry for him, but it had to be done. I raised my magic wand. The officer in front of me swallowed.

My phone rang.

And then something went *zzzsst*, and hit my chest, and I felt as though my insides were boiling away in a blue electric current. I blinked. Another *zzzsst*.

The world bounded to one side and I found myself lying with my cheek on the pavement. My phone was still ringing. Luz. It might be Luz. But when I tried to reach into my pocket, nothing happened. I wasn't sure where my arms were.

The phone rang and rang and rang. The world tilted again, and jerked, and then I was sitting in the back of a car and slowly toppling sideways. My nose came to rest on the vinyl seat. "It smells," I said, but no one was listening.

My phone rang and rang. My door opened and a small animal jumped into my jacket pocket—no, it was the woman's hand—and then she was talking to someone on my phone.

". . . Officer Matsuo. And you are? Yes, sir, Seattle PD. Torvingen? That's the owner of this handset? White female, weird pale blue eyes, about six feet tall. English accent, or— Say again? Her mother is who?" A long silence. "I see, sir. Yessir. Um-hm. Bye." She closed the phone, said, "Shit," very softly. "Shit."

I fell asleep for a while and woke when the seat bumped and mysteriously turned into a hospital gurney. A harassed-looking triage nurse in greens said,

"Christ, not another one. What's her name?" A man said something. I turned my head—it was very heavy. The police officer. Henry. "Aud," the nurse said, "look at me." Bright light. "No, keep your eyes open. Aud, I need them open." It was difficult. Strange dry-warm feeling on my eyelids: latex-clad thumbs. More bright light, moving from side to side. "Aud, are you one of the movie people?"

I said, No, or tried to, but my mouth seemed glued shut—

"She says she's from Atlantis," Henry said helpfully.

—but then I remembered a woman with blond hair talking about cameras and falling and—

LESSON 3

ALL TEN WOMEN WERE DAMP-SKINNED. OUTSIDE IT WAS IN THE HIGH FORTIES BUT THE repaired thermostat was clearly set by people upstairs who weren't doing much in the way of exercise. I'd shown my class the axe kick, a coup de grâce delivered with the heel and used to break the spine when your assailant was down—though none of them, of course, had really understood the implications of that; I was just showing them how to kick a bag—and the side kick, which used the edge of the foot like a guillotine and was perfect for either neatly displacing the kneecap or more messily wrecking all the ligaments that hold the knee joint together, depending on the angle of attack.

The bag, which I'd unhooked for the exercise and rested end-up on the floor, sagged sadly at knee height. Therese and Kim were braced against it while Katherine let loose a good one.

"Again," I said. "You might not be accurate with the first kick. Always keep kicking. Once is almost never enough." She whomped it again. "And once more, this time with some noise. Use your lungs. They're like bellows, pumping oxygen. Fuel for your fire."

This time when she kicked she squeaked like a furious guinea pig, a sound that at least had the startle factor in its favor.

"Good, thank you. These kicks are what you use when you are in a serious fight, when you have to put them down long enough to get away."

"How long is that for?" Katherine said, breathing hard. She kept eyeing the bag as though willing it to straighten up and act threatening so that she could kick it again.

I looked at the class. "How long do you think?"

"It depends," they chorused.

"Exactly. Long enough to ensure your safety, whatever it takes. And every situation will be different. Let's say you're in the parking lot at Kroger. How long then?"

"Two minutes?" Jennifer said.

Tonya shook her head. "It doesn't matter how long, just as long as you've got the time to get to your car."

And get in and lock the doors.

"Or maybe just long enough to get back into the store and get help," said Therese.

"Also good. Now, what about being in Piedmont Park at night? Suze?"

"It would have to be longer, because it's a big park, and it's dark."

"How long do you think?"

"If you were in the middle of the park? Twenty minutes. It would take about that to get to the lights, and people."

"That's on a normal day. If you're hurt or in shock, you won't be thinking clearly or moving fast. You'll need even more time."

"Or you could call nine-one-one and hide," Christie said.

"Calling nine-one-one is a good idea no matter what," I said. "But just because you call doesn't mean they come. To be safe you take them down long enough for you to reach safety."

They thought about that for a bit. Tonya was the first to see where it was heading.

"Twenty or thirty minutes is a real long time. . . ."

And now Therese was folding her arms: she saw where we were going, too, and she didn't like it one bit.

I nodded. "Sometimes the only way to survive is to disable your attacker, not just hurt them. Hurting them makes them not want to run after you, but disabling them means making sure they can't."

No one said anything.

"In this kind of extreme case, you go for the eye, the knee, or the throat. Eyes, because if they can't see you, they can't find you. Knee, because they can't chase you if a leg doesn't work. Windpipe, because if they can't breathe they can't do anything."

Compromise oxygen supply, structural integrity, or visual acquisition of the target—though Jennifer, of course, might want to know how you'd deal with a blind attacker who was already used to following people they couldn't see.

Therese tightened her arms and lowered her chin. "If you're talking about cutting someone's air supply for twenty minutes while you're not there, you're talking about maybe killing them."

"Yes." Another way to cut off oxygen would be to cut off its medium of transport, the blood supply—open the carotid, for example—but I imagined she would like that idea even less.

"I can't believe that would be necessary."

And that was the problem, mine as well as theirs, because part of me hoped they never had to believe, never came to a personal understanding of the necessity for these techniques.

"Could you kill someone to save yourself?" Therese said.

"Yes."

"You sound very sure."

"If you decide to hurt someone to save yourself, you need to commit to it completely."

"Do or don't do, there is no try," Nina said in a Yoda voice.

"Something like that," I said over the nervous laughter. "But about whether or not learning this is necessary, think of all the other things you learn that you'll probably never need. Like fire drills. It's unlikely that you'll ever need to scramble from your workplace at three in the afternoon because of a massive fire, but you learn the procedure just in case." But fires weren't directed personally at their target, they didn't sneer and call you bitch, and if you got burnt, your friends didn't think it was your fault. Women weren't reared from infancy to fear fire.

"So," I said, "the knee, the eye, the throat. The knee is a good target, difficult to protect against one of those kicks we just learnt. The eye is extremely vulnerable." Tonya made a pecking motion. "The throat is more complicated. There are two targets. The larynx, or voice box, which you can feel if you tilt your head up and run your finger down your windpipe until you feel a bump, your Adam's apple. No, higher up than that, Christie. Kim, would you show her— about where her mole is, yes. It's easier to find on a man. If you hit that bump hard it will fracture and swell. The windpipe closes."

"Sounds easy enough," Pauletta said.

"It is."

Easy did not mean fast or clean. Suffocation takes minutes, and when the victim clutches at his swelling throat it grates, like a knife point dragging along a brick wall.

"It sounds easy, but how many of you think you could do it?"

They looked at one another.

"You need to know you can do it. You need to know it will work. We ended last week with Christie saying that feminine means vulnerable. And that's what we're told, yes, but here's a question. If an average man attacks a woman, intending to rape her, what do you think will happen if she struggles?"

"It'll just make things worse," Jennifer said. "He'll get mad and hurt you worse."

"No, not according to Justice Department statistics. Their latest available figures say that women fight off unarmed rapists successfully seventy-two percent of the time."

They were quiet.

"But what if he has a knife?" Jennifer again.

"Then she'll fight him off fifty-eight percent of the time."

"A gun?"

"Fifty-one percent."

"More than fifty percent, even with a gun?"

"Even with a gun. Government statistics." The media wouldn't say that, though, because fear is what sells papers and commercial spots. "And we're talking about untrained, unarmed women. Even before you set foot in this class the odds were in your favor: if you fight back, you'll probably win. Most stranger attackers, even serious ones who have planned their attack extensively, rely on the attack being fast and quiet. An attacker will watch you: read your body language. Depending on the situation they will test you, to see how easy you'll be: they'll spin some story about needing your help. They'll flatter you, flirt with you. They imply that you're being unreasonable or not nice or impolite or illogical. You have been brought up—programmed, if you like—to respond to these suggestions."

"Those fuckers," said Suze.

"You have been trained to seek approval, to please, to not draw attention to yourselves. It's powerful training. Don't underestimate it. I can teach you to snap spines with your bare feet, to break free of a stranglehold, to fracture a larynx with the side of your hand, but if you're too worried about a stranger's disapproval to even tell him you want to sit by yourself on a park bench, you won't be able to use any of it."

"So what's the goddamn point?"

"Remember the first class, hitting the bag?"

"*Blam,*" said Nina.

"It was a way to think around the programming. A mental trick. Therese, how many children do you have?"

"Children? Two. Twins, boy and girl. Six years old."

"How would you have felt if you had seen that man, the one Sandra played last week, sitting on the bench next to your daughter?"

"I would have dragged her away fast, and maybe reported him to the police."

"Why?"

"Because she's a child!"

"But he was just talking about his dog."

"No, he wasn't. He was a creep and a liar."

"How did you know this?"

"Because I could tell."

"How?"

"The way he sat, the way he looked at me."

"People who lie expertly with their words give themselves away with their bodies. And your body knows that. It's a language clearer than English. If words and actions conflict, believe the body." I would explain why another time. "You read him correctly, Therese. You were willing to act on that knowledge to protect your child, but not yourself. Why's that?"

"Because it's cool to go all mother lion if it's your kid," Kim said.

"Exactly. So next time you're in a situation like that, ask yourself what you'd do if it was your daughter sitting there, or your frail, elderly mother. If you'd be willing to risk embarrassment for their sake, why not your own? And then ask yourself this: what's the worst-case scenario if I act on my belief?"

"You're totally wrong and end up feeling like a dork," Christie said.

"Right. But then ask yourself: what's the worst-case scenario if I don't act on my belief?"

Silence, then "Huh," said Pauletta.

I nodded. "Right. I end up dead."

"You make it all sound so easy," Katherine said, "like it was a . . . a . . ."

"Cost-benefit analysis," Tonya said.

"That's what it is. When you go home tonight, get out your list and add another column: feeling like a dork. Compare that to how it would feel to being dead, or being raped, or having both arms broken, or your cat tortured or your car stolen, and make some decisions."

A couple of them looked thoughtful.

"For now, let's move on to some physical tricks. Remember that MARTA station from last time? We'd just left a scared young woman about to be attacked. Who wants to play that part?" Christie stepped forward. "Do you remember how she was standing?"

Christie put her hands in her pockets and turned her head from us.

"I'm going to play the attacker. I won't do anything to hurt you, so try to relax. Okay, the rest of you, how should I attack her?"

"Grab her from behind," Nina said. "Like you're going to drag her off into a dark corner."

I wrapped my arms around Christie. "What can you do from there to escape?" She struggled halfheartedly and subsided. "Not much."

"See how having her hands trapped in her pockets means she's lost one whole set of body weapons," I said to the class.

"But even with her hands free she couldn't do much with them from there," Pauletta said.

I let go of Christie. "You grab me this time." She did, gripping her own wrists and getting a solid base. "Okay, my arms are still trapped by my side but this time my hands are out of my pockets. My attacker's expecting me to try to pull them free." I made as if to do that and Christie tightened her grip obligingly. "But think about what I can reach if I move the other way." I moved both hands easily to her inner thighs. "The groin's very vulnerable from here, but he won't be expecting me to go for it because he thinks I'll be struggling to escape. Okay, what else can I reach? Think about the different body weapons."

"Kick him," Katherine, sounding excited. Kicking seemed to be her thing.

"Yes, right foot or left: a stamp straight down onto the top of his foot would hurt, especially if I was wearing heels. There are also lots of nerve endings in the shin. You could scrape"—I lifted my left foot and ran the bare heel gently down Christie's shin—"or I could kick back, like a donkey." I demonstrated in slow motion. "What else?"

"Nails," Kim said, with a *ha!* look. "'Specially in summer."

"Yes, if his legs are bare you could get his thighs, maybe even behind his knees if he's really tall. Lots of blood vessels behind the knees, and the hamstring. The femoral artery in the groin. Perhaps you could reach forward to get the back of his hands. Very sensitive there." And a lot of tendons. "What else?

What about his face?" Blank looks. "Think. Use your head, literally." I did a slow-motion head butt. "It would depend on his height, but you could get his nose or chin or collarbone." Break the collarbone just right and bone splinters would tear up the big blood vessels that lead up to the neck.

"Wouldn't that hurt?" Jennifer said.

"The skull's very thick at the back, near the top, and there aren't many nerve endings. What else? What would he be expecting? Think about different dimensions."

Silence, then "Downwards," Nina said. "You could go down, to the floor. Wriggle out like a kid would. He wouldn't expect that. Unless he had three-year-olds at home."

"Good. Or if he's trying to drag you off, you can go limp, like a child, make it really hard for him to carry you. Okay, thank you, Christie."

She let go and I flexed my arms a couple of times.

"There are endless ways to deal with any situation. What I want you to do is find ways to use an attacker's expectations against them. If they expect you to go forward, go back. If they think you'll pull, push. You could do worse than remember Nina's words: like a kid would. A very badly behaved kid. Be loud, be definite, be badly behaved, kick up a fuss: refuse to do as you're told. Don't be afraid to call attention to yourselves. Think in three dimensions. Be stubborn, be contrary, be totally self-absorbed. It doesn't matter what anyone else thinks, especially your attacker. You don't owe anyone an apology, or explanation, or information, or help, or even understanding. Be selfish. If you wouldn't let it happen to your child or your parent, don't let it happen to you."

That would help only so much. Their training was bone deep. I wanted them to leave today with one thing, just one, that would make it permissible for them to hurt someone to protect themselves, a way for them to impersonalize the choice.

"Imagine it's summer. You get a new grill that burns so clean you can't see flame, all you can see is the heat shimmering over it. You invite your neighbors, all adults, around for a barbecue, but you warn them, each and every one, about the grill—that it's hot, they're not to go near it—yet the woman next door sticks her hand in it and gets burnt. Whose fault is that?"

"Wouldn't be mine," said Pauletta. I looked at Katherine, who nodded, then Jennifer, who said, "The neighbor's. Absolutely."

"So, what?" Suze said. "We should set ourselves on fire?"

"Yes. In a way." They gawped at me. "Split into two groups, one this side of the room, one that. Each group subdivides into a two and a three. The two face the three. I want the twos in the center facing out." The room would be just about big enough. Nina and Tonya faced Pauletta, Katherine, and Kim. Suze and Christie faced Sandra, Jennifer, and Therese. Nina grinned and started to click her fingers: the Sharks versus the Jets. "So, Nina and Tonya, and Suze and Christie, you're two friends out somewhere—where?"

"The parking lot outside Kroger," said Nina.

"The soccer fields in Piedmont Park," said Suze.

"So you're walking along, minding your own business, when these three shady characters"—I couldn't imagine a less shady trio than Therese and Sandra and Jennifer—"step across your path. It's already clear—maybe from what they've said, maybe something they've already done, but there's absolutely no ambiguity—it's clear that they intend to hurt you. You either have to hurt them back, or get badly injured."

Each immediately edged closer to her partner.

"Now what?" Nina said. "Is this where we get six feet tall?"

"This is where you set yourselves on fire. Start to swing your arms in a circle perpendicular to the floor. Big, easy circles. No muscle tension." I demonstrated. "Start slowly. Backwards or forwards, doesn't matter. Try it. Good. Feel the blood rush to your hands. A little faster. Clench your fists. Remember the first lesson: *blam, pow, zap!* Feel the blood bulging in your fists, making them heavy. Ever seen a kid windmilling on the playground? Charging at a group of other kids? That's what you're going to do. Faster. You're on fire. When you charge, if they don't get out of the way, it's not your fault. *Blam, pow, zap.* Faster, as fast as you can! Charge."

Suze bellowed like a bee-stung bullock and charged, with Christie a split second behind; Tonya leapt forward with a screech and Nina followed, laughing. Their opponents, sensibly, ran away. Tonya, still screeching, galloped after them, chasing Pauletta and Katherine, then Jennifer, who had run all the way around the wall to get away from Suze.

"Okay, quick, Therese and Sandra, Kim and Katherine, in the center. Pump your arms, charge!"

Therese did not make a sound, but I didn't worry about that. Sandra's silence was more troubling. Katherine squealed and Kim hooted, and the other women were shouting or laughing so much that it didn't matter.

"And Jennifer and Pauletta, and Suze and Christie again. Mill those arms. Go!" This time I definitely heard Christie, and Pauletta made a sound a bit like a police siren. "Yell," I said, "anything, any sound you like. All of you, attacker and defender. Make it loud. Anything. Your lungs are bellows pumping the fire." The noise was deafening. Through it I heard Jennifer making a thin *Eeeeee!* like an otherworldly kettle about to boil over. Pauletta's ululating siren began to climb in pitch, then soared into a scream that sliced across the room and brought the action stuttering to a halt like a video glitch.

"Enough. Good." They were all grinning. Pauletta was high-fiving Nina. "If you charge like that at a bad guy and he doesn't get out of your way, it's not your fault he gets hurt. Clarity of communication is the key."

"But what if one of them had a knife?" Jennifer asked.

"In that case you'd break for one of the unarmed assailants."

"What if they all had knives?"

"I can show you variations on the hand technique to protect blood vessels and tendons, but in all likelihood you'd get some kind of cut."

"What if one of them had a gun?"

"Handguns are notoriously inaccurate, even when the shooter is well trained. And it's very hard to be accurate when someone is charging at you, screaming."

"What if they all had guns?"

Or a flamethrower, a tank battalion, a tactical nuke . . . We could play this game forever. "You would use all that you know to stay alive. You know more today than you did yesterday. In every class you'll understand more. But let's be clear, there is no magic bullet, no funny handshake, no secret decoder ring. Nothing and no one can keep you perfectly safe. There are only probabilities. We prepare, we practice, we do the work, and then we try to forget about it, because no matter how big and fast and strong you are, how heavily armed or well trained, there's always going to be someone out there who is bigger, faster, or stronger. Always."

FOUR

I LAY IN A BED, ON MY BACK. I COULDN'T OPEN MY EYES. BREATHING FELT LIKE AN effort. Silk clung to my calves and forearms—clothes, no, pajamas—and I could move my arms and legs a little. Firm mattress, good-quality cotton sheets tucked in neatly, warmth but no weight—a down comforter. Very quiet. I listened to my breath: no echo, which meant soft surfaces. Not a hospital. I focused on the air moving through my nose and mouth and caught a hint of . . . perhaps cologne, perhaps high-end toiletries. A hotel. I couldn't move my head. I listened harder, and felt someone outside my line of sight, watching, assessing, waiting.

MY MOUTH tasted vile. I could make out dim, reddish shadows on the ceiling that moved a little then stilled. I turned my head slowly—the signals from brain to muscle seemed to be routed through another dimension—and saw glowing numbers. A clock. A bedside table. The numbers changed again, from 5:03 to 5:04.

Someone had drugged me. They'd put it in the wine, or the kamikazes, or the coffee; sprinkled it on the food, or sprayed it on the flowers.

When I tried to sit up the world tilted violently and I had to lie down again. I panted for a while, but couldn't seem to get my breath. When the world steadied, I raised myself cautiously onto my right elbow. I reached out and up with my left hand, which swung back and forth like a weather vane before I managed to put it on the cold lamp base and find the knoblike switch. I pushed at it three times before it clicked on. The light was cozy and yellow, but bright enough to see the phone, some clothes folded neatly on a chair, and heavy drapes. Definitely a hotel, a good one.

The dizziness hit again before I could pick up the phone.

THE LIGHT was still on. There was a woman standing by the bed. Phone, I thought, but I couldn't stop staring at her head.

"Are you awake?" she said.

"Your head is pink."

"Yes," she said, then realized what I was worried about, and touched her hair. "It really is pink. Fuchsia."

"Um," I said, so I didn't have to nod.

"Dizzy?"

"Yes."

"I'll be right back." She came back, too quickly for me to sit up or reach for the phone, carrying a blood-pressure cuff, stethoscope, and clipboard. "My name's Suzanne. Left arm, please."

It was more of an effort than it should have been to lift my arm. As I straightened it, I felt a twinge inside the elbow. She pushed up the pajama sleeve—whose? I don't wear pajamas, but they weren't new—and I saw the neat hole in the vein. "Let's use the other arm."

She wrapped the right biceps in the pressure cuff, and pumped. The back of my right hand started to ache. There was a hole in a vein there, too.

"Please keep still." She let out the air, listened, made a note on her clipboard. Unwrapped the cuff and took my wrist in her hand.

"What—"

"Hold on." She finished counting, made another note. "Sorry. What were you saying?"

"What day is it?"

"Saturday. Five-thirty Saturday morning. Can you sit up?"

I did, very slowly. She rubbed her stethoscope warm, then listened to my lungs and heart. I studied the clothes folded on the striped chair. They were mine, but not what I'd been wearing last night. The door to the left of the chair was double, and louvred. I was in a suite. Then I recognized the coffee and cream stripes on the upholstery: the Fairmont.

I'd been in a hospital. Police.

"You okay?"

Pioneer Square. Those things I'd said to Kuiper. Someone had done that to me.

"If you're too warm I could strip off some of these bed covers."

"I'm fine." Snuffle my truffle. That's my vehicle. Tongue palace.

She took a penlight out of her pocket, turned it on. "Look at the light, please. Sorry," she said when I flinched. "Touch your nose with your index finger." I had to move slowly. "Good. Other hand." I was panting again. Someone had done this to me. "You can rest now. I'll get you some water."

I'd been in a hospital, and now I was in a hotel suite. Someone had moved me and I didn't remember a thing. She came back with a pitcher and a glass on a tray. She poured for me, only half-full.

"Can you manage?"

I took it from her grimly, managed to drink most of it before the glass began to slip. She eased it from my hand. "Lean forward, please." She cradled my forehead on her shoulder and efficiently rearranged my pillow. "There. Lean back. Comfy? Good. I have to make a call. I'll be right back."

My muscles felt hot and hollow and soft, like just-blown glass. A red light on the phone winked as Suzanne talked on another extension. I heard snatches of her side of the conversation. ". . . sit up . . . pressure low but not dangerous . . . talk to her?"

The chair holding my clothes stood about six feet from the end of the bed. I could do it if I had to.

"Aud."

I didn't realize I'd shut my eyes until I had to drag them open. My mother stood several feet away. Not in the wine, then. She wore black yoga pants and a charcoal fleece zip-up. Her face was clear and clean and her hair caught in a clip at the base of her neck.

"How are you?"

In the kamikazes at the hotel bar? Just as I remembered Dornan slugging back the rest of my cocktail, it struck me that I had gone to all that trouble to wear the right clothes last night and here I was at half past five in the morning, half-naked in a strange bed, and my mother perfectly poised and coiffed, as usual.

"Aud?"

I forgot what I'd been trying to remember. "Tired."

"That's only to be expected." She came a little closer. "I am very glad you are all right."

"Reta—*rela*tive term," I said. I still couldn't get my breath.

"Indeed." She cleared her throat and gestured at the edge of the bed. "May I?"

I nodded. She sat gently, careful to not rock the bed.

"Is Suzanne treating you well?"

"Pink hair."

"Yes. But her references are excellent." In the silence my breath sounded light and gasping, like a frightened girl's. "They wanted you to stay in hospital but I believed you'd prefer a less . . . structured environment. The nurse was Eric's idea. She says you're doing well. Your blood pressure is a little low, but your pulse is strong and steady." Her eyes moved in a search pattern: my eyes, my mouth, my chin, my chest, and back again. "She says you have good hand-eye coordination, your pupil dilation is improving rapidly, and your eyes should be back to normal in a few hours." Her eyes never kept still. "The breathlessness might take a little longer. A day or two."

"I'm fine."

"Yes."

"Fine."

"Yes, and very lucky. After what you took—"

"Given."

"Of course. Were given, yes." Her gaze settled on a spot between my eyebrows. "I'm told that so far they have identified MDMA, barbiturates, amphetamines, opiates, psilocybin, and PCP, and some other substances that haven't yet been classified. Quite a cocktail."

Ecstasy, magic mushrooms, oxycodone or something similar, angel dust, speed.

"The medical team wanted to give you a stomach pump, but as Eric pointed out, it would have been a needless procedure given the fact that you'd ingested the drugs in liquid form. In the coffee, they think. Most of the damage would already have been done. Plus it was clear that you had been vomiting."

I frowned.

"Your clothes," she said gently. "Apparently you can thank the wine you drank for that. Those who hadn't had any alcohol weren't so lucky."

Lucky. Dancing around in Pioneer Square with vomit on my clothes.

I lifted my right hand, needle hole towards her. "This?"

"Saline IV. Dehydration apparently is one of the main side effects of MDMA, or ecstasy. Suzanne will be insisting that you drink plenty of water."

"And this?" I nodded at my left elbow.

"Blood draw."

I remembered none of it. Someone had done this to me.

"Your clothes are being cleaned, but I thought you'd want to have something to hand immediately."

"Yes." Thank you, I wanted to add, but didn't have the breath.

"Aud." She started to reach for my hand.

"You said. Others."

"I'm sorry, yes. A score of people from a film set were admitted to Harborview Medical Center before you arrived. I thought I had told you." She smoothed her eyebrows with her fingertips—for my mother, a shocking expression of fatigue, which reminded me of my surprise when she had repeated herself yesterday, and why.

"Dornan?"

"Your friend is unaffected."

"Information?" I was too tired to say more, but she understood.

"Perhaps when next I speak to the police liaison he will be able to tell us something."

The coffee urn. Had to be. Kuiper? No, she had been surprised when I'd said, when I said those things. Somebody had made me say and do things that . . . Somebody had rendered me helpless, somebody . . . "Uh," I said as my heart skipped a beat and then slammed against my rib cage in the wrong place.

"Aud?" She was leaning over me. "Aud?" I didn't have the breath to speak.

Suzanne ran in from the other room, brushed my mother aside, thrust her stethoscope through a gap in the pajama top.

"Fine," I said. "I'm fine."

"*Shssh,*" she said, and frowned—the skin between her eyes rolled in a plump sausage—and moved the stethoscope slightly.

Whatever it was seemed to be over. My heart pulsed neatly, in the right place.

Suzanne straightened and slung the stethoscope around her neck. "Mild arrhythmia," she said. "Not too worrying, but a doctor might be a good idea."

"I'll see to it," my mother said.

Suzanne hesitated, then nodded, and went back into the sitting room. No one had asked my opinion. I struggled to sit up.

"Please, Aud, try to rest. I don't think you realize just how serious this could have been." She smoothed her eyebrows again. "I consulted with your friend about your accommodations and we agreed to install you in a two-roomed suite so that Suzanne can remain here as long as you feel she can be helpful. Your friend also has been very helpful." Oh, yes, very. "The police have promised an extensive inquiry, and I'll keep you updated with any developments. All your belongings have been brought over from your hotel. If there is anything else you need, ask Suzanne or call me. Now I will speak to your friend, and to Eric. He should be here within the hour."

Her back was very straight as she walked away, despite the fact that, on top of jet lag, she must have been up all night taking charge of my life.

It took a long time and a lot of effort but I eventually dragged the room service menu from the bedside table to the bed, and dialed the right numbers. I knew exactly what I wanted, but found I kept ordering random words from the menu ("delicious," or "sales tax"). After a few tries I found that if I kept my sentences to two words or less—scrambled eggs, two please, tea, English breakfast—I could manage. I concentrated on the fact that I could manage, not the fact that I had to.

Breakfast arrived ten minutes before Dornan. The food tasted like something forced from a crack in the earth.

"Well," he said, looking at the tray on the bed, "it doesn't look as though that was a success."

"Taste those eggs."

"Thank you, but I've already—"

"Taste them, Dornan, or at least get the tray out of my sight. They taste vile, and they smell even worse." Or at least that's what I tried to say, but it came out as a river of muddled syllables. I stopped. Tried again. Stopped. His eyes glistened. "Bad," I said. "Bad food."

"The eggs are bad?"

"And the butter is rancid and the milk for the tea curdled." Cremble degg. Runny kid. I took a deep breath. "Butter. Milk. Ranky—*ran*cid."

"I see."

"Do you? My taste. They've done something. The drugs. Everything tastes of sulfur." I stopped, this time in surprise, because I had made sense, and was shocked to see Dornan half close his eyes in relief. Brain damage. My mother hadn't mentioned that possibility. He hopped up, lifted the tray, carried it to the dressing table, grinned as he popped a strawberry in his mouth. "Shame," he said, sitting down again. "They're delicious."

"The fruit was all rall—*right*," I said.

"You want me to bring that back, then?"

"No. Yes. I don't know. Forget the food. Why did you let my mother take over?" Mumbly ho-taker. But most of it had come out all right.

"All her suggestions seemed like sensible ones."

I said carefully, "Why her hotel?"

"Better than being in hospital under restraint."

"Wasn't that bad." I should have signed those papers, made sure he had power-of-attorney for health care.

"You weren't making any sense whatsoever. And you were seriously alarming the natives. One of the police officers who was brought in had to be treated for a bruised shoulder and seemed pretty cross about something. They had to Taser you, Torvingen. Twice. I'm guessing that if it weren't for your mother you'd have a few bruises of your own and be facing charges."

"You were at the hospital?"

"I was. I have to say you seemed to be happier when you were stoned. You might have been talking gibberish, but your smile was radiant."

Poison had made the world so beautiful. But I wouldn't be able to say that. "Strawberries," I said. "Bring me them."

He brought me a napkin, a fork, and the dish of fruit and put them by me on the bed.

I ate one. "Still at the Edgewater?"

He nodded. "I've kept your room there, too, just in case. But I thought you might like to stay here, perhaps, for some privacy." He said that with a slight question, but I had no idea what he meant by it. When I didn't respond, he said, "Your mother wanted me to stay with you. She isn't easy to refuse."

"No." We sat in silence for a moment. "So. You met her. Tell me."

DORNAN FORGOT to take the tray with him when he left and I was too tired to call out to Suzanne.

When Eric Loedessoel arrived five minutes later, his eyes strayed to its contents while he explained why he was there.

"I have an M.D. but am not a practicing physician. I can't treat you or formally advise you in a medical capacity, but I have consulted with colleagues at Harborview Medical Center, and believe I can help you with any questions you might have, on a stopgap basis. But I want to make it clear that in my opinion tomorrow you should consult a fully qualified and licensed physician."

"Thank you," I said. "For your help so far."

He looked at the tray again. "I see you didn't eat much," he said. "Was it the taste? But you can still smell?"

I nodded.

"Many of the other victims are displaying similar symptoms."

Victims.

"Those that are conscious, that is. One of the as yet unidentified compounds has a tendency to depress the autonomic nervous system. Two of the victims are being assisted with their breathing. There was a third, but he is already managing to breathe nicely on his own again. The reasonable conclusion is that the effects are probably temporary."

I had never been a victim before.

". . . worry about, as long as you avoid over-exertion. I'd like to look at your notes, if I may?"

I nodded.

He left and came back with the clipboard. This time I noticed his faint scent of cologne, and knew whose pajamas I was wearing.

". . . few days, probably an unnecessary precaution." He was looking at me.

"I'm sorry?"

"Suzanne noted an arrhythmia. It's probably nothing to worry about, a result of toxic stress, but I'd suggest avoiding taxing your heart in the next few . . ."

I lost track again of what he was saying. All these favors mounting up. Reduced to relying on the kindness of strangers. I had to get back to my own hotel.

". . . emotional lability . . ."

It was all that caterer's fault. Kuiper. She should watch her coffee more carefully. Dancing in Pioneer Square.

". . . hallucination flashbacks . . ."

I woke midafternoon. My breathing was a lot better. When I sat up, the walls shimmered but didn't dance.

My clothes on the chair were carefully chosen: Eileen Fisher trousers in black linen, with pockets; a layering T-shirt, white; a V-necked silk sweater; underwear; cashmere socks; low-heeled boots. They would do for any occasion and temperature. I knew as surely as though I'd seen my mother do it that she had chosen them. I looked around the rest of the room: my laptop on the dressing table, not where it belonged, but where I would see it when I was well enough to sit up for any length of time; my jacket laid casually over the back of an armchair; my luggage stowed beneath the window, again, not where it belonged, but where I would see it and infer that the rest of my belongings were in the closet. My wallet, I knew, would be in the pocket of the jacket; my toiletries would be in the bathroom.

After five minutes of sitting and turning my head this way and that without dizziness, I felt confident enough to drag myself to the bathroom.

I sat on the toilet, and thought about beauty and poison, and the fact that my mother knew me so well she could use my own belongings to send the kind of message that would get through the drug fog: I was able to leave anytime I needed to. I stared at the silk pajama bottoms pooled at my feet and kicked them off, then unbuttoned the top and dropped it on the floor. My skin still smelled of cologne, but faintly.

I came to with a start, cold, and hauled myself to my feet, and flushed the toilet. Suzanne came into the room just as I got to the bed. The left side of her hair was flat; she must have been taking a nap, too.

"Need some help?" She reached out, but hesitantly, unwilling to touch naked skin without permission. Or maybe she had just never seen healed knife and bullet wounds.

"No. Thank you." I climbed onto the bed, trying to look as though it cost less effort than it did, wondering, even as I did so, why I bothered. Suzanne wasn't a predator waiting to pounce at the first sign of weakness; she was a nurse.

"Actually, yes. You could help. My laptop. It's on the dresser." Four-word sentences were now easy.

She brought me the laptop, set it up—it didn't take long; the signal here must have been better than at the Edgewater—and refilled my water glass. "Make sure you drink it," she said, and left.

I had two e-mails. One was from Luz, one from Rusen: the information I'd requested. While it was downloading, I fell asleep.

When I woke up, it was dark again. After midnight. I was viciously hungry, but couldn't face the idea of fruit. Rusen's document blinked at me. I scrolled through it. The text bulged and shrank on the screen like a squeezed accordion. I found I was stabbing the keys so hard the casing creaked. I drank the water. The fact that I had to annoyed me. The nasty nylon laptop case, the fact that my laptop was there—that I was in bed in this room—that my clothes were laid out neatly on the chair, that some strange woman was sleeping in the room next door and that I had had no say in any of it made me want to hurl the glass at the wall. I wasn't even sure if I could. I didn't even know if the room was registered in my name. Was I being treated like a dependent, like a child? I was wearing Loedessoel's pajamas. Even my skin smelled of him, the man who had married my mother. My mother, who had crooked her finger and said, Come, and I'd climbed obediently onto a plane.

I put the glass down. My heart squeezed and released, squeezed and released as my adrenal gland pumped hormones into my bloodstream and arteries widened and surface capillaries shut down. The muscles in my jaw pulled my teeth together, my thighs twitched, I was too hot. And somebody had done this to me. They had dumped a cup of powder in a coffee urn and turned my life inside out, like a sock.

They wouldn't have been able to if that bloody woman, Kuiper, had been paying attention. And why did she think I was out to hurt her precious Rusen, anyway? No doubt she was laughing, laughing right now, telling a friend all the stupid things I'd said.

And then I was hunting for her information, and found it: Film Food, Kuiper, Victoria K. prop., 4222 Myrtle Avenue, in Wallingford, just four blocks from the Jitterbug, according to MapQuest. And it made perfect sense to get out of bed and put on those carefully selected clothes, collect the draped-just-so jacket, complete with wallet and car keys, and leave.

MURPHY'S, the pub on the corner, was shut. Restaurants, bars, and movie theaters were dark. Lights changed at an empty intersection. It was so quiet I could hear the new leaves of the maple tree under which I'd parked hiss and shiver. The moon was small and bright. Wallingford slept. Well, Kuiper wasn't going to.

Number 4222 was a small, wooden bungalow, original pre–World War I cedar shakes painted sage green, woodwork bright white. No light on the porch. No light on most of the porches; obviously a low-crime area. Sodium streetlights pooled like pale brass on sidewalks, whose concrete had been wrenched out of true decades ago by the growth of tree roots. Here and there it gleamed more palely, where the concrete had been replaced. Still silent, no tree frogs, no crickets—just the river of interstate traffic about a mile away. The scent of spring flowers, delicate as lace, there and gone again. Utterly unlike Atlanta.

From the path, three concrete steps—dark, with moss growing on the uprights—led to eight wooden steps, painted a darker green than the cedar shingles, to a wooden porch. The door had glass insets, and a brass lock plate that hadn't been replaced for forty years.

Both sets of steps had rails, but added recently, sometime in the last five years, though not very competently; the right-hand rail wobbled. Cheap, gimcrack thing; aluminum painted black to look like cast iron. Out of place.

There was no knocker on the door, no doorbell. I banged on the white gloss-painted panel between the glass. The house boomed. The sound rolled up and down the silent street. I banged again, thumping the door panel with the meaty part of my fist, five times, putting some weight behind it.

"I know you're here," I shouted cheerily. Her van was in the driveway. Bang. Bang, bang. Not a single neighbor's light flicked on. Polite, circumspect, incurious. Very Scandinavian.

"It's me"—bang—"a victim"—bang—"of your coffee." Bang, bang. "I don't"—bang—"even like"—bang—"coffee." Bang, bang. "Kuiper." Or whatever she called herself. "Kuiper." Bang. "Come out." Bang, bang.

Between one bang and the next, the hot, tight clarity of adrenaline drained away and I found myself panting. Something in my peripheral vision fluttered. My palm squeaked as it slid down the glossy woodwork. I locked my knees.

"No," I said. "You won't. You will not." And I hung there, between standing and collapse, smelling the mysterious flowers again, wondering what they were.

The porch vibrated briefly, and with an effort that made the scar near my jugular tighten, I pushed against my hands and swayed back onto my heels before a deadbolt rattled and the door opened.

Bare feet on a lovely, ribbon-work inlaid oak floor. They must be cold. White toweling robe to her knees, and hair trapped under the collar where she'd pulled it on in a hurry. Phone in her left hand. Didn't she know that the time to call the police was before opening the door? I opened my mouth, but the graphite sheen under her eyes, her drawn face, shocked me silent.

"What—" she began, but the flutter in the corner of my eye turned to flapping, and I lost the lock on my knees. "Fuck," she said, and grabbed me under the arms before I went down. The phone dug into my armpit. For a moment my face hung near the opening in her robe, and I breathed the soft, buttered-toast scent of sleepy, naked woman. Then she shifted her grip, stepped in close enough to lean my forehead on her collarbone, and stuffed the phone in her pocket. "Fuck," she said again, and half dragged me across the living room to a three-seater sofa. She dropped me awkwardly, but the old leather was soft. Luz would have liked it.

She rearranged her robe, then leaned across me and switched on a table lamp. She looked down. The exertion had given her a bit of color. "Tell me why I shouldn't call the police"—she bent and peered at me more closely—"or maybe an ambulance."

"I'll be all right," I said, sitting like an abandoned rag doll. I was so very tired of feeling helpless.

"What are you doing here? No, never mind. Just keep still. I'll call you a cab." She straightened and turned this way and that, as though looking for something.

"No need. I have a car."

"You're not fit to drive."

"I drove here."

"Right. And that worked out so well for you." She wasn't really paying attention, still scanning the room for whatever it was.

"I'm fine."

"Of course you are."

The color was fading in her cheeks, and she looked ill again. "Did you take some, too?"

"What?"

"Drugs. Did you take any?"

She looked at me this time. "No."

"So why do you look so terrible?"

She folded her arms. It took me a minute to understand that her strange expression was hurt.

"No, that's not . . . I didn't mean it to sound . . ." I wanted to shrink to the size of an ant and creep into the cracks of the sofa.

"You do seem to have the gift of tongues. Speaking of which, you'll have to explain the 'tongue palace' reference to me sometime." She went back to scanning the room. Stilled. Sighed. Fished the phone from her pocket. "Now, a cab."

"No cab. I'll call my friend, Dornan."

"Oh," she said. "Him."

I couldn't interpret her tone and she didn't offer any hints. "His number's—"

"I have his number." She crossed to an enormous chair, in the same battered-looking leather, at the other end of the living room, consulted a notebook, and dialed. While it rang she pulled her feet up under her, tucked her hair behind her ears, brushed an imaginary fleck from her robe. "Hey," she said, "it's Kick."

Kick?

"Oh, don't worry, I know. Three-thirty. Yep."

Her name was Kick?

"That's right," she said, staring up and to the right at nothing, as people did on the phone. "Because I have a friend of yours prostrate in my living room. Uh-huh, the very same. Yes. Well, fairly lucid. Soon? Okay."

She put the phone down and wiped her face with her hand. "He might not be able to get here for half an hour. Depends how long it will take him to get a cab." She stood wearily. "I don't imagine you want coffee."

I shook my head. Three-thirty in the morning. What had I been thinking, banging on her door at this time?

She walked into the kitchen, carefully, as though she were not sure of her step. An injury? Might explain why she didn't do stunts anymore. Water ran in the sink, then a kettle. A cupboard opened and shut. Half an hour. How many more stupid things could I say in half an hour?

I woke to find her draping me with a blanket. I struggled upright. She stepped back and pulled her robe tighter, and I got another waft of that soft, naked smell.

"I woke you," I said. "Before. Earlier." The smell had unmoored me. "It's late. I'm sorry."

She sat at the other end of the sofa, and tucked her legs up again. Her toes poked out beneath the robe. Small, like her hands. I imagined them soft between my palms.

"I'm sorry," I said again.

She nodded tiredly. "I don't need this. The police already kept me for hours. Did I have a grudge? Why? And when they got past that, it was, Did I know who did have a grudge? Did I know against whom? Did I know why? Had I seen any strangers on the set?"

"What did you say?"

"That you were the most suspicious character I'd seen all day." She glanced at her wrist, realized it was naked. She got up again and tucked my blanket in around my shoulder. "Sorry. But it's true. Besides, you know the police won't come after you. Lift your hand." She tucked my arm in. "Whoever you are, you're off limits. To the reporters, too. My face was splashed all over the papers—and Sîan Branwell's, of course. You? Nowhere to be found. But me, all anyone will think of now when they see the name Film Food is poison." Her voice sounded distant, almost dispassionate. "The mad poisoner of Seattle. I worked so hard."

I didn't say, Don't blame me. I didn't say, It's not my fault. It didn't matter. It wasn't her fault, either, but people were still blaming her. She had still lost her reputation. "Did you? See any strangers on the set?"

It seemed an effort for her to come back from her bleak internal landscape. "No."

"Then I'll get it all back. Your reputation."

"Why would you care?" she said wearily.

Because your feet are turning blotchy red with the cold and I don't want to think about why I want to warm them with my hands, why I want to make you tea, bring it to you, right here, and stroke that heavy hair—which gleams like soft metal that's been cut with a knife—back from your cheek and tell you not to worry about the stain on your white coat, not to worry about anything.

"I'll find them."

She nodded, but she wasn't really listening. She was too tired to care.

I carefully folded back the blanket and levered myself to my feet. The least I could do was let her get back to bed. "I'll wait outside."

She also stood, but this time with a slight smile. "No, you won't."

"I won't?" I said, stupid in the face of my own horrible, insidious tenderness.

"No. Because I hear your ride."

All I could hear was the uneven lumping of my heart. I concentrated. Outside, a car door thunked and a diesel engine rattled as the cab pulled away. She opened the door before he could knock.

He looked at me, then her. No one spoke. Then she stood to one side. "Can you walk?" Dornan said to me, and I nodded. "Keys?" I touched my jacket pocket, nodded again, and stepped forward. My knees held. "Tomorrow?" he said to Kick, who also nodded. She looked ill and tired and walking once again in her bleak world.

"I'll find them," I said.

Dornan walked by me down wooden steps, then concrete. I didn't hear her shut the door behind us, but I couldn't afford to split my concentration to turn and see if she was watching. I leaned both hands on the car roof while he opened the passenger door. He stood close while I eased myself into the seat, made sure my fingers were out of the way before he slammed the door. Then I looked. Kick's door was closed.

Dornan fussed with the seat and seat belt and then the mirrors, the way people who rarely drive do.

"Do you know the way?"

"Mostly. I think." He started the engine, released the brake, and we rolled down the street. There was absolutely nothing on the road, but at the traffic circle he checked his mirror twice, indicated, and drove counterclockwise all the way around to the left before turning.

We reached the interstate without incident.

"What happened?" he said.

I shrugged tiredly. I didn't really know. He nodded as though I'd answered, and drove some more.

"Sîan Branwell," I said.

He spared me a quick sideways glance.

"The name of the star, of *Feral:* Sîan Branwell."

"Yes. I found out yesterday."

That wasn't the only name he'd found out. "Why did she tell you her name and not me?"

"Maybe because I asked her nicely."

And then the freeway was passing beneath what looked like the hanging gardens of Babylon. I blinked and tried to refocus, but the vision remained, and it was real: a park built over the interstate. It wasn't hard to imagine the city overtaken by forest, fifty years after the apocalypse. For a moment I thought I smelled the rank breath of an unseen predator, big and lithe, pacing the car, hidden by trees.

THIS WEEK THERE WAS STILL LIGHT IN THE SKY WHEN I PARKED, AND UNDER THE greasy hydrocarbon fumes of drive-time traffic, a hint of life scented. Twigs were swollen at their tips.

The white board was gone, but magazines were stacked under the peg-board. I tried to imagine how this space was used when I wasn't here. Some kind of low-rent group-counseling space? A beggars-can't-be-choosers law clinic? Sandra was absent. I wondered if she would come back. No matter. My guess was she already knew the most important things I would be teaching today.

We would begin, though, with action. Make them all feel big and strong.

"The larynx," I said. "To fracture it, you use the edge of your hand, like this." I showed them how to make a knife-hand. "The tension is in the fingers, the thumb is bent. It's easier and faster to strike outwards, palm down. Practice with both hands. If your attacker is on his back, you can come straight down, like a hatchet. If he's on his stomach, you'd be better off with an axe kick to the spine."

They spent a minute or two slashing the air, then I ran them through a few attacks on the prone bag. After that I hung the bag back on its frame, and we did some side strikes.

"The knife-hand will work very well, though obviously you'd have more reach with a pipe, even a length of hose. No," I said, as Nina opened her mouth, "not panty hose. Garden hose." Suze punched Nina on the upper arm and grinned. "Any other household objects that might work?"

"Wrench," Suze said.

"Hammer," said Katherine, after a moment's thought.

Objects from Man World. "What about the kitchen?" They looked blank. "Anything fairly flat to get under the chin." Silence. "A cake slicer," I suggested. "A spatula. Even a dinner plate, if you hold it in both hands and jab forwards."

"A dustpan?" Kim said.

"A skillet. Swing it."

"Good, Tonya. What else?" Another pause. "Anything can be a weapon if you think about it that way."

Therese folded her arms. *"The Joy of Cooking?"*

"A little unwieldy if you're going for the larynx, but it would work well against the back of the neck or side of the head, or even slammed down on a hand. One of those thin hardcovers would work, though, just like a plate."

"Man," Pauletta said. "You sit around all day thinking up this shit?"

"More than fifty percent of attacks on women happen in the home. It makes sense to have weapons close by. Imagine your house not only as a refuge but as a garden of weaponry." I might as well have been talking Farsi. "So think. What else? What's in the kitchen, apart from recipe books and cooking utensils?"

They just couldn't seem to make the connection between the kitchen and violence. The one who would have understood that bad things happen more often in sunny breakfast nooks than in midnight alleys wasn't here.

"Food," I said. More blank looks. "Anyone here cook with linguiça or andouille or chorizo?"

"Sausages?" Suze said. "You're saying if some wacko breaks into my condo I should hit him with a fucking sausage?"

"Why not?"

"Because it's *food.*"

"So," Nina said after a moment, "an andouille sausage. Should it be fresh or frozen?"

"That, of course, depends. Fresh might be a little slippery for a proper grip, but you'd get that whiplash effect for extra power. Plus you could dispose of the evidence more quickly because it's faster to cook and eat the weapon if you don't have to defrost it first." I smiled to show them I was being witty. They seemed to find that disturbing.

"Pasta!" Jennifer said. "You know, that dried spaghetti in the packet. Well," she said to herself, "it's flat."

"Cooking with weapons," Nina announced brightly. "A book of recipes for the modern woman!"

Their hilarity lasted almost a minute; they would remember it, and the lesson.

"Just because we're talking about the larynx and blunt-edged weapons doesn't mean you can't use something sharp. In the kitchen, the perfect tool for this kind of job would be a cleaver. Now," I said, while they looked at me uncertainly—was this another joke?—"let's move on to the second target, which is here, in the hollow of the throat." After a moment they changed gears and started touching their throats. "Careful. Don't press too hard. The trachea there is close to the surface, very fragile, vulnerable to swelling. It's a small target, so if you've no other weapon but your hands, your best bet is your fingers. Like this." I made a slow, upward stabbing motion. "It's the same basic form as the knife-hand, but this time you strike forwards, like a spear tip. The thumb is curled again, but this time keep your fingers slightly bent." I went along the line and bent and pointed and curled. "Hit the bag a few times. Start gently on this one, you'll see why. Kim, you do this instead." I showed her an extended knuckle strike. "I don't want you to rip the bag." Or split her nail bed to the cuticle.

Suze, of course, went a little too hard to begin with and jammed her knuckles. "Shake it out," I advised. "Use the other hand for now."

I watched for a minute to make sure no one was going to break her fingers.

"Okay, good. Now we'll start putting some of this together. Stand closer than you think you need to. Strike through the target. Good, next. Strike more than once. And again. Strike harder now, harder. Next. Good. Next. Strike fast. Remember: that's what gives you power. And, good, speed it up. Fist strike, knife-hand, fingertip. Next." They were trotting to the bag now. "Good. And a little faster." Now they were running. "Lungs, I want to hear your lungs working. Fist, finger, knife. Right hand, left hand, right hand. Fist, and finger, and knife." Now they were moving to a beat, *fist* and *finger* and *knife, fist* and *finger* and *knife,* hearts filling and clenching, pumping shocking red blood to muscles greedy for oxygen. Heat bloomed under their skin, their lips opened, and the room filled with the susurrus of breath. My nostrils flared at the sharp tang of adrenaline-charged sweat, my own breathing deepened, and they were like a vast horse I rode bareback, skin to skin, gripping that muscle and bone between my thighs, moving with its rhythm, urging it on—more, faster, harder— as it stretched out and its hooves cut into the turf and it thundered over the plain, running without effort, without fatigue, without end. And then Jennifer stumbled and Katherine ran into her and the rhythm broke and it was just women hitting a bag.

"Good. Stop a minute. Get your breath."

They did, bending over, some with hands on each other's backs, chests heaving, skin pink and damp, faces smooth.

"Sit," I said. They sat differently, more loosely, more present. I could still smell them. "So, you're back in your house. What weapons would work on the hollow of the throat?"

"Knife," Tonya said promptly.

"Fork," said Jennifer.   .

"Broom handle."

"Beer bottle." That was Suze.

"Good. Now think of something that doesn't fit in the hand like a spear, or something that's not hard."

"Like what?"

I rose, crossed to the pile of bags and shoes, picked out a blue pump with a three-inch spike heel. Kim's. "Hold it with the sole in your palm, strike sideways. Or"—I went to the pegboard and the magazines—"how about this?" I picked up an *Atlanta* magazine.

"It's just paper."

I rolled it into a tube, slid it through my right hand until I held it like a stumpy ski pole, took a step sideways, and slammed the end into the pegboard. It punched right through. I examined the edges of the round hole: painted particle board, not metal. Cheap. I put aside my irritation.

"Magazines make good weapons. They can be two different kinds of tools—deadly"—I pointed to the hole—"or not." Now I held the magazine like a flyswatter and slapped it against the edge of the board. "They're particularly useful in a situation where your actions are legally dubious, or could be made to seem so. Very few prosecutors would be prepared to charge you with assault with a deadly weapon if you were armed only with a magazine." I hadn't meant to mention prosecutors at this early stage.

"Can I have a go?" Suze said.

I handed her the magazine.

She rolled it up, hefted it a couple of times, then whipped it viciously into the board. A neat circle of plywood popped out the other side. "Awesome!"

"Anyone else?" I'd have to buy the center a new pegboard anyway, and nothing brings home a blow's power better than the satisfaction of destroying something. It would also distract them from my mention of the law.

Six people stood at once. Therese and Jennifer were only seconds behind.

Five minutes later, after a combination of backwards, sideways, up, down, single- and two-handed blows, the board was reduced to a metal frame and a pile of splinters.

"So, what else in the room would work as a weapon? Set aside a moment the idea of throat strikes."

"Man, I was just getting used to that."

"So what should we be thinking of?" Jennifer said.

"Remember the first lesson, when I asked you to list the reasons you came here in the first place. And a couple of reasons why your friends and family would encourage you to come. Pick one of those friends and family situations. Doesn't matter how trivial you think it is. It's not your reason. It's theirs." I let them take thirty seconds to pick something. "So. The room as weapon. Someone, anyone, give me a situation, then give me what you could use."

"If some guy is, like, making kissy noises and all his friends are laughing, you could hit him with a purse," Christie said.

"It would certainly send a strong signal, which is useful in a social situation. If you wanted to do some damage, though, it would depend on the purse. But think about the room itself."

"You mean the bar?"

"All right, the bar."

"Well, there's bar stools . . ."

"Beer bottles."

"Glasses."

"Tables."

"You can't just pick up one of those tables," Pauletta said. "It's not like on TV. Those mofos are heavy."

And the bottles wouldn't break if you used the closed end, and the chairs wouldn't conveniently splinter. The fighters wouldn't grin afterwards, either, then belly up to the saloon bar and order each other rotgut whiskey.

"You don't have to lift the table, you could use it another way, particularly if it's low. If you push someone a little and the table's behind them it will upset their balance and they'll go down. But supposing this drunken guy has pushed you up against the wall and is still making kissy noises at you. What then?"

"Kick him," Katherine said.

"Head butt right in the fucking face," Suze said. "Wham."

"Both would work."

"Yes, but what did you mean about using the room?" Therese said.

"Think about what we did last week, using expectations against your attacker. Christie, stand against the wall." I faced her, leaning against the wall, a hand on each side of her head, face nine inches from hers. "What would he expect you to do?"

Everyone's face went blank.

I sighed to myself. "What would a TV character playing a young woman in a college bar do?"

"Depends on the show," Tonya said. "She'd either cry and hide her face until her boyfriend showed, when she'd watch the creep get stomped, or she'd tough it out, give him a big smooch so that he went red and his friends laughed, then she'd sort of strut away."

Everyone nodded. I had no idea what kind of shows they watched.

"Let's swap roles," I said to Christie. I bent my knees considerably so that we were the same height. "Now lean in, as though you're going to kiss me." She hesitated. "Don't worry, I won't let you." She leaned forward. I put my right palm on her sternum and pushed back, just a little, just enough to make her feel her own strength. She leaned harder. I heaved an exaggerated sigh, tilted my face up as though about to give in, and slipped my left hand to the back of her neck: just like a starlet about to kiss the hero. In one move I slid down the wall, jerked Christie's face down and forwards, and twisted, and shot my right hand up fast enough to catch her forehead just before it smashed into the painted cinder block.

"In real life, of course, you wouldn't catch his head. Thank you," I said to Christie, who was still blinking. She touched her forehead a couple of times to make sure it was still there.

"What I did was use the wall as both a weapon against my attacker and an aid to balance. I could bring my entire weight to bear on his neck because I was using the wall to keep me from falling backwards. If you practice this at home with unsuspecting spouses, I'd recommend you put a mattress against the wall first."

Therese folded her arms. I gestured for her to speak.

"You're in a bar. He's drunk. You shouldn't have hurt him like that."

"The fucker deserved it," Suze said, chin out.

I looked around. "Anyone else?"

Pauletta stirred. "Now I think about it, then maybe yeah, it could be a bit harsh. Dude only wanted a kiss."

"Yeah, but he should've stopped when she said stop," Suze said.

"I didn't hear her say stop," Therese said.

"So what should she do?"

They all turned to me.

"It depends."

"Man, how did I know she was going to say that?"

"It always depends," I said. "Always. Every situation is different. What do you do if your car breaks down on I-75? You don't call a tow truck and say, 'It's Tuesday, bring a wrench,' or 'It's Thursday, bring gas.' You look at the context. This is a college bar. This man is drunk. He has friends. We don't know if Christie has friends—Christie, do you have friends?"

"Well, yeah."

"In the bar. And how old are the man and his friends?"

"Twenty-one?"

"In that context, yes, you shouldn't have needed to get to the face-smashing stage. Therese, come over here and play Christie. I'll be the drunk."

Therese stood straight. I leered and staggered. "Give us a kiss, then."

"No. Go away."

"Oh, don't be like that. Smile, go on." I moved closer.

"No." She backed up half a step but didn't turn away, didn't smile. "Go away."

"Just one kiss . . ." I started to reach out.

"Don't touch me," she said loudly.

"Jeez, lady, I just wanted a—"

"Don't you dare touch me. Lay one finger on me and I call the police." Her pupils were small and tight, her whole face pointed at mine. "If you touch me I'll have you sued for assault. You'll never get your degree, you'll never get a job. Don't touch me!"

I turned to the others, raised my eyebrows. They applauded. Therese grinned, fiercely.

"It all goes back to what we were saying last week: communication and body language. Don't let them use embarrassment against you. You won't die of embarrassment. But let's suppose he's pushed you against the wall and he's leaning in for the kiss. At that point are you warranted in using the maneuver I showed you earlier?"

"Yep," said Suze.

"Not in that kind of bar," Christie said.

"Just what kind of bar is it?" Suze.

"Suze, come and play the drunk who's got me against the wall. Okay. Suggestions?"

"Just say no, like before. Real loud," Kim said.

"Let's say I'm so scared my mouth's gone dry and I can't shout," I said. I would teach them another time how to deal with fear and its effects. "Let me show you one or two other tools you could use. Remember the knife-hand." They all made knife-hands. "Watch." I laid the edge of my hand against Suze's larynx. "If she tries to press towards me, that's going to get very uncomfortable. You're not deliberately hurting him, but you've drawn an unmistakable line. You've set yourself on fire. If he pushes harder, any damage is his fault. Try it. Gently."

I let Suze try it on me, but kept the muscles in my throat expanded protectively.

"Good. One other thing. Kim, remember that knuckle extension I showed you?" She held out her arm obligingly. Everyone copied her. "Good. Now support your middle knuckle with your thumb and tuck the other fingers in, as though making a fist. Face your partner." I moved Suze into position. "There's a spot right in the middle of the breastbone where the nerve lies very close to the surface. Feel for it. Now put your knuckle on your partner's breastbone and push."

"Ow!"

"Shit!"

Everyone sprang apart rubbing their sternums.

"This is a very useful little tool. Appropriate for delicate situations, particularly those times when you have no wish to draw attention to yourself." Appropriate. My mother would approve. I knew Therese would go home and practice that until it hurt to breathe. "Remember, the right tool for the right job. Even naked in an empty room you have plenty of tools. But the first tool you should practice is communication: Know what you want and don't want, be prepared to communicate that clearly. Make sure your body and your words send the same message. Don't apologize, don't explain, don't threaten. It's all information they don't need, and information is currency. It's power. It's a tool."

They frowned. I thought for a minute.

"Jennifer." Her jaw twitched. "When was the last time you got a wrong-number call?"

"A wrong number?"

"Yes. When?"

"About six months ago."

"Remember how it went?" I picked up an imaginary phone and held it to my ear. "They called, and you picked up the phone and said . . . what?"

She picked up a phone, too. "Hello?"

"Hey, is this Annie?"

"Er, no."

"Well, who is this?"

"Jennifer."

"Is Annie there?"

"No, no one called Annie lives here."

"Annie Contin. Are you sure?"

"Of course I'm sure, it's just me and my husband."

"And it's not Contin?"

"No, I'm sorry."

"Well what number is this?"

"555-2658."

"Well, that's Annie Contin's number and I'm supposed to deliver a load of dog chow this afternoon. What's your address?"

"We don't have a dog. We have a cat. And . . . and you don't need my address!" and she slammed the imaginary phone down. Everyone was giving her sympathetic looks, the kind that in the South mean Dear Lord, what a moron. In the space of half a minute she had given a total stranger her name, her phone number, the fact that only two of them lived there, that she had a cat and no dog, and that she could be browbeaten without too much effort.

"Anyone think they can do better?"

"Yep." Suze picked up the imaginary handset. "Hello."

"Hey, is this Annie?"

"Nope, fuck off, asshole." Slam.

"That's always an option," I said. "But similar to using a pile driver on a picture nail. Anyone else?"

Therese raised a phone to her ear. She smiled. I nodded. "Hello."

"Hey, is this Annie?"

"No. What number are you trying to reach?"

"Is this Annie? Annie Contin?"

"No. I believe you have the wrong number. Good-bye."

"Excellent," I said. "The less people know about you, the less they can hurt you. Think about it: who in your lives has the power to hurt you most, to wound you cruelly with a word?"

"My mother."

"My husband."

I nodded. "The people who know us best can hurt us the most because they know us, know how we think and what our vulnerabilities are. Any information you give a stranger can be used against you. Anything. Information is valuable. Don't give it away."

F I V E

I WOKE AT NOON ON SUNDAY WITH MY MUSCLES STEADY AND MY MIND GATHERING speed, cold and clear as a bobsled in its ice run. I got out of bed without having to think about it, called room service without referring to the number listings, and ordered breakfast—fruit and cheese—without a hitch.

The shower fittings were solid nickel-plated steel, heavy and cool. I twirled taps, watched the steam curl up from the tile floor. Even the water smelled different from the water in Atlanta; no heavy chlorine tang.

The water pressure was strong, the shower like a fizzing drill on my skin. I soaped thoroughly, found the light blue stain of small bruises on my inner upper arms, where the police officers had taken a grip, a scrape on my left shin and three tiny cuts on my right ankle, like paper cuts. I'd probably never know where they had come from.

Hard white tile, as in a hospital room. I increased the hot-water flow and my goose bumps went away.

My mother had moved me here while I was unconscious and had no say in the matter. But the Edgewater was a dark and damp place. Despite its money-eyed smugness, the Fairmont was lighter and brighter, and my room accessible only via the door, not the water. So I'd stay. I didn't need Suzanne anymore, so she could go.

I toweled my hair dry, smoothed moisturizer methodically on my back, and shivered—as I hadn't for more than six months, since the nerves healed—when my hand ran over the bullet scar on the underside of my left arm.

AT THE breakfast table by the bar, Suzanne did her best to take it philosophically. "Well, I guess it's good that you're feeling better. I mean, it is good, definitely." She looked around wistfully while I wrote her check, and indeed the suite looked beautiful: thick glass tabletop gleaming in the sunshine, flowers vivid, Barber playing on the Bose.

I signed the check, handed it over. "I'm sorry about the lack of notice, but I've added a bonus."

When she saw the amount, her pupils, clenched tight against the bright sunshine, expanded briefly. She folded it and put it in her pocket.

I stood. "Do you have more work lined up?"

"Oh, well, I work through an agency. It'll be okay." She touched her pocket unconsciously, and stood. "I'll be okay."

Even in Seattle I imagined it wasn't too easy to get work as a private nurse with pink hair and a nose ring. I doubt my mother would have hired her if it hadn't been a middle-of-the-night emergency.

She shrugged. "Well, hey, time to pack." She gave the silk upholstered sofa one last pat and went into her room.

I set up my laptop on the table and opened Rusen's spreadsheet, the employment information. It looked as though he'd been thorough.

No one knows for certain if it was Einstein who said, *Everything should be made as simple as possible, but not simpler,* but it is a useful guiding principle. This wasn't, as the police appeared to think, a one-off grudge or a prank. There had been trouble with my property for two years. The trouble had continued with Hippoworks Productions. The drugging incident meant more trouble. It seemed entirely possible that there was some kind of connection. Also, as William of Ockham said, *pluralitas non est ponenda sine necessitate.* And Kick had seen no strangers on the set.

Hippoworks LLC had two partners, Rusen and Finkel, and two permanent employees, both of whom worked at their Culver City office in California. For the *Feral* production, they employed about four dozen others on a contract basis. They were nonunion contracts, but at scale, with the exception of Sîan Branwell, who, being the star, had a few extra clauses and a bit more money. The end-date of her contract surprised me: less than a week away.

I scrolled to Kick's information. Not much: addresses, references, a City of Seattle business license for Film Food, plus a notation that Rusen had checked her bond and insurance information and had two outside references on file. I opened a Web search bar and typed in KUIPER, VICTORIA K, and got several dozen hits, all relating to Film Food. Her website was rudimentary: a few menus, contact information, a professionally shot photo of Kuiper in white coat and hat, knife in hand and smiling self-consciously.

I changed the search to KICK KUIPER, and this time got several thousand hits. IMDb had a list—a long list—of her films. *Stunt!* had a cover interview with "Top Diving and Driving Artist 'Kick' Kuiper" from four years ago. The picture was of a woman in a red harness suit smiling brilliantly, bright with that reckless shine that comes only from riding a wave of adrenaline to survival. The caption read "Kuiper on the set of *Tantalus.*" I remembered that film. The action hero had been too old for the actress. The action scene with the actress had been good—Kick's scene, I now realized.

There was also a smaller piece, about a year later, another interview, with Kick saying, "Hell yes, I'll be back. The docs say the pins will be out in a month. Two months after that I'll be as good as ever." She sounded like a character from a fifties western, not like Kick at all. I backtracked, and found the news item—reported in *Variety* and *Hollywood Reporter,* even a one-liner in *EW*— about the fall that went wrong. I paid the subscription fee for the first two and read the articles.

"It's pretty much a miracle she survived at all," Benton "Buddy" Nels told us. "You fall from a hundred feet and you have to land right, you have to hit that sweet spot. You miss it and the bag flings you sideways at a wall or the sidewalk, hard, and real fast. Like shooting an egg from a catapult. You just break."

And break Kuiper did, cracking two vertebrae and several ribs, and shattering her pelvis and right hip. Fortunately she landed on dirt that had just been dug over and fluffed for a horse-fall scene minutes earlier.

"They're saying it was the dirt that saved her, and I understand that, but that's not the whole story. Beyond that, there's her superb physical condition. And beyond that, hell, I can't explain it. There must've been some angel looking out for her that day."

The word *miracle* cropped up three times, along with *unbelievable* and *inexplicable.*

Something caught my eye: a report a year before her accident from *Business-Week,* about product liability and various industry insurance rates. There was a thumbnail photo of Kick, *noted stuntwoman Victoria "Kick" Kuiper,* and a quote from her about why she wasn't planning to sue the makers of her harness. "Stunts are dangerous," she said. "***t happens." I followed the link and found that that time it had been a broken scapula.

All that work, all that risk, and now she cut fruit for a living. Maybe she was good at it, but did it ever make her smile like the sun?

I looked up. Suzanne, eyes tired and cynical, held out the check. "You forgot to date it."

I took it. "So I did. Do you have—" She handed me a lime green plastic pen. "And what is today's date?"

"May seventeenth. Holy shi— I mean, are you okay?"

"Absolutely. Yes, fine."

I watched as though from the wrong end of a telescope while she picked up the piece of splintered pen that had skittered across the glass-topped table. Where I had snapped it, the lime green plastic had turned milky pale, like the sepals that protect new tree blossom in spring.

"My apologies for that," I said. "I will of course reimburse you for the damage."

"It's a pen," she said, and bent to pick up the rest of it from the carpet. I got another from the laptop case, took off the cap, tested it on the back of the check. Blue. I turned the check over, aligned it carefully with the edge of the table, and wrote in the date. My hand didn't shake. I capped the pen, returned it to the bag, refused to look at the photo of the woman who still smiled because she hadn't lost anything.

"Excuse me," I said, and stood. "Please see yourself out."

I stood with my back against the bedroom wall until she left, thinking nothing.

I WALKED TO the waterfront. Waves slapped and seagulls squabbled, as at any other beach, but traffic fumes wafted over the grass. It was crowded with smiling people wearing sandals and shorts, even though it was only in the mid-sixties, and they seemed unreal, though I couldn't put my finger on why. I walked north, to the Seattle Aquarium, but I remembered pictures from the guidebook and couldn't bear the idea of being trapped beneath the surface with marine otters swimming ceaselessly from one side of their tiny concrete tank to another. I kept going north, the water to my left. Past the Edgewater— I wondered what Dornan was doing today; I should call him and invite him to move to the Fairmont—past the Pacific Science Center, which on another day would be interesting, and on through Seattle Center, the theater district. At some point I found another park with fewer people. Instead of gulls, this one was full of crows. One strutted along the path in front of me. In the sunshine its feathers shone with a dull, oily sheen, as though carved from slate.

I watched the water and the sky, where cumulonimbus massed on the eastern horizon, zinc and pewter.

After a while, I headed back south and then east, down more of a gradient. For the first time that day I found myself panting slightly. A few days, Loedessoel had said. I slowed, and breathed more easily.

South again, Boren Avenue, Howell Street, where the city began to look like any inner urban wasteland: empty blocks, patched pavement. In Atlanta the air would have felt heavy and tired; here it was light and capricious, as contradictory as the waterfront park.

It was as I was walking past a low, industrial-looking building with the unlikely name of Re-Bar that I realized I was being followed: a white man sixty or seventy yards back. About forty, my height, casual dress, not an athlete but moving easily enough. Usually I was the one doing the following. I stopped, and pretended intense interest in the sign that said, Open at Eight. The man slowed, took out a phone. I shook my head at the sign in mock regret, and started back south, but slowly, hoping he would close the gap. He didn't.

A professional, which made it unlikely I had been picked at random. Which raised a very interesting question. Was he connected to the people who were steering the warehouse mess, the people who were systematically reducing its value? Time to start getting answers.

I turned, as though going back to something I'd just seen. Once again, he slowed. I kept walking. He stopped. He put his phone away.

I ran at him.

After a split second, he ran, too. He ran with concentration, no backward glances, no tension in his shoulders, but I began to cut the distance. Fifty yards. Forty. My lips skinned back in a grin. Thirty. Soon we'd find out what was going on. Twenty. Then we hit a hill. In five seconds I was breathless and in fifteen he was gone.

It took me half an hour to get back to the hotel. No one followed me. I wasn't sure what I would do if they had. I thought of the laptop as I'd left it: Kick's smile as brilliant as burning magnesium. *I'll get it back for you,* I'd said. No one could ever give her that back.

THE CONCIERGE, whose name was Benjamin, was African-American, which surprised me, and I realized what had seemed so unreal about the crowds by the waterfront, and nearly everyone I had seen in Seattle so far: they had been ninety-five percent white, with a handful of Asians and a sprinkling of Hispanics and Native Americans. Nothing like Atlanta, where more than half the population was black.

I introduced myself. He smiled—he had a tiny birthmark just to the left of center on his bottom lip—said he knew who I was, and asked how he could help me this morning.

I didn't like the idea of anyone knowing my name.

"I'd like to arrange for the delivery of a large floral bouquet, today. Special delivery, if necessary."

"Certainly."

"Whatever's in season will be fine."

"A particular occasion?"

"A thank-you."

"Formal or informal?"

"Formal. And a note, to read, My apologies once again for the disturbance. Thank you for your kindness. Best wishes, Aud Torvingen."

"Return address?"

"No." And that was that.

I DELETED the search results and Kuiper's picture flicked out. I read Rusen's file for five minutes, then closed it. I hadn't even been able to understand that Seattle was almost wholly white. There was absolutely no point scanning a document in the hope of spotting an anomaly. I simply didn't know the city well enough. I shouldn't have come. In Atlanta, I knew law enforcement and criminals, journalists and politicians; I understood the lines running between money and power. Here, I knew nobody; nobody knew me.

Perhaps I could do something about that.

BENJAMIN LOOKED UP. "Ms. Torvingen. More flowers?"

"No. Something else." He smiled, to indicate that he was sure that whatever it was, it was within his capabilities. I wondered where concierges went to school to learn that responsive, intelligent attentiveness. "This is my first visit to Seattle and I don't know a soul. I was hoping you might help me overcome that."

"Of course." Face still open, still attentive, but eyes speculative. "Perhaps you could be more specific."

"This evening I'd like to relax privately here at the hotel in the company of someone attractive and discreet."

"Attractive and discreet. Certainly." I could have been asking to rent a car. "Should your companion have any specific attributes?"

I pondered. "I require a certain level of maturity. A grown-up." Someone who paid attention to the world.

He nodded courteously. "What time would it be convenient for him—or her?—to visit?"

It was about two-thirty. "I'd like her to be here as soon as possible."

"Very good. And for how long would you like the pleasure of her company?"

How does one time such things? "Perhaps she should be prepared to devote the entire afternoon and evening."

"I'll make arrangements and fax them to your suite."

WHEN I GOT back to my suite, paper was churning silently from the fax machine: *Four-hour sessions max. available, $1,100 per. Poss. negot. consecutive sess. at time of payment—cash preferred, credit card accepted. Meeting scheduled 4:30 pm.*

One hour and fifty minutes from now.

I turned my laptop on again, and opened the e-mail from Luz.

I just finished a book by Lloyd Alexander have you read any? They're okay but not as good as Narnia I borrowed them from my friend Natalie.

Had she mentioned Natalie before?

Natalie says they're for kids but I might like them, she's also lent me one called Eragon that she says is excellent. I read the first page but then Aba told me to turn the light out and not read anymore tonight so I'm writing to you instead.

Perhaps I should write to Adeline about the need to explain the spirit as well as the letter of the law when making suggestions to Luz. Adeline still thought of the computer as a complicated typewriter. It wouldn't occur to her that with the lights off, Luz could send e-mail, surf the Web, work on her LiveJournal, add to her Sims family. It was doubtful that she knew Luz and I talked to each in any other way than the stiff little thank-you notes Adeline made her write, fountain pen on lined paper—*Thank you very much for paying for my new dresser and desk. They are mission style, stained medium oak, and will be very useful when I do my homework*—and then included with the progress report she dutifully sent every month, a list of expenses, church events, and health or educational matters. The handwritten notes were grammatically perfect. I suspected Luz wrote a rough draft and Adeline then went over any mistakes and had Luz copy it out in her best hand. Perhaps that's something I should be doing with these e-mails.

But it was Adeline's role to correct Luz's grammar and tend to her manners, not mine.

It doesn't matter what she calls you, Mama or Tante or Aud, if legally you are her mother, somewhere inside she will one day expect you to behave as one.

But what did that mean, exactly?

IN MY mother's suite, the afternoon sun fell against the eastern corner of the sitting room and spilled over the carpet and up the legs of the coffee table. It flashed on her wedding ring, white and yellow gold, geometric Italian design, and the enameled Norwegian flag pin in her lapel. She was talking about her day: meetings at Microsoft, a tour of the Nordic Heritage Museum in Ballard, and an honorary marshal spot in the Syttende Mai independence day parade. She saw me looking at the flag. "I forgot to take it off," she said, and pulled it casually from the silk. She dropped it on the table and cradled her coffee, and continued her account of all the Americans celebrating their Norwegian heritage, eating *polse* and ice cream, the children wearing bright red *bunad,* the Sons of Norway with their heavy banners and the fiddlers dancing behind them. Every now and again she would pause, and wait for me to add something, and when I didn't, she would go on.

Every now and again, too, she tilted her head. She knew I'd come to talk to her about something.

Help me, I wanted to say. *Talk to me about how it was. Tell me about family.*

". . . realize that today is short notice, but perhaps tomorrow? If you're well enough."

Dinner. "Yes, tomorrow would be fine. Thank you."

"And your friend, would he like to come?"

"I'll ask him." It was quarter to four. I had to get cash. "Yes, probably."

She put her cup down, smoothed her dress. "Good. Tomorrow it is, then. Although if you don't have plans for tonight . . . ?"

"I have plans."

She nodded, and we stood, and I was struck by how she moved. She wore a dress—not a suit, not a gown, but a dress—and she was happy. She was tired and a little tense, but underneath it all she was at home with herself in a way I'd never thought I'd see. When I was a child, I had dreamt of how she might be in a perfect world—the grin, the hug, the surprise trip to the zoo, the maternal mysterious knowledge of my innermost secret desire for a ham sandwich or chocolate biscuit—but I'd never imagined this lightness, a woman who finally had some air folded into her mix, who had risen like a fairy cake.

"I'm . . ." But there wasn't time. "Thank you. I'm happy for you. It's good to see you."

She laid her hand on my upper arm briefly—her fingertips touched the hidden scar. "Audhumla." The giant cow from the beginning of the world, who was made of frost, and licked the frost from stones. I had forgotten. She had first called me that when I was five, and she had found me sucking the creamy ice that had risen from a milk bottle left on the doorstep at dawn and frozen. Then she had laughed. Now she didn't.

ROOM SERVICE had called and left the champagne. I counted out eleven one-hundred-dollar bills, and then again, and left the two slight stacks next to each other on the sideboard. I stowed the rest in the drawer beneath the TV, with the remote. Now I had half an hour to shower, and arrange the furniture and lighting. The welcoming ambience wasn't strictly necessary, and might not make any difference to the end result, but I wished to acknowledge that although my companion might be bought and paid for, she was a human being. It seemed only polite.

AT 4:32, there was a confident knock on my door.

"I'm Isabella," she said, in a voice like myrrh, and I let her in.

She took it all in—the chilling champagne and two glasses, my bare feet and still-damp hair, the lack of underwear beneath silk shirt and trousers, the closed inner drapes in the sitting room and the bedroom door standing ajar and showing a hint of shadow and candlelight—in one sweeping glance, and said, "Thank you," when I offered to take her wrap. It slid from her bare shoulders into my hands like an offering. Her skin smelled of heat and spice. I carried the light wrap to the closet, and took my time hanging it.

The cash was gone when I returned, both piles.

She looked out over the city while I poured the champagne, and when I sat on the sofa, she sat at my feet as though it were the most natural thing in the world, and laid her hand on my thigh.

"Aud," she said, "it is very good to meet you," and I wanted to believe her. Her eyes were sunlit honey. Summer eyes. Nothing to do with frost or snow or death.

"It's very good to meet you, Isabella," and then I couldn't think of anything else to say, because her hand had started to stroke my thigh, almost absentmindedly, and she was looking at me as though I were her queen.

"Aud, it's an unusual name."

"Yes."

"Are you visiting from another country?"

It felt like it.

"Aud. Am I pronouncing it right?"

"Yes. It's Norwegian, after Aud the Deepminded. She founded Iceland."

"Iceland," she said. "I hear it's a beautiful country. Contradictory. Ice and glaciers and molten lava. And hot springs."

And so controlling of its citizens: only certain things on television, certain names legally allowed.

"You have such lovely muscle here, such strength." She stroked down, paused thoughtfully, stroked up, ending just a fraction higher than she'd started. Her cheekbones shimmered, as though gilded. Through the thin silk of my trousers her hand was warm and alive. "Do you like to work out?"

"Um?"

"You work out?"

"Yes."

She propped her cheek on her fist and went on stroking. "Swimming? Or perhaps some other kind of sports." She knelt like a handmaid, eyes never leaving mine, waiting for a signal. "Tell me what kind of sports you like."

"Competitive." I tried to organize my thoughts but she was calling heat from me as effortlessly as flame from a lamp, and my mind was drowning.

She bent and pushed off her shoes—her scalp was white and clean, her hair smelled of attar of roses—then leaned across me for the champagne. Her breasts plumped warmly on my legs for a moment and then she topped up my glass. I should be doing that. I should be doing all sorts of things. But all I could focus on was her hand.

"Your champagne," I said. "Don't you like it?"

"It's delicious, a very good choice. But this evening is for you. I'm here to make you happy."

She rested her palm, very gently, on my belly. If I let her, she could make me very happy. All she had to do was turn her hand and her fingers would brush between my legs. I took her wrist, and I meant to put her hand away, to say something, to explain, but I couldn't help it, I turned it palm up and leaned forward and kissed it.

She arched, until her throat was inches from my mouth. "Tell me what you want," she said, and I watched myself take her head in my hands and kiss her. I hadn't meant to, but then I found her mouth hot and sliding under mine and I couldn't stop. I folded down next to her and, and hands still in her hair, eased her flat on the carpet and knelt over her. She reached for my leg and tugged, gently, insistently, until I lifted it, and straddled her. Her dress rode up over smooth, golden legs and a tight curving belly. She was small in my arms, and her heart beat as fast as a rabbit's.

She reached up and brushed my left nipple through the silk very lightly with the back of her hand, and I groaned. She blinked at me, very slowly, and touched my top button, and undid it, and touched the next one, and unfastened that, and the next, and I didn't stop her, and she freed my left breast and held her palm beneath it, not touching, until I lowered my breast to it; and she drew her hand down another inch. Again I bent, until my breast was three inches from her mouth. She moved her hand. Her breath was feathery, her lips red.

"Give it to me," she said, "make me take it," and opened her mouth.

I wanted to stop. I wanted to weep. I wanted to make her take my whole breast in her mouth and slide off my trousers and straddle her naked belly, hot and soft.

Someone knocked on the door. She went very still beneath me.

"Aud, it's me." Dornan.

I couldn't think. I felt dazed, too hot and swollen for my clothes.

"Aud?" He knocked again.

I sat back on my heels and took a ragged breath, and then another. I fastened a couple of buttons. Isabella closed her mouth and ran her hands through her hair. I breathed some more and stood.

Isabella sat up. "I don't do couples." She pulled herself onto the sofa and tugged her dress into place.

Dornan knocked again. "I'm not going to go away until I know you're all right."

I wiped my mouth with the back of my hand—her lip gloss smelled the way all makeup does, waxy and womanly—and walked to the door and opened it.

"I'm sorry," Dornan said, walking in. "I should have remembered earlier." I closed the door mechanically. "We were in a bar in Ballard, and these men came in dressed as Vikings. So I said, What's going on? And someone told me it was Syttende Mai, and I said, What's that when it's at home? And they said, May the Seventeenth, Independence Day, and so I thought of you, and how you must be feeling, so I . . ."

He saw the champagne, the two glasses, and stopped, puzzled. Then he noticed the woman on the sofa with smudged lip gloss and no shoes, and turned to me and took in my half-buttoned shirt, my still-flushed cheeks, and swollen eyelids.

"I see," he said. "I find I've been foolish." He spoke slowly, in the educated, guarded accent he hadn't used with me for years. "It seems I've been making unwarranted assumptions. Well. I apologize for the interruption and will be out of your way as soon as I may."

He nodded politely to Isabella, gave me a distant, measuring look, said, "I really don't understand you at all," and left, stepping briskly.

Isabella ran her hands through her hair again, then picked up her champagne glass and took a hefty swallow.

I hung the DO NOT DISTURB sign and locked the suite tight. For the first time since her wrap had slid into my hands and her smell had punched into my brain, I could think, and I did. "A friend," I said. "I'm very sorry about him bursting in like that. Please finish your champagne and let me pour more." In her world, unplanned interruptions no doubt tended to have dangerous repercussions, and I needed her relaxed and willing to take a risk. "You're safe with me. You can leave anytime you like. However, I'd like the chance to make it up to you, if I may. We could talk a little, and relax, and later I'll order us dinner, if you're willing."

"I would love to talk," she said, with only a fractional pause. Whatever it took to make me happy. Twenty-two hundred dollars was a lot of money, and satisfied customers were more likely to return. She patted the seat beside her. "Sit with me." The myrrh was back, the promise of damp skin and tumbled sheets and hoarse cries in the dark.

I sat, and sipped, and she took my hand and held it, and looked at me with those honey and amber eyes.

"Let me help you relax," she said.

"You've had a fright. I feel bad about it. You're not under any obligation."

"But I want to. Being with a woman is different. Special. It's not like a job, not at all. It's pure pleasure."

It was a lovely fiction, and she told it so well. She read the temptation in my face and smiled.

It's nonsense that the eyes are the gateway to the soul. The smile tells all. Broken people can lift the corners of their lips and crinkle the skin around their eyes, but the center is always missing: the tiny muscles at their brows and beneath the eyes, at the curve and bow of mouth, the hinge of the jaw. The smile is empty.

I lifted her hand, put it gently on her lap, and let go. "I don't want sex," I said. "I want information."

She looked at my hard nipples and then between my legs where the silk was dark, and laughed. She put her arm along the back of the sofa. "Certainly we can talk first, if you like."

"I'll rephrase. I will not have sex with you. I want information."

"What do you want to know?" She touched the back of my neck. You know you want me, her hand said, and I'm paid for.

I stood up. "Excuse me one moment."

I closed the bedroom door behind me, found underwear and jeans. Even while I pulled them on, part of me was listening, heart beating high, hoping she would tap on the door and I would open it to say no, and she would kiss me and crawl onto the bed, and then lift her face from the sheets and turn back to look at me, and I wouldn't be able to help myself. I might even be able to make her feel good. What was so wrong with that?

And now the extent of my self-delusion was obvious and pitiful. The lack of underwear, the open door—good manners, yes, put Isabella at her ease, yes, lull her suspicions so she would give me what I needed. *Give me what I needed.* A way to have sex without guilt: She made me do it, Officer, I couldn't help myself.

But that wasn't the point. The point was that Seattle as a city was closed to me. I needed a way in.

I laughed at myself, fastened every button, and went back in.

"Five thousand dollars," I said. "You give me a name and address, and anything else I need to talk to the man or woman who sets things up for you."

"I'm an independent."

Perhaps that's what she liked to pretend, but a hotel with a client list like the Fairmont would not deal with a random service provider. They preferred the reassurance of organization; the kind of people who could short-cut my search for whoever was trying to devalue my real estate. "Who gets a cut of your price?"

She didn't like that. "It's a referral fee."

I opened the drawer under the TV and pulled out a brick of cash.

"Five thousand, cash, on top of the twenty-two hundred I've already paid, and not a soul will know the information came from you." Which meant no one would take their cut.

"Thank you, no."

After what had occurred between us, I couldn't bring myself to force her.

AFTER SHE had gone, I tidied away the champagne, blew out the candles, and stripped naked. I could smell my own need.

I placed my feet exactly, put my palms together, and reached for the ceiling. I breathed out, slow and controlled, and reached some more, until two vertebrae popped and settled, then I bent to the floor, palms flat, and breathed four smooth breaths, six seconds in, seven seconds out. I began the slow-motion movements of a tai chi form.

When I was done, I began again, even more slowly. And again, until sweat coursed down my body.

LESSON 5

THEY WERE ALL THERE. ALL EXCEPT SANDRA APPEARED HAPPY AND RELAXED: GLAD for it to be spring at last, finding it easier to travel to a strange part of the city now that it was no longer dark when they arrived, now that they no longer had to be afraid when they got out of their cars.

"Sit for a minute," I said, and they folded to the floor with varying degrees of ease. Sandra moved more carefully than usual. I wondered what color her torso was. "Let's talk about fear."

"Let's not," Nina said, and though she was smiling, as usual, she wasn't joking.

"Fear," I said, and waited. "What is it?"

"There's all kinds," Kim said. I raised my eyebrows. "Like scary movies are good."

"But being pulled into your supervisor's office is bad," Tonya said.

"And worrying that you're being followed." Katherine, of course.

"The Goliath at Six Flags is kind of cool." Suze.

"But thinking you might have cancer isn't." Nina.

Silence. "And all these things are fear?"

"Well, yeah."

"How are they different?"

"Some are good, and some are bad."

"Why?" Blank looks. "All right. How do you feel when you're afraid?"

"Frightened," Nina said in a *duh* voice.

"How do you know you're frightened?"

They all stared desperately at the carpet, saying with their entire beings: don't like this, won't go there, la la la.

Finally Christie offered, "I shake."

"Yes," I said, "and probably your mouth goes dry."

"Damn," said Kim, "that's right."

"It's the same for everyone. Fear is a physical response to real danger, immediate danger. It's glandular and fast as lightning. There's nothing you can do about it."

They looked appalled.

"But fear isn't the enemy. Fear is your friend. It tells you the truth about what's going on. In that sense, it's a bit like pain."

"Pain is not my friend," Therese said.

"Reliable messenger, then. We don't always want to hear what it's got to say, but once it's arrived, it doesn't pay to ignore it."

Pauletta was frowning. "That's it? I paid good money to hear you say we're gonna get hurt and scared and there's nothing we can do about it?"

"That's not what I'm saying. I'm saying that when you're in danger, your glands release all kinds of hormones that are instructions your body cannot disobey."

"So some guy scares us and we run shrieking down the alley, that what you're saying?"

"No." I put on my earnest, friendly face. "One of the most important hormones involved in the fear response is adrenaline. Its prime function is to shunt power to necessary systems, basically to make sure you're ready to fight or run or both. So, Christie, when you tremble, that's adrenaline flooding your long muscles, your arms and legs, with power. If you're not running or fighting, you shake, like a shuttle trembling at the launchpad."

"I'm not a shuttle," Kim said. "I start to shaking, and the next thing I do is pass out."

"For real?" Pauletta said.

"Once. Went down, whap, like someone broke my legs. Busted my teeth out on the ground."

"No shit?"

"Just baby teeth. Loose anyhow." She shrugged.

Jennifer was breathing far too fast for it to be healthy, and her upper lip glistened. "You pass out? But if you pass out, you're helpless. . . . I'm going to buy a gun," Jennifer said. "I am. A big, big gun."

"Guns don't help," Sandra said. The whole class looked at her.

"Okay," I said. "All right. I'm going to tell you what happens and what can happen when we're scared. And then I'm going to show you some ways to get around some of those things. No one has to pass out with fear ever again—"

"You said there's nothing we can do about it."

"—and no one has to buy a gun."

Now I had their attention.

"Fear is an emotion, a glandular reaction. It's physical. It affects what we do, how we think, and how we feel. Fear is the body's response to an understanding of real and immediate danger. Remember those key words: real and immediate. Your glands flood your body with a variety of hormones, like adrenaline. Adrenaline instructs your body to rev up the parts and processes essential for you to fight or run, and to shut down the nonessentials. So, for example, the capillaries in your face close, making you go pale. Your digestion—from saliva production to excretion—turns off, so your mouth goes dry."

"Is that why I get sick to my stomach?" Tonya.

"Yes. You get queasy because your stomach, usually churning away constantly, essentially freezes. Your heart and respiration rates go up—your heart pounds, you feel breathless—to get oxygen, lots of oxygen, to the long muscles of your arms and legs, getting you ready to respond at your maximum. Fear is a good thing."

"But getting scared isn't." Pauletta was stubborn.

"There's nothing good about being in danger, no." Except that it means you're not yet dead. "But fear, when you are already in danger, is a good thing. Adrenaline also affects the way your brain works."

"Panic," said Jennifer, nodding.

"Not necessarily. What happens in times of real and immediate danger is that your unconscious brain, a kind of emergency expert system, takes over. Panic is a system conflict. It's what happens when your conscious and unconscious brain fight." And melt down, and all sense just runs and hides. That had happened to me for the first time last year, in New York. Tonya was saying something. "I'm sorry."

"I said, like a robot trying to compute when the scientist says, I always lie."

Nina made robot-in-a-loop motions, like something from a bad 1980s music video. The tension was beginning to ease.

I blinked. "Yes. Very good. Just like that. And just as a robot in these stories is always naïve, our conscious mind can be, too. It can persuade itself of things an idiot child wouldn't believe." I shook off memories of last year. "I'll come back to that, because it's important." It was the heart of everything, but I couldn't get there from here. "For now, I'd like you to think a bit more about what fear is and where it comes from."

I stood. They watched warily as I walked to the back of the room and my satchel. Tension was high again. I retrieved the packet of blank three-by-five index cards and the box of Sharpies and handed them out.

"On this card I want you to write the one thing you're afraid of, that you hope taking this class will help with."

"Small card, big pen," Nina said.

"That's because I want you to keep it short. And add, at the bottom right, a simple yes or no, in answer to this question: Have you ever been assaulted? By which I mean physically or sexually attacked." There were a dozen ways to define assault, but for my purposes, that would do. "You won't be reading these aloud, and I don't know your handwriting, so be honest, be specific."

Caps popped as they came off and the air filled with Sharpie scent—Tonya sniffed hers meditatively; she'd have a headache later—there were lots of faraway looks, some scribbling. Sandra's pen moved vigorously but never touched the paper.

"Time's up. Cap the pens, please, and pass them back to me."

"What do we do with the cards?"

"Hand them to Nina." There was some standing, some timing of the thrust of card from their hand to Nina's: attempts to disguise who had given what. "Nina, shuffle them and give them to me."

She did. While they sat down again, I sorted the cards rapidly into the yes pile, three; the no pile, six; and the blank card. I set the cards to one side, facedown.

"According to the 1985 London WAR study, eighty-one percent of women sometimes or often feel frightened at home alone in the daytime. This percentage rises for when we're outside or it's night or both." I looked around the circle, waiting until everyone but Sandra stopped looking at the cards and met my eye. "So what, exactly, are we afraid of?"

Sandra lifted her head. Her face was waxy with intensity, the tiny muscles in her brown irises pulled so tight that in this bad light the plump fibers had an amber sheen. I'd seen a woman look like that once whose boyfriend had their son in a cupboard with a gun against his head. She was ashamed. She couldn't tell me; she wanted me to know.

"In an earlier class I gave you Department of Justice statistics on the chances of avoiding rape if you fight back."

"Seventy-two percent if he's unarmed, fifty-eight percent if armed with a knife, fifty-one if armed with a gun," said Tonya.

"Many of you expressed surprise at that." Nods. "That's because the information we get, every day, from TV and newspapers and online, is all about the rapes that are completed, the lives lost, the pain suffered—preferably with blood and body parts and panicky eyewitness accounts. Why? Because that's what gets an audience, and the bigger the audience, the more the media can charge for their commercials. More than eighty percent of us spend our lives afraid because that helps soap makers and computer manufacturers sell product."

"Same old same old," Nina said. "The military-industrial complex."

"The capitalist system," Christie said. I couldn't have been more surprised if she'd turned purple and exploded. "Someone was talking about this at school last semester. The patriarchy."

"The patriarchy," Nina said. "Haven't heard that word since I did women's studies in college."

"They had college back then?" Pauletta said.

Nina ignored her; she was getting excited. "I remember now. Some big feminist, one of those dead ones, said men teach us to be afraid to control us."

Andrea Dworkin: "We are taught systematically to be afraid. We are taught to be afraid so that we will not be able to act, so that we will be passive, so that we will be women . . . ," in *Our Blood,* though I had no doubt she's said it in some form or other in all her books. The male conspiracy against women. When it came to the media I had always thought corporate greed was a much simpler explanation.

"It's been estimated that the media publicize thirteen completed rapes for every attempted but uncompleted rape. If you round up the chance of getting away from an unarmed attacker from seventy-two to seventy-five percent, that means you have a three in four chance of getting away."

"Or kicking his fucking head in," Suze said.

"And then if you take the thirteen-to-one completed-versus-uncompleted-rape media figure, it means that the papers and the news underreport fight-back stories by five thousand two hundred percent."

"Math makes my head hurt," said Katherine.

"Imagine you're listening to WSB while you drink your mocha and drive to work. Imagine it's a slow news day, so you hear about a grandmother who fought off a rapist with her umbrella. Think about the other fifty-one women who got away."

Tonya got it. Her eyes shone, and it was a different shine than Sandra's.

"Much of what we call fear is actually worry about imaginary situations," I said. "It's learned. It can be unlearned. When you read about someone being raped, remember the three others who got away. On those rare occasions where you do hear about a woman getting away, remember the fifty-one others who did, too. Better yet, don't read or listen to that kind of news."

"Not listen to the news?" Jennifer looked shocked.

"The news exists to make people anxious, so that they keep watching, so that the provider—the website, the network, the publisher—can sell advertising space. But anxiety and worry are not the same as fear. There's very little useful about them. Worry, or stress, or anxiety are responses to long-term or persistently imagined danger, not real danger, not immediate danger. Horror and dread, again, aren't usually about the immediate, but about the future: the suspense of waiting for what you think will come. Note that: think. When you lie awake at night and start imagining mad axe murderers or hooded rapists, we're not smelling them, not hearing them, not feeling the vibration of their footsteps."

I picked up the cards and turned them over.

"Let me tell you something about what's written on these cards. The ones with no in the bottom right list fears like 'being raped,' 'being followed,' 'dark places,' and so on. Do you see any similarities between them?" I waited.

"Horror-movie stuff," Tonya said. "Kind of generic."

"Yes," I said. "The ones who wrote yes were more specific."

"Like what?" Suze, one of the Nos.

"Waking in my hotel room to find the bellboy exposing himself, my old boyfriend getting drunk and paying me a visit, being beaten with a garden rake." I looked around the circle of faces. Therese and Kim's faces were closed, Nina looked particularly detached. "Some of you seem unhappy."

"You just said we're afraid of make-believe things," Pauletta said.

"Those of you who have never been assaulted are worrying about the wrong things. You've paid for my advice, so listen to me now. Fear is a good thing, worrying about fear is not. All right. On your feet."

"What?"

"Up." I stood. "Stand in a big circle. Good. Fear releases adrenaline. Adrenaline will make your heart pound, and make you pant. It's the panting that leads to hyperventilation, which leads to passing out. Some people pass out because they're so frightened, they forget to breathe at all. So if you're not breathing, start. A good way to do that is to exhale sharply, even if you feel you've got no air, and that'll trigger an inhalation. It's enough to get you going. But then you have to not hyperventilate. I'm going to show you how."

Their chests rose and fell with rapid, shallow breath.

"Stand in a stable, comfortable position. Push your tongue up into the roof of your mouth and clamp your back teeth together. This will control your jaw and neck muscles, in case you're shaking, and also, if you get hit on the jaw, it's less likely to break. Keep your back straight." Their notion of straight was pitiful. "Try to feel your spine in one long line, like a plumb line. Don't stick your chin in the air because that will put a strain on your vocal cords, which we'll need nice and relaxed for later." Though there was a good physiological argument, too, for lifting the chin: it reduced the emotional response and promoted blood flow to the frontal cortex. But one thing at a time. "Keep your shoulders down. Not only does that look more confident and relaxed but it reduces muscle tension and therefore speeds any emergency response. Breathe through your nose, breathe deep from the diaphragm. Feel your belly swell. Put your hand on your stomach. There." I walked around, adjusting posture. "Make that hand move out. Your chest should hardly move at all. In through the nose, deep and slow, your belly swells. Out, a long gush through the mouth. In, deep and slow, and out. In. Out."

Their faces grew pink.

"Now that you're breathing nicely and there's no more danger of passing out, it's safe to address some of the other fear symptoms. If your arms and legs are trembling, but you don't yet know if you should run or fight, try clenching and relaxing them. If your mouth is really dry, open your mouth slightly—if it's safe to do so—and run the underside of your tongue over your bottom front teeth. That should make your mouth water. Do this for a few seconds, and swallow a couple of times, and gradually the dryness will go away and your larynx will relax. So now we're ready to use our voices."

Ten pairs of shoulders rose. Well, they were going to have to get over that.

"Voice is an important body weapon. In its way, it's as useful as a kick or punch. Voice can embarrass or frighten a potential attacker. It can summon help, give warning, and say no, loudly and clearly. It can give you confidence, and deafen your attacker, actually damage an eardrum. Voice can immobilize an attacker or potential attacker for a split second." Therese made a slight *huh* of skepticism. I started walking around the inside of the circle. "Voice increases the power of any physical move you might make because it helps you focus your attention and your strike. Voice depends very much on the way we breathe. Make the voice come from deep down, as though it's from your thighs and stomach, not your throat and head. You want a deep, explosive sound." I stopped in front of Therese. "Like this:

"Huut!"

The sound slammed into her face and blew her backwards. Her arms pinwheeled. I resumed walking while she shook her head and pulled herself together.

"Spread out just a little. We're going to do some squats." I demonstrated. "Slow and easy. Breathe out through your mouth as you go down, in through your nose as you come up. Down, out." The less self-conscious made a kind of *ooourff* as they went down. "Up, in. Down, out. Up, in. Now a little faster. Down!" More *oourffs*. "Up. Down! Good. Let me hear some noise now. A deep sound, a boom. Feel it blast out of you, like a train from a tunnel. *Ooosh!* All together. *Ooosh.*" The entire circle dropped, like a falling hoop. Half made a noise. "Up, and in. And *oosh.*" More of the hoop sounded. "And up and in and *oosh.*" Gaps in the hoop only from Jennifer and Katherine and Sandra. "And up and in and *oosh!*" Katherine sounded. Not much, but something. The circle was almost closed. "Up and in and *oosh!* Up, in, oosh!" An uncertain *ooh?* from Jennifer. Almost. "Up and in and *oosh!*" Jennifer's ooh firmed and strengthened. Katherine was as loud as the rest. "Up and in and *oosh!* Louder. Ooosh! Louder. Ooosh!" I walked around, breathing, booming, listening. And there, at last, a thin, hesitant sound, wavering like a ghost. "Louder. *Ooosh!*"

The hoop dropped, the sound flared up, unbroken, like a ring of fire. My face stretched in a fierce grin: you breathe, you make a noise, the next thing you know you're talking back, and then, next time he thinks about hitting you, you leave.

Ooosh.

Ooosh.

Ooosh.

"Louder! Blow your attacker into the back of next week. Use that fear, use that anger. Louder. And up, and in, and one last time. *Ooosh!*"

The sound was tremendous; I felt it through the soles of my feet. If there had been a window, it would have rattled.

"Yes!" Suze said, pumping her arm.

Everyone was grinning. Tonya turned away briefly, but not before I saw the sparkle on her cheeks. Sandra looked as though she had seen God.

"*Whoo!*" Kim said. "We kicked *ass!*"

The basement door opened.

It was like watching a pride of lionesses lift their dripping muzzles from the belly of the dying zebra and zero in on the giggling hyena.

The face of the long-haired woman in the doorway went white. Classic fear response. The scent of mass-produced incense, and the whine-and-tinkle of Crystal Gaze's sound system—three women with nasal problems singing Om-mani-padme-hum—drifted into the basement. The woman swayed, clutched for the doorknob, missed, nearly fell.

"Breathe," Nina advised.

Everyone laughed. The woman in the doorway looked as though she might cry. I recognized her from behind the cash register upstairs. "How can I help you?"

"I, uh."

"Breathe, honey," Nina said again.

We all waited politely. "You, uh, that is, the customers were wondering . . ." She didn't seem to know how to proceed.

"Were we too loud, honey?"

"Yes. Loud. You were loud."

"They heard you upstairs," I told everyone. "Through the concrete and the floors and over the sound system."

"Excellent!" Christie said.

SIX

I CALLED DORNAN BEFORE BREAKFAST. HE WOULDN'T PICK UP. I LEFT A LONG MESSAGE. When I called again, half an hour later, he answered.

"It didn't look like work," he said.

"No."

"In fact, it looked to me as though I showed up just in time."

An image popped into my head of Dornan in baggy blue shorts and sagging tights, cape askew, kicking down the door to my suite to the accompaniment of melodramatic music.

"I did, didn't I? Show up in time?"

Depends how you look at it. "Yes." Though I hadn't got the information I'd wanted.

"Aud, don't take this the wrong way, but are you sure you're all right?"

"How do you mean, exactly?"

"Last night just . . . well, it's not like you. The whole idea strikes me as baroque and too complicated, all that potential for things to go wrong. And the timing. It's almost as though you set yourself up for it. At best, it seems unchar-acteristically silly."

Irresponsible. Then a victim. Now silly. "Every week a new high."

"Yes, well, that's probably some sort of joke, but those drugs were truly wicked. Most of those other people are still in hospital. One of the carpenters just had to go back on a ventilator, for God's sake."

He was very well informed.

"Look, why don't we just go back to Atlanta? You don't really care about your warehouse anyway, and you've seen your mum. I've seen enough of the Seattle chains. I have some ideas to be working on, and, besides, the business is probably dissolving with no one looking after it. Let's just leave. Don't get distracted. What happened with the drugs is irrelevant, like, like an earthquake. It affected you, yes, but it wasn't aimed at you. It wasn't personal."

"Oh, but it was."

"More than a dozen people—"

"Dornan, think about it. This whole thing has been aimed at getting me to sell the warehouse cheaply. Who I was didn't matter, it was the fact that I owned the warehouse. They began by reducing my cash flow sharply, by calling OSHA and EPA to harass my leaseholder, which they hoped would make whoever owned the warehouse view it as a liability. It was a liability. But then Rusen came along. He started trying to deal with the problem, he tried to talk to EPA and OSHA, so then whoever was engineering all this had to start messing with the production itself." The day-as-night exposures, the lighting setup, the props. "And when Rusen, with his unexpected corporate efficiencies, starts trying to find ways to finesse that, and keeps making his payments to me, they start to scramble and dump drugs in the coffee. Which I drink. Ironic if you stop to think about it. Two months ago all they would have to have done is make me an offer. As you've said, I didn't really care. The only reason I came out here in the first place was to *be* distracted."

"And because of your mum."

"Yes. But mainly to get away from Atlanta. Only now I find I'm being manipulated again."

"This is different."

"Is it? They drugged that coffee, and I drank it. They slid their nasty little hands inside my head and paddled about. I can't rely on myself anymore. Is what I see real? Can I walk up a hill without my heart faltering and the oxygen not getting to my lungs because some compound that I can't even name has altered my metabolic cycle? If I have to run I don't know if I can. If something, someone comes for me, I don't know if it's really happening. Do you know what that's like?"

"No."

"So, yes, now I care. I'm going to get these people. And you know what?" And it slowly dawned on me that this was true. "I'm going to enjoy it. Because, as you say—and you're obviously more well informed than I am—someone is still on a ventilator, and the people who did this to her—"

"Him."

"—him deserve whatever I can mete out. This is something I can do something about. It won't be easy, because Seattle isn't my town, and I'll have to do things differently, but I'll find them."

"I'm getting that."

"I'm going to get information from Corning's office and follow it. And if, in order to get to these people, I have to deal drugs or talk to kiddie-porn merchants or get naked with gorgeous women I've given a lot of money to in the privacy of my own suite, I will."

"Though you didn't. Get naked."

"No."

"Though she was very decorative."

"She was, wasn't she?"

"But not really your type, in the end."

"No."

"Maybe if she'd pissed you off," he said. "That seems to work for you."

I said nothing.

"Well, I don't imagine there's any way I can help, but if there is, let me know."

"There is something," I said, and imagined him flinging himself skyward and hurtling around the earth faster and faster until it slowed, and reversed, and the film of my life ran backwards through the last year to the afternoon when Julia sat on my lap by the fjord and said she was going to Oslo and there was no reason for me to go with her, she would only be gone twenty-four hours, and I said all right. "Have dinner with me tonight."

"You're eating again?"

"Not by choice. Come be my moral support. With my mother and Eric."

Silence. Then he sighed. "What time?"

"Seven. I'll pick you up."

THE SUN was bright and the air soft. It was going to be a hot day, for Seattle. The sunshine seemed to puzzle and provoke the normally placid local drivers. Crossing Fifth Avenue, I heard the tire squeal and horn honk of two separate near misses.

I got to Corning's office at two minutes to nine. Gary was hovering by the door, already agitated.

"Miz Corning's been . . . there's . . . I'm afraid your appointment is postponed."

I moved him aside gently. The reception area was brightly lit, and the adrenaline coursing through my system made it seem brighter still. Corning's door was ajar, and her lights off. "Don't move," I said. I listened.

"She's . . ."

I walked in, turned on the lights. Perfectly tidy and normal, apart from a lone piece of paper facedown on the floor. I picked it up. Page two of a standard commercial lease, blank. "Gary?" He ventured in behind me. "Where is she?"

"That's just it. I don't know. She hasn't been in, and she hasn't called. It's not usual." Emphasis on the last word.

I turned and waited.

"She's very particular about clients. Always here half an hour before an appointment, always wanting the file so she can appear to have remembered everything about the client. The personal touch, she called it."

Past tense. "When did you get here?"

"Usual time. Eight o'clock. Well, five minutes late, so I was worried she'd . . . I've been working on a presentation on the new . . . on the presentation she was going to give later this week."

Was going to give. He was young, but not stupid. Perhaps he knew something he didn't know he knew. "Why are you so worried?"

"I just am. It's not usual. When she still wasn't here after I'd finished my coffee, I waited another minute or so, then called her cell, in case she was stuck in traffic, so I could ask her if there was anything I could do to prepare for her meeting, you know, so she wasn't cutting it too fine, but there was no answer. She always answers her cell. So I thought maybe she was sick, so I called her home. Nothing. So I checked her appointment calendar, and she hasn't canceled anything, so I was thinking maybe she'd had an accident."

"Yet you haven't called the police."

Silence.

I sat in Corning's chair. "Why don't you take a seat and we'll have a little chat."

He sat stiffly.

"How long have you worked here?"

"Fourteen months."

"Fourteen months. Long enough to know that not everything that happens in this office is aboveboard. You're smart. You know that you should probably have reported some of these things to somebody. But it's your first real job and who could blame you if you listened to your boss when she told you that everybody does things this way. Business is business."

His face was set.

"But, as I say, you're smart. And no doubt you understand by now that at least one of your clients, me, does, in fact, blame you for conniving in irregular, unethical, and very probably illegal activity. But perhaps you and I can work something out."

He wavered for a moment, then sat as straight as a plumb line and lifted his chin. How annoying. I could break something—it probably wouldn't have to be a bone, a desk lamp would do—but he was young, and I'd bought him chocolates last time I'd been here.

"Do you know what money is, Gary? It's a lubricant. Money makes the things you want possible. It can't buy love, but it can buy sex, and respect. Money gets you security and attention. It can buy health and it can pay for justice. So if I said I would offer you an undreamt-of sum, what would you do? If you could have anything in the world, what would it be? Take a minute to think about it."

He crossed his left leg over his right, linked his hands over his knee, and began to sweat.

Dornan would ask for an empire of some kind, six thousand coffee shops all over the world, and guaranteed bargains every time he shopped. Maybe he would ask for Tammy back. My mother? For all political and business negotiations to be reasonable and rational. Luz would want a pair of leather trousers and permission to have the light on all night. Kick, oh, I would bet my bank account I knew what she wanted: the impossible.

Gary cleared his throat. "To be in charge. I'd want to run my own real estate office."

It's impossible to look at someone and know whether they are being brave. For an agoraphobic, walking down the street is a heroic act. For someone with absolutely no imagination, running into a burning building to save a baby is not hard. Bravery is relative. Perhaps it's the same with dreams.

"Staying out of jail would be the first step, and I can help you with that. Let's begin with you bringing me my file. I'll make us some coffee."

There was no espresso machine in the break room, but I found a French press and an interestingly scented light Arabica blend. While the kettle boiled I leafed through the magazines and newspapers on the table. One was the *Seattle Times* with the story about the drugging.

Back in Corning's office, Gary was kneeling on the floor by the filing cabinet, looking baffled.

"It's gone," he said.

I considered. "What else is missing?"

"How did you—"

"What else is missing?"

"A lot."

"How specific is the loss?"

"I don't understand."

"Particular files, files that are connected in some way, or random chunks?"

"I don't know."

"Find out. Do you want cream or sugar?"

He was still riffling through files when I brought back the coffee. I settled comfortably behind the desk and sipped, content to wait now that he'd begun.

"I'm going to have to cross-check the computer records file by file against the paper files to know for sure what's gone, but I can tell you one thing I've noticed. She'd had me make calls about three lots in the last couple of months that are connected. More or less. I mean, literally. They're next door to each other. Contiguous."

"Is one of those lots mine?"

He nodded.

"You said more or less."

"That's the thing I don't get. There's one lot between the others that isn't for sale. It's the Federal Center. You can't buy that. Also, I don't remember any calls to other investors about these other three lots."

"You think she wanted it for herself?"

"I don't know. And it's pretty useless land, anyhow. Warehouses. Who wants those?"

"Close the file cabinet and come sit. Talk to me about real estate here in Seattle."

I **TOOK THE** *Seattle Times* with me and read the story carefully in the car. I tried to imagine I was Corning. I highlighted the names of those admitted to Harborview Medical Center. I asked the MMI for a map.

At Harborview, I found that they had all been released, except for one man, Steven Jursen, who had been transferred that morning to the University of Washington Medical Center.

According to the MMI, the UW Medical Center was less than a mile from Kick's house. I drove down her street, even though it wasn't strictly on my route. Her van wasn't in the driveway. I wondered if she had got the flowers. Of course she had. Benjamin was an efficient concierge.

The lobby of the medical center was stuffed with art. The floors were clean enough to eat from, if I'd wanted to eat. Nothing was white. The elevator took an age.

Jursen was in a private room. The door was partly open. I stepped close, lifting my hand to knock, and the smell hit me: that hospital scent of disinfectant and fear and floor polish, of bleached linens and sugary drinks, of sleek equipment with its contacts recently wiped down with alcohol and ready to lie cold and stinging against warm skin. I knocked. No response. There again, if he was on a ventilator, there wouldn't be. I pushed the door open.

He was asleep. Sunshine poured through the large window, gilding the brushed steel and putty white of the equipment standing ready around the room. He was breathing on his own. On the set, I remembered a man in his late fifties with hard hands and grey hair who wore overalls and walked with slightly bowed legs. A manual worker all his life, whose parents or grandparents had come from Sweden and had expected a hard life of hard work. No great ambition for success, just a steady job with one company, maybe in construction, who paid him on time and took care of everything. A mid-twentieth-century man trying to live in the twenty-first.

Asleep, he looked quite different, not younger but purer, untouched by the experience and compromises of age. A preacher from the eighteenth century, say, who knew he was doing God's work. I looked at his chart. He'd been off the ventilator since midnight. There were EKG records and an order for an echocardiogram and something called a MUGA test. Under *marital status* a woman had written in blue ink: *divorced.* I adjusted the slant of the blinds so that the sun wasn't in his face, and watched his chest rise and fall, then went to find a doctor.

I DROVE A circuitous route—no one followed me—to a café on Boat Street that I'd read about. I pulled into the parking lot. It was lunchtime and I was hungry, but I didn't get out of the car; I doubted my hunger would stand in the face of food that tasted of sulfur and burnt rubber.

Jursen had congestive heart failure. The overdose had nearly killed him—an overdose he'd been fed because he was connected to me. His near-death was a consequence an order of magnitude greater than spoiling a few rolls of film, and very public. Corning was running scared, scared enough to try to erase her tracks, starting with pulling the tail on me. Good. I would let her stew in her own juices another day or so. Fear would do my work for me.

KICK'S VAN was parked outside the warehouse, but it was her assistant at the craft-services table. Rusen stood by one of the soundstages, talking to Peg and Joel.

"—can't," Joel was saying. "It just doesn't make sense to do it that way with these time constraints."

"You're always saying what you can't do," Peg said. "Why don't you try looking at what you can, just for once in your miserable, whining life. We've—" She saw me and broke off. They all turned.

"Don't let me interrupt," I said.

"No, no," Rusen said. "Are you looking for your friend?"

"Dornan? He's here?"

"He was. Or maybe that was yesterday . . ." He pushed his glasses up his nose, realized that it was him I'd come to talk to, and turned to the other two. "Sorry, guys. Later."

"But—"

"Later, Joel, okay?"

As we walked through the set to his trailer, someone dropped a microphone boom, someone else started shouting. Rusen's stride was small and tight.

His trailer was painfully neat. He took his customary seat behind his keyboard and began organizing paper clips into rows.

"Things seem a little tense," I said.

"Sîan Branwell has to be in Spain in four days to shoot a feature. We're having to reorder the production sequence to get all her scenes in the can. It's causing . . . complications. Disagreements with the director and stunt coordinator. And money is, well, you know how the money is. And Finkel isn't coming back tomorrow, after all."

"His son is worse?"

"He's dying." Silence. "Boy howdy, it does seem wrong to be worrying about money and production schedules and bickering crew when a boy is dying."

"Letting your dream go won't keep him alive."

"That's right," he said. Then, more strongly, "That's right. And, anyhow, our people need these jobs. The industry's in a bad place with Vancouver siphoning off business. We can't . . . But, hoo boy, you didn't come here to listen to me. What can I do for you?"

"We should start planning our strategy for OSHA and EPA. Let's begin with payroll and benefits. How's health insurance?"

It turned out that his people had major medical but both co-pay and deductible were very high, and the company's secondary insurer was making a fuss about covering the difference.

We talked about that for a while. He began to look a little less harried.

"I took a long look at your payroll and I don't see any information on the young person I noticed the other day. Even if he's an unofficial intern, we need some paperwork."

"Bri's not an intern. He's Finkel's son. Bri Junior."

"I thought his son was dying."

"His other son."

I mulled that. "How old is he?"

"Bri? Fifteen— no sixteen now."

"Unless he sits around reading comics all day, get some paperwork going and formalize some kind of payment. Figure out what would make OSHA happy. And how old's his friend?"

"Mackie? Oh, he's twenty at least."

We talked for another hour. When I stood to leave, his tension was no less but it was focused. He had a plan. "We can keep it together," he said. "It'll work."

Back on the set, I wandered over to the craft-services table. The woman behind the counter was standing around looking bored.

"Kick around?"

"Nope. Taking a break."

"Know where she went?"

"Nope. For a walk or something. Said they'd be back in"—she looked at her watch—"I guess about forty-five minutes from now."

They.

"Hey, want some coffee?"

"No. Thank you."

"That's what everyone says these days."

I COULD GO talk to the *Times* reporter. I could go to the police and use my mother's name. I could forget letting Corning soften herself up in a fear marinade and go find her. But if anyone gave me information I didn't know where it might lead me, and yesterday, on the hill, I had found myself breathless. There might be other shortcomings I wouldn't notice until I leaned on them and found them wanting.

GOOD DOJOS are often found in bad neighborhoods. Seattle Aikikai was on Aurora alongside Korean massage parlors, a gun shop, and several love motels.

The dojo smelled deeply familiar: chalk, sweat, the white vinegar used to keep the canvas mat clean and bleached. One young woman and five men were stretching on the smaller mat. They were friendly enough. A heavyset Chinese-American introduced himself as Mike. The woman said her name was Petra and that if I didn't have a *gi*, I could see if any of the ones hanging in the women's changing room would fit. The changing room was tiny, with flimsy walls and a crooked shower stall no doubt installed by a hapless volunteer. The pleasantly amateur feel reminded me of my first martial arts classes in England. I hung my dress on a hanger and contemplated the *gis*. None of them would ever see bright white again, but one tunic was reasonably clean. The cleanest trousers were too small, and the white belt stiff and difficult to tie.

There were covert glances when I came out to stretch, but it was considered impolite to ask questions or appear to be interested in another's level of training. Aikido is built on Taoist principles; competition is frowned upon.

When the bell chimed twice, we moved to the large mat and knelt in a line along the long side. Despite the supposed lack of competition, it was tradi-tional to line up according to rank; as the newcomer, untested, I politely took the low-rank spot on the right. Mike took the left-hand position. The sensei, full of his own dignity, descended magisterially from upstairs, *hakamas*, the bloused trousers of *dan* rank, swishing like a long skirt. The students exuded awe; I guessed he was very high-ranking, sixth or seventh *dan*. He was in his early forties, and his hands were reddish around the knuckles. His hair was very dark brown, and crinkly, and his forehead crinkled to match when he saw the newcomer in the ill-fitting *gi* in his dojo, but the ceremony had begun and there would be no talking until after the final bow.

We all bowed to the *kamiza* in the center of the long wall, then he turned and we bowed to him and said in unison, *"O-ne-gai-shimasu."* Please practice with me.

He moved through what was obviously an unvarying set of warm-ups, which began with loose shoulder swinging, moved on to spine stretching, wrist working and blending exercise, and ended with *shikko,* a kind of duck-walking on the knees, and finally roll-outs, forward and back. Everyone moved easily, and I guessed none had been studying less than a year. Serious students.

We knelt in our line again, and the sensei motioned Mike onto the mat as his attacker, or *uke.* They stood in *hanmi,* though Mike began with right foot forward rather than left and had to change. Probably left-handed.

"Shomenuchi," the sensei said, and Mike stepped forward smoothly with a right-hand knife-hand chop at the sensei's forehead.

In karate or judo, the *nage* would block solidly, meeting strength with strength, the muscle-sheathed arm bones clashing like swords. If you were good, if you struck at the right angle and speed, your opponent was already off balance and in pain by the time you punched out his floating ribs, if you were a *karateka,* or took him crashing to the mat, if you were a *judoka.* It was a wasteful way to work, with so much effort expended in negating one force with another.

When Mike's hand came down, there was no bone-on-bone shock, no meeting of force at all. The sensei stepped out of the way, an easy turn at the hip and glide back and out, and laid the side of his right hand on the *uke's* right wrist, the left hand behind his right elbow, then was behind the *uke,* guiding him, helpless in a stiff arm bar, along his original path, facedown to the mat, where he was pinned. It was like watching a leaf get sucked into a whirlpool.

A young man made a late entrance and hurried through his bow and rushed into the men's changing room.

"*Shomenuchi ude osae,*" the sensei said, describing the technique, and Mike slapped the mat twice, and the sensei let him up. He demonstrated twice more, slowly, and then once at full speed. The final time, Mike slapped the mat in earnest, and when he stood, he was sweating.

The newcomer came out to the mat, still tying his belt, but instead of kneeling he waited for me to move down a space. When in Rome.

Sensei gestured us to our feet. The others paired off instantly, which left me with New Boy. He bowed at me sulkily, and assumed *hanmi,* waiting. I dutifully stepped into *shomenuchi.*

He was rushed, and clumsy, and if I'd been a beginner he might have sprained my shoulder, but he was uncertain enough that my arm was not fully extended, and he moved stiffly, using muscle rather than technique, and I could control him without appearing to and go down without injury. He frowned. He knew something wasn't exactly right, but had no idea what.

Part of the noncompetitive ethos of aikido is to help and guide each other: the *uke* helps the *nage* with the technique; the *nage* ensures that the *uke* goes down without injury. The greater the disparity in skill, the greater the responsibility. A ninth *dan* should be able to take down a rank beginner with speed, grace, and precision, without anyone getting a bruise. He should be able to help the beginner do the same to him.

The woman who had taught me aikido in Atlanta, Bonnie, had talked about sensing *ki,* and blending energies. She showed me an exercise called the unbending arm. We faced each other, and she asked me to hold my right arm out straight and make a fist. Then she turned it palm up and laid my right forearm on her shoulder. "Don't let me bend it," she said, and interlaced her hands, and began to press down at the elbow. I gritted my teeth and locked my arm. "You're strong," she said, but after three or four seconds, my arm bent. She smiled cheerfully. "Want to see if you can make me bend my arm?" So we exchanged positions, and I pulled on her elbow, and nothing happened. She looked bored, even pretended to yawn while I grunted and exerted more and more pressure. "You look like you're going to burst something," she said. So I asked her what the trick was. "Trick? It's not a trick. Here, put your arm back up." I did. "Now bend it a little. And spread your fingers wide. Relax, relax your shoulders and neck and back. Root your feet to the earth." The earth was covered in concrete foundation, steel I-beam construction and bamboo flooring, but I didn't comment. "Now feel the energy coming up from the earth and through you and down your arm. Stay relaxed, keep your fingers open. Channel your *ki* through your fingers. It's pouring out of you in a stream of light." And my arm didn't bend, and it took absolutely no effort. And I didn't understand it at all.

"Are you really trying?" I said, and she said she was. Later that day, I found Frank King, my first APD partner, six-feet-three and two hundred thirty pounds, and put my arm on his shoulder and said, "Bend it," and he couldn't.

I didn't believe in *ki,* or the energy from the earth, or light shooting out of my fingertips, but the fact was, when I relaxed and thought about energy flowing smooth and liquid through my arms, my arm didn't bend.

I wrestled with the idea for a week, and I told Bonnie the idea of *ki* was nonsense, and she shrugged and said, "What does it matter?" and after a while, it didn't. I could feel when I got into the zone and became fluid and unbendable. And then one night Frank and I were called to a fire. The firefighters were already there, herding people back, unspooling their hose, locking down the connection, but just as the water began to stiffen and bulge through the flattened canvas, a chunk of burning roof pinwheeled in orange flame onto the lead hose man, and he'd gone down. The hose whipped and snapped like a dying moray eel and snaked itself ten yards across the pavement, leaping and spraying the crowd before I got to the hydrant and cut the water supply. When another firefighter took the nozzle and shouted, "I'm good!" I opened the hydrant again, and watched the hose turn into a live thing, and something I couldn't articulate clicked in my brain.

In one of those strange coincidences, when I got home, too wired to sleep, I turned on the Discovery Channel and saw a program about crocodiles. "This twenty-two-foot croc can run more than twenty miles an hour," the narrator said in an Australian accent, "but when you take a look at its spinal structure, that doesn't seem possible. Researchers at the University of Melbourne tell us that the key to this incredible strength and flexibility is hydraulics." And they showed two geeky-looking academics draping an empty hose over two saw horses fifteen feet apart, turning on the water, and watching the hose transform from a limp tube to an arcing, stiff sausage. They hung weights from it; it didn't bend.

Hydraulics. It wasn't the bone and ligaments and tendons that made an arm strong, it was the blood pumping through the vascular system, the plasma in the cells of sclera and muscle.

New Boy didn't yet know this. Directing him, from my position as an *uke*, was a little like trying to direct a high-pressure hose from the hydrant end instead of the nozzle.

Then it was my turn as *nage*. It would have been very easy to breathe in two long gushes and take him down in a perfect moving spiral, pin him helpless to the mat, nod unemotionally when he slapped, let him up, do it all again. But he wouldn't learn anything, and neither would I. And so the first time, I took control very gently, like sliding my palm under a tap runoff and tilting it so it was almost, but not quite, perpendicular and the water landed an inch to the right of the drain. For a moment, he tried to fight. He tried to draw his wrist up, but my palm on his elbow was firm and I guided him kindly to the mat.

He slapped, and leapt up, rubbing his shoulder, and then looked confused when it didn't hurt. But the sensei had seen it, and came over.

"Everything okay here? Jim?"

Jim looked at me, then nodded slowly.

"Continue," the sensei said, and watched while I assumed *hanmi*, and Jim came at me, and I took him down, just as before. The sensei nodded, and gestured for us to swap roles, and I attacked Jim. I used my body to guide his hands and he took me down with the same puzzled look as before.

The sensei motioned Jim away, said, "Watch," assumed *hanmi*, and nodded for me to attack.

We barely touched each other, but we felt each other's strength clearly, and it was the difference between the exuberant rushing together of two mountain streams and the vast movement of ocean currents—the Kuroshio gliding past the North Atlantic Drift, separated by the continent of North America. I went down, and slapped, and stood.

He bowed with a thoughtful look.

When we sat again for the next demonstration, it wasn't in rank order. I sat between Petra and an older man with red cheeks and grizzled hair, and the sensei held his wrists out behind him for a man with a tense face and long, black hair to take in *ushiro tekubitori.* The student flinched, even as he grabbed the wrists, and the sensei stepped backwards into *tenchi nage.* The student was already up on the balls of his feet, longing to go down so that he wouldn't have to anticipate it anymore. Sensei threw him; the student rolled out well enough for me to guess he was perhaps *yonkyu* rank and to wonder why he would keep studying if he were so afraid.

We stood. Petra hesitated just a fraction before turning away and bowing to the student on her left, which left me with Mike.

Mike knew what he was doing. When he took my wrists, his arms were relaxed. It was clear he was ready to deal with a complete beginner or a master. I swept my right hand up and left down, stepped back smoothly with my left foot, then scissored my arms and sent him flying into a forward roll. He rolled like a big cat and came up grinning. I grinned back.

This time when we knelt, sensei beckoned me onto the mat to be his *uke*, and held out his left wrist. I grasped it in my right, careful to grip with my little finger, which so many people forget. We didn't look into each other's eyes, not yet, because this was for the class, not between us, but he paid me the courtesy of not holding back when he whipped me into *kotegaeshi*, and I had to twist in midair and break-fall to save my wrist and ribs, and when he flipped me onto my stomach, he moved fast and not gently and he not only put me in a wrist pin but locked out my elbow and braced my upper arm against his thigh to torque my shoulder at an uncomfortable angle. I slapped. When I stood, the row of kneeling students were sitting very straight, eyes wide, except Mike, who was grinning even harder.

This time when we paired, Petra didn't hesitate.

She was light and whippy but I took particular care to guide her neatly. "Wow," she said, when she came up. Her eyes were wide-set and hazel, under straight brows. "Your energy is, like, really clear."

I smiled and held out my other wrist, and she took it. It was like playing with a lariat: twist this way, twist that way, and everything is neatly coiled on the floor and perfectly still, with no more ability to get up and move without permission than a piece of old rope.

She held her left wrist out, and I took it with my right, and she frowned in concentration, turned her left hand over and out, stepped back with her left foot, pulled her elbow close to her body, put her right hand over mine and turned. I went down, but in real life I would simply have moved behind her on the diagonal, put my hand up, and kept turning until she was unbalanced and I could flip her over my hip. Or I could have twisted faster in midair and turned out of the wrist lock. But I went down, and waited patiently until she decided which way to step over me to flip me onto my stomach. A bit more fiddling and she had me in a decent shoulder pin.

I got up and took her wrist again, but this time before she moved, I said, "Spread your fingers. Just imagine it for a moment, then do it." She frowned again. "Relax your shoulders. Imagine you can do this perfectly, and then do it."

She did. She beamed. Held her left wrist out eagerly.

"This time, with your right hand, guide mine, turn it as though you're rolling a fat sausage over in the air." She did, and it gave a tighter, faster torque to the wrist lock. This time I wouldn't have been able to do anything but go down.

"Cool," she said.

The dojo was not air-conditioned. Soon everyone was glowing with sweat. Mike was drenched. Every time he rolled, sweat spattered the mat.

The tense student, whose name turned out to be Chuck, was hard to work with. It was like dealing with a panicked deer. When he was *nage,* he would begin a technique, then stop and say, "Shit, shit, no, no, let me try again," pleading as though I were a judgmental father who would beat him for any mistake. I found myself moving very, very slowly, breathing loudly so that he would take an unconscious cue from my respiration rate and slow his own, and keeping my face quite still. Once or twice I found myself trying not to get between him and the light in case he bolted.

The grey-haired man was Neil, and although he was competent, it was clear he was not well. His cheeks acquired a faintly purple tinge and he ran out of breath very quickly, and had to rest every now and again. Everyone seemed used to that.

We knelt again. Sensei surveyed us, paused, and said, "Free play." Electricity rippled down the line of students. Petra and Jim moved regretfully off the mat and sat to one side. Free play is not for beginners.

Chuck, Mike, Neil, the two men I hadn't worked with, and I ranged in a circle around sensei, Mike looked around, nodded, said *"Hei!"* and Neil charged at sensei, and then flew through the air in a tucked ball, and one of the anonymous students ran and was flung on his back, and then Chuck, whom sensei stepped to meet so he couldn't collapse with fear before making contact, and then Mike, who rolled backwards, then me. I ran without breathlessness, smiled as the currents brushed and I described an elegant spiral and rolled out and was on my feet again even before Neil came charging in once more.

The more truly expert an aikido player is, the more closely movement

on the mat during free play resembles the Brownian motion of particles in sus-
pension. Sensei moved slowly across the canvas, flinging bodies random dis-
tances, never letting the group close in or a pattern develop. But against six
opponents no one can keep that up forever without taking them out perma-
nently, one by one, which is why, generally, only those who aren't too far from
being *yudansha* take part in free play: gradually, no matter how good one is,
things start to get just a little ragged, just a little rough. The goal becomes one
of *pushing away* rather than guiding. I've seen more than one person get hurt
in such situations.

Sensei lasted two and a half rounds before the raggedness became serious.
He stiff-armed Mike in the center of the chest and he went down with an
ashen-faced thump; sensei immediately stood straight and clapped his hands
twice. Everyone sagged a little. Neil was gasping; the others were breathing fast.
So was I, but not in distress.

Sensei offered his arm to Mike, who came off the mat looking fine.

"Angelo," he said, pointing to the student with the mustache whom I hadn't
worked with, and we began again. Angelo was ragged after two people: shoulders tense, fists clenched, steps small and abrupt. Sensei let everyone have a go
at him before pointing to someone called Donny. Then Neil.

And then it was my turn, and Mike charged first, like a young bear, and I
smiled and bowled him neatly into the path of Chuck and they went down in
a tangle, and then I turned to help Neil fly, and then sensei ran at me and dived
to roll and come at me feet first and I refused the challenge and leapt over him
like water bursting over a stone and sparkling clear and bright in the sun, before dipping and rising under Angelo, tossing him up like a whitewater rapid
flips a raft, and joy fizzed under my skin as he turned turtle and came down flat
on his back and I was spinning, taking Donny into a headfirst fall that would
have broken the neck of anyone who didn't practice falling two hours a day.
Blood rushed sweet and hot under my skin and laughter bubbled up through
me and I loosed it. It was a lovely day.

DORNAN WORE black jeans and a jacket and had taken the sapphire out of his
left ear.

"What are you smiling at?" he said crossly as we drove north to meet my
mother and Eric.

"Not a thing."

He wriggled uncomfortably, tugged at his jacket cuffs and then his seat belt. I wasn't sure why he was so tense. He'd already met my mother. She hadn't eaten him.

"We're going to be early," he said.

"Yes." If you were early, you could check out exits, and crowd choke- and vantage-points before you had to settle down. You could scan the clientele, get a feel for who might do what. Except that when we parked by the massive totem outside Ivar's Salmon House and went in, my mother and Eric were already at the far side of the enormous room at a table cornered by two picture windows, sitting drenched in the westering sun that poured across Lake Union and turned their chardonnay to bottled summer, but they rose with such glad smiles, such open shoulders and wide hands, that I smiled, too, and felt a jet of the same joy I'd experienced that afternoon.

I walked to the table slowly, absorbing the vaulted space, the forty feet of native canoe suspended from the roof beams, the rounded faces of the Inuit and Aleut servers—not unlike the Sami in the north of Norway and Finland—the deep reds and creams of painted native carvings on the walls. Even the music sounded Sami, too, which made sense when one considered the fact that Alaska and Siberia were separated only by the narrow Bering Strait. The smell of salmon did not fill me with horror.

They had thoughtfully left the two chairs facing the best view, which meant I had to sit with my back to the door, but if I turned in my seat slightly I could watch reflections in the window. There were three possible exits.

We all sat as though we meant to stay: shoulders down, feet flat, back relaxed. To start, everyone but me ordered the clam chowder. I opted for the green salad, on the theory that if I could manage fruit, I should be able to manage green leaves. The chowder arrived first. It smelled like pale, thick brimstone. I swallowed. When my salad came, I found that if I avoided the cheese, it would be edible.

We talked of our day. I told them about aikido, about Petra obviously thinking it was a stigma to work with another woman, about the joy of falling at speed.

Dornan talked of his morning, lunch at a French bistro downtown, the growing franticness of the film production. "Time is getting short. They only have another four days on their star's contract, and she wants to leave before that. The director is threatening to go, too, and take the stunt actor with him."

Eric wanted to know who the star was, and he and Dornan talked happily about favorite TV shows. My mother and I smiled at each other, and I realized that I was quite relaxed.

We talked of Eric's day at Spherogenix and then Encos, the companies' focus on bioengineering specific immune-system proteins. He sounded urbane and relaxed, but it was clear he was passionate on the subject.

"You're a scientist?" Dornan said.

"I have an M.D., but I don't practice."

"Why is that?"

He paused. "I was twenty-five. I was a doctor. Patients would put their lives in my hands and trust me to help them. I found myself unwilling to play God. I don't mind playing business but people's lives . . . I was afraid."

I had been wondering why he didn't practice, and Dornan had simply asked.

"Are you still afraid?" he said.

"No. Or at least I don't think so. Plus I've come to see that negotiating development licenses ultimately affects many people's lives. It's different, though. Doing so at one remove."

The difference between squeezing someone's warm neck with your hands and launching a smart bomb from two miles up. I nodded.

"Plus," he said, "I get to have lunch with all the big-shot investors, mostly famous CEO-type people."

Else laughed. "But what he really likes is the people the famous CEOs attract."

He smiled at her, then at me and Dornan. "I admit it. I like the shallow glitz." And he and Dornan talked about the relationship between celebrity and big business, and when the conversation morphed back into a discussion of what was going on with Seattle biotech, I watched a cormorant airing its wings on one of the dock pilings.

"But of course a lot depends on a proposed South Lake Union real estate development project."

I focused. "Real estate? How does that tie into biotechnology?"

"One of the city's major developers is trying to get various concessions from local government—a spur from the proposed light rail line, relaxed commercial/residential zoning, and so on—in order to essentially create a biotech hub on the lake's south shore." I tried to visualize the area: the northern edge of downtown, then I realized that those were probably its lights shining across the water. "If he succeeds, then half the people I'm talking to would relocate, at favorable lease rates and certain city and county-level tax breaks. But in order to assure those favorable terms, they would in turn have to make concessions, commitments to employment levels, diversity quotas, environmental controls, and so on."

Something in my brain began to tick.

"Naturally, all this affects pricing and long-term product viability, which are my major areas of concern."

"So if the city's getting less tax money, why is it a good thing?" Dornan said.

"Hubs are good because they attract other businesses. Like, for example, software nexuses in Silicon Valley and here in Seattle."

"Coffee," Dornan said, nodding. "Tully's, Starbucks, Seattle's Best."

"Exactly."

"Also beer and tea and chocolate," he mused. "Seattle's Best Chocolate, Dilettante, Fran's, Red Hook, Stash, Tazo—though those might be Oregon, now that I come to think of it."

All delivery mechanisms for nice, respectable drugs; all things that would get a Scandinavian through the winter.

"That's the way it seems to work," Eric said. "Once an industry perceives that the business climate is favorable, that the employee base has the right education, that others will travel to a particular city in order to take employment there, then it will relocate. Others follow." He made a rolling motion. "It snowballs."

"Ah." Dornan nodded wisely. "Fashion."

Eric laughed. "Of course. Though they'd hate to admit it."

The cormorant launched itself from its perch and flew out over the water.

"Zoning," I said. "Is it hard to change?"

"Not as hard as it should be," my mother said.

"It depends," Eric said, with a glance at her. "There are some good arguments for keeping zoning flexible. But perhaps there's a particular reason you asked?"

"My warehouse." My mother looked at me. Dornan looked at his wineglass and sighed. "I was thinking of selling it, only now I discover that that's exactly what someone wants." And I explained what I believed had been happening.

"This morning I found out my agent has run off, and taken my files and a few others with her. Her assistant tells me that she'd been negotiating to purchase several properties along that stretch of the Duwamish, all industrial property. Only he couldn't figure out why, who she was negotiating for, or who would be interested in it. So I was just thinking, maybe she's found a way to change the zoning. How would she go about that?"

"City or county council vote. Most of the time they just rubber-stamp the recommendations of a zoning committee chaired by one councillor and half a dozen civil servants. They will usually indulge in a pro forma public meeting before formulating their recommendations. For high-visibility issues, though, the individual councillors will make up their own minds. That is, they'll let interested parties make it up for them by means of campaign contributions, promises of future development dollars, and public and behind-the-scenes support for the councillors' pet projects."

"Buying votes—that simple?"

"Pretty much."

"The way of the world," my mother said. "Favors for favors. For example, that's one of the reasons I'm here: the Norwegian government's licensing agreement with a large software company is ending shortly and there are interesting new parameters to explore, particularly relating to security. I'm talking to the executive team purely informally, as a favor to the Labour Party."

I forgot the zoning issue. "The party, not the government?"

She nodded.

Party politics operated only in the domestic arena. "You're thinking of going back to Norway."

Her face smoothed into that automatic pseudo-candid expression all career diplomats—all politicians—learn, but then she paused and glanced at Eric. He shrugged: your daughter, your decision. She took a deep breath. "Yes."

"What have they offered you?"

"The Ministry of Culture and Education. For now."

"Well, well, well."

"What?" Dornan said, looking from me to Else to Eric and back again. "What?"

Eric took his wife's hand. "Aud has just discovered that her mother has greater ambition than she knew."

"You're aiming for the top," I said.

"Yes." Now that she had made up her mind to tell me, she seemed quite calm about it.

"What's your timetable?"

"Move back later this year, assume the junior cabinet position next year, then . . ."

"Madame Prime Minister." We all looked at each other. "But why?"

"Victor Belaunde," she said. "Do you remember?"

It had been a long time, but Belaunde, onetime Peruvian ambassador to the UN, had been quoted in our household all through my childhood. My mother was very fond of quotations.

I said from memory, "When there is a problem between two small nations, the problem disappears. When there is a problem between a big country and small country, the little country disappears. When there is a problem between two big countries, the United Nations disappears."

"It's even more true today than it was then. Norway needs to be bigger. We have work to do. But the sense of importance must come from inside. That's what I want to do."

"You want to change the world."

She didn't deny it.

Dornan looked around the table, shook his head, and said, "It's genetic." Which everyone seemed to find funnier than I did.

"Aristotle," Eric said, with the air of a magician producing a rabbit from the hat. "Humans have a purpose in the world, and that purpose is to fulfill their destiny."

"Destiny is a pretty creepy word," Dornan said, and then, with a disarming smile, "depending on the context."

"Quite so. There again, Aristotle also said that greatness of soul is having a high opinion of oneself."

"Yes," Dornan said in his best Trinity debating voice, "but do we believe him or Socrates when it comes to moral action? Socrates declared that it's impossible to know the right thing and not do it. Aristotle, on the other hand, asserted that one can have the knowledge but fail to act because of lack of control or weakness of will." He was enjoying their surprise. "Straw poll: Aristotle or Socrates?"

"Aristotle," said Eric.

"Aristotle," my mother said, but more slowly.

They looked at me. "Socrates," I said. "Because it's all about what you mean by 'knowledge.' And 'the right thing.'"

They looked interested.

"There are hierarchies of knowledge. It depends on which you privilege: somatic knowledge or extra-somatic. If you tell a child the fire will burn if she sticks her hand in the flame, she'll only believe you if she knows what hot means."

"You mean like the razor?" my mother said.

"Razor?"

"You were seven, or perhaps eight—old enough, anyway, to have had more sense—and you found a razor blade on the turf at York races, and picked it up, and I said, 'don't touch it, that's sharper than any knife,' and you just couldn't help yourself, you had to see how sharp it was. You tested the edge on your thumb and bled all over your new shoes." She turned to Dornan. "We had to spend half an hour in the first-aid tent until she stopped bleeding."

Dornan grinned. I looked at my thumb.

"You were saying?" Eric said.

"Oh," I said. "Well, think of religion. If you believed, really and truly, that you would spend eternity burning in hell for having sex with your brother's wife, you wouldn't do it."

"Unless you couldn't help it. And if you're nineteen and in the grip of powerful hormones, you're next to helpless. Reason might not exist."

"Yes, but while you're feeling the rush of hormones, at that moment, you know—physically, somatically—that having the sex is the right thing. It doesn't matter what your frontal cortex is trying to tell you. Except that I sound as though I think our minds and our bodies are separate things, and they're not."

Before I got myself even more muddled by trying to explain how I thought of the layered brain—the limbic system not under conscious control, the cerebral cortex being a lightly civilized veneer over everything—Dornan stepped in.

"So," he said, with a Groucho Marx eyebrow waggle, "if Aristotle is right, are we to believe that (a) most politicians are weak, or (b) uncontrolled, or (c) just not smart enough to know the right thing?"

"Politicians are like con men," my mother said. "They persuade themselves to believe ridiculous things, and then pursue them in all sincerity."

Startled silence.

"Which is why powerful people need people they love by them, to say the unwelcome thing, to help them believe what is right."

It was the first time I had heard her use the word *love*. We had never said to each other, *I love you*. When I was little, it had never occurred to me to believe otherwise. By the time I was old enough to wonder, I would not make myself vulnerable enough to ask.

Over after-dinner drinks we talked about politicians, and family members and lovers who had damned or saved them, and Eric paid the bill, and we walked outside and stood on the dock for a while. Dornan and Eric moved down the ramp a little, and a Canada goose waddled fatly behind them, hoping for a handout.

My mother and I watched the water. It was the blue-black of an old-fashioned Beretta that someone had oiled lovingly for twenty years. It heaved lazily, constantly, and the reflected boat lights smeared and ran like Day-Glo paint.

My mother and I watched the water for a while. "You didn't say what you thought of my plan for national politics."

"Eric seems as though he would be willing to say the unwelcome thing. I would, too."

"Thank you," she said, "I would listen." And I imagined us clasping hands in the dark, though neither of us moved.

LESSON 6

AS I GOT OUT OF THE CAR AND STARTED UNLOADING THE TRUNK, THE SLANTING SUN turned my windshield to gold. It wasn't just the light, it was a faint dusting of pollen. Yesterday there had been one minute less than twelve hours of daylight, today one minute more; it was twenty degrees warmer than the past week; tomorrow there might be rain: spring gamboling as senselessly as a new lamb.

I opened the basement door with difficulty at 6:01. That familiar scent of dust, competing perfumes, and carpet.

"Sorry I'm late," I said, and kicked the door shut behind me.

"What the hell is all that?"

"Swords," I said, dropping one bag, "or maybe they're lightsabers, it's hard to tell." I dropped another bag, the one full of T-shirts and the sponges and the red ink, and set down the cheap gas station cooler. I pulled one of the plastic toys, lime green, from the first bag and examined it. "No, it's a sword. A cutlass, I believe."

"This has got to be a lightsaber," said Pauletta, picking up another and holding it like a shocking pink banana.

"Let me see. No. It's meant to be a *katana*."

"A what now?"

"*Katana.* Japanese sword." A hollow plastic imitation of the one I had at home, with a braid-wrapped ray-skin hilt and signed tang and a blade that shone like watered silk.

"I think I'm pretty safe in saying that is not a sword." Nina pointed at the white polystyrene cooler.

"Take a look inside."

She toed off the lid and peered in. "Water pistols."

"Unfilled," I said. "Two volunteers to fix that." Suze and Christie won the privilege and practically ran from the room. "And a volunteer to kick the cooler to bits."

Katherine and Tonya decided they could manage that between them, and did. The polystyrene squealed and squeaked. I half expected Nina to say, "Scream, sucker," in an action-hero voice but she just watched. Perhaps she didn't like mysteries, perhaps it had been difficult for her last week admitting, even to herself, that she'd been assaulted.

"Everyone else, stretch out and warm up." They were doing that, and the cooler was a pile of jagged polystyrene splinters by the time Suze and Christie got back with the loaded guns. Christie's hair was wet and the back of Suze's T-shirt was sticking to her spine. Clearly they'd felt obliged to test-fire a couple.

They settled into stretching with the rest. "Today we're going to talk about weapons: guns, knives, sticks, and swords. What they can do, what you do if faced with one."

Several laughed, some nervously. Weapons weren't made of Day-Glo plastic; plastic couldn't hurt them. Right?

I picked up the shocking pink *katana*, twirled it like a baton, then balanced it on my index finger, thinking. "Who thinks they can stab my hand with this?"

"Me. You bet," said Kim. I tossed it to her. She caught it on the blade. A martial arts class would have stopped everything to explain about taking the weapon seriously, treating it with exaggerated respect, but that was not what I was after.

From the bag I took two large white T-shirts, a sponge, and a bottle of red ink. I pulled one of the T-shirts over my head, then poured a little red ink into the sponge. "Give the sword back a minute."

I squeezed the wet sponge around the sword below the hilt and pulled the blade through my fist so that it gleamed redly. I gave it back to Pauletta, then wrapped the second T-shirt around my hand like a cartoon bandage and held out my hand.

"Stab this. Leave a big bloody mark in the middle." I stepped back a little. She edged forward. I edged back.

"No fair. Keep still."

"If someone was standing opposite you with a sword, or a knife, or a gun, would you stand still?"

"Then how can I stab you?"

"Good question."

She charged, stabbing madly, and I moved away, and she missed. She looked mortified.

"It's very hard to hit a moving target—with a blade, or a bullet."

I gestured for her to give me the sword. The ink was dry; I leaned it against the wall, picked up a water pistol.

"Who wants to have a go at shooting my hand with the gun?"

"I'll do that," said Suze.

"Choose your weapon."

She picked an orange-and-red ray gun and held it in two hands, like a TV cop.

"What kind of gun is it?"

"A big one," she said with relish.

"Anyone, give me the name of a handgun."

"SIG-Sauer P210," Therese said. "Or a Smith and Wesson 627, if you prefer revolvers."

Everyone looked surprised, or perhaps impressed. I certainly was.

"That's a heavy gun," I said.

"Nearly three pounds, unloaded. But it takes eight rounds."

"How many's the other one got?" Suze asked her.

"The Sig? Eight in the magazine, one in the chamber."

"Then that's what this is."

"All right," I said, and stood about ten feet away. "Shoot me." I sounded like something from a bad porn film.

Suze took a wide-legged stance, aimed, and I waved the T-shirted hand very slowly to one side just as she began to squeeze.

"Shit." She squirted again. I made the wave a lazy, three-dimensional figure eight. She began to swear and pump furiously with her index finger and I simply walked up to her, still waving one hand, though a little more randomly, and took the gun away.

"Of course," I said to the class, "I doubt I'd be as calm if that were a real gun. Then again, with the noise and the weight and only nine bullets, she probably wouldn't have been as accurate."

"She missed!" Pauletta said.

"Yes. Most people do, most of the time."

"Handguns are more accurate than water pistols," Therese said.

"In the hands of an expert, and on the range, wearing ear protection and aiming at a stationary target, yes. In real life, no. A shooter will hit a running target only four times out of a hundred—and even then the bullet is extremely unlikely to find a vital organ. You can improve even those overwhelmingly favorable odds by not running in a straight line."

"But . . ." Nina said, and couldn't think of anything to add.

"If someone pulls a weapon on you, keep breathing and start thinking."

"Start running."

"Yes, if you can. If you can't, start asking yourself questions. What weapon is it? What kind of person is holding the weapon?" They all looked monumentally blank. "Ask yourself what they want. If you know what they want, you can make some good guesses about what happens next, where your advantage might lie. So, what do they want?"

"To hurt you."

"Sometimes."

No one else had anything to offer. I decided to approach from another direction.

"Remember that they can't hurt you with a stick or a knife unless they can touch you with it. They can't hurt you with a gun unless they can hit you. That means stay out of reach, and start moving."

"What if he's already behind you in the car?"

"He won't be, because you will have parked in a well-lit spot, and before you get in the car, you have looked through the window."

"I will?"

"Yes. As you approach the car, you have your keys ready. You are not overburdened by bags. You examine the car by eye as you get closer, noting whether there are any extra shadows under or inside the vehicle." Why didn't they know this?

"Underneath?"

"Attackers have been known to hide there."

"Jeez, I never thought of that."

If they spent time worrying about being attacked in the first place, why didn't they spend time considering realistic possibilities and responses?

"So what do we do if there's someone under the car?" Jennifer said.

I looked around with raised my eyebrows and waited. "Leave?" said Christie.

I nodded. "If he can't touch you, he can't hurt you."

"Unless he has a gun."

Either they were unable to listen or they couldn't connect the dots. "The hit rate of four times in a hundred only applies under usual circumstances. If the assailant is squeezed under a car I imagine the number is even smaller. Also, as we've learnt before, you can use almost anything as a weapon. You could throw your groceries at him before you run. A can of tomatoes makes a formidable weapon." Or a cup of hot coffee. Or a good yell. Or a spray of oven cleaner.

Nina made a rock, paper, scissors hand. "My tomato beats your gun." They all laughed.

I wasn't in the mood for it today. "I've given you statistics," I said. "Now you tell me what it is about guns and knives, even toy ones, that makes you all so nervous."

No one offered an answer. Katherine shifted from foot to foot. Kim started flicking her nails.

I sat down. "You may as well make yourselves comfortable. This may take a while."

They sat one by one.

"This is a serious question. Why do knives and guns scare you so much?" Flick, flick, flick. Tonya's faint wheeze.

After a long thirty seconds, Therese said, "We're afraid of getting hurt."

"Let me tell you something about the times you've been hurt, all of you, every single one: it didn't kill you."

"But getting hurt . . . it hurts." Pauletta.

"Certainly. So does having routine blood tests. Or dental work. Having children, spraining your ankle, menstrual cramps. A hundred and one things you've all been through before and survived."

"But a knife. Being cut."

"None of you has been cut while chopping vegetables?"

"Do you really not understand?" Therese said. "It's the malice. It's the fear. It's the idea of some masked man with a knife threatening to torture you, and you being so scared that you do anything he says. Anything. You humiliate yourself just so he won't . . . damage you."

"So he won't cut your nipples off and rape you with the knife!" Jennifer said.

There was a gelid silence and they all looked away.

The bogeyman with a knife. Afraid of the bogeyman, because they didn't know that 76 percent of women who are raped and/or physically assaulted are attacked by a current or former husband, cohabiting partner, or date; that for women ages fifteen to forty-four, domestic violence was the leading cause of injury. They have met the bogeyman and they are married to him, at least according to the *Journal of the American Medical Association.*

I had encountered ignorance before in my brief stint as a community liaison officer. They didn't understand, they didn't know. They hadn't been twelve when their mother had visited a London domestic violence center in her ambassador's clothes, chatted politely to the executive director, and been given a green-covered, amateurishly designed book titled *The Women Against Rape Study.* Their mother hadn't given that mysterious-looking book to her assistant. They hadn't taken the book from the assistant's desk the next day and leafed through it, trying to understand who their mother was and what it was that other people thought interested her.

I had gradually become fascinated by that book, with its columns and tables of statistics, its quotes from women who had been attacked by husbands and brothers and boyfriends, by bosses and transport workers and babysitter's fathers.

I had read that green-bound book over and over, in between novels like *The Lord of the Rings* and *Narnia* and *Dune,* and had gradually come to believe it was my job to be the wise and powerful one, the wizard, the warrior, the seer; my job to lead my people and protect them from harm. I was the one with the noble brow and the secret book of runes, I was the one who knew. And so I became that person. I taught myself. I read that book, and others. I watched people. I studied their faces, their hands, their words. I learnt karate, and later wing chun, and boxing, and aikido, and tai chi. Killed a man who pointed a gun at me when I was eighteen. Joined the police force. And gradually forgot that I had ever had to learn, that I hadn't been born this way, that nobody is.

I stood and pulled my shirt off.

"The fuck . . . ?" Suze said.

I pointed to a silvery line about three inches long on my left side, just above my hip.

"This thin scar here, that was a knife. At the time it felt as though someone had drawn a pen along my ribs. I barely noticed. Adrenaline does that." I walked slowly around the circle of women. Look. See. Know. This is what it's like to have your skin opened like the thin skin of a peach and watch the juice run out. "It bled a fair amount, but I didn't even need to go to the emergency room, I just bound it up."

"It didn't hurt at all?" Tonya looked as though she wanted to put her fingers on it, in it. Doubting Tonya.

"It hurt the next day, a kind of deep ache, a bit like the worst time I sliced my finger when cutting up carrots."

I showed them that scar on the tip of my left index finger. There was a scar on my thumb, too, but I couldn't remember what that was from.

"Cutting carrots?" Katherine said, with a look that said, Are you fooling with me?

"I took naproxen and that helped."

"Like for period pains."

"Yes. Pain is pain, whether it's 'natural' or not."

They chewed on that.

"Were you afraid?" Jennifer said.

"No. It happened too fast. It often does."

"Was he trying to kill you?"

"No."

"What did he want?"

"He, they, wanted to escape. I was in their way. It wasn't personal."

"Not personal!"

"No, I don't think so. He wasn't expecting me there in the first place. He didn't care whether I hurt or not, whether I died or not, he only cared about himself."

I couldn't tell what they were thinking.

"This"—I bent my left arm and put my fist on my shoulder to show the pink furrow running along the line between triceps and biceps, then turned so they could see the entry wound by my left shoulder blade—"this was a rifle bullet, fired from a scoped weapon. I couldn't tell you if that was personal or not. It was for money. He was an expert, who was lying prone and ready in the snow. Snow. I was a dark target against a white background. As you see, it missed all my vital organs. I was hit here on the shoulder and the bullet traveled just under my skin, down my arm, and out near the elbow. I lost blood but was able to drive myself back to safety eventually. I'm told that the scar can be repaired nicely. This—"

"Wait. How did that feel?"

"At the time, it felt as though someone had punched me in the back." And then I had been worrying about not getting shot again, about hypothermia, and bleeding too much, and, overwhelmingly, worrying for Julia.

Therese said something.

"I'm sorry?"

"After that? After the punch in the back?"

"It hurt. But pain is just a message. Just a note to let you know that something is wrong. You can ignore the message."

"You can't ignore a hole in your back."

"You can. You can ignore anything if your life depends upon it. Pain is just a message. Of course, I did take some morphine."

"Morphine."

"Yes. And later I went to hospital."

"Did the police catch him, the guy?"

"They found him."

"Did he go to jail?"

"No. He didn't make it that far."

Most of them didn't get it, but Sandra was looking at me, face very still, eyes like a photograph of an eclipse: pupil a black hole, iris blazing, almost writhing, like a corona. I didn't understand her message. "That one," she said, pointing to my neck, "that looks personal."

"An addict. An adolescent with a straight razor. I couldn't tell at first if it was a boy or a girl. It turned out to be a boy." I had seen his naked, skinny little chest when I had taken his sweater. I could have killed him. I nearly did. "As I say, an addict, or schizophrenic." Funny, that had never occurred to me before.

"Were you scared?"

"I thought I was going to die, but I'm not sure I was scared."

"What did you do?"

"He had the blade against my jugular. He'd probably seen how from television. For a little while, I gave up. I just started telling a story." I had spent months trying not to think about that night, how I had known, really known, I would die, how sordid I found the situation, the understanding that this was it, right there, in the dark, in a park full of homeless people in a city where I knew nobody while wearing the clothes of a man I had just beaten half to death, and that there was nothing, nothing to be done.

"A story. Like a Dick and Jane type story?"

"No. I don't remember, exactly. I just talked and talked, and then he wavered, because he was young and he needed his drugs, and his arm dropped, and I took the razor away from him."

"Did you hurt him?" Suze said.

"No." But there had been a moment when I considered cutting his throat, watching his blood gush out and down his chest. It would have been black in the faint city light among the trees. "No. I left."

"Don't tell me, no hospital, right?"

"Right. A plane, to North Carolina. Then healing. There was some . . . some blood loss."

"No shit."

"But not everyone's like you," Kim said. "We can't let someone shoot us, stab us, slit our throats, and then go home and take an aspirin."

"The human body is very strong, very difficult to kill, unless you're facing an expert." If I put a razor to someone's throat, they'd die. "And they, I, you heal. Look." I sat down and pulled up my left pants leg, past the two-inch white scar just below the back of my knee. "This happened when I was nine. Or eight, something like that. A nail sticking out of a piece of wood. I was running around in the garden, jumped over something, felt a little scratch, then—"

"Blood for days," Nina said, nodding. "Cuts on the plump parts, near a joint, they just gush. 'Specially if you've been running. See this?" She flexed her right arm, showed a very similar scar just above her elbow. "Barbed-wire fence. And this"—she showed us four neat indentations across the tops of the fingers on her left hand—"a steel tape measure. We were running around on this construction site when I was a kid, three of us holding the tape, only I tripped over my own ankles and fell over and, *zzzt*, they ran on and the tape cut me open."

"I have a burn scar," Katherine said, and then they were all rolling up or unbuttoning or pushing down something and showing scars, and saying, "You're right, it didn't hardly hurt to start with," or "It bled like crazy," or "I had nineteen stitches! Hurt like a motherfucker the next day."

Sandra talked about her crooked middle finger, how it got caught in her sweater sleeve when she was trying to take it off and running to catch the school bus when she was eleven, how she'd tripped and fallen and her finger was broken to pieces. She didn't mention the burn on the back of that hand that looked much more recent. She didn't point out the damaged thumbnail.

Nobody asked her about those things, either, though Pauletta did say to Kim, "So, that scar on your chin. That's from when you bashed your own teeth out on the pavement?"

"This? Nah. That was from going facefirst down a slide and forgetting to put my arms out."

So then the conversation became about playground mishaps, and I was struck by the fact that none of them talked about being hit or strangled or knocked down with malice by the school bully; though Pauletta admitted to having been a bully when she was a kid. "That was my momma. She told me I needed to take care of my business, so I did. And then I started to take care of business that wasn't mine, you know? You look at me crosswise and I slam you against the lockers. You don't ask me to your party and I trip you up and kick you in the stomach and take your lunch money." She saw the way Therese was looking at her and shrugged. "Hey, I was a kid. I don't do that now. You never hit somebody?"

Therese shook her head.

"What, not ever, not even as a kid?"

"I never did, either," Tonya said.

"Nor me." Jennifer. "Or me." Katherine.

They stared at each other and I stared at them all. Sandra stared back. "You've hit people," she said. "What's it like? Does it feel good?"

"No." But surviving did, feeling brilliant with life, huge, vital. Winning: one life between us and it is mine.

She nodded slowly, knowing there was more to it, knowing, too, that I wouldn't talk about it. This was private, the way being hit and burned and cut and strangled at home was private. We could acknowledge it between us, as long as it remained unspoken.

"So what's the broken-up cooler for?"

I stretched across the carpet and lifted a shard from the pile. "This?" It was a little over a foot long. "It's a KA-BAR."

"A what?" Jennifer said, clearly prepared to be frightened.

"A hunting knife. The blade is about nine inches long, partially serrated." I handed it to her. "This"—I picked up another piece, a bit shorter—"this is a broken bottle. Who wants it?" Tonya held out her hand. I picked up another piece, small and slim. "What should this be?"

"A razor," said Sandra. "I'll take it." I wished I could read her mind.

I took two more pieces of polystyrene from the pile, which turned out to be a bread knife for Kim and an ice pick for Suze. "Everyone stand. Those with a weapon choose an unarmed partner."

Several of them looked at the wall clock, but there were six minutes left.

"Stand opposite each other. Attackers, move in until your weapon touches your partner on the chest. Now look at your feet. None of you are more than eighteen inches apart. Some of you only a foot or so. It's not too hard to make sure you don't get that close to someone, especially if it's a stranger. If you're paying attention to your surroundings, to what's going on around you, no one will get that close to you. Unless it's a public situation: a line at the grocery, a seat on MARTA, getting in an elevator." It occurred to me that I had no idea what a PTA meeting was like, or singing in the church choir, or a ladies' coffee morning. But from what I had gathered, these were not things that frightened them.

"You can't watch everyone all the time," Therese said. "You'd be stressed out of your mind."

"But you'd be alive," Sandra said.

I found I didn't like being on the same side as Sandra. "You don't watch everyone all the time. Not consciously. You don't spend your life on red alert. More like amber, except in your secure home. You take simple, automatic precautions, like having your keys ready, taking the corner wide, parking under a light, checking the car before you get in, not giving out information you don't have to, never unlocking the door without looking and putting a chain on first, and so on."

"That's a lot to remember," Kim said.

"Not really. You'll get used to it and eventually won't even think about it. You all already remember to turn the gas off, to check both ways before you cross the road, to not pick up kitchen knives by the blade, to avoid broken glass, to not breathe water, to not pick up a roasting pan without an oven mitt, and a thousand and one other things. Checking your car and carrying a phone and locking your door are like that. Just sensible precautions."

"You'll have to make us a list," Nina said. Jennifer nodded vigorously, forgetting the hunting knife she was holding at Therese's breastbone. A list was something she understood, something she could master. Better than nasty knives.

"I will. And we'll go through it together." Because the best defense was to need no defense, to see them before they saw you. "Meanwhile, back to our weapons."

They all straightened. The women with the polystyrene shards assumed vicious expressions and their partners looked nervous.

The clock clunked as the hour hand moved.

"We'll have to pick this up next week." I handed out Sharpies. "Write your name and weapon on the polystyrene and give them to me until next week. Meanwhile, everyone who had a weapon, decide what it is that you want. Money? Your victim's car keys? Murder? Rape? A nice long chat about state politics? Are you hungry? Are you cold? Are you bored? Young? Smart? Angry? Frightened? Who are you? What do you want?"

Jennifer looked panicked. Decisions are hard.

"Unarmed partners, remember that no one waves a knife at you just because. They want something. Something tangible or something emotional. You have to figure out what. Think about that before next week."

SEVEN

I WOKE LATE AFTER A LONG, DREAMLESS SLEEP. I EXERCISED IN THE HOTEL GYM, showered, then sat in my underwear and opened the file Rusen had sent. I looked through it with growing frustration. I had no more idea of what might be relevant than I had before Isabella. Outside, clouds scudded by and the tops of trees shivered in bright sun. I closed the laptop, put on a summery silk dress and jacket, and set off to learn some Seattle neighborhoods.

Queen Anne was rather staid, even twee, the Seattle equivalent of Atlanta's Virginia-Highland area. Farther north, I walked around Greenlake in the breezy sunshine. I attempted to eat a sandwich in a café by the water but was defeated by the extraneous aiolis and mustards and strange pickled vegetables. Even before the destruction of my taste buds, my idea of a good sandwich was simple ingredients: fresh whole-meal bread, Danish butter, chicken roasted at home without garlic or rosemary or anything else. Chicken, butter, bread, perhaps a little fleur de sel. Nothing to clutter the essential flavors.

I considered returning to the hotel but doubted the spreadsheet would have become any more meaningful. I needed to go to the set, talk to people, get a feel for what was going on. Perhaps SPD had missed something.

Mercer Street was choked with traffic. I checked the time. Just after four o'clock. Later than I thought. The light had fooled me; I was used to more southerly latitudes.

I called Dornan. "I'm heading for the set. Want to join me?"

"Already there."

"Oh." Traffic was at a complete standstill. For the first time since I'd got to Seattle, someone started honking.

"Hello?"

"I'm here." It was getting hot. Without movement there was no airflow. More honking. Despite the noise, I didn't want to close the windows and use air-conditioning. "Hold on." I unfastened my seat belt, took off my jacket, re-fastened the seat belt.

"Look," Dornan said, "things are getting busy here." I heard Kick's voice in the background, and Dornan said something about the director, and the stunt actor, but in the rumble of stationary traffic and honking horns, I missed it. "I have to go," he said.

I eventually merged with traffic on Alaskan Way, and watched my rearview mirror. Nobody followed me. How disappointing. Today, he wouldn't have got away. Today, I would have got some answers. I lifted my left hand from the wheel and flexed it, then my right. I sat up straight and stretched my spine as I drove.

A MAN STOOD in front of the closed side door, brown hair parted on the left, feet in Velcro-fastened cross trainers that looked like bowling shoes, set wide. Near the door, the asphalt was turning to greying gravel crumbs, which could prove dangerous underfoot. A potential liability issue; I made a mental note to mention it to Bette, and put on my jacket. The late afternoon was a little too warm, but it freed up my hands and would protect my bare arms. When I approached, the man held up his hand, palm out. Left hand. The right stayed at his side, but not limp. The tendons at the wrist were relaxed, brown eyes alert. I stopped about ten feet away.

"ID?"

I reached into my inside breast pocket. His eyes followed my hand, but despite his right hand remaining conspicuously free, there was none of that subtle body turning that meant he was ready to pull a gun, that he was thinking of the gun under his arm or at his belt, that he had a gun at all.

"I'm glad to see they've finally got some security," I said.

He nodded, but didn't take his eyes off my hand. I took out my wallet and extended my driver's license. He beckoned me forward a little, stepped to meet me, accepted the license with his left hand, and stepped back, still trying to make his body lie. His gaze flicked down, then back up at my face. After a moment he nodded and transferred the license to his right hand, then extended it towards me between the tips of his index and middle fingers, again leaning forward slightly, moving back when the transfer was complete. He didn't step aside.

"Is there a problem?"

"Nope," he said. "It's a closed set today."

"A closed set?"

"No one in who isn't on the list."

"I see. Any idea why?"

"Nope." But his eyes moved side to side; he was about to confide something. "Closed set is usually when they're doing naked stuff."

Wisps of steam. But I'd had the distinct impression that that had been filmed already, and that Rusen and Finkel were aiming for a teen audience. I still hadn't read the script, though, so I couldn't be sure.

"I need to talk to someone inside. Any idea how I should go about doing that if you don't let me in?"

"Nope." A sudden gust of wind blew a stiff, finger-wide hank of hair over his right eye.

"I've been having a relaxed day," I said. "It seems a shame to lose that tranquillity." I resisted the temptation to do a quick hamstring stretch. "Step aside."

"A closed set, lady, means you can't just walk in."

Personal space is adjustable—in a crowded room, for example, we expect less; in a deserted park, more—but we always know when it's being invaded. Various bodily signs from a stranger prepare us for the possibility: heavy sweat and a pale face hint at high adrenaline levels; muttering alerts us to craziness; hunching of shoulders or raising of hands shows preparation to move forward, as does a show of teeth or narrowing of the eyes. We send and receive a myriad of signals. But if you give a warm smile and wear a pretty dress and stay relaxed, their conscious mind overrules their subconscious understanding of the signals.

I smiled and walked right at him, shoulders down, arms swinging freely, and got to within eighteen inches of his face before he finally processed the information and grabbed at my upper arm. I swayed slightly to the left, clamped his hand firmly to my right shoulder with my right hand, and turned clockwise so that his arm locked out and I stood behind him, left palm on his skull, behind his right ear. His hair was crispy with hair spray. Gravel crunched under his feet as he maintained his balance. I shifted the grip on his right hand to turn it into *sankyo*, a wrist lock.

He froze. "What—"

"Be quiet and keep still." I lifted my hand from his neck to the thin metal skin of the warehouse wall. Lots of vibration: lots of noise. No filming in progress. I released him, slid open the door, and went in.

It was as hot and active as a termite nest ripped open by an aardvark and exposed to pitiless light, only here, instead of the South African sun, it was arc lights, dozens of them, and rather than a heaving mass of insects around the grublike queen, three cameras on cranes and nearly a score of people surrounded and focused on Sîan Branwell. And this was merely the inner circle.

She was younger than I expected, still soft with the remnants of teenagehood. Her hair was the soft brown-black of mink. She was saying, "Fuck, fuck, fuck," to herself, like a chant.

"It's going to be great," Rusen said to her. "It's going to be amazing. Okay, people. We need this. We need perfection. Sîan, you'll be just great. Okay. Okay, people."

He was talking to himself, too. Everyone was talking, and sweating, and pale. I could taste the adrenaline in the air as one person powdered Sîan's face; another tweaked the fold of her formal ballgown; someone changed a filter on a light; Joel said "Check" into his headset; Peg pointed like setter at a leaf out of place on the soundstage; and an assistant scurried forward, bending like someone approaching a helicopter, and scooped up the errant greenery. The greenery reminded me of that long-ago trip to York races with my mother, when I had picked up the razor blade. Bright silks, a humming crowd, the racehorses moving to their gates, something they had done a hundred, a thousand times before. Their nostrils were wide and red, their tails twitching, the muscle and skin over their withers shivering, a trickle of sweat, great hearts pumping. Then the last gate closes, the starters' assistant nods to the booth, the crowd focuses, the flag goes up, jockeys lean forward—

I heard the door open. "Freeze!" shouted the security guard.

White faces swung in my direction, focused past me. I turned. The guard had followed me and now looked vaguely foolish with nothing to point.

"Fuck, fuck, fuck," Branwell kept saying, only more loudly now, and more insistently, like an autistic child keeping the world at bay.

Someone to the side of the soundstage moved her head in a tight, clean turn: Kick, standing behind an empty craft-services counter and mostly obscured from view by a sweating man in tight black clothes. She wasn't wearing her white coat, but striped cotton trousers and sandals and a form-fitting long-sleeved white T-shirt with a neckline that showed her collarbones. Something hung from a black cord around her neck.

I stepped forward but, "Out!" shrieked Peg, and ran at the guard as though she would hack his head off with her clipboard. "Out! Do you have any idea how close you came to— Do you realize— Have you any idea—"

"Hush," I said, and touched her on the shoulder.

"You," she said, puzzled.

"It's all right."

"He nearly . . . Three cameras! You have to— I mean—"

"It's all right." Joel pulled his headset from his ears until it hung around his neck. He was frowning. A restive ripple ran through the crew. "Don't let it disturb the shoot."

"But— Everything's riding on this, it—"

Once at the races I'd seen a horse buck as it came out of the gate. Four horses had crashed into him, delicate patens snapping. Two had had to be destroyed. The race was canceled. "There now. It's all right. I'll take care of it. There now. Look, Joel needs you."

"What?" But she turned around to look.

"They need you."

"All right," she said, and took a half-step backwards. Rusen looked indecisively from his set dresser to his star to the security guard. I made a *Don't let me interrupt you* gesture. He hesitated, then nodded.

"All right, people," he said. "Okay. One more time . . ."

I turned to the guard. "This way," I said, and gestured to the open door—the breeze was lovely. "And don't say a word. If you make a noise when the cameras are rolling the producer will sue you for damages. I'll also sue you for trespass." I motioned him through the door. "If anyone tries to get in, stop them, but be polite. Think customer service. Do your job." I shut the door behind him. Took my jacket off.

The atmosphere began to swell and tighten again, focusing, and the hum of voices, mixed with the occasional *Fuck, fuck* and *Okay, people, all right,* began to build.

I tiptoed to a sidewall where I'd remembered there being clothes racks. Now there were piles of stacked scaffolding poles. I was glad to see they were strapped together securely. Rolling steel could be dangerous.

"No need to creep," Dornan said from a few feet away. "At least not until the klaxon." His eyes were alight with the kind of intensity I hadn't seen since before Tammy had left him. For some reason it made my stomach clench.

"Why is everyone so tense?"

"Three cameras," he said.

"So Peg said." And it hadn't meant much the first time.

"The director walked out, as I said, and the main stunt actor, and now Rusen is risking everything on one throw. This is the last day Sîan will be here, and instead of breaking the scenes down to separate angles, he's going to shoot from three at once for the close-action sequences and dialogue. If we don't get it in the first or second take, everyone, we're screwed. The film cost alone is huge."

We, I thought. We both looked from Branwell, still chanting to herself, seemingly oblivious to the tweakers and powderers, to Rusen.

"Rusen's directing?"

"Yep."

"He's done it before?"

"In film school. The real director walked out. Said he couldn't work under this kind of pressure."

We looked beyond Rusen, who no longer looked like a chess prodigy but like a teacher on a field trip with twenty psychopathic schoolchildren, to Kick.

"Who's that standing with her?"

"Bernard. The stunt guy."

"He's not the same one who was here the other day."

"No. He left with the director. Bernard's a beginner. Kick says that if she doesn't babysit him, he'll bolt. It's a something-and-nothing scene: jump over a table, roll, pretend to hit someone. But he's pretty inexperienced."

Kick was talking intently to Bernard, who was nodding. He was only an inch or two bigger than Kick. I wondered why she didn't do it. Dornan probably knew; he always seemed to know these things. Without her white coat, the deep V-shape of her torso and the wide shoulders and narrow waist were clear: a high-diver's body, or a trapeze artist's. Her hair was clipped up, and tiny muscles in her neck moved under the skin.

She looked different. Better. "She seems . . . less tired."

"Yes," Dornan said.

He sounded almost smug, and I started to feel prickly and restless. "It's hot in here."

"The air-conditioning is so noisy we have to keep shutting it down. People keep forgetting to turn it back on again between takes."

As I watched, Kick mimed a ducking turn for the stuntman, who was looking dubious. She moved easily, a quarter horse to the racehorses: powerful, nimble, responsive, intelligent, present. The thing around her neck swung out and banged back against her breastbone.

"So what's with the rent-a-cop?" Dornan said.

"Um? No idea. But he won't be around long. What's that thing around her neck?"

"A fan. She doesn't do well with heat. I wish she'd use it."

I hadn't known her long but I couldn't imagine Kick buying something like that for herself. "So is it going well, the filming?"

"Well, yes. I think. People are focused, and Rusen seems to know what he wants. Though they haven't actually done any filming yet today."

"No?"

"No. Rusen's been running everyone through the rehearsals. It's complicated. The second-biggest sequence of the whole pilot."

I nodded, not really listening. Kick was now turning her chin into her chest, gesturing to the stuntman, watching him do the same.

"You still don't know the plot, do you?" Dornan said.

"No."

"Have you even read the treatment?"

"Whose treatment?"

"The treatment. The story outline."

"Why don't you tell me it?"

"And you'll listen?"

I turned to face him. "You have my undivided attention."

"Okay." He seemed mollified. "There's this woman, Vivienne—that's Sîan, of course—who wakes up one night and she's naked, and alone in the middle of a big city."

I nodded. Wisps of strategic steam.

"She has no idea who she is or how she got there. And she's just recovering from the shock when she sees the dawn, and as the sun rises, *phhttt,* she turns into a fox."

"A fox."

"It's pretty cool—metaphor made concrete: foxy woman and all that. Anyhow, the fox, naturally, has no clue about anything. I mean, it's a fox. So then night comes again, and, *phhtt,* the fox turns into the naked woman, Vivienne, who once again has no clue, et cetera. Only this time, she remembers, after about an hour of shivering naked behind a Dumpster, that she woke up the day before in the same position and then somehow lost time."

It was interesting how he assumed a vaguely American accent to tell me all this.

"So she spends the rest of the night thinking and planning, stealing some clothes, scrabbling for food in the Dumpster, et cetera. Day comes, *phhtt,* she turns into a fox—"

"You don't have to keep saying *phhtt.*"

He blinked. "Oh. Well, so she turns into a fox. Fox runs around, eats a bird, all that fox-type stuff. We can use stock nature footage for that. Did you know that foxes live all over the city?"

"Yes. Go on with the story."

"So night comes"—he made a flicking *phhtt* gesture with his right hand—"she turns back into Vivienne—that's easy, apparently; you just do a shimmering dissolve—"

"Dornan."

"Right. So, anyway, she's Vivienne again, she doesn't know anything, but this time she remembers in about ten minutes that she's done this a couple of times before and trots off immediately to her Dumpster, where she finds the clothes. Which she puts on. And this goes on for a while, with the cycle getting shorter. Eventually she makes friends with other people—street people, to begin with, of course, all of whom, for budget reasons no doubt, seem to live in the warehouse district—which is complicated by the night-as-woman, day-as-fox shapeshifting."

"The Ladyhawke part."

"Right. Eventually, through a series of events that, frankly, seem a bit muddled to me, but Kick says will get cleared up in the editing, she gains allies, learns about the fox transformation, makes sure she's protected while she's an animal, and starts trying to work out who she is, where she came from, and what happened. With me so far?"

I nodded.

"And it turns out, there's this bad guy—I don't know if he's an evil corporate research scientist or an evil government agent, but he's evil—"

"And lives in a florist's shop."

"What? No. That's one of the friends. Lots of friends. It's an ensemble show—that's the *Dark Angel* part, that and the government thing, and that it's in Seattle. Where was I?"

"Lots of friends."

"Well, there will be, if we ever get to do a series and not just this backdoor pilot. Anyhow, this guy does something to Vivienne, only that, it turns out, is not her real name . . ."

Kick was . . . not frowning, exactly, but getting tight around her cheeks and eyes. The stuntman was looking young and frightened.

". . . this afternoon's sequence comes just before the end, where the bad guy has followed her to her friend's place, the florist, and is sending in the hard lads." Now the American accent was slipping and he sounded very working-class Dublin, the way he did when he was ebullient. "Lots of action. Viv and her friends fighting for their lives. But all surrounded by greenery, d'you see, instead of the usual shite blowing up. It's cheaper. And what that means is it's all internal work for the actor."

"In addition to the stunts," I said.

"Well, yeah. The stunts. No one's exactly sanguine about that. Rusen asked Kick to give Bernard some unofficial coaching."

Now Kick was pushing the sleeves of her shirt up in frustration. "As well as doing the food?"

"No one's exactly eating the food. Partly, you know, because of what happened. Partly because, well, who could eat in this kind of atmosphere?"

He was right. The tension was building again. Kick slapped the stuntman on the arm, and he clenched his jaw and walked forward into even more intense light towards what I assumed was his mark. The tweakers left Branwell, who now drew herself up to her full five feet five inches.

"Okay, everyone. Going hot in thirty. Let's go."

The building hushed. "Twenty-five," a voice said. Branwell looked like a brown-furred fox: sleek, well fed, bright-eyed. The stuntman looked like a moron. "Twenty."

The countdown continued. Joel listened intently to his headphones, then gave a thumbs-up to Rusen, who looked at the camera operators, who appeared to ignore him, the way heavy machinery operators always ignore lesser mortals.

"Ten."

Branwell had her eyes closed. Rusen smiled at the stuntman encouragingly. He looked as though he needed it.

"Five. Four." Rusen pointed to the cameras, and to the clapper operator, and nodded to Branwell. "Go now."

The lights seemed suddenly brighter, the greenery more green, Branwell's face more alert. She took a great, shocked breath, swung around, flinched—and, "Cut!" shouted Rusen, and the entire set burst into applause.

"Fantastic," Dornan said, "bloody fantastic."

"That's it?" Bernard hadn't even done anything.

"No, that's just the beginning. But she nailed it. First time. That's great. That's a good omen."

All around me the termite mound was heaving again: swinging of lights, the rushing of hair and makeup, the nervous pacing of the stuntman, the furious note-taking of two different people. I started for the craft-services table, but Kick was no longer there.

"Okay," Rusen said, "ready again in thirty."

And everyone hushed, and this time the scene lasted almost seven seconds, and again Dornan's face brimmed with delight, and again everyone clapped. Bernard still hadn't done anything. I watched the intent, focused bustle.

I didn't understand a bit of it, but it was mesmerizing, as urgent as a trauma team working at the scene of an accident. In the middle of the fourth scene, Branwell's key light went out with a pop.

"Hold!" Rusen called, and everyone froze to the spot. Branwell closed her eyes and went even paler. Rusen looked at Joel.

"I can have it changed out in about five minutes," Joel said.

"I need it in two, Joel," Rusen said.

"The engines willnae take it, Cap'n," someone said—Peg—and everyone smiled.

"Aye, aye, two it is," Joel said, and I understood that for two minutes you could hold together the mass delusion that this was possible, that one could make a sellable, watchable film from two bobby pins and a roll of sticky tape. Five minutes would leave time to question the miracle. Every person in the room was willing the impossible to become real with every fiber of his or her being. Magic wouldn't wait. Technicians worked frantically, stripping gels, repositioning, rechecking light levels.

Kick appeared at my shoulder. She looked supple and alive. She nodded at the stuntman. "He's in a flop sweat."

She wasn't sweating at all, I saw. And her breath smelled of strawberries. On my other side, Dornan shifted.

"Makeup," Rusen said conversationally, and pointed his chin at Bernard. They rushed up and started powdering his face and neck.

Without the surrounding dark rings, Kick's eyes seemed brighter and softer. Every individual cell seemed to be humming.

"Places," Rusen said. "In thirty."

And again, Bernard did nothing. Again, Branwell nailed it. Everyone was grinning. There were high-fives.

"Don't get cocky now," Kick murmured to herself, leaning forward so far I thought she might topple over. The black plastic fan on its black cord hung down like a plumb line. Her waist was tiny. My hands could span it easily. "Not yet. Not yet."

"Just this one, then we'll break for a half hour," Rusen said. "Places."

The whole room was focused on Bernard, but my focus was split between the actors and Kick, who was practically quivering.

"Going hot. In five, four, three, two. Now."

And Bernard ran under the lights, tripped over his own feet, rolled with a crash into a stand of greenery, and got up again, looking dazed. No one yelled cut, no one made a sound, but Kick twitched. Bernard leapt over a chair and rolled again.

"And cut."

No applause.

"Bernard, are you good to go again?" Rusen said.

He nodded.

This time he ran, leapt, rolled, and by Kick's gush of relieved breath I understood it had gone well. Everyone was grinning. I was, too.

"Thirty minutes, people," Rusen shouted. "Thirty minutes."

"Excuse me," Dornan said, and headed to the bathroom. The huge main doors rolled open, and the brilliance of the lights dimmed for a moment until my eyes adjusted to the different spectrum of the sun. A roar started near the ceiling. Someone had remembered the AC. People flowed out into the sunshine.

Kick and I turned to each other. We stood close enough for me to see the loose weave in the stripe that ran over her hipbone.

"I got your flowers," she said. "Thank you."

"You're welcome. You're looking well."

"You've lost weight."

"It's hard to eat when food tastes like something shoveled out of a crematorium."

Her face sharpened with professional interest. "Still?"

"Worse, if anything."

"And I thought it was just people not wanting to get drugged again—not eating my food. Jesus. Okay." She nodded to herself. "Okay. What tastes the worst?"

"Scrambled eggs."

"Other eggs?"

"Any eggs. Especially boiled. And milk smells terrible. I've been drinking my tea without."

"Butter?"

"Not good."

"In what way?"

"Sulfur and smoke."

"Fish?"

"Some are fine. Some aren't."

"But fruit is good."

"Yes. Not all vegetables."

She was nodding again. A wisp of hair slid gracefully from its clip. "Like broccoli."

"Yes. How did you know that?"

She brushed aside the question, briskly, impersonally, like a doctor. *This isn't about me, it's about you.* "I have some ideas about what might taste good. Though, hmmm, is it the taste or the smell?" She was talking mostly to herself.

"Everything would taste better if I could find whoever did this and bang their head on the wall."

She laughed. "That sounds like you mean it."

I shrugged. "It's what I do."

"I thought you owned things."

"That, too."

The stripes in her trousers flared and stretched from waist to hip, ran in muscled lines down her thighs. Someone brushed by me. I turned, glad of the distraction. Peg and Joel, carrying milkshakes, laughing for a change. Behind them was Bri, the bony-faced teenager, and his friend, with greasy paper sacks. His brother was dying, and he could still eat.

"Fast food," Kick said, misinterpreting my look. "No one even drinks my coffee anymore."

"Then why do you stay?"

"Because I'm stubborn. They won't be willing to eat fast food forever. And the minute they change their mind, I'll be ready."

"All right. How about now?"

She looked me up and down, raised her eyebrows. I nodded. "Okay, then." She took off the fan, dropped it on the counter, and busied herself with the urn. "It'll take a minute to make fresh."

"No cream."

"No cream."

People were flowing back in. Cool air eddied from the door and the ceiling. Once she had the coffee on, she got a can of soda from the fridge. Instead of popping it open, she ran it across her forehead and the inside of her wrists.

I laid my hand on hers. "Not the wrist." Her hand was so small. "Lots of nerves in the wrist and the side of the neck. If you put something cold there for long enough, those nerves will send a message to the rest of the body saying, Hey, it's cold out here, and all the peripheral blood vessels will close to preserve heat. Those blood vessels are what dissipate heat. So if they close, you won't cool down. Here." She let me take the can. I ran it slowly down the outside of her arms, smearing condensation over her smooth skin. I took her hands, one by one, rubbed the can over the backs then palms, tilted her chin, followed the curve and hollow of her face, slid the can to the back of her neck.

She looked up at me. "It was good, what you did with that rent-a-cop. Just leading him out without fuss. Maybe you just act nicer when you wear a dress." I didn't say anything. "You said last week that you wanted my help."

"Yes."

"Let's trade. I talk to you, I get you as my food guinea pig."

"All right."

"Then come to my house for dinner. Supper. Nine o'clock. You know where it is."

"Yes." I brought the can back to her cheek. Moisture from the can trickled down her neck, as far as her collarbones, which rose and fell, rose and fell. I wondered if the water would still be cool or whether it would have warmed running down her skin. "If you really want to stay cool, you should wet your hair. The heat generated by your head will dry it, and the evaporation will cool you down."

"What are you doing?"

We turned. Dornan. Holding a red-cardboard-bound script.

Kick stepped away and took the can from me in one smooth move. "She's telling me to go soak my head, in the nicest possible way." She put the soda back in the fridge, got herself a bottle of water.

"You should use the fan I got you." Kick pretended not to hear him.

"Is that the script?" I said.

"What? Oh, yes. Here." He held it out. "You should read it."

The air conditioner fell silent.

I hefted the script in one hand. Nine o'clock. "I'm going back to the hotel," I said to him. "I'll give you a ride."

"Oh, I think I'll stay awhile," he said. "But thanks."

LESSON 7

OUTSIDE, IT WAS STILL OVER SEVENTY DEGREES. INSIDE, THE BASEMENT AIR-CONDITIONING unit set in the wall rattled like a garbage disposal with a spoon stuck in it. I turned it off. It would get hot. Tough.

I handed out the five polystyrene weapons and lined the women up opposite their unarmed partners.

"A lot of us are scared when we face an edged weapon—a big knife, a broken bottle, a razor. If and when that ever happens to you, the first thing you do is breathe, the way we learnt two weeks ago. Do it now." They did. In. Out. "Now that you're sure you won't pass out, the next step is to demystify the weapon. Look at the weapon—Tonya's bottle, Kim's bread knife, Sandra's razor, Suze's ice pick, Jennifer's KA-BAR—and ask yourself: Why is your attacker carrying a weapon in the first place? To boost their confidence? To instill fear in you, his victim? To hide behind it in some way? Then you ask yourself what the potential power of the weapon is. How sharp at the tip? Is it edged? How long is it? What kind of damage can it do? So, for example, an ice pick isn't very long, and it's not much use for slashing or bludgeoning, but it's great for stabbing."

Suze gave Kim a superior look.

"And Kim's bread knife," I said to her, "while it might not be very sharp, nor have a stabbing point, can be used, with sufficient force, to take your nose, or your head, right off."

They nodded, but they had no notion of the sheets—the rivers, the lakes— of blood, or how much muscle it took to saw through flesh and then bone.

They were waiting for me to continue. I forced myself back into their southern lady shoes.

Suze's ice pick was traditionally a tool of men, or sexually predatory women in the movies. A bread knife was a tool of the home and hearth, something they handled every day, or that their mothers, at least, had. Not hard to guess which these women found more frightening.

"Next you have to ask yourself how expert the attacker is likely to be with the weapon. We've already seen how difficult many of them can be to wield. Bear in mind that very few people are experts with things like razors or bread knives or ice picks. Remember that a weapon has no power of its own. It depends entirely on its user." And the magic the victim invests in it.

"What's the point of all this thinking?" Pauletta said.

"Assessment. You can't know what to do in any situation until you've assessed it. Keep your eye on the weapon and remember: It's just a tool. Not magic."

None of them looked as though she believed me.

"Once you're breathing, we go on to other questions: What does your attacker want? Will you be in more or less danger in a few minutes? Pick your moment to act. When you do act, begin with a distraction."

"Wait," Pauletta said. "Can we go back to the part about—"

"I'll take questions later. An attacker with a weapon will be concentrating on that weapon. It will be a kind of talisman, a psychological crutch. The armed attacker's focus will be very narrow indeed."

"I'm getting lost here," Pauletta said.

"Sandra, give Pauletta your razor. Pauletta, come and stand here. Threaten me with the razor. Sandra, where were you, as the attacker?"

"Getting my oil changed."

"And what did you want from Pauletta?"

"To make her weep," Sandra said matter-of-factly. *Weep.* Very biblical. Very melodramatic. *I'm special,* her tone implied. *My life is worse than anyone here can possibly imagine. Except you, of course.* But I was tired of her nonsense.

"All right," I said to Pauletta, who was staring at Sandra. "We're in a garage. Pauletta, you're going to try and make me weep."

"I don't . . . Okay." She waved the polystyrene self-consciously. "Kneel down, bitch. Kneel right here."

"Okay," I said, putting my hands up in the universal "Hey, whatever you say" gesture. "Just tell me what you want."

"I'm gonna make you cry." Her hand went to an imaginary zipper. Always the same. Too many movies. "Get on your knees."

"Right," I said, pretending to be about to go down on one knee, and then started to retch.

"*Eeeuw!*" Pauletta said, and stepped back.

"There. That's a distraction. Other distractions could include picking your nose . . ."

"Gross!"

". . . drooling, shouting, acting like a crazy person. The point is to break your attacker's vision of the event. Don't let him orchestrate. Don't, ever, buy into his world." They weren't getting it. "In this instance, as soon as my attacker gestured towards his fly, it was clear he wanted close personal contact. He was having some kind of power and sex fantasy. Vomit has probably never figured in them. Vomit is visceral: wet and hot and stinking. Nothing like the vision he's been constructing for months, years, decades. The point of vomiting or picking your nose is to break his vision of you. You are not a victim. Don't act like one."

Jennifer looked as though she wanted to cry. Tonya seemed confused.

"Which part don't you understand?"

"Me, I don't understand why you're so pissy today," Nina said.

"Pauletta wanted to ask a question earlier and you just steamrollered over her."

"Yeah," Pauletta said.

It was true. I didn't want to be here, in the closed basement. I wanted to be outside, bare feet in the grass, breathing fresh air. But I had agreed to teach these women. No one else would. "I apologize. Pauletta, what was your question?"

"I was wondering, when you said you have to know what they want and pick your moment to act. What did you mean? How do we know what he wants?"

"Yeah," Nina said. "You said no one is a mind-reader."

"That's right. No one is a mind-reader. You don't have to be. With an attacker with a weapon, you most probably won't even have to ask. Just listen."

They were nodding even before I could explain, taking my word for it.

I said, "Most attackers who arm themselves do it because they're nervous. If they're nervous, they're very likely to be verbal. They'll be talking from the first second they threaten you: 'Give me your purse, lady, give me your purse, put the fucking purse on the ground,' and so on. That's the simple situation; if someone says that, nine times out of ten the best thing to do is to give them the purse and they'll go away. But you can't always trust what someone is saying. For example, if your attacker is saying, 'Don't scream, don't say a word, I'm not going to hurt you, keep quiet and I won't hurt you,' you might not want to believe them, because, generally, if someone is saying something over and over again, it's for a reason. It means they're thinking about it."

"Even if they're saying the opposite thing?" Kim sounded more puzzled than skeptical.

"Yes. You'll be able to tell the difference."

"How?"

"You will know. You'll feel it." The body always knows. "Feeling it, knowing it, is the easy part. The hard part is trusting that knowledge and acting on it."

"I don't understand," Therese said.

"It's women's intuition," Katherine said.

Suze snorted.

"Women's intuition makes it sound like magic, and it's not. In reality such knowledge, a visceral understanding of a situation—you could even say empathy itself—is based on a biological system. Your mirror neurons."

They looked perfectly blank.

"Tonya, you and Suze and Christie, go get me three of those chairs, and, Pauletta and Nina, bring the bench. Chairs here, bench here, as though these are stools by a bar. Sandra, bring me my satchel, please, then sit opposite me. Therese, you sit there, you're drinking quietly, idly watching me and Sandra talking while we drink." I rummaged in the satchel, found a big flat-ended Magic Marker, and set it on the bench so that it stood up. "Imagine Sandra and I have shot glasses and this"—I gestured at the marker—"is a bottle of whiskey. We're just drinking and talking. Everyone is relaxed. We're talking quietly. Therese can't hear a thing we're saying." I leaned confidentially towards Sandra, and she adopted a matching pose. "I pick up the bottle, like so, to pour. Then suddenly I stiffen, and start to hold the bottle differently." When I changed my grip Sandra swayed slightly: a sudden, instinctual urge to move backwards, out of harm's way, negated by her conscious mind. "What's going on? Therese?"

"I don't know."

"Trust your first instinct."

"Looks like you're about to slam that bottle across his, her face."

"Anyone disagree?"

None of them was ready to commit, either way, though it was clear from their body language—tilted heads, hands clasped in the small of the back—that they knew what Therese knew, they just didn't understand how they knew and they weren't ready to say so.

"Therese is exactly right. I was getting a better grip, getting ready to break this bottle on Sandra's face. You all knew that, instinctively." Sandra in particular, but she had also learnt from long experience not to fight back because she was never going to make her defiance permanent, never going to run away and get to safety, and in the long run, the more she resisted, the worse her beating would be. "You saw the way I changed grip, and the act of watching me do that triggered a cascade of signals in your inferior parietal cortex."

And I'd thought they'd looked blank before.

"You've probably all seen the way children imitate things to understand them. They'll pretend to roll out a pie crust right along with you, they make noises and pretend to change gears as you drive. This happens in your brain, too. When we see someone pick up a bottle, a whole set of nerve fibers, called mirror neurons, pretend to be picking up the bottle, too. Whether you're actually picking up the bottle or just watching someone do it, those neurons fire in the same pattern. Your body understands intimately how it feels. So when I shift grip, your brain shifts grip, too. And these mirror neurons are hooked into your limbic system, to the part of your brain that handles emotions. So your brain knows what it means when I'm turning the bottle like that. You know, deep down, in that intuitive part of you, what's going on, in a way that your conscious mind probably doesn't."

Katherine looked thoroughly confused.

"You can look it up when you go home. For now, think of the mirror neurons as re-creating the experience of others inside ourselves. We feel others' actions and sensations in our own cortex, in our own body, as though we ourselves are having those sensations, doing those things. In a very real way, we are doing those things. Think of your mirror neurons, your hunches, your intuition as a powerful adviser, an interpreter."

"So," Nina said slowly, "when you said the first week that no one is a mind-reader, you lied."

Next time I taught this kind of class, I was going to do things differently. Completely differently.

"Well?"

Next time. I set that aside to consider later. "Think of the two concepts as complementary. The body knows, the body doesn't lie. But our conscious mind doesn't always want to believe what it knows. It's not convenient. This is true for an attacker, too. They will tell themselves a story about how the attack will go. They'll ignore what they know—they'll ignore the mirror neurons telling them that you don't want to talk to them, that you don't want to be their friend—and believe what's convenient. Because they don't want to hear what you have to say they'll pretend you're not saying it, so it's good to state your wishes and intentions clearly."

"Loud and often," Kim said with the half smile that meant she was thinking of her children.

"If you say something clearly and specifically to a potential attacker, two things will result: One, he won't be able to pretend to himself that he doesn't know you don't want his attentions. Two, you yourself won't be able to pretend that everything's fine. Your conscious and subconscious mind will be aligned. That's a very powerful feeling."

"The power of the righteous," Sandra said.

Silence.

"It could be described that way, yes: knowing you're doing the right thing, even if others don't understand. Sometimes self-defense or the defense of others requires actions that no one understands. Sometimes you have to do them anyway."

Everyone pondered that.

"Now, let's go back a little, to the importance of knowing what your attacker intends. Any ideas about why that's important?"

They all shook their heads.

"It's important to know what they intend so that you can judge whether the situation will get more or less dangerous, more or less opportune for you to act. For example, Suze, what do you want?"

She blinked.

"You're threatening Christie with an ice pick. Why? What do you want?"

"Okay, yes. Her money."

I looked at her polystyrene. She raised it menacingly. "All right. Christie, what did I say about ice picks?"

"Good for stabbing, not cutting or throwing or bludgeoning."

I smiled. I hadn't said anything about throwing; she'd come up with that one all on her own. "All of which means your attacker has to be very close indeed to do you any terrible damage. So what would you do?"

"Throw my purse on the ground and run."

"Good. Why?"

"Because."

"Think about it."

"Just because." I waited. "Because he's mentioned money?" I nodded. "So throwing the purse would be a distraction?"

"Yes. Excellent. Because even if he wants more than money, you know money is on his mind because he's mentioned it. If you judge it's time to act immediately—and this sounds like a situation in which it might be—a distraction is often a good first step. Then you remove yourself from danger. Nine times out of ten that will mean what?"

"Run," Katherine said.

"It depends," Tonya said.

"Yes," I said.

"But which?" Jennifer said. "It can't be both."

"It is both. Everything always depends. In the absence of other data, in this imaginary mugger scenario, leaving if you can is a good option. This is an example of a situation where it appears to be a good idea to act immediately, whether by running or engaging. Other examples of times to do that are when you think your attacker plans to put you in an even more dangerous situation, where your options will be narrowed. For example, if he traps you by your car and instead of saying, Give me your keys, he says, Get in the car and drive me."

"What about, what about if . . ." Jennifer couldn't bring herself to say it. She was very pale. The make-believe KA-BAR hung loosely in the hand at her side.

"What if he wants to rape or torture you?"

I think she nodded but her neck was so stiff with tension it was difficult to tell. I'd never had this problem with rookies. I thought for a moment.

"Jennifer, I want you to relax, if you can, and breathe. I'm going to ask you to imagine some bad things, but they're not real." I looked at the others.

"We're all right here," Nina said, and stood close enough for Jennifer to feel her body heat. "No one's going to hurt you."

Suze stepped up, too. "We'd kill the fucker."

Jennifer smiled tremulously.

"So. Jennifer, you're planning to rape Therese." I raised my eyebrows at Therese: Are you all right with this? She nodded and, too late, I remembered that Therese was probably one of those who had answered yes on the have-you-been-assaulted exercise. There again she was confident and contained, she had trained with guns, she had what-iffed. With luck she wouldn't have a meltdown. "You have a KA-BAR. It's big, it's frightening. You have it at Therese's throat. You want to rape her. She knows that"—again I checked with Therese, who nodded minutely—"and she's too frightened to do anything but what she's told. What do you do now?"

"I don't, I don't . . ."

"Rape. What does it involve?"

"Sex."

"How can you have sex if you're both fully clothed?"

"Oh. Well. Okay." She jabbed her polystyrene in Therese's general direction. "Take your clothes off!"

Therese, also pale now, put her hands to the buttons of her polo shirt.

"See how we're all staring at that, waiting to see if she'll actually take off her shirt? Someone who is contemplating rape will be staring, too. His focus will be split now between the weapon he's holding and the deliciousness of getting a grown woman to be his puppet. This would be an excellent moment for Therese to act. But let's say she understands that there will be an even better moment soon. So let's imagine that she's taken off all her clothes. Now what?"

"Now I guess I rape her."

"So will you push her against the wall? Onto the ground? Let's try the wall." The class parted like the Red Sea and Therese walked to the wall.

Most stranger rapes are fast and brutal, an overwhelming battering force, with no time to think, only to act immediately. Violence, like love, always happens when you least expect it. But that was not an analogy I wanted to use in a self-defense class.

Therese stood, back against the wall.

Most rapists who preyed on a stranger literally couldn't face their victim. But this wasn't a real-life reenactment. This was a lesson.

"So, Jennifer, now what?"

Jennifer swallowed.

"To fuck her from there your dick would have to be about a yard long," Pauletta said.

Jennifer looked involuntarily at her crotch and everyone grinned.

"Pauletta's right. You're going to have to get very close. Let's . . . Therese, you step out. I'll take over." Therese, stiff-legged with tension, pushed herself away from the wall. "Jennifer, would you like someone else to take over for you?"

She shook her head.

"All right then," I said to her. "You know I won't let you hurt me. You know I won't hurt you."

She nodded.

"Where's your knife?" She showed it to me uncertainly. She was going to need some direction. "Put it against my throat." I turned to the rest of the class. "Now what would he do?"

"Whip out his whanger," said Nina.

"Can you pretend to do that?" I said as gently as I could Jennifer.

She looked down again at her crotch.

"At this point he's distracted again. This would be a good time to take some action."

"But what if he was strangling you, too?" Katherine said.

Pauletta hooted. "He can't strangle her, hold a knife at her throat, and pull out his dick at same time. He's a rapist, not a three-armed superschlong."

I could have kissed Pauletta but settled for smiling with everyone else. "That's absolutely right. So this is an ideal moment to do something. What?" Blank. "Let's try it. Everyone without a weapon, against the wall. Everyone with a weapon, put it against your partner's cheek. Closer, Suze, you're not even touching her face with that ice pick. So, now, those against the wall. He's fumbling with his zipper—everyone, put your hands on your fly." No one moved. Southern women. I sighed. "Okay, just hook your thumb into your waistband and let the hand dangle in roughly the right place. Good. Now, remember, a weapon has no power in and of itself. If you knock away the arm holding the weapon, you've knocked away the weapon. Give that a try."

No one moved. "How would you do it?" Katherine said.

I gestured her away from the wall and took her place under Tonya's bottle.

"It's always best to knock the weapon away from your body, not towards it or across it. So here I would knock her right arm away from me to my left, her right. If she had the bottle on my other cheek," I tapped Tonya's wrist and pointed; she shifted the bottle obligingly, "I'd want to knock it away and to my right, her left. Think about that for a minute." I could see them mentally thinking *right*, then *no, left, no, right.* "A forearm block is best. If the bottle is here, on my right cheek, I would use a left forearm block." I demonstrated in ultra slow motion as I talked. "See how that means I twist to my right, and that moves my right cheek back out of reach of the bottle and at the same time presents less of my body towards my attacker as a target."

Lots of frowns. Clearly too much information at once.

"Just remember to knock away from your body." I demonstrated again, very slowly. "Try it." I gestured Katherine back into place and walked up and down the line of pairs. "Slowly, very slowly. Imagine it's a game of slow motion. Pivot, bump your forearm into theirs. Yes, good." It wasn't, but it would get better. "No, Pauletta, see how that drags the razor right across your face if you knock it across your body and Sandra's? You want to spin the other way, knock with your left arm, to your right."

"But I'm right-handed."

"All right. Sandra, for now, hold the razor against her other cheek."

Sandra gave me an amused we-know-it-wouldn't-be-this-convenient look, and swapped hands. She was beginning to annoy me.

"Now," I said to Pauletta, "try again. Pivot, yes, cross slam, yes. Excellent. But try to use the outside of your forearm, like this."

"Why?" said Pauletta, as though it were just another detail I was using deliberately to confuse her. Sandra maintained her veiled-secret expression; she already knew.

"Because there are fewer important nerves, blood vessels, and tendons to be damaged on the outside. Also, it will hurt less when you take the impact on muscles when you're hitting as hard as you can. Also," I said, raising my voice to the whole class, "when you move, yell. Not only will it remind you to breathe, it will be a further distraction to your attacker. You can never have too many distractions or too much noise." I plowed ahead before they could get twisted up about that. "We'll do it together. On the count of three. Okay. Knives on cheeks. One. Deep breath. Focus. Three. Yell! And pivot. Slam. Excellent. And again. Knives. Breathe. Yell and pivot. And again."

"Ow!" said Jennifer.

"Slow motion, Therese, but very good." Pauletta had hit Sandra twice as hard, but Sandra hadn't made a murmur. "And again."

"Ow," Katherine said, too, as Tonya's bottle ran across her throat for the second time.

"Try again," I said.

She did. Same result. "I can't do this," Katherine said.

"Sure you can," said Tonya.

"I can't."

"Not yet," I said. "That's why you have to practice."

"If Tonya was a great big guy and that was a real bottle, do you think I'd really have a chance?"

"Yes."

"It's ridiculous. I can't do this."

"All right," I said.

"All right? All right?!"

"I'm not going to force you."

"I just, I want . . . I want you to teach us how to not get hurt."

"Infallibly? I can't. No one can. There is no perfect security. Yes, most men are taller and stronger than most women. That's not the point. You can be seven feet tall, and in fighting trim, and there will always be someone out there who is bigger and stronger and faster. The point is to do the best you can, then stop worrying."

"Stop worrying? I dream about this stuff every night now. I worry that someone is lurking under my car, that they're assembling clues from my e-mail conversations, that they'll watch my every movement and rape me on the subway platform."

"The fact that you're worrying about these things now makes it less likely for them to happen. You'll never be carjacked by someone lying underneath your car because now you look."

"Maybe you'll die of worry," Suze muttered.

"I heard that."

"Hey, then at least you're not deaf, just stupid."

"All right," I said. "Everyone, swap roles. Five minutes. Then we're going to sit."

When they were done, I carried around the bin so they could ceremonially throw away their polystyrene weapons.

"You did well. Yes, even you, Katherine. You've all learnt a lot in the last six weeks. You're not perfect killing machines, no, but there again, that was never the goal."

"Hey, speak for yourself," said Suze. Surprisingly, Therese nodded agreement.

"My goal is to make sure you've thought and planned and practiced so that you can relax in everyday life. Here's something that might help." I handed out the list I'd compiled after last week. "Read it carefully and we'll talk about it next week."

"Hell," said Nina, flipping the page, "now we're all going to die of worry."

"Next week?" said Jennifer. "Next week's a holiday. I'm going out of town."

"Then the week after is fine."

"We should get together anyhow," Katherine said. "Have a picnic or something. Leave the guys at home."

"A field trip," Nina said.

"I'll be out of town," Jennifer said again.

"I'm gonna be here," Suze said.

"And me," "Me too," "I'm not going anywhere."

They were all looking at me.

"How about my place on Lake Lanier," Therese said. "A social event, not a class, so it doesn't matter if some people can't make it. A covered dish."

EIGHT

WE DRANK CHAMPAGNE. KICK WAS AT THE SIX-BURNER STOVE, STIRRING A HUGE POT WITH a wooden spoon. "The stew sticks if I don't watch it," she said. She was wearing the same striped trousers and white T-shirt, but no sandals. Her feet didn't look cold. I sat on a hard chair by the counter.

The windows were open but screened. The breeze had died to a sigh and the night that seeped in was soft with moisture, potent with change. In the low atmospheric pressure the voices of moviegoers leaving the theaters on 45th, the sudden metallic judder of engines flaring to life, the music from the Jitterbug restaurant and Murphy's Pub carried clearly and mixed with earthy blues from her CD player. The city-lit sky swam with clouds, sleek as seals.

The kitchen was big, and open, all cherry and pine—even the ceiling was pine—and continued to the dining room. I carried my champagne over to the dining room windows. Judging by the slight unevenness of the floor and the change in windows, it was an extension built less than ten years ago. It jutted out over a patio. A pear tree rustled against the left-hand window. On the other side, a little farther away, the silhouette of a cherry tree overhung the extension and the garage. Beyond the patio the garden seemed stepped, maybe to a lawn.

The house smelled like Spain in April: bread and olive oil and simmering beans and lemon juice and garlic. Some kind of unctuous meat roasting. If it were Spain it might be kid, but it was probably lamb. I went back into the kitchen. My mouth watered.

"Ah," she said, "want something right away?"

I nodded.

She got two small dishes from a cupboard near my head, and turned off the gas under the pot. "Spoons in that drawer in front of you. Napkins in the drawer underneath." She got busy with a ladle. "Here." She handed me a bowl without ceremony. "Pond-bottom stew."

It was a reddish-brown soup. I put it on the counter and handed her a spoon. She refused the napkin and just ate a couple of mouthfuls, leaning back against the stove.

I spread a napkin on my lap and balanced the bowl carefully.

"Spilled stuff cleans up. Just taste it."

I dipped my spoon into the stew cautiously. "It smells a bit like *fasolada*."

"Same basic principle. Lots of olive oil and celery and garlic, some lemon, but instead of just white beans, I've added kidney beans and carrots. Really it's a fall stew, hearty, warming. But it seemed like something you'd enjoy. When it's cooked as long as it should, it gets sort of sludgy, like something you'd scrape off the bottom of a pond. Eat."

I ate.

"Well?"

It tasted as fresh and clean as a shoot bursting free of winter-hard dirt. It filled me with hope that I might enjoy food again. I had the ridiculous urge to burst into tears.

"Do you like it?"

I showed her my empty bowl. She smiled. I eyed the pot on the stove.

"No. No more right now. I've made half a dozen things. I thought we'd try a bit of this and bit of that, just graze, see what works."

Graze. Maybe that roasting smell wasn't for me. "Is it all vegetarian?"

She smiled. "You don't strike me as a vegetarian. Let's move to the table so it doesn't get messy."

There was no ceremonial laying of places or careful positioning of silverware. No candles, no shimmering crystal. Just the music, and the champagne, and the food.

We began with salad: greens and sprouts and grated carrots and sunflower seeds. "Try both dressings," she said. "This one is tofu and basil." It was astonishing—creamy and smooth and clean. "The vinaigrette's flaxseed oil and balsamic." Totally different, warm and aromatic, as subtle and rich as cello music.

I didn't say anything, but I didn't have to. Her cheeks pinked with pleasure.

"Now for the hummus." It didn't smell like any hummus I'd ever encountered: toasty, almost sweet, but also tangy, with the familiar sting of lemon and garlic. She slathered it on black bread and handed it to me. "Here."

I bit into it. It was coarse and hearty, much rougher than any hummus I'd ever had before.

"And here—" She crossed in three light steps to the fridge, brought back a bowl and a jar of mayonnaise, and went back to the cupboard for two dishes. Her hips were round and tight with sheathed muscle.

"Homemade cole slaw," she said, and mixed up the shredded vegetables with mayonnaise in her dish. "Put it on the hummus." She heaped it on the bread-and-hummus mixture. "Here. Try it." I tipped and mixed and heaped. "Just pick it up. It's messy, but that can't be helped. At least you're not wearing that nice dress."

I bit into the bread and hummus and cole slaw.

"I thought you'd enjoy the different textures."

I did. I didn't know how she'd known that I would. The cole slaw fell off, smearing over my hand and plopping onto my plate. I picked it up with my fingers, finished it, made myself another slice.

"How much weight have you lost?" she said.

"I don't know." I chewed a few more times, swallowed. I wanted to stuff the world in my mouth.

"You like food."

"Yes."

"It must have been hard."

"Yes." I hadn't realized just how hungry I'd been. Still was. "Thank you."

She nodded. "When you were talking on the set, I thought: It sounds like what happens to people's tastes when they have chemo. And I know what to do about that. It's partly a saturated-fat thing. Stick with things like olive oil and flaxseed oil. Avoid your dairy and your eggs and your beef, especially aged beef."

"And broccoli."

"Yeah, well, I said partly. The rest . . . I don't know. But have you ever noticed that broccoli sometimes smells sort of fishy?"

I nodded, surprised.

"Whatever makes it smell like that is one of the things that your taste buds, or what's left of them, won't like. Very, very fresh seafood should taste okay. Oysters, for example." She grinned. "Hold on."

She disappeared into the living room. The music stopped and restarted with Ella Fitzgerald singing Cole Porter. . . . *oysters down in Oyster Bay do it.*

"The taste buds," I said, when she returned. "Chemo destroys them?"

"Yep." She settled back on her chair. "Though I've never heard of it happening so fast, or after just one dose."

"And does it come back, the taste?"

"Most likely. Might take a while, though. Months. Even a year or two."

A year or two . . . *Let's do it, let's . . .*

"Until then, distract them with other tastes, anything aromatic is good. Ginger. Garlic. Lemon. Vinegar. Tomato. Thai, Indian, Greek, northern Italian. And texture. I guessed that you'd like things that contrasted, that were unexpected: cold and crunchy cole slaw with room-temperature tangy hummus, unrefined bread. Also something you could build, literally. You like being in charge."

"An arrogant toad?"

"Well, no. But you looked like you might be, that first time. And then you came hammering on my door—but you seemed so, I don't know, reduced. I wanted to make you feel better, but I couldn't even feed you. Though the crack about how awful I looked made me worry less about that."

"Yes." The gift of tongues.

"Is it true you're paying everyone's hospital expenses?"

Rusen. I shook my head.

"It's not true?"

"No. It is true." I just didn't want everyone to know.

"And then I saw how you dealt with that rent-a-cop. And you, I don't know, you looked different in a dress." She poked at a shred of cabbage on her plate.

"You look different in shoes." Inane. She seemed to bring it out in me. But she didn't look up from toying with the cabbage and I understood that what mattered here wasn't the words. I poured the last of the champagne. "I have more in the car. If you like."

Now she looked up. "What, you always drive around with a six-pack of bubbly in the backseat?"

"Not always." I stood, waited. She nodded.

Outside, I could still hear the hum of pub music from Murphy's. Judging by the smell, someone across the street was getting high. I felt every stir of light Seattle air on my forehead and cheeks. The food was pleasantly present in my stomach, but did nothing to blunt the other, growing hunger.

I went back in. Definitely lamb. "It smells like Catalonia at Easter."

"Never been there," she said. "Been just about everywhere else, but never Spain. Or France."

I put one bottle in the fridge and opened the other. I would have to buy her a champagne bucket. "Can you cook French food, too?"

"I can cook anything."

I can cook anything. I studied her, one bare foot tucked underneath her, the other swinging back and forth, and remembered the scent of sleepy, naked woman.

She flushed. "It's my job."

"Yes," I said.

"At least it is, now."

"Yes."

"Why did you come?"

I gestured at the food, but she shook her head.

"No. The first time. At three in the morning. Why did you come?"

Because she had stained her white coat and I wanted to know if anyone would wash it for her. Because she needed someone to bring her tea when she was tired, hold her when she saw her career falling about her in ruins.

And that wasn't me. Couldn't be me.

"I'm sorry," I said.

"I know. I got the flowers." She leaned forward. In the slanting light the tops of her breasts looked as if they had been dusted with gold. "But why did you come?"

She leaned closer, tucked her hair behind her ears. She missed a strand. I reached out and tucked it back for her. It felt as slippery as a satin camisole.

"Tell me why."

I tucked hair back behind her other ear. "I was angry." I reached for her hand. She tensed slightly, then let me lift it to my mouth. Her knuckles smelled of garlic and, faintly, that naked, sleepy, buttery-toast scent my back brain was already beginning to recognize. I turned her hand over. Blood bloomed under the skin of her breast and throat. I kissed the center of her palm. Her head fell back, and I caught it. The back of her skull felt as small and hard as a cat's. I lifted her hand again, and this time kissed the inside of her wrist. All those nerves. She made an unconscious pushing motion with her feet on the floor. Her hips lifted slightly. I bent until my lips were inches from hers. Her breath pistoned in and out. Her eyes were black.

I kissed her. It was like opening my mouth to a waterfall; it fisted through me. I pushed the table to one side, picked her up, and laid her on the rug.

"God," she said hoarsely. "God."

TWO HOURS later I found myself kneeling on the floor next to the rug. The CD player had turned itself off. The wooden floor was cool on my shins. Kick was on her back, naked.

"God," she said. She sat up. There was a carpet burn on her chin. She shivered.

"You're cold." I handed her a random assortment of clothes, hers and mine. She stared at them blindly. "Here." I sorted through the heap, found her T-shirt. It was inside out. I pulled the sleeves carefully back through the shoulder holes. "Lift your arms." Dazed, she did, and I slipped the T-shirt over her head. Her face emerged, blinking and puzzled, then frowning.

"Tell me you didn't plan that," she said.

I shook my head.

"You're right," she said. "Who the fuck could plan that?" She found her underwear. Paused. "The lamb will be ruined."

IT WASN'T. It was more well done than lamb should be, but it was good, fatty and strong and grass-fed, and we ate, and talked carefully, and gradually she started to flush again, but when I reached out she tensed.

I put my hand in my lap and waited. "You don't live here," she said.

"No."

She got up and closed the windows, and put on the kettle, and brought me a cut-glass plate of rich, dark French chocolate, and stood next to me, hip against my shoulder, and I breathed in her sharp, buttery wood-smoke scent and stared at the chocolate, and told myself it didn't matter.

She stood, and I sat, very still, and the kettle began to rumble. I turned my face so that my cheek rested against her thigh. The faint vibration of her femoral pulse alongside her femur became a trip-hammer. Her legs shook. I put my arm around her waist.

I meant simply to steady her, but she softened into me, almost sagged, and my arm tightened, and my need, and she let herself go so that I was holding her up with one arm and pulling her pants down with the other.

"Bed," I said, and my voice was tight and savage. She pointed at the stairwell, and I carried her.

THE SKYLIGHT showed a night sky of brass and acid. The thick scar that snaked through the crease between the top of her thigh and her hip bone looked dark grey, though downstairs it had been the color of raspberry sorbet. To my fingertips it felt like soft old leather trim. It was a clear, clean incision.

"How long has it been?"

"Two years." She was very still, her face in shadow.

"Does it still hurt?"

I felt her shrug.

I kissed it. The skin under my hand moved as the muscles in her belly tightened. I slid on top of her. Kissing her was not like kissing Julia, who had been all length and plum softness, and whose messages had been very clear. Kick was like a powerful trapped beast. She stirred restlessly, one hand in the small of my back pulling me closer, one on my shoulder pushing me away. I eased to one side, weight on my right elbow, head propped on my hand. I stroked her belly. The muscle loosened. She sighed. The sigh sounded as though it had a smile in it. I smiled back in the dark. She ran both hands up my left arm.

"You have scars, too. But they all feel different."

"That one was a bullet."

She explored it carefully. No one had done that before. "When?"

"Almost exactly a year ago. In Norway."

"Norway."

"Yes."

"And this one?" She stroked the thin line just above my waist, on the left side.

"A knife. Two or three weeks before the bullet."

She nodded. I dipped the tip of my little finger in her belly button, stroked my thumb over the jut of her bottom rib. Then the next one, and the next. I ran the back of my hand under the curve of her breasts. Her breathing was rhythmic and strong. I kissed her. This time both hands slid to the small of my back and tugged. I eased on top of her, slid my arm carefully under her head.

"Ummn," she said, and began to move, and I moved with her. This time, when we were done, she was definitely smiling.

I lay on my back and she knelt by me and ran her hands up over my face, down the sides of my head, my neck, across my collarbones, down to my breasts, around and around, down to my waist, up again to my neck. The sky had softened to the color of old buttercup petals.

"And this," she said, touching the scar on my throat. "This must have been very bad."

"That was just six months ago."

"I didn't know owning things could be so dangerous."

"The danger is an unavoidable by-product."

"Of owning things?"

It seemed to be working that way with the warehouse. "I used to be police."

"But not now."

"No."

Silence while we both thought our own thoughts. "Why did you come?"

"Because you invited me."

Her laugh, a silvery, delighted squeal, like the laugh of a six-year-old thrilled by some childish wickedness, astonished me. I sat up. She poked me with her elbow. "To Seattle."

"To sort out my real estate problems. To get out of Atlanta for a while. To see my mother and meet her new husband."

"Ah."

"What do you mean, 'ah'?"

"She's a somebody, isn't she?"

"You met her?"

"I saw her, at the hospital. Everyone paid attention. And then there were all those no-mentions of you in the press. Tell me about her."

She has hands like mine, I wanted to say. "Her name is Else Torvingen." It suddenly occurred to me to wonder whether she had changed it when she married. No. She hadn't changed it when she married my father. "She's the Norwegian ambassador to the Court of Saint James's."

"The court of— The ambassador to England? She got the job because she's rich?"

"She's not rich."

"But you are."

"From my father. They divorced when I was thirteen. He died three years ago. He left me— It was a surprise. The amount." It still was, sometimes.

"So what's she doing here?"

"Semi-official trade negotiation. Computers, mainly. And seeing me."

"But you—"

"Live in Atlanta. Yes. Like Dornan."

The tension ran through her like a current. She pushed herself away, got up, and found her robe. She stood by the window, looking out.

"Kick?"

"I'm having dinner with him tomorrow."

I got up and stood a little behind her. I wanted to pull her to me, cradle her, but I knew she would pull away.

"That's Queen Anne Hill," she said, pointing south across rooftops to three radio towers blinking with red lights. It looked better from this perspective. "And down there is Gas Works Park. During the day, seaplanes come and go, landing on Lake Union."

"Kick."

"You should come here and see that sometime before you go away, back to Atlanta." Her arms were wrapped around her body. I couldn't tell if she was cold or feeling defensive.

"Kick," I said again. "Kick." She turned slowly. "I'd like that, like to go to the park. I like you."

"He's a kind man."

"Yes." I held out my arms, and she stepped in and I held her.

THE SMELL of baking woke me a little after nine. I dressed and went downstairs. Kick was taking a tray of muffins from the oven. Her hair was damp. I hadn't even heard the shower.

She looked a little tired, but the smile she flashed was bright: it was morning; all doubts and revelations of the night before were done. "Banana raisin oatmeal rice flour muffins. Invented fresh this morning. But you woke up too soon. They have to cool."

"I should go shower."

"Do it later. Open the windows, would you?"

She disappeared into the living room, and a moment later oboe music flowed through the kitchen.

Sunshine and baking had made the kitchen and dining room warm. A house fly explored the windowsill, back and forth, like a confused, hunchbacked old man. I pushed up the two side windows but it couldn't get out because of the screens. The breeze was cool and soft on my face.

She had cleaned up the kitchen, moved the table back in place, showered, dressed, and baked while I'd lain naked and blissfully unaware. I had relaxed completely. I had a nasty feeling that I knew why.

The kitchen began to smell of . . . "What is that?"

"Nutmeg. And smoked salmon—it should be haddock, but I didn't have any." She opened a plastic tub. "And brown rice. And—pass that dish, would you? Thanks—boiled egg."

Kedgeree.

She stirred, turned down the heat. "You remember where the napkins and silverware are."

I laid the table. Now that I wasn't dazed with drugs or hormones, I saw that it was an old piece, solid cherry carcass, with a polished mahogany veneer. I found cork place mats piled on the stretcher of a battered-looking secretaire in the corner, gave us two each. Green cotton napkins. Knife, fork, spoon.

She dished onto two plates. Carried them to the table. Nodded at the kettle, from which steam was still easing, which I took to mean *Make the tea.* A small teapot, some green tea, and two beautiful mugs stood ready. I brought the pot and mugs to the table. Put a mug each on a place mat, got out another for the pot. Sat.

Albinoni streamed as clear as the sun into the dining room. The old mahogany glowed like bronze. The flatware winked. The smoked salmon in the kedgeree was flecked with nutmeg and nestled amid nutty, moist rice. Kick wore blue and grey.

Soon I'd be flying back to Atlanta with Dornan.

"You look as though you don't know if you're in heaven or hell."

"Kedgeree is my favorite breakfast food."

She smiled, as playful as an otter. I leaned over and kissed her. The fly ran back and forth. I poured tea for us both. This was where I asked her what she was doing tonight, but I already knew. The silence grew. The otter slowly submerged.

"Will I see you on the set this afternoon?" I said.

"I'll be busy."

"I see."

"No, you don't. We have location shots." The otter popped back up. "But tomorrow is another day. Now I have to eat and run."

She ate at lightning speed, with clean, deft movements of fork to mouth, cup to mouth, napkin to mouth and then plate, and rose from her chair like an acrobat, with no visible effort.

"You take your time." She kissed me, not a millimeter of lip in the wrong place, not an ounce of weight on the wrong leg, perfectly balanced. She scrutinized me for a full two seconds, but gave no hint of what she thought. "Let me know how you like the muffins. Drop the latch on your way out," she said, and left.

I finished my kedgeree, poured more tea, and listened to the rest of Albinoni.

TEN O'CLOCK. Sixty-nine degrees, light breeze, cheerful pedestrians. I drove carefully.

She had left me in her house. I could have done anything: stolen her things, searched out her secrets, fingered through her most personal possessions, spat in her milk. But she knew I wouldn't. She probably knew I would look for airtight tubs to put away the remainder of the kedgeree; find a tin for the muffins; make sure the kettle was unplugged; rinse the dishes and turn on the dishwasher; make the bed. Turn off the CD player. Check that the lights and oven were off. Leave my cell phone number on her table. Just as she had known that I liked food with different textures. Just as she had known that I liked to wrap my arm around her waist and hold her tight against me as she moved. Just as I knew nothing of what she thought, or why.

I pulled over on Westlake, dialed her number, and after three rings got the machine.

"It's Aud. It's . . . There's a fly. In the dining room. It can't get out. You'll probably have to take off the window screens. You'll need a ladder to get at them from the outside. I can do it, if you like."

Or she could just open the front door and shoo it out. Or catch it in her hands. I imagined her small hands cupping the fly. The scent of her fingers.

I'm having dinner with him tomorrow. I closed the phone. Stupid, stupid, my forebrain said. But another part of my brain, the old, animal limbic system, sat back on its heels, raised its face to the sun, and crooned. And, unbidden, the underside of my arms remembered the soft swell of her breasts as I turned her in bed, the press of her lips and slick of her tongue, and the car felt as alien as a mother ship.

A truck rumbled by, the driver singing to something on a classic rock station, looking pleased with and in charge of his world.

I shut my windows. Opened them again. Breathed in, deep and slow, and out again, long and slow and steady, using the muscles in my abdomen to force the air out in a steady hiss. In again, for a count of ten. Pause. Out, to ten. In. Out. Then I called Dornan.

It rang and rang. I imagined him looking at my number on his screen and deliberately turning it off. I hung up before his voice mail finished inviting me to leave a message.

IN MY suite I walked naked and dripping from the shower to my laptop, where I searched randomly through Norwegian and English dictionaries. *Elske. Elsker. Forelske seg.* That disposition or state of feeling with regard to a person that manifests itself in solicitude for the welfare of the object, and usually also in delight in his or her presence and desire for his or her approval; warm affection, attachment. The affection that subsides between lover and sweetheart and is the normal basis of marriage. The animal instinct between the sexes. *Liker.* To feel attracted to or favorably impressed by. *Kjæreste.* One who is loved illicitly . . .

I called Dornan again. This time I left a message.

WE MET for lunch at a bistro on First Avenue. The menu was aggressively French. I chose the soup—lentils and chicken livers, with a Rainier cherry compote—mainly because I couldn't imagine how it would taste. It also had the sets of ingredients Kick had recommended.

We ate without saying much, and I wiped up the last traces of lentil and cherry with bread. "Good soup."

"But it's a shame about the service."

"Yes." West Coast hipsters trying to do French attitude.

"Seattle," he said. "If you don't like the weather, wait ten minutes; if you don't like the service, wait ten minutes."

It was Kick's phrasing, Kick's intonation; she could have been sitting between us. I didn't know how to begin. How did friends talk about something like this?

The sun spilled right down the center of the avenue as we walked to the gallery. Before I met Julia, I never went to art galleries. When she died, I began to visit them, because they reminded me of her. Now it was merely a habit.

The gallery wasn't as empty as I'd expected, but there were few enough people that we could move from painting to painting at our own pace. I worked along the right-hand wall, Dornan the left.

The heart-of-pine floor creaked as I walked from picture to picture. Hyperrealist still life in oils. It seemed to glisten, as though coated with glycerine. An American artist. Interesting, but not something I'd want in my house. A series of fuzzy-looking black-and-white lithographs of cityscapes viewed from second-story windows, empty industrial complexes, a stand of silver birches in the snow. None of them worth more than a minute. Two huge abstract French pieces, nine feet by six, of what looked like something between Christmas ornaments and the insides of a clock. Then a woman in a red silk Chinese robe, bending over a guitar, glass beads in her hair. I paused. It was ugly, drenched with hatred—the woman's face wasn't deformed, but it made me shudder—but the beads were irresistible; like a child, I wanted to scoop them up and put them in my mouth, and something about the light slanting across the floor intrigued me. I leaned in close. The brushwork was textured and confident. The next was by the same artist, a nude reclining on a couch, her back to the room. It was a twenty-first-century painting in the style of a nineteenth-century Russian or French master, every tassel of the velvet rope hanging from the bedpost, every strand of hair exquisitely rendered, yet the background was curiously abstract. The model's profile was Asian, but the body was fleshy and

Dutch. I went back to the first painting, and the block of text about the artist. Lu Jian Jun. Forty-two. Chinese, winner of several national prizes, now living in San Francisco.

I don't know how long I stood before the third painting. At some point Dornan came and stood by my shoulder. Neither of us spoke for a while.

A woman in a silk robe leaned back in a chair and looked straight out. She formed a diagonal slash across the square canvas. Behind her was an antique dressing table, with beads piled on the distressed wood. The colors—her face, the robe, the slant of light across the floor, the jewels piled thickly on the dressing table, the table itself, the chair—were all the same palette: pinks, greens, and browns. I had no idea how he had done that. The pigment was brushed, and layered, and slathered—even, here and there, troweled. There were two places where it looked as though he had smeared it so forcefully he had cut through the canvas. But the woman was serene, a Chinese-American Mona Lisa. There was nothing to hint at the time period. It could have been the nineteenth century, or the twentieth, or the twenty-first. The woman could have been sixteen or twenty-five. She could have been a prostitute, staring into space after servicing a client, an actress who had just left the stage after a particularly fine performance, a young girl dreaming of her love. A face of many stories, some finished, some beginning.

Antique Dressing Table, 2002.

"She reminds me of Kick," I said.

"Yes?" he said. "She is beautiful."

Silence. "Do you like her?"

"Oh, yes, very much."

"No. Dornan, do you like her?"

He met my gaze. His eyes were very blue. "I like her very much."

"Will you—" I dropped my gaze, turned back to the painting. "Is it the kind of thing you would buy, do you think?"

"I couldn't say. It would be a big decision, with many things to weigh carefully. Look now, look at this." He tapped the price placard. "That's more than I paid for my house six years ago."

I struggled on doggedly. "But you like her."

"I do. Though I wonder if she might look ridiculous on my wall. Maybe she'd be better suited to a glittering palace, to a great and terrible queen whose eyes are as pale as diamonds, who drinks bloodred wine, and trails a cloak of dark glamour."

I didn't know what to make of this fey mood. He was the one who was supposed to make conversations easier. "You could change your house."

"Ah, but maybe I don't want to change my house. Maybe I like it just as it is. Maybe when I come home at night I want comfort and the smell of coffee and to feel safe. But I'm not sure yet."

"Maybe you'll find out tonight."

"Maybe I will."

We stared at the painting. So beautiful but so flimsy, just daubs of oil on thin canvas. How did one keep such a fragile thing safe?

I dropped Dornan at his hotel, and then drove around for a while to find a video rental store. I talked to a pimply, concave-chested clerk about movie stunts and all-time best performances, and left with six DVDs, four of them featuring Kick.

I RERAN IN slow motion a scene of Kick dropping from a ninth-story window in what was meant to be London's financial district but looked more like Chicago. Her face had been digitally erased and replaced by the star's, but I would have recognized anywhere those shoulders and tight waist, the way she turned like an eel thrown through the air, as though she had all the time in the world.

I paused the film, and called my mother. She answered on the second ring. The sound quality was awful. I could hear traffic.

"Where are you?" I said.

"Just about to get into the car to drive to Redmond."

"What's on the agenda today?"

"More of the same. Security concerns. Details on limited source code sharing. Licensing." Noise. Movement: the car.

"Yes," I said. Traffic noise, cutting in and out as she started to move. She'd be sitting in the back, her driver in the front. "When you move back to Norway, won't you have to drive yourself?"

Pause. "Aud? Are you all right?"

"Mor, when did you know?" *Mor.* Mother.

Noise. "Aud?"

But I knew the answer: you never knew. Love wasn't a state change. Romance might be, and lust, and like, but they were just the preconditions. Love was the choice you made; day in, day out. I could choose no.

"Never mind. The night the police took me to Harborview. I assume you pulled some strings to keep my name from news reports."

Traffic noise. "Yes."

"I assume this was just reflex. I assume you wouldn't mind if I correct the press's lack of information?"

"No." Noise. Muffled conversation. A suddenly better connection: she had asked the driver to pull over, so that we stayed on one cell. "You are an adult. You must feel free to tell them anything you think necessary. As always, though, I recommend caution." Pause. "Are you all right?"

"Why wouldn't I be?"

Silence.

"Yes. Yes, I'm fine. It's just . . . There's been some fallout for a woman who isn't . . . I just want to make sure that no one else suffers who doesn't have to."

"I see. Aud, I'm busy for the next two hours, but would you like to join me for dinner?"

"And Eric?"

A longer silence. "No. Just you and me. You can tell me what you've been up to for the last couple of days, and we can talk some more about the newspapers. I might be able to be of some help."

"Dinner, yes." Help, no.

MINDY LEPTKE had a large corner cubicle, with a window view. She looked like a stoat: small and bright-eyed and probably vicious when cornered.

"I usually get the quirky stories, the ones where no one gets hurt and there's some heartwarming moral at the end that makes everyone feel good while they swallow their last mouthful of coffee."

I wondered how many of her readers that morning had paused, coffee hot in their mouths—did it taste just a little odd?—and got up to spit in the sink.

"But I persuaded the editor to let me go for it this time." She tapped the issue of the *Seattle Times* with the page-three headline, "TV Pilot Poisoner," and its lurid tale of vomit and madness, followed the next day by an update on chemical analysis of the drugs, and a no-holds-barred graphics sidebar of just what happened to brain cells under that kind of toxic load.

"Excellent piece," I said.

She nodded in satisfaction. "Espresso sales were down for nearly sixty hours." She looked at the clock, no doubt wanting to go home. Everyone else had.

"But you didn't get all of it."

She shrugged. "You never do."

"I want you to do a follow-up," I said.

"There's nothing to say."

"What about a political exposé, tying together Seattle real estate developers, the influence of foreign governments on the media"—I hoped my mother would forgive me—"the film industry, and corrupt city and county councillors?"

"Your proof? No, wait, don't tell me. You want me to find that, right?"

"No. I will."

"Right." She rolled her eyes. When I didn't wither under her cynicism, she said, "What's your interest in the matter?"

"I was one of the people who drank the coffee that day. Those people drugged me."

"They drugged a lot of people."

"I own the warehouse where it happened."

She turned to her keyboard. Tap tap tap. "And you are?"

"Aud Torvingen."

"Torvingen . . . Torvingen . . . Not seeing your name." She fished a spiral notebook from the bag hanging over the back of her chair, flipped back a few pages, flipped forward one or two. "Nope. Some corporation owns the warehouse."

"I own the corporation."

"Can you prove that?"

"Yes."

"Okay. We can come back to that." She picked up a blue plastic pencil and twisted it until the lead popped out. "You say you drank the coffee prepared by Film Food?"

She didn't have to check for that name. It was a good name, no more and no less than it had to be. Did Dornan make fun of it in front of Kick? "The coffee. Yes. I did."

"How come you're not on my list? I have sources both in the SPD and Harborview."

"My mother is Else Torvingen, the Norwegian ambassador to the U.K." I gave her a second to absorb that. "She has been in town just a few days." Only a handful more to go.

"I see." Now her pencil was poised. I wondered why she didn't use a voice recorder. "And your name again is Aud Torvingen?"

"Yes." I spelled it for her.

"And you're saying your name was deliberately withheld from the media?" As though CNN had been camping on my doorstep.

"No. Not in the sense that there was any particular reason for doing so. It's more of a reflex action." *Tighten. Control. Assess.* My mother's PR mantra, or one of them. Another was: *Drown them in unnecessary detail.* "You see, if you grow up with a diplomat as a parent, they do everything they can to protect you from even a whiff of scandal, even if you've done nothing wrong, because your name is inevitably linked to theirs, and then theirs to their government. Diplomacy is all about low profile." War with smiles and firm handshakes. "But in this case there's no reason to keep it secret. I didn't do anything illegal or unethical. Nor did my mother or the Norwegian government. I was a—" In this context there was no avoiding the word, and I'd said I would get her back her reputation. "I was a random victim. As was Victoria Kuiper, the proprietor of Film Food."

"They withheld her name as well?"

"No. That's the point. She and her company were named. You named her."

"It sounds vaguely familiar."

"But none of this was her fault, although it would be easy for most readers to infer otherwise. Her business is suffering. I want you to write something about that—about how it wasn't her fault." She wasn't writing anything down. "You could set the record straight."

"No one would care."

"Make them. You could talk about her stunt career. You could write about her wonderful food."

She was looking at her watch. It was almost six o'clock.

"How do you feel about heights?"

She shrugged.

"Stand on your desk."

"What?"

"I want to help you understand something."

"By standing on my desk."

"Humor me." I stood and pushed aside her mouse and telephone and a few sheets of paper. "I'll help you up." I held out my hand and looked as though it were the most normal thing in the world to ask someone to do.

She stood. "What about my shoes?"

They had broad, two-inch heels. Stable enough. "Leave them on. But put the pad down. Sit on the desk first, that's right, then scoot over, get your feet under you, I'll balance you, then . . . up you go."

She stood there, swaying. She might have fallen if it were not for my hand on her hip, anchoring her. A pillowed hip, utterly unlike Kick's.

"You are less than three feet off the ground. Feels farther, doesn't it? A long, long way down. Perhaps you can feel your stomach churning just a little." The power of suggestion. "Now imagine it's a hundred feet. Kick Kuiper was the first woman to take a hundred-foot dive for film. That's thirty or forty times higher than this. Higher than the whole building. Look out of the window. Imagine it." The swaying got worse. "Now imagine the wind rushing. And imagine you're wearing high-heels and a thong bikini." I had to use both hands to keep her steady. "And now imagine you're not just standing there, but that you have to walk to the very edge, and look down, and jump."

"Let me down."

"All right."

"Let me down right now."

"Take my hand. And the other one. Sit down slowly." She sank to her haunches. Sat. Pushed her feet out in front of her. Eased off the desk. Sat in her chair.

"Now imagine you did all that, you jumped, you fell forward, face-first. A hundred feet. Falling for about four seconds." I nodded at the big clock on the far wall. We watched four seconds pass. "It feels like a long time, but there's just time to close your eyes and breathe a prayer. And then you hit. And then you realize you're alive. You did it. You broke the record, and you're alive. And everyone's clapping you on the back. And fifteen million people in darkened movie theaters will watch you take that fall and feel their hearts slam under their ribs, then grin with relief when you walk away. And you're going to get a big check for it. And then imagine one day you can't do that anymore, but you love the movies so much you start from the beginning in some other field, and you work—day in, day out—clawing your way back into people's good graces, doing your best to ignore the fact that they pity you, that you could do their jobs six times better than they could, if only you didn't have a hip held together with a dozen steel pins, ignoring the fact that it hardly pays, and that cutting tomatoes is just not the same as falling through the air like a stooping eagle. And then imagine that some fool takes even that away."

She started writing. After a minute, she slowed and looked up. I could see the cynicism reasserting itself. "Human interest isn't enough. Before I start in on the work, the hours of backbreaking, mind-numbing work, asking people questions, searching archives, combing the Web, bring me something."

"If I bring you proof you'll write about Kick?"

"Bring me proof of government corruption and I'll write about anything you want."

MY MOTHER and I turned to face the elevator door. I pressed the button for the lobby. *I'm having dinner with him tomorrow. Today, now. Tonight.*

She raised her eyebrows, nodded at my thumb, which had turned white against the steel button. I let go. "The newspaper woman I saw today was less than cooperative," I said.

"Ah."

The bell dinged. My mother got out first. We headed for the hotel's oyster bar.

"Journalists," she said. "Very annoying. Particularly photographers."

"Yes."

"One understands how they get punched so often."

We found a seat at the bar. The bartender brought us menus. My mother ordered a glass of cabernet. I chose champagne.

"I have never punched a person," she said as our drinks arrived. "I don't believe I've ever punched anything."

I shook pictures of Kick and Dornan from my mind, kept my place in the menu with my finger, and looked up. "Never?"

"No."

"But . . ." If my mother said *Never,* she meant not even a cushion when she was a child. I sipped my champagne. My mouth bubbled, as it had last night. "Would you like to?"

"Now?"

I pushed my champagne away. "There's probably a bag in the gym."

She slugged back her wine and stood, prepared for battle in her cream silk sweater, taupe linen pants, and delicate evening sandals.

In the gym, a woman with hair pulled back and ears sticking out was yanking at the handles of a lat machine as though trying to pull the legs off her boss; a young, slightly overweight man knelt on all fours on a blue yoga mat, morphing from cat to cow and back again. His back was very flexible. In the best hotel gym tradition, everyone ignored everyone else.

The bag was a heavy boxing bag, and my stomach squeezed: it was the same brand as the one I'd used for my class. This was my mother, I told myself. I was just teaching her to punch. It would not end in blood and death and the feeling that I'd done more harm than good.

The bag looked brand-new. I checked the hook and chain, nonetheless, ran my hands over the casing. Smooth and soft. Acceptable for her beginner's hands.

I had a sudden flash of Kick's small hands. *I like her very much.*

"If you're going to hit with both hands, you'd better take off your wedding ring." She touched it, then twisted it off and put it in her pocket. No tan line. *Maybe you'll find out tonight.* "And your shoes." Her sandals were low-heeled, but I didn't know enough about her balance to be sure. She slipped them off. She seemed more comfortable in bare feet than most of my class had. I held my hands up, curled my fists. She copied me inexpertly. "Imagine the pads at the base of your fingers are an iron bar. Don't clench too hard. All tension should be in the wrist. Okay?"

"Okay." The whiteness around her knuckles eased.

"There are seven basics to learn about striking. One, strike from a firm base. Two, most of your power comes from the torque generated by—" She was shaking her head. "What?"

"Show me."

"All right." Different rules for my mother. "Hold the bag for me like this." I showed her how to get behind it and brace it against her shoulder. "Ready?" She nodded seriously. I hit it, hard. *I like her.* She moved back half a step. I hit it with the other hand. *I like her.* She set her feet and her face. I let fly with a right-left-right combination. *I like her very much.*

My mother's serious expression smoothed, replaced by a bland mask. I didn't have to turn around to know that Yoga Boy and Bat Ears were watching.

"Show me again," she said. And I obliged with a left-right-left. "Do I have to make that noise?"

"What noise?"

"That 'ush' sound. Sometimes a 'hut.'"

Ush. Hut. Well. "Make whatever sound you like. Anything. Just as long as it pumps air from the deep part of your lungs."

"Does it hurt?"

I looked at my fists, the pinking knuckles. As we swapped places I started worrying about her spraining a wrist, breaking a finger, crushing a knuckle. Not being able to get her wedding ring back on. "Start gently."

She assumed the same position I had, took a moment, then punched. Coordinated, but too careful to be graceful.

"Again. Try the other hand."

She stepped into it, and connected squarely, but the bag didn't move.

"Stop being careful now."

She hit the bag. She was only two inches shorter than me, and despite having gained ten pounds or so in recent years, she was strong. I had seen her wallop a tennis ball hard enough to smash an opponent's teeth out. She should have made me stagger.

"Again," I said. "Remember to breathe."

She hit the bag, and huffed as though trying to blow out the candles on a birthday cake. Tidy, controlled, self-contained.

"Don't think about those people watching you." I said it loud enough for the man and the woman to hear. The woman's ears turned beet red. She looked like Mickey Mouse after a gallon of Thunderbird.

"Comics," I said. It was faintly embarrassing talking about this to my mother. It felt more personal than talking about sex.

"Comics?"

"Comic sounds." I gestured for her to swap places. "When Spider-Man hits the Green Goblin. Pretend that's you. Blam!" Thump. "Pow!" Thud. "Whap!" Movement would carry me through. My blood pumped. "It's not you standing there, not a recently married career diplomat in the gym of the Fairmont. You're on the wild *fjell*. You're a troll, or the Hulk smashing the farmhouse." Thump, thud. "A golem destroying an SS Panzer division."

Her eyes kindled. I braced the bag.

"Norway fighting the Danes."

"Ha," she said, "Hothead Paisan!" and walloped the bag. I staggered back. She crowed and thumped it again. "That surprised you!"

The whole of the next ten minutes surprised me. After Hothead Paisan, it was characters from newspaper strips, then TV cartoons. She began to laugh like a berserker, sending me staggering back six inches every time she hit the bag, sending Bat Ears and Yoga Boy sniffing from the gym in high dudgeon. We took turns, running through all the Loony Tunes characters, then the Wacky Races—she was particularly fond of the Slag Brothers and their clubs—and ending with Roadrunner. Every time her fist thumped meatily into the bag, she seemed to expand, glow more brightly.

Her knuckles were glowing, too. "Time to stop," I said. "Your hands will hurt if you don't ice them soon."

She looked at the bag, slitty-eyed as a cat by a mouse hole.

"And I'm getting hungry." My muscles hummed, coursing with oxygen. If someone cut me now, the blood that splashed on the floor would be crimson.

WE HAD prairie fires—tequila shots with nine drops of Tabasco—and oysters on the half shell, followed by more shots. She clenched her fists and stuck them in the crushed ice where the shellfish had nestled.

I remembered our first night in Seattle, Dornan looking at the last oyster. *For once I'd be prepared to fight you for it.*

"So," I said. "Hothead Paisan?"

"That surprised you."

"It did."

"Eric has all the comics. He has a roomful of comics. Comics spin-offs from TV shows, too. He's partial to the strong-woman genre. Xena, Warrior Princess. Buffy."

All the ones where the troll doesn't win in the end. Mostly. "Are there any Norwegian comics?"

"Do you know, I'm not sure. But Eric would know."

We talked about Eric and his biotechs. About her day with software companies and wrangling over source code and security intellectual-property issues. I told her about my run-in with Mindy Leptke at the *Seattle Times*. "I just wanted her to print a follow-up about Kick. The caterer. It's not fair that her business should suffer."

"Indeed," she said.

"So now I have to get her proof."

"Will that be easy?"

"I don't know. The basic rule is, follow the money. I know who is behind this—a woman called Corning—but I don't know how far it goes, how deeply woven into local politics. I don't know who she hired. Once I know that, I can take it to the papers and get Kick's name cleared. So, on paper, yes, it should be easy. But . . ."

"But life rarely works like that. There are often so many other matters that require our attention."

"Yes." *Maybe you'll find out tonight.*

After a slight pause, she said, "I never did meet your other friend. Julia."

"No."

"I had thought perhaps, when you first mentioned Dornan . . . but then I realized not."

"No."

"No," she agreed. She took her wedding ring from her pocket and slid it back on. Yellow and white gold. Clean style, heavy gauge. Substantial. "Eric and I will be here only another few days."

"Yes."

Someone tapped a microphone. We turned to look. A jazz trio was getting ready to play. We turned back to the bar. I shook my head at the bartender's raised eyebrows and made a signing-the-tab motion. "It might be nice to meet Kick before we leave," she said.

"It depends."

"I see." She stood. "Meanwhile, with that reporter, before you present her with information, insist on a final review and veto for her article."

"Yes."

"And don't worry, you'll know what to do."

LESSON 8

FIFTY YEARS AGO THE U.S. ARMY CORPS OF ENGINEERS DAMMED AND DIVERTED THE waters of the Chattahoochee and Chestatee rivers to form a twenty-six-mile-long lake, Lake Sidney Lanier. It's named after a poet who, ironically, wrote about the natural beauty of Georgia, including "The Song of the Chatta-hoochee," which, these days, was being reduced to a moribund murmur as cities, farmers, and recreation-seeking citizens took a bite out of it.

Housing surrounds the lake like scum on the edges of a stagnant pond, everything from rentals to log cabins to palatial CEO second homes.

Therese's place was an eighties-built four- or five-bedroomed social-climbing recreational space. There was parking for a dozen cars, and decks visible from every angle. I was hoping I'd arrived late enough—six o'clock instead of five—to avoid the inevitable Tour of the House, complete with requisite "Oh, my goodness," "Oh, how cute," and "How in the world did you come up with such amazing colors?"

I rapped on the frame of the screen door and Therese opened it wearing the modified country-club casual wear usual for these things, including boat shoes. I deposited my dish—green beans sautéed in bacon fat, with lemon and oregano and chopped tomato—on the kitchen counter with a dozen other containers and made my way through French windows to the deck that jutted out over the water. On the east side was a huge hot tub, big enough for a congressional delegation, steaming aggressively in the sixty-five-degree early evening. Built-in benches ran around the perimeter of the deck.

Suze, in cut-offs, muscle-T and Keen sandals, clearly hadn't got the country-club-casual memo. Nor had Kim, the only other person out there, who glittered in a sparkly halter top, deep-blue nails, and a fancy hair clip. Even the heels on her pumps glittered. I sat next to Suze, who gestured with her can of Coors to a cooler under the bench.

"What'd you bring?" she said as I popped my can.

"Green beans. You?"

"Three-bean salad."

We drank beer.

"Lotta beans," Suze said eventually.

Kim joined us. She held a frosty pink cocktail, which she raised in my direction. "Hey."

I nodded. "Where's everyone else?"

"Getting changed."

Suze squeezed her can and tossed it in a box lined with a garbage bag. "Therese just happens to keep around bathing suits in, you know, fifty zillion sizes. For her guests. So they can either throw themselves in the lake or parboil themselves like lobsters in the party hot tub. Or the pool."

"You didn't fancy a dip?"

"Hot baths should be private, and it's getting too cool for the other kind."

When I looked at Kim, she flicked her nails in the direction of her hair and makeup: she wasn't going to get wet for anybody after all the trouble she went to.

THE EIGHT of them—Sandra hadn't shown up, either—had forged a classroom relationship based on common ignorance, but here on the deck overlooking Lake Lanier, as the sky shaded from Limoges butterfly blue to Wedgwood to inky Delft, even level-the-playing-field bathing gear could not disguise their differences. Tonya's hair had been carefully ironed for the occasion, and she kept smoothing it, worried about humidity; rings winked on four of Christie's fingers—probably from her toes, too, though those were in the tub—and in her left nostril, and a rose tattoo twined over her shoulder; Therese's arms and legs were bare of any ornament but fabulous grooming—nails manicured and buffed but not polished—and glowing great health; Nina wore spiderwebbed varicose veins on thighs and calf and spent more time than probably was comfortable sitting up to her waist in the hot tub. She was also drinking a lot, something bright green.

They had all left their shoes right by the tub, as though bare feet were somehow unnerving.

Balanced between the cool March lake air and the warm foaming tub water, between social situation and a meeting of strangers, alcohol, food, and the southern woman's gift for small talk held the evening together: recipes, husbands, pets. Inevitably, the talk turned to children: Therese's twins, a boy and a girl, Kim's two girls, Nina's grandchildren.

"I don't have kids," Suze said.

"Well, of course you don't," Pauletta said.

"What's with the 'Oh, of course'?"

Pauletta adjusted the gold cross hanging between her breasts, splashed idly at the water foaming by her leg and said nothing.

"I don't have kids, either," Christie said.

"Nope," said Nina, "but you will. I can tell." Perhaps it was just the confidential, you're-one-of-us tone, but I thought I detected a slight slur.

"How do you mean?"

"With some people you can just tell these things. Some people you can't. So how 'bout you, Aud. You got kids?"

"Not as such, no."

Pauletta flipped her ponytail from one shoulder to the other. "The hell does that mean?"

"It means I don't want to talk about it."

Everyone in the tub closed up slightly, like water lilies preparing to shut for the night, and smiled extra hard. Suze and Kim looked away, as though not wanting to be associated with such a blunt breach of the social code.

"So," Nina said, "where you come from they don't talk about their kids?"

Where you come from. Planet Different.

Therese stood up. "It's getting cold out here, don't you think?" No one admitted what she thought. She stepped out of the tub and slipped her shoes on. "Wouldn't it be nice if we all went in and ate some of the lovely food we've brought."

One by one they began to climb out, and I noticed how each one, before even picking up a towel, put her shoes on.

Nina stayed in the tub. I didn't think she felt confident of getting out without falling down. When we were the only ones left on the deck, I took a towel from the pile, shook it out, and carried it over to her. I held out my hand.

"Haul yourself up on this," I said.

She reached for my hand but instead of pulling herself up she pulled me close. "I gave a daughter up for adoption once, too," she said sadly. "She'd be about your age. I think about her. I wonder what she's doing, if she's all right. I wonder if she keeps herself safe. It's so hard to keep kids safe in this world."

"Yes," I said. "Come on, now. Let's get to the kitchen before the food's all gone. I'll help you. Wrap this around your shoulders. Sit here. That's right. I'll get your shoes. Okay now? Good."

Once she was standing she was fine, but just in case, I stayed close as we walked through the living room to the guest room where her clothes were.

"So. Your daughter. Why did you give her away?"

"It was before I was married. I thought she'd have a better life. But now I don't know. How can I know? I just hope her adoptive mother was kind."

"What would you want from an adoptive mother—who, what kind of person would you want for her?"

"Someone kind but stern. Kids like boundaries, you know? I learned that too late for my two . . . my two that I kept." Her face crumpled.

"Hey," I said. "You have grandchildren, though, yes?"

"I do. Four of 'em. And, trust me, they're being brought up right."

"Brought up right." I nodded. "So tell me more about your vision of the perfect mother."

"Perfect?" She looked muddled. "Nobody said anything about perfect. No such thing. But who I imagine for my little Katie, my little Katie's mom, she has no . . . issues, you know? Nothing to take out on Katie. No money worries, no problems with health or other members of the family being weird. Normal. Good, strong values. And consistent. She's consistent. Oh, thank you." She took the cardigan I'd held out. "And kind. Did I say that?"

"You did." We sat quietly on the edge of the bed, then I stood. "You ready for some food now?"

She nodded. "I think you should teach us about kids," she said. "You should teach us how to keep them safe."

"I'll give it some thought."

IN THE KITCHEN—there were four varieties of beans, but Therese had provided a ham—Nina worked hard to include me in conversation. "So that 'bam, pow' stuff in the first class—you like comics?"

"I'm not very familiar with them."

"My son, Jason, used to bring home comics and I'd say, Read a real book! And he'd say, This *is* a real book, Mom! And he gave me a couple. And, you know what? They were pretty good."

Everyone looked at her blankly.

Therese stepped into hostess mode. "Isn't this lovely potato salad? Kim, can I have the recipe?"

"Sure. I'll e-mail it."

"We could set up a chat group," Nina said. "Everyone should give me their e-mail address."

"What about Sandra?" Katherine said. Then, "Wonder where she is?"

No one said anything. No one was willing to say it.

NINE

WHEN I WOKE, MY JAWS ACHED WITH TENSION. WHAT LITTLE SLEEP I'D HAD WAS FILLED with dreams of paintings and cold, empty chairs.

According to Gary, Karenna Beauchamps Corning lived in Capitol Hill. The address turned out to be one of those high-priced, high-security condo buildings that went up five years ago and would probably come down in ten: all marble facing on porous concrete and inferior-grade rebar. Morning sun gilded the polished steel letters (lowercase, Helvetica) that spelled out the name of the building: *press.* Press what? I rang her buzzer. No response. I got back in the car and phoned. Nothing. I watched for a while.

A man with a very small white dog headed for the main door. I got out of the car, pretending to talk on the phone, feeling in my pockets for a nonexistent key.

"—goddamn it, Jack," I snapped into the phone. "I promised Harris we'd have those projections by tomorrow noon and we'll goddamn well have them by tomorrow noon. Am I making myself— Hold on one sec." The man was opening the door. I swapped the phone to my other ear, felt in my trouser pocket. "Yeah," I said, "yeah. Are you listening, we've— Hold on." I swapped sides again, felt in my other pocket. Spared a harassed glance at the man and his dog. He obligingly held the door open for me. "No, Jack. No. Absolutely not. Tomorrow. Look—" I swapped the phone one more time. "Thanks," I said in an undertone to the man, waved him ahead when he looked as though he was about to hold the elevator door for me. The dog cocked its head at me. "Tomorrow is the absolute—" The elevator door dinged shut. I put the phone away.

I took the stairs down to the parking basement. The slot marked 809 was empty. The oil spot wasn't fresh. I walked up to the eighth floor. The air in the stairwell felt thick and unused.

The door was good quality. Pine stained to look like oak, but solid. Heavy brass fittings. One simple mortise lock. I pulled on latex gloves.

I was out of practice. It took three minutes to open. I listened. No beeping: no alarm. Or maybe a very, very expensive alarm. Given the lock, I doubted it.

I checked her bedroom closet, only two hangers empty, and then the bathroom: a gap on the second shelf of the medicine cabinet where three or four things might usually sit. I looked in the fridge: eggs, juice, a wilted head of lettuce. An opened and restoppered bottle of chardonnay. Thai takeaway cartons, limp with grease that had had four or five days to settle. I went back into the bedroom and looked in her dresser. The lingerie drawers seemed more than half-full.

I prowled through the rest of the condo. One lonely paperback in the living room, a *Da Vinci Code* knockoff. The second bedroom had been converted to an office very recently: it smelled of new carpet and plastic electronic component cases that were still out-gassing. Fake wood-grain filing cabinets, fax, phone, computer, paper shredder. The bin beneath it was empty. I looked in the kitchen. The garbage can was also empty.

I sat on her Italian leather sofa and stared through the picture window at Elliott Bay. A container ship plowed heavily south and west to the docks. One ferry was slicing its way out, one in. Overhead the sky was bright and clear, but bluish grey clouds were slipping over the western horizon.

I reconstructed what had happened. Already shaken from my visit on Thursday, on Friday she had taken any incriminating files from her office. On Saturday morning she had picked up the newspaper and read with mounting panic that someone had drugged half the crew on the *Feral* set: her minions had overstepped their bounds and someone had nearly died. She had stuffed a few days' worth of underwear in a bag, with some vague notion of keeping out of the way until things blew over. But keeping out of whose way? Mine? The police? Her political cronies? Someone else? And where had she gone?

I opened her filing cabinet. It was mostly empty; the green cardboard hanging files, the buff folders, the files, the paper, all smelled new. The labels on the hanging folders were unfaded, and there were very few of them. I leafed through what there was, but nothing occurred to me.

I turned on her computer. No password screen. A green Carbonite backup icon at bottom right. I went to her most recent documents, scanned the folders, found one labeled Da Vinci, and smiled. I opened it. A quick look confirmed my guess: it was a list of passwords and user names, including the one for Carbonite. Sometimes people made it too easy. I copied it to the flash drive on my key ring, and found myself humming.

The odds of getting caught on the premises of a break-in increase exponentially once you pass the ten-minute mark. One more minute at the screen, in case something unexpected happened with Carbonite, then two minutes searching her papers.

I found her calendar and pulled it up.

It was all in personal shorthand: *5/14: JB 10:30. Usual. Wtd upd. 5/15 11:45 dtwn lun. push harder. 1:30 upd. Will JB get ETH? 5/18* . . . I wasn't scheduled, which meant these entries were from before our encounter. I scanned the rest. An entry for the coming Monday caught my eye. *5/22: 11:00—ETH!!* Whoever JB was, she or he had come through.

I copied that, too, just in case. Some of it was easy enough to guess at—wanted update, downtown lunch—but I wouldn't know who was pushing whom harder or about what until I identified JB and ETH.

It took more than two minutes to find her bills because, rather than being filed neatly, they were tossed in a kitchen drawer. I found her cell phone bill, and noted the phone number, her car insurance information—she drove a Lincoln Navigator—and her credit card details.

IN ATLANTA I would have taken the information to Benny or Taeko and had what I needed an hour later. In Seattle, I had to do the grunt work myself. At least I could do it outside.

Gas Works Park. I'd seen it from Kick's bedroom window. She'd said I'd like it. After mapping it on the MMI, I drove north, detoured past Kick's house. Her van wasn't there. Maybe it hadn't been there all night. I refused to think about that.

Gas Works Park was the southern spit of Wallingford, a green tongue poking into Lake Union. It was the old city gasworks, turned into a park thirty years ago. Kick obviously liked this place, and perhaps Dornan would appreciate the postmodern picture of rusting gasworks surrounded by parkland, but to me it felt wrong. Natural beauty and heavy industry did not belong together.

I carried my laptop case along a broad path. To the east of a big hill, surrounded by grass, two of the old gas towers still stood, covered in graffiti and quietly rusting to themselves. To my left, the exhauster-compressor machinery left from the fifties had been bolted firmly in place and painted thickly with cheerful enamels, an industrial jungle gym for small children. I couldn't imagine wanting to bring children to play in a place like this. The grass might be green and the engines brightly painted, but the dirt must be drenched in contaminants.

Ahead of me, framed by sparkling water, a man threw a Frisbee for his red setter. The dog writhed impossibly up and up toward the sun and snapped the yellow plastic from the air and brought it to its owner, who threw it again. Over and over, joyously, tirelessly.

The breeze off the water was steady and strong. I climbed the hill by the water's edge. At the top was a huge sundial. It took me a minute to work out how to tell the time and date, a task complicated by the fact that the clouds that had been on the horizon only an hour before now kept obscuring the sun. I wondered what kind of faith in the universe the artist must have had to create and build such a thing in Seattle. The city rose in a sheen of glass and chrome beyond the water, the Space Needle off to the right. Small craft plied to and fro. An arrowhead of geese sliced in to land, followed by a tiny seaplane. The sun came back out and the water turned navy blue, the various waves like cream lace. It looked like a sixties fantasy of what a science-fiction city of the future should look like, and I realized that that was the point, that this was a new kind of city for the New World, proud to show its history and heritage and dreams, even if that history was, to European eyes, sadly stunted.

I found a bench that looked down and across the water but was sheltered from the breeze. I took out Corning's cell phone bill, wrote down the numbers that appeared more than once, and started calling.

"Hey, it's Janice," said a recorded voice. "I'm running errands but call me back, 'kay?" Janice: JB? No way of knowing. I tried the next number. "You have reached the law offices of Leith, Bankersen, and Heshowitz, how may I help you?" A male voice. Seattle had the highest number of male receptionists I'd ever come across. "What kind of law do you specialize in?" I asked him. "We are corporate tax specialists." "Could I have the names of your principals?" "Certainly." None of them matched the initials. The next number. No reply. The next. Another male voice, but this one an entirely different animal. "Thank you for calling the reelection campaign offices of Edward Thomas Hardy. I appreciate your support. I'm afraid all my lines are busy right now but your call is important to me, so please do leave your name and contact information, and I'll try get back to you as soon as humanly possible." Wordy. Like all elected officials. ETH. I circled the number.

I called the others, but got nothing of note.

I opened my laptop, hooked it to my phone, and while the networks sorted themselves out, I downloaded the calendar information from my flash drive, and read it thoroughly. Then I ran a Web search on Edward Thomas Hardy.

It was slow work, using the cell network, but eventually I started getting results.

He was a Seattle city councillor, running for reelection. He had started fifteen years ago as an environmental zealot and was now the current chair of the Urban Development and Planning Committee. He had been instrumental in pushing through several of the zoning changes on the South Lake Union biotech development. An image search turned up pictures of a worried-looking man in his late forties. White. Unexpectedly deep-set hazel eyes. ETH. And someone called JB had "got" him for a meeting with Corning next week.

The Seattle City Council website told me that, in addition to two councillors and two alternates, the zoning committee had three legislative assistants, one of whom was Johnson Bingley. JB.

Bingley turned out to be twenty-eight, recently married, and to have blond hair (and an expensive haircut) and a political science degree from UC Irvine. With a bit of work I turned up the abstract of his dissertation: a piece of nonsense about interstate politics that was all generalities in a blatantly cut-and-paste plagiaristic style. Bingo. Criminals looked for shortcuts. Entry-level politics were full of them.

I did another long, slow search to make sure Bingley was the only staffer with the initials JB. He was it. But ETH was his boss. The question now was, on which side of righteousness did ETH fall?

A cloud scooted away from the sun and I shaded my eyes. I closed the lap-top and unhooked my phone, weighed it. I didn't know whom to call, Kick or Dornan, and I didn't know what I'd say if they answered.

I plugged it back in and started a deeper search on Edward Thomas Hardy.

I DROVE BACK up Myrtle, past Kick's house. No van in the driveway. It was only midday, but traffic on 45th was almost stationary. It got hot in the car, but I didn't want to roll up the windows and turn on the AC.

Traffic crawled over the bridge, and again through downtown. As I got closer to the warehouse my stomach tightened.

Kick's van wasn't in the parking lot. Where were they? What were they doing?

The set rang with the clang of hammer and wrench on metal pipe: people putting together a huge scaffold. It was hot. Joel hovered, looking worried, oc-casionally consulting what looked like a wiring diagram. Everyone—the cos-tumers, Bernard, Peg—was carrying pipes, hauling on command, or standing back to admire the growing edifice.

There was no sign of Kick or Dornan, and the food on the craft-services table was conspicuously packaged sandwiches and a coffee urn with the lid taped down.

"Any idea where they are?" I said to Peg.

She put down her end of a piece of scaffold. "Where *who* are?"

"Kick. Dornan."

"Dornan's her friend?"

No, Dornan's my friend. "How about Rusen?"

"Editing."

"Where?"

"On the Avid."

I said merely, "It's probably a good idea to wear gloves when you do this kind of work."

I went back out into the parking lot, to the trailer, and knocked. Traffic roared in the distance. I knocked again. The door opened. Hot, rebreathed air rushed out. Rusen blinked at me. He had that can't-change-focus look of someone who has spent twelve hours sitting in one place staring at a screen. He hadn't shaved for at least twenty-four hours. He'd had even less sleep than I had.

"May I come in?"

"May . . . ? Sure, sure."

Inside, images were frozen on six screens. He sat on the chair in front of them, seemed momentarily confused when I remained standing.

"Something urgent?"

"Not urgent. But we do need to discuss your problems with OSHA and EPA."

"Problems? Right. OSHA. EPA." He focused on the screens, reached for the console, paused, hand above the big hockey-puck frame-by-frame advance control. "Do you mind if I just finish this . . ."

Scene? Act? Track? I had no idea. As soon as his hand touched the controls, he seemed to lose touch with his verbal centers. I looked around until I found a chair, rolled it over, and watched for a while.

He turned the big dial on the console, and one of the pictures would move forward. He'd dial it back, and forward again. He'd look at one of the other screens, punch a button, dial that back and forth. And another. Sîan Branwell stood and sat, stood and sat, stood and sat, turned and turned back, over and over. He muttered something to himself, chewed the cuticle on his right-hand ring finger, dialed again. Nodded. Punched other buttons. Ran one of the pictures again. The turn of her head was subtly different. Perhaps two frames missing before the screen cut to her beginning to stand, then back. Or—no, he had zoomed in. I didn't know you could do that. It was like watching someone play God, rearranging time, making the puppets dance differently. It didn't look as though he were going to stop anytime soon.

"Rusen."

"Um?" He didn't look at me.

"Rusen." I leaned forward, laid a finger on the back of his hand. He blinked, focused on it. Blinked again. Looked at me. Reluctantly withdrew his hands from the console, tucked them under his thighs.

"Sorry. Boy howdy, that thing's addictive."

"Yes. We need to—" But he was focusing on the screens again. Visual capture. I studied the console. Identified what appeared to be the master power switch. I had no idea, though, if it was all saved to disk or whatever one did with these things. I looked again, until I began to understand the layout. Then I reached out and turned off one of the screens.

He jerked as though he'd been shot. I turned off a second.

"No," he said. "No."

"It's just the screens," I said. And extinguished the others in rapid succession. "You haven't slept, I'm guessing you haven't eaten. There isn't enough oxygen in here to sustain a bacterium, and we need to talk about a few things. I think you should take a break."

He considered it, then reached out and punched a button. A background whine I hadn't noticed powered down. He stretched. His spine cracked. He looked at his watch. Frowned.

"Let's go eat something."

He squinted and shielded his eyes from the sun before stepping down from the trailer, like a drunk leaving a bar in the middle of the day. I let him adjust and didn't talk until we were sitting down in the corner of the set farthest from the scaffolding and he was biting into a turkey sandwich. I let him chew and swallow, chew and swallow, and look around for a minute.

I looked around, too. Where were they? I turned back to Rusen.

"How's it going? The editing?"

"Good. Better than good. Working with the Avid's making me wonder if I shouldn't have shot in digital to begin with."

I gestured for him to explain.

"The digital editing. It feels so fluid. And the quality . . . I don't see the difference. I thought I would. We shot on film. Expensive, but better visual quality. Or that's the conventional wisdom." He shook his head. "So, anyhow, we take the film and make a digital copy, and I edit the copy. That way it doesn't matter if I mess up. I'm just doing a rough cut. A real editor will do all the fine work, and cut the negative." He bit, chewed, swallowed. "But editing is . . . well, I'd no idea. The possibilities are pretty much endless. Imagine if we'd shot digital from the beginning. The effects, boy. I can make this film say anything on this machine. It's like . . . it's like statistics. I can rearrange the story completely. Which is good, because I've completely changed the ending. Or I think I have. Which means we have to change the beginning. Otherwise it won't make sense when we blow everything up."

"You're going to blow up my warehouse?"

"Not literally. But we'll build around that scaffolding, shoot some stuff on the soundstage, then take it outside, and blow it all up in the parking lot. At least I think we will. The director was supposed to figure all this stuff out with the stunt guy. But if we'd been doing this in digital, there's all kinds of effects . . ." His eyes lost focus again.

"So why didn't you just shoot in digital to begin with?"

"Because . . ." He shrugged. Chewed. Swallowed. Sipped coffee. "It's my first film."

"It's a backdoor pilot."

Someone dropped some scaffolding. Hoots, shouts. All good-natured.

"Boy, I know that. Finkel reminded me of that just today. But it's a film, too. And I can cut it that way, so it gets its time in the light."

"Finkel is back?"

"Didn't I tell you? No, clearly. This morning. He buried his son yesterday and got on a plane. You should meet him."

I had absolutely no wish to stare grief in the face. "Later. Meanwhile, it might be an idea not to try to penny-pinch on the set, particularly when it comes to safety. Those people building the scaffold should be wearing goggles, and gloves." They should be professionals, but that was his business. "And you should be running the air-conditioning."

He half stood. Looked around. "We're not?" I let him work that one out for himself: the shirt sticking to him, the scaffolders stopping to wipe their brows. His body was also beginning to realize it was exhausted. His eyelids drooped, the muscles over his cheekbones sagged. "You're right. We should fix that."

"It would make OSHA happy. As would gloves and goggles and protective headgear." I reminded myself that getting involved in others' problems led to nothing but trouble.

He put the half-chewed sandwich down, too tired to eat any more. Or maybe it was just that his appetite was ruined knowing that, had OSHA walked onto the set while he was lost to his digital edit world, they would have closed it down.

"The editing's important," he said.

"If you say so."

"I'll pay more attention."

"Someone should."

"I need to look at the budget. Protective gear . . . But the editing . . ." His focus began to drift again.

This wasn't my problem. And Kick wasn't here.

I stood. "Well, I'm glad Finkel's back. He can help."

"Finkel. Of course." He stood, and walked with me to the door.

"AC," I reminded him. After all, Kick would be back at some point.

"Right." He called over to Joel and suggested the AC. Joel, in turn, called over one of the hands who didn't seem to be doing much. Bri's young friend.

The sun was still shining. After the heat of the warehouse, the air in the parking lot was cool and refreshing. I pointed the remote at the Audi, but Rusen beckoned me over to the second Hippoworks trailer, opened the door.

"He'll want to meet you," he said as we went in, at which point it was too late.

Finkel stood when we entered. He was a little under average height, and his eyes were wide and his hair parted just to the right of where it should be, for his cut. Grey showed strongly at the roots. Grief was a strong wind, blowing away the habits and vanities of a lifetime. There were no papers on his desk.

"Anton, this is Aud Torvingen. The owner. The one I told you about."

"Pleased to meet you," he said, and shook my hand, and gave me a huge smile that belonged to someone else, perhaps the person he had been before his son died.

"I'm very sorry about your son," I said, and because there is no possible reply to that, other than thank you, which to me always felt like thanking your executioner, I said, "I'm afraid I don't know his name."

"Galen," he said. "The last two years he always told people to call him Len. I hated that. But I understood. I called myself Tony when I was twenty." He smiled at some memory. His lips were the color of old-fashioned rouge at the center, but the edges were dry. He had probably forgotten to drink plenty of water on the plane.

When Julia had died, I hadn't slept for days. "Well, it looks as though you got back just in time. Rusen needs help with some production details."

"Yes?" he said, turning to Rusen.

"Nothing that can't wait," Rusen said.

"No. Tell me."

"Protective gear. Goggles and things."

"The crew won't wear them?"

"Money. Do you have any idea what these things cost?"

"Do you?" From the straightening of Rusen's neck I took this to be a flash of the pre-grief Finkel. "Besides, who says we have to buy new? Is there a clause somewhere? Half the people on set will have something at home they could use. Or maybe we could work out a rental agreement with a hardware store for product placement."

"Product placement? We've finished all the shooting except for the finale and a couple of effects."

"Never too late for product placement," he said, though with an abstract air, as though he couldn't believe he was talking about such things when his son lay dead, dead.

"Right," I said. "I can see that you two are going to be pretty busy. I'll leave you to it. It was good to meet you."

I closed the door quietly, and stood for a moment on the tarmac with my eyes closed, remembering the feel of the world when I was grieving—like a cold wind on a chipped tooth.

Kick's white van was backed up five yards from the warehouse door. Someone, hidden by the back doors which were both open, was pulling something heavy along the bed preparatory to hefting it out, someone humming Kevin Barry. Dornan.

A pause in the humming, followed by a low *oomph,* and a murmured, "What do they put in these things?" He stepped backwards into view, holding two cases of soda with one of bottled water balanced on top. He started to lift one hand to push the van door closed, but the weight was too much for one arm. He pondered. Tried with the other hand.

I stepped up behind him. "I've got it."

"Christ almighty." He clutched convulsively at the water, which nearly slid off, and started a smile which was abruptly extinguished. "Torvingen. What are you doing here?"

I raised my eyebrows. "It's my property." The words glinted between us, naked as a sword jerked halfway from its sheath. My property.

"So it is."

Nothing on his face but wariness. "Do you need a hand?"

"I've got it. Thanks." No. More than wariness. Resentment? Anger?

"I'll get the doors, then." I put my hand on the warm metal. Kick's van. "You'll have to back off." After a moment he backed up two steps. My biceps bunched as I swung the doors shut. "Kick around?"

"She's at her sister's."

"Her sister's."

The case of coffee slipped a little. He had to grab it with one hand. I made no move to help. Her sister's.

"You should carry those in."

"My time is my own, I believe."

"They look heavy," I said.

"Well, yes, I suppose they are." He didn't budge.

We measured each other. I could break his spine with one hand. We both knew it. "Is she coming here later?"

"I'm not her keeper," he said.

"No?" He lifted his chin, and it would have taken just one step, one swing with a crossing elbow, to break his jaw. "You look tired. Did you have a long evening?"

His pupils were tight and I saw him swallow, but he kept his voice steady. "We had a perfectly lovely evening, thank you."

He had cried when Tammy left him. He had helped me countless times. He was my friend. I breathed, in and out, and took a step back. Gravel rolled and crunched under my boots as I walked away.

I got in my car. Reversed carefully. Signaled before I merged with Alaskan Way, then I called Corning's cell phone. "You know who this is," I said. "You missed our Monday meeting, but don't worry, I'll find you."

I would find Corning and slam her head in a car door. First I would find Edward Thomas Hardy and break both his thumbs.

I hadn't even known Kick had a sister.

I CALLED AHEAD, and this time a bouncy-voiced assistant answered. I explained that I was in Seattle visiting some real estate interests and checking up on the yacht they were building for me down at the lake. I was considering the possibility of moving here, of making a significant contribution to Hardy's campaign, assuming I liked the cut of his jib. The assistant was very happy to slot me in, right away. I gave my name as Catherine Holt. I'd be there in fifteen minutes. They wouldn't have time for meeting prep or any kind of background check.

Hardy's reelection offices were in Fremont, a neighborhood immediately west of Wallingford, along the ship canal. I drove back north. The Audi's lack of connection with the feel of the road annoyed me. I drove faster than I should, longing for the bite of tire on pavement.

When I got there, the assistant ushered me into Hardy's office—which, with its pressed-wood furniture and artificial-fiber carpet did not give the impression of wealthy corruption, though perhaps he was just smart—and left us alone.

Old Ed Tom Hardy stood and smiled a politician's smile, and came out from behind his desk. He extended his hand.

I studied him. Medium height. Face thinner than his body.

"Hardy," he said, in a resonant voice, hand still out. "It's a pleasure."

"Not really," I said, and sat.

He wasn't stupid. He pulled in his hand and studied me in turn. "I take it you don't really intend to make a huge campaign contribution."

"No."

"And that your name isn't Catherine Holt."

"No."

"Should I call the police?"

"Have you done something wrong?"

"You look as though you want me to have." His voice buzzed very slightly and he edged prudently behind his desk, but like Dornan, he wasn't going to roll over without a fight. The difference was, Edward Thomas Hardy wasn't my friend.

"I'm considering making you eat your chair."

Unlike Dornan, his chin went down, rather than up. "I have no doubt you could do that." His Adam's apple bobbed, but when he spoke again his voice was admirably steady. "We could begin by you telling me what you think I've done."

"The zoning committee."

"Ah." He sat wearily. "I'm sorry if your parents have lost their lease, or your brother his job, but Seattle needs the South Lake Union development."

"I don't have an opinion about South Lake Union."

"I don't understand." No apology, no irritation, no fake smile. He was pretty good.

"Do you know somebody called Karenna Beauchamps Corning?"

He opened his mouth, and his lips began to shape *no,* but then his eyes flickered, up and left, as he remembered something.

I nodded. "You're meeting her Friday. Johnson Bingley set it up."

"He's one of the council admins." No guilt in his voice. But perhaps he was an excellent poker player.

"I know."

He was smart enough to wait and see where I was going.

"Did you read about that drug incident in the warehouse district last week?" Wary nod. "The drugs were administered by Corning's proxy. She wants the leaseholder to go bankrupt and leave the land vacant so that she can buy from the owner at a reduced price. I think she's meeting you on Friday to ask for a zoning variance on a lot, or several lots, along the Duwamish, which she'll develop for a profit. I think Johnson Bingley will get a cut of that profit for introducing you."

There was a very long pause. "That's illegal."

I knew that tone. I'd heard my mother use it at a press conference when she'd been sandbagged by a question about improprieties by one of her staffers.

"Yes."

"You don't appear to be accusing me of improper behavior."

"Not at this time. I understand some of the realities of politics. Sometimes there are good reasons for zoning variances. I'm simply pointing out that Corning is a criminal."

"Perhaps you should take the matter to the police."

"Perhaps I should."

He acknowledged the called bluff with a long blink.

"The police can't help me get what I want. You can."

Another pause. "I don't even know your name."

I made a decision. "Aud Torvingen." I leaned forward and held out my hand. He shook. A good handshake, the kind my mother would classify as under siege but not overwhelmed, morally or politically. "I'm the owner of the property Corning had been devaluing—she was my broker. I'm hoping that we can help each other."

"And how do you think I could help you, exactly?" He didn't need to ask how I could help him; he was a politician running for reelection, and if I owned industrial property, I had money.

"Information. About zoning and development in Seattle. How much would Corning have made if she'd succeeded?"

It took him a moment to change gears, but politicians live or die by their ability to seize a proffered alliance. "Let's start at the beginning. Tell me about your warehouse."

"It's a cross-shipping facility on Diagonal Avenue South."

"Near the Federal Center?"

"Yes."

"That whole swatch of Duwamish is designated wetland and the environmental lobby want it declared an estuarine restoration site. We couldn't buy your land, of course, if you didn't want to sell, though the recent rulings on eminent domain are interesting, but if the surrounding land were purchased by the city and protected, your plot would be almost impossible to develop."

"Almost?"

"Impossible, period, if you want to make a profit."

"It's just a profit thing, then?"

"What else is there in real estate?"

I studied him. "I've read your first campaign statement: it is part of a city councillor's job to be a steward of the city's natural resources."

He swiveled his chair this way and that. "That was a long, long time ago. In the years since, it has been represented to me, forcefully, that my job is jobs and profit."

"Let's pretend, just for a minute, that you still believe you are a steward of the city's natural resources. Tell me about the wetland zoning, the estuarine restoration."

"You really want to talk about the environment?"

I matched his former, light ironic tone. "What else is there in real estate?"

His expression didn't change, but his cheeks pinked slightly and where his collar was tight against his neck, I could see his carotid pulse. Hope was something to be feared in politics.

I upped the ante. "I don't need to make a profit. Tell me about the wetland."

He tapped his appointment book, thinking; opened it, checked his schedule. "Would you like some tea or coffee?"

I accepted. He left the room for a while. When he came back he was carrying two mugs of coffee and a large rolled map tucked under his arm. His face was damp and his hands smelled of lotion. He unrolled the map and anchored it to his desk with his coffee mug and appointment book.

"The Duwamish," he said, pointing, unfastening one shirt cuff. "It used to teem with salmon and heron. You could dig oysters and shoot duck."

I looked at the concrete-straight lines.

"Harbor Island, here, is a Superfund site."

Spiky, industrial geometry of piers and jetties and pipelines where the Duwamish met Elliott Bay.

"As warehouses and industrial complexes close, we've been buying up land, slapping restoration orders on it, and waiting for the economy to turn around so we can remediate."

"How much?"

"To do it properly?" He rolled up his sleeves while he mused. "Hundreds of millions. Just labeling the land 'wetland' costs a fortune. The regulations are tortuous." He opened a filing cabinet and selected a stack of paper. "Here. Director's Rule 6-2003, City of Seattle Department of Design, Construction and Land Use: The Requirements for Wetland Delineation Reports. The whole thing is a rule about the presentation of the rules of the mapping of wetland. Thousands of words, none of which even begin to say what wetland is, and why it's important."

"But my land has already been designated wetland."

"Yes, and that makes it possible for us to bid on it, when it comes up for sale, because of funds allocated in previous budgets and held in escrow. But the designation is wide open to challenge if someone wants to take our bid out of the running. Somewhere along the line, someone is bound to have broken some of the regulations, which means the designation can be thrown out. And right now the city doesn't have the money to spend on resurveying. Even if it did, it would take a couple of years."

"So getting the warehouse and adjacent land rezoned wouldn't be hard."

"No."

"What would you do with the land if you wanted to make a big profit?"

"Mixed light commercial and residential. A marina, a restaurant, condos."

"In the middle of an industrial area?" But that was European thinking.

"There's already a park." He pointed more or less at my warehouse. "It's a pocket park. Here, between your land and the Federal Center. On the water, opposite Kellogg Island."

Kellogg Island was a tiny lump of land in the middle of the river that I hadn't known was there. "It's not marked."

"It's too new. But I opened it eight months ago. It's a very sexy combination of industrial district surrounded by nature. Someone willing to drop seven figures on a pied-à-terre would buy one in a heartbeat."

I wouldn't have understood that a month ago, but I was beginning to. I studied the map. Gary had said that Corning had been talking about four adjacent plots of land. "Is the Federal Center up for sale?"

He paused, consulted some interior ethics monitor, and nodded. "They're moving to facilities in Renton, though that's not general knowledge."

"Show me what's their land." He did. "And if you included my land, and the park, and, say, the two plots north of that, how much would it cost to develop as the kind of place you were thinking of?"

"Hard to say. Mid–eight figures."

"Easy to get investors?"

"Very. With that park as the natural centerpiece, profit could be forty percent."

"If the zoning were changed," I said.

"If the zoning were changed."

I WALKED along 34th, and between the bricks and mortar of the software industry, Getty Images, Adobe, Visio, I caught glimpses of the ship canal. I stopped and leaned against a low wall. A dilapidated fishing boat chugged by. I watched it as I called Gary. "Get me everything you can on those plots Corning was looking at. Get me estimates of value. Find out who the owners are, and if Corning has been in touch with any of them."

At the corner of 34th and Fremont I passed a sculpture, of five people and a dog at a bus stop. Someone had recently added balloons and blinding green wigs, and signs around their necks saying *Happy Birthday, Alyssa!!* The sculpture was called *Waiting for the Interurban*. A hundred years ago the Interurban had been an electrified rail line running from Renton to Everett, cutting through the warehouse district. Not a bus stop. A commuter light-rail stop. Pity it had closed. I couldn't remember when. Kick might know.

We had a perfectly lovely evening.

I drove back to the warehouse. I wanted to hear what Kick thought.

IN ATLANTA, the afternoon sky would be bluer, the sun yellower, the trees and grass more green, and the pause before rush hour would have sweltered, sticky with sap and insect song, only lightly sheened with hydrocarbon. Here, rush hour had already started. The Alaskan Way viaduct poured as slow and thick with cars as a carbon dioxide–laden pulmonary vein. I kept pace like a good little molecule, let myself be funneled in due order onto Diagonal Avenue, noting unmarked turnoffs, rail spurs, then the Federal Center, and pulling eventually into the half-full lot of the warehouse. I parked next to Kick's van, but didn't get out of the car.

I called Dornan. He answered on the second ring.

"It's me. Is she there?"

"Where are you?"

"In the parking lot. Is she there?"

"She is not. But stay there. Please. I'm coming out. I want to talk."

I got out of the car and leaned against the hood. The air was slithery with diesel but now that I was hunting for it, I also smelled the unmistakable rolling underscent of estuarine river. I closed my eyes and visualized the map in Hardy's office. Very close.

Dornan emerged, holding two cups of coffee. He held one out wordlessly.

I took it. It had cream in it. "I can't drink this."

"Why not?"

"It has cream in it."

"Ah. Not because you're pissed off at me? You were pretty pissed off earlier. And you pissed me off, actually, which is why, well, why I might have let you take away a false impression."

"False?"

"You pissed me off. You're always— Well. There it is, yes: false. Though we did go for a walk, and we did talk a lot, and I do like her very much. But it'll never go further than friendship. Though friendship, I've heard, can go a long way, with the right wind."

False.

"Do you want to know what we talked about half the bloody night, with the sea soughing gently and the moon out almost full?"

"I don't know."

"You." He sighed. "Move up a bit." He leaned back against the hood, too, and sipped his coffee. We both turned our faces to the sun. "She's a fine woman."

"She is."

"And she's very— Oh, stop clutching that coffee as though it's your long-lost puppy. Looking pathetic doesn't suit you. If you're not going to drink it, put it down, for heaven's sake."

I set it carefully on the gravel. "You talked about me?"

"Among other things." His eyes were distant for a moment. "She's very fond of you."

"Me, too, her."

"I'm glad to hear it. She's not . . . That is, she needs . . . Ah, well. What she needs is her business."

"Yes." Hers and mine. He wasn't the one she had fed. He wasn't the one who had seen her eyes go black and run a hand down her naked spine. I started to smile.

"You look particularly fatuous when you do that."

He sounded petulant and it suddenly occurred to me how he might be feeling. "Are you all right?"

"All right? Why wouldn't I be?"

I didn't say anything.

He sighed. "I like her, and I think it could have been fine between us, but . . . Well, just but. It's like a jigsaw piece that doesn't quite fit. We could hammer it in and call it good, but the pattern would be wrong. I live in Atlanta, for one thing."

"As do I."

"So you do." He could sound very much like my mother sometimes when he used that *I know things you don't* tone. "But, Aud, the pattern is very nearly right, very nearly. She means a lot to me. Don't toy with her."

Silence. "So. Is she in there?"

"No. But—"

"Do you have her cell phone number?"

"She doesn't carry one—" He knew so much more about her than I did. *Because I asked nicely.* ". . . me finish, she's not on the set, but she is here."

"Where?"

He nodded at the second Hippoworks trailer, just as the door banged open and she jumped down. She wore jeans and work boots and a salmon tank top. The arms of a cardigan were tied around her waist. Her skin was golden. From here you couldn't see the freckles on her shoulders. She said to Dornan, "Floozy and the Winkle aren't—" And then saw me. "Aud."

Her hair was down. I wanted to plunge my hands in it, pull her to me.

"Well," said Dornan. "I should be getting back in to help with that scaffolding."

Kick and I just looked at each other.

"It's still hot in there," he said to her. "Maybe you should stay out here for a bit."

She nodded.

"Pass your cup, then," he said to me. I bent and retrieved it, handed it over obediently. He sighed, shook his head, and went inside.

"It'll be hot in there for a while," I said.

"Okay."

"We could go for a walk."

"What, in traffic?"

"Not exactly."

THE POCKET park was on the other side of a deserted side road and hidden by a row of straggling hawthorn. If I hadn't known it was there, I would never have found it.

There was a patch of grass and two benches overlooking the Duwamish, connected by a short path to a grassy clearing. We held hands and sat on a bench, watching the river slide by below, as brown as overbrewed tea. I felt my lack of sleep the night before, and if the wind hadn't been so strong, I might have dozed. Every now and again the water glinted, like a powdered old lady throwing a roguish smile.

The rocky shore was green-slimed and smelled of rot. Northward, in the direction of Harbor Island, four Canada geese stood splay-footed on the pebbles and honked. Beyond them arced the concrete spans of a massive bridge.

"What's the bridge?" I asked Kick, stroking the back of her hand idly with my thumb.

"The West Seattle Bridge. And, funnily enough, what it's connecting to is West Seattle. Typical of this city."

"Dornan finds all the names in this city amusing."

"Um." She sounded relaxed, or maybe she was just sleepy.

"I hear you two were up late last night, talking on the beach." She was staring out over the water. "So. What was so interesting that it kept you up until two in the morning?"

She turned to look at me, and searched my face the way my mother had done just a week ago. "Oh, this and that." And she laughed, and kissed my cheek. I put my arm around her.

Gulls wheeling over the old, crumbling pilings that poked like broken teeth from the low water on the shore of Kellogg Island squabbled over something I couldn't see. Power lines ran here and there, and steam, white as the smoke in a movie magic spell, coiled up from a plant on Harbor Island. The clouds in the west looked like yellowed Styrofoam.

"There's nothing like this in Norway," I said.

"Um." She settled tighter against me. In this light, her hair was like twisted gold wire. I would have been happy never to move again.

A tug plowed by, heading south, upriver, tight and rolling and muscular, cocky as a rooster. Its engine throbbed but the stink of diesel was whipped away by the breeze. Silver flashed in its wake. Salmon.

In the other direction, downriver, near the geese, more movement made me turn.

"Look," I said, and she lifted her head.

A green-backed heron came in to land, like an inexpertly piloted Cessna. She sat up. "If a stunte dived that badly she'd be fired."

"Not as graceful as you," I agreed. "I watched *Tantalus*."

"That old thing?" But she sounded pleased.

"You dive like a cormorant."

She smiled but didn't say anything. The wind began to pick up. Another heron slipped and slid through the air and splashed tail- and feetfirst into the shallows right in front of me. It plunged its ugly, ancient-looking beak into the opaque water but missed whatever it had been after. Disgusted, it took off again, flapped heroically for a moment, and finally hauled itself into the air, legs dangling.

"I had no idea they were so clumsy. And small. It was a heron, right? I always thought they were bigger."

"Great blue herons are big."

"And what's that?" She pointed.

"A grebe, I don't know what kind." And then I was seeing wildlife everywhere, and naming it for her: a kingfisher, some kind of coot, more fish, a bumblebee humming over the mossy grass, a ladybug snicking its wings in and out as it crawled across the back of the bench. I knew that the shallows would creep with crabs and be bobbled with oysters, that the smell of rot meant that living things grew here and then died. And I knew why people would pay a million dollars for a condo in an industrial district.

Kick slid close again, laid her palm against my cheek. Small, cool hands. I turned. Her eyes were very grey. She leaned in and kissed me. "Sometimes your face looks like something carved a thousand years ago."

I ran my hands over her shoulders, down her arms, around her waist. The muscles in my thighs and back strained and trembled. She was shaking, too, but although her pupils were big, I realized it was with cold as much as desire. I untied the cardigan knotted around her hips, lifted her with one arm, and pulled the cardigan free with the other. I breathed fast. "Put this on," I said.

While she pushed her arms into the sleeves and tugged I watched the sky. The clouds had grown denser, firming from Styrofoam to incised stone, subtly colored, chiseled and layered and polished. "It's beautiful," I said.

She buttoned with her left hand, laid her right on my thigh. "Isn't Atlanta like this?"

I shook my head. "In Atlanta, in May, the sky is always blue. Later in summer there are storms in the afternoons, and for an hour or so there are clouds overlaying a sky the color of pink grapefruit, but this . . . it's like intaglio-cut stone." I pointed. "There. Mica. And amethyst. Rose quartz. Carnelian, and, look, see that grey? That's what natural, uncut diamond looks like."

"Kiss me," she said.

I did, and I wrapped my hands around her tiny waist, then slid them around the swell of her hips, pulled her to me. Her bottom was warm and luscious. I cradled her cheeks, ran my hands back to her waist, dipped my fingers under her waistband. Our mouths were wide. Another tug hooted.

I looked at the grass, decided there were too many goose droppings, and sighed.

She pulled away, grinning, as though she knew what I was thinking. "Oh, well," she said, "nice park anyway."

"Glad you like it."

"I had no idea it was here. Be nice if it was more private, though." She laughed to herself as she straightened her clothes.

"There's a woman called Corning who wants to pave all this over with condos."

"Will you buy one?"

"No." She shivered again, and I put my arms around her. "Because I'm not going to let her build them."

She started kissing me again, then stopped. "What time is it?"

"About four o'clock, I think."

"Shit. I have a— I have to run." She kissed me again. "Meet you at the house? Around seven?"

AT AIKIDO, the sensei wasn't there. Mike was leading the class. It was informal and boisterous. I made people fly, and flew in my turn.

Afterwards, as we swept and wiped the dojo, Mike and Petra separately invited me to the Asian Art Museum to see a new display of Chinese art—Mike in a *whatever* kind of way, and Petra shyly. I declined but suggested they go together, and managed not to smile at their consternation.

THE HOUSE cooled and darkened. We lay under her duvet. My face hurt from smiling. She butted my hand, like a cat; I stroked her head. There were no lights on in the house, and in the long, northern dusk her hair gleamed, dark and light, layered, sometimes pale and silvery like bamboo pith, sometimes heavy and dark, like freshly split pine. "Wood," I said. "That's what your hair reminds me of."

"You think my hair's like wood?"

"I love wood." I rolled onto my stomach and stroked her hair, over and over, rounding over the back of her head, feeling the sleekness, like the oak finial of a three-hundred-year-old baluster that has been polished by twelve generations of hands. Figured oak. That was it, exactly.

She rolled onto her stomach, too, so that we were lying next to each other like eight-year-olds looking over the edge of a cliff. "So you know a lot about wood, and about herons and oysters. You didn't learn that in the police."

"I wasn't always in the police." And I told her of growing up in Yorkshire and on the fjord, in London and in Oslo, while my mother worked her way up the political and diplomatic ladder. Of my travels in the wild parts of the world, working on my cabin in North Carolina: the trees, the birds, the wood.

"It sounds beautiful," she said. "My parents had a cabin in the North Cascades. It was hot and dusty—dust everywhere. Jesus. It's basically a desert out there. But that's where I learnt to ride. Do you ride?"

"I do."

"English saddle, though, I bet."

"That's how I learnt. But I can ride western."

"I can ride anything. With or without a saddle."

I can cook anything. I can ride anything. Simple statements of fact. "Even bulls and broncos?" I stroked the small of her back, very gently, running my palms over the tiny hairs there.

"Anything. When I was a kid, I did stunt riding of things like ostriches and goats and llamas. I've ridden elephants and alligators and, once, even a very large dog."

Her backbone was entirely sheathed in smooth muscle. I ran my fingertips down the soft skin. The slanting light threw fillets of muscle into sharp relief. What Kick was saying suddenly registered, and I paused. "When you were a child?"

"It's a family thing. My mother did stunts. My uncles do stunts. One of my brothers is a stunt rigger. My sister did makeup. My father, in case you're wondering, is in trucking. How old were you when you learned to ride?"

"Eight. Or maybe nine."

Downstairs her phone began to ring.

"Pony or horse?" The machine beeped, and someone with a deep voice started leaving a message.

I thought about it. "Pony, I suppose."

"You suppose? What was his, or her, name?"

"I haven't a clue." The voice stopped and the phone machine beeped again.

"You must remember. That moment when . . . You really don't remember?"

"I don't really remember learning things." I cast my mind back to being a girl, nine, on a pony on the moors; twelve, my mother and the WAR study; a year or so later in Yorkshire's West Riding, a horse. "Judy," I said. "One of my horses was called Judy. When I was twelve or thirteen. She was a hunter. Fifteen hands. Her mane was very pale. A bit like yours." I ran my hands through her hair. "Yours feels better." I pushed it away from the back of her neck, which I kissed, then some more, and swung my leg over her so that now I sat in the small of her back, like a soft saddle.

"Um," she said. I reached around and took a plump breast in each hand. She groaned and began to move.

LATER, she said, "Let's eat pizza."

When she went downstairs to find the number, I wrapped myself in a sheet and stood by the window. Eastwards, the radio towers on Queen Anne Hill blinked with red navigation lights. I heard her taped voice in the background, then the beep and deep voice of the replayed message. The sun was setting on the other side of the house, drenching the western slope. The stairs creaked as she came back up.

"You're doing that noble statue thing again," she said. She wrapped her arms around me from behind, rested her head between my shoulder blades. "What's so interesting?"

I nodded at the hill, at the sunset reflecting from the windows on Queen Anne in the growing dusk. "They look like campfires. Like an army camped in the hills above Troy."

Her arms were tight. We stood there a long time. I wondered who had left the message.

Eventually, she stirred. "Get dressed," she said. "It turns out I have an early appointment tomorrow, so I'm going to kick you out after we've had pizza." She smiled, but it was brief and distracted. "We'll do something tomorrow."

"Good."

"But I don't know my schedule. I'll call you."

LESSON 9

APRIL. OUTSIDE, NUTHATCHES SANG AND AZALEAS BLAZED ON EVERY LAWN. INSIDE, WE all sat on the scratchy blue carpet that smelled less new now, and ten women stared at their copy of the list of general pointers, specific dos and don'ts and miscellaneous hints I'd given them the week before Lake Lanier.

I knew the list. I looked at the women. We'd had a week of solid sunshine since I'd seen them in their bathing suits. A few—Suze, Therese, Nina—were showing the first hint of the gilding common to middle-class Atlanta white women in summer. Many were in short sleeves. Sandra wore short sleeves for the first time, too; things must be going through one of those periodic honeymoon periods at home. She felt me looking at her—she had the sensitivity of a prey animal—and looked back. Her eyes did that brilliant shining thing, trying to share some message that couldn't be put into words, and I made a mental note to visit Diane at the Domestic Abuse Alliance sometime in the next couple of weeks and chat. From my early days in uniform I knew that simply asking Sandra would send her scuttering back into her burrow, but whatever she was trying to tell me was getting more urgent.

"I'd like to say a word about appropriate clothing. This carpet will take the skin off your knees and elbows when you fall. Soon we'll be trying out some moves where you will be making contact with the floor. From now on I'd advise long sleeves and long pants. Also, from next week, I'd like us all to be working in bare feet."

Those who worried about their feet would now have a week to take care of them before exposing them to the world. "Before we set the papers aside, are there any questions?" Shuffling of papers. Silence. Two months ago I would have said the list was entirely self-explanatory, but I had learnt that silence was a bad sign. "Page one, then. The first principle: See them before they see you. Remember the gunfighter metaphor. The Kroger exercise."

"Don't stand and blink in the light," Jennifer said, fast and loud, in a star pupil voice.

"Yes," I said. "Don't draw attention until you know what's going on. It's one of the most important maxims on the list. It's connected to many of the simple dos and don'ts on page two." Flip, flip of pages. "Take the corner wide. Never get in your car without looking. Don't walk by large shrubberies—"

"Don't walk under an overpass!" Jennifer said.

"Yeah, jeez," Pauletta said, momentarily forgetting her list. "There's this overpass right by my mother's that I park near and walk under every day. And these big-ass bushes along the sidewalk. But then I read this thing and got to thinking."

I nodded. "In England in the early eighties, the Yorkshire Ripper used to stand against a corner wall—or on an overpass—and when women walked past, he'd bash them on the head with a paving stone." It was something I'd never been able to drill into my rookies those years Denneny had asked me to supplement their academy training: when you blow into a building expecting trouble, gun out, don't forget to look up. "Always look," I said. "Not looking never saved anyone. Don't look at the ground while you walk."

"And in a public place sit with your back to a wall and facing the door." Tonya.

"Or facing the majority of the room," I said. "It depends. For example, if it's a place where people come and go and tend not to stay long—a coffee shop, a laundromat—you would face the door. If it's a restaurant or bar or club where people may be for several hours, you would face the majority of the room."

"And," Tonya said slowly, "I guess you could even maybe say that's kind of connected to the information thing, on page four."

"It is. But maybe you'd like to explain that to the rest of the class."

"I don't know, exactly. So, okay, someone can walk into a bar all smiley and nice and then after four hours of Jim or Johnnie they get mean as a junkyard dog. So what you see at one point, the information you've got, isn't the information you get later. Information . . . changes."

That was a subtle realization, one I hadn't bothered to set down. Tonya was beginning to connect the dots.

"Huh," said Suze. "Information changes. Okay. But I like this list of practical stuff, at the end."

That was the miscellany that didn't fit anywhere else.

"Don't hit bone with bone. Be the hammer, not the nail." She made a swinging-mallet gesture. "I seriously dig that." She turned back one page. "And I like these, too, these general sorts of . . . These Zen-type things. Like, you don't have to be nice, you don't have to be polite."

"Oh, like you ever are," Pauletta said.

"Shut up." Suze pointed about halfway down the page. "If someone abuses you, make them stop. If you're inside their reach, that means they're inside yours. If they want one hand, give them both. But I like the last page best. The simple stuff, where you just tell us what to do." She turned to it. "Protect your neck. Don't kick higher than the knee if they're still standing. Yell fire, not help." She looked up. "But I kind of don't get some of those completely."

"Or at all?" Pauletta said.

"Then I'll explain," I said. "Lists down. Everyone stand. Tonya, Kim, Katherine, help me with the mats." We carried the four big mats from their place against the wall and to the middle of the floor. "First, I'll demonstrate why you should never kick higher than your own knee." I gestured for Suze to join me in the center. "Come here and try kick me in the stomach."

She stood about eight feet away. "You remember I play soccer, right?"

"Yes." I patted my stomach.

"Just don't sue me."

She did that semi-skip followed by a short run-up that all soccer players do, and launched her right foot squarely and at speed for my diaphragm.

I stepped back, caught her ankle and jerked—though slowly enough that she understood she was going down and could take precautions. She thumped back on the mats hard. I gave her a hand up. She stretched cautiously. "They don't do that on the field."

"No." I turned to the class. "Even for a trained soccer player, kicks are slow and the direction and target are obvious. Your attacker has plenty of time to get out of the way and take countermeasures. Kicking high will unbalance you. So if you decide to go for a kick, and your attacker is standing, aim for the knees, shins, instep, Achilles tendon. If your attacker is on the ground, go for the spine or head."

"Not the nuts?" Tonya.

"Most men are supremely conscious of their testicles. It's a strike they expect—unless you're already down and they're standing, or unless you're already in their arms. Suze, you up for more demonstrations?"

"Sure."

"Stand there, as though you'd just knocked me to the ground." I knelt before her in an approximation of a woman clubbed to her knees. "From here, you'd go for the genitals with the forearm swing." I made a fist and swung my whole arm through a vicious arc between Suze's legs, pulling the blow at the last second. "That's a strike that's difficult to defend against. Most men, when they see a woman on her knees, don't expect it."

"Wonder why," Nina said.

I unfolded and stood. "Next we'll look at what I mean by, 'If they want one hand, give them both.' Suze, grab my wrist. Tug a little, as though you're trying to drag me off somewhere." I resisted for a split second, just long enough to get her to pull harder, then moved straight at her, aiming a slow-motion palm strike at her nose with my free hand.

"They want my left wrist so badly, I'll be generous and throw this one in for free."

" 'If they want one hand, give them both,' " Suze said to herself, and nodded. She grinned. "I like that."

"It's unexpected, which comes under an item on page two: use their expectations against them. Suze, wrap your arms around me from the front. Good. Now, watch. See how I'm sliding my right leg back about a foot. I'm taking my weight on the left foot and moving my center of gravity just a few inches away from my attacker, who then has to follow. I'm using the attacker's expectations against him."

"His balance," Tonya said, "right?"

"Yes."

Tonya, face lighting with understanding, said, "I get it."

"I don't," Kim said.

Tonya would explode if she couldn't talk, so I nodded for her to go ahead.

"Look, see how he, she—Suze. See how Suze thinks Aud's pulling away, and how Suze starts tipping off balance. So Aud could strike Suze now, while she's off balance. But she didn't, and now Suze is reacting by pulling back harder. And the legs are opening, too." She looked at me. "That's what you were waiting for, right?"

"Yes." She was beginning to see patterns, learning how to think. "First of all, Suze had to widen her stance, which means opening her legs. Now she is yanking me towards her, so any strike I make at this point is helped along by the momentum of my attacker. So here is where I would strike up and forward with my right knee. Suze, step aside a moment."

She did.

"Imagine he's got me, arms around my chest or shoulders. Now I wrap my arms around his waist, too, and drive my knee between his conveniently open legs."

I demonstrated, pulling down hard and fast with my arms, and snapping my knee up.

"Voilà," said Nina. "Balls for earrings."

Katherine giggled.

"Practice it. Just the stance."

They did that for a while, with lots of grins.

"Next from the list: Protect your neck. When I threw Suze on the floor, she knew instinctively to protect her neck and head. That's what you do. If you are ever about to go down, protect your neck. If you get grabbed, protect your throat. I'll talk more about the neck and head another time, when we do falling. For now we'll focus on the throat." And I would add to that something else on the list: Where there's a joint, there's a weakness. "Christie."

She stepped onto the mat.

"No more throwing until next week," I said, to reassure her. "Someone give me a suggestion as to how Christie should grab me around the neck."

"One-handed," Sandra said, "with her other hand grabbing you by the wrist."

A very specific scenario, not one that came to mind out of thin air. The class understood this, and stirred uneasily at the implications they couldn't, or wouldn't, consciously grasp.

"Christie?"

She was left-handed, so I lifted my left wrist for her right hand to grab, and lifted my chin for her left. Her hands were cold with nerves, and her grip tentative. Perhaps these women would never feel confident.

"See how I tuck my chin down," I said, my voice deep as vocal folds stretched over my larynx. "It's the first thing you do. Protect your throat. Now, Christie, tighten your grip around my wrist without gripping too hard on my throat." She tightened obediently. "What should I do?" I asked the class.

"Knee to the groin?" Jennifer said.

"Kick him on the shin," Katherine said.

"Good," I said. "Lots of nerves on the shin. Good distraction." I still remembered the pain of a kick I'd received on my shin from a fellow beginner in karate. I'd ended up in Accident & Emergency, thinking my bone was broken. X-rays had shown extensive bone bruising. I'd limped for months. "Now we tackle the stranglehold. How?"

Blank looks.

"Where there's a joint, there's a weakness. Watch." I reached up with my free hand and peeled away Christie's left little finger, bending it back, until she let go. "Even the biggest attackers have little fingers." I gestured for Christie to renew her stranglehold. "There's also her wrist."

"Wait," said Pauletta. "I can't remember all these details."

"Then don't. But we can forget the wrist for now. The best thing to do in this situation is focus on the elbow."

"The elbow." She looked rebellious. She wasn't the only one.

"Yes," I said with blithe cheer. "If your attacker's arm is straight out, like this, then a move very similar to the one we learnt last week would be appropriate: a twist and forearm slam. In this instance, on the outside of the arm." I demonstrated in slow motion. "Try it."

Southern women can't resist cheer. They gave it a go.

I went down the line. Jennifer hadn't remembered to strike with the outside of her forearm. I reminded her. Therese was managing a little less neatly than usual. Tonya was frowning with concentration and muttering to herself. Sandra was red-faced.

"Remember to breathe." I gestured her aside and took her place. Katherine draped her limp hand around my throat. "Like this. Tuck the chin, kick the shin, twist, noise with the slam."

"Chin, shin, twist, and hiss," Pauletta said to Nina, next to us.

"Or maybe chin, shin, slam with a blam." Nina liked blam.

I wondered what it had been like to be my mother and patiently teach me to tie my shoes, hold a knife and fork. Kind but stern. I plowed on. "Now, if the arm is bent, like Nina's, Pauletta might want to come up inside the bent joint, up the center line of your attacker's body, and then out across the joint with the forearm." I demonstrated. "Practice that."

I walked the line again, this time showing them how to pivot in the opposite direction.

"Chin down. Down," I said to Nina.

The only one who seemed to be getting this up-inside-the-guard, outwards strike was Sandra. It disturbed me, though I couldn't put my finger on why.

"Good," I said. "There's a fourth possible response to this one, which involves—"

"Whoa," Pauletta said. "Overkill. Seriously. Just tell us the best one."

"There is no best one," I said. "That's the point. I'll explain later."

Stubborn silence.

I ignored it. "This last technique is a trapping move. Take your free arm and point your hand at the ceiling." Five women hesitated, then pointed halfheartedly. "Point hard. Stretch for the ceiling. No," I said to Jennifer. "Without going up onto your toes. You need to maintain your balance. Keep your legs very slightly bent—as the list says. Always keep your knees slightly bent. It aids balance, and reduces reaction time. Keep your weight over your feet—Kim, pull that knee back a bit until it's over your foot. Good. Now stretch up, up, that's right, Therese, good, without lifting your chin—keep protecting your throat—"

"Jesus," Pauletta muttered.

"—point, point, then pivot inwards and swing the whole arm scything down, also inwards . . . No, move the arm as a unit, the whole thing." I demonstrated again. "Pivot, breathe out, a loud out breath, as you swing your arm down, and you trap the strangling arm under your armpit. Then you can whip your elbow back into his face when you pivot the other way, by which time—"

"Nope," she said. "Too much to remember."

"Just try it."

"Besides, how will I remember what to do when he's strangling the life out of me?"

"Just try it," I said again.

She lowered her head, like Luz preparing to get really stubborn. Good practice for my visit out to Arkansas next month.

"All right. Try the other things I've already shown you."

"I can't remember them."

"You can remember one, I bet. The little finger."

She nodded grudgingly.

"Practice that one, then. Everyone else, give the pointing a try, then run through each of the other techniques, once each, then swap partners, then come and sit down."

I went around the circle giving pointers, and then sat as the first few did. Christie and Suze were the last; Christie patiently kept showing Suze how to do the trapping move. As soon as Suze got it halfway right, I clapped and gestured them into the seated circle.

"Some of you think that the things I'm showing you won't work in the real world. Some of you think I'm throwing too many things at you at once and want me to show you just one thing for each situation, to show you the best. But there is no best. There are literally hundreds of moves I could show you for each situation—"

"Not helpful," Pauletta said.

"Shut up," Suze said. Tonya and Nina nodded. Pauletta shut up.

"—in a stranglehold situation, all of them would involve protecting your throat, distracting your attacker, and aiming at a weak point. Today I chose joints."

Jennifer bit her lip, trying to remember everything.

"There is no best technique. There's only what's best for you. Remember the first lesson? Katherine." She came to attention with a jerk. "Remember how you didn't like punching but thought kicking was all right?" She nodded. "I've been showing you several ways to deal with every situation and, no, of course you don't need to know them all. But you do need to try them all. I'm showing you so many so that you get some notion of patterns—chin, shin, twist, hiss, as Pauletta would say—but then also you get to find what fits your particular body type and emotional response. For example, my favorite strike is the back fist." I showed them, the sharp, uncoiling, snakelike back-of-the-knuckle strike that came as naturally to me as turning my face to the sun. "It's not as powerful as many other strikes. I could tell you it's a perfect, always-retain-your-balance strike, how it's unreadable until you do it, how it's hard for your opponent to catch or trap, and that's all true, but the real reason is that, to me, it just feels good."

Funktionslust, the handy German word for enjoying what you do well.

"I showed you four ways to deal with a one-handed front strangle, and you'll have found that one of those techniques feels better to you than any of the others. Jennifer"—she straightened—"liked the little-finger move. And Christie was good with the arm trap. Therese also liked the little-finger, but Suze preferred hitting the outside elbow. Sandra, on the other hand, liked coming up inside the elbow. The rest of you probably need to practice all four a few more times until you find the one that works best, the one that will spring instantly to mind if someone wraps his or her hand around your neck."

Tonya and Christie both touched their necks.

"I could show you two dozen variations on how to deal with a stranglehold—"

"Which is your favorite?" Christie said.

Information is power. But I'd started this.

"The trap, followed by an elbow drive to their nose or throat."

"How come?"

"Because it works on a front or back strangle, one- or two-handed. It's flexible, adaptable. But also . . . because being strangled is personal." I had a sudden image of Sandra, coming up inside the strangle of a shadowy figure, with that upward strike, putting her face close to her strangler's. "The pin traps them instantly, so they feel how I just felt." *Me,* the imaginary Sandra said. *See the face of the one you would hurt. The one who is fighting back. I am real.* "The elbow strike is a very strong blow. It says, you can never do that to me again."

Sandra paled and her pupils expanded briefly. Fear, lust, hatred? I couldn't tell.

I tried to remember what I was saying. "No one knows everything. You don't have to. In these weeks I want you to learn one or two things thoroughly, your own things, not mine. Things that you will practice until they are muscle memory, until someone can touch your throat, even by mistake, and your muscles know instantly what to do. No," I said, as Katherine opened her mouth, "it doesn't mean you'll be attacking your hairstylist by mistake if she touches your neck. It means you'll know how when you need it, that's all."

Kim flicked her nails and Suze frowned.

"It's like mathematics."

"Oh, that's just great," Pauletta said.

"Yeah," Suze said. "Math sucks the big fat one."

"No. It's part of how you think. It's automatic. You use arithmetic every day. How many are there of us sitting here? It's second nature. But do you remember how hard it was when you started in . . ." For a moment my brain stumbled trying to convert to the American educational system ". . . in kindergarten or first grade? Self-defense is like that. You don't need to learn astral physics, you don't need non-Euclidean geometry, you just need arithmetic."

"Or a calculator," Nina said.

"How many of you need a calculator when you're in the supermarket? You look at the prices on the meat counter. You know whether you can afford steak or if you have to get hamburger. You know it without laborious calculation, because arithmetic is second nature. Now, on your feet."

Moans and groans. But they all stood up.

"Partner with someone different. Try all four strangle breaks. Pick your favorite. Practice that three times, swap roles. Fifteen minutes."

I walked around the practice circle, reminding them about a tucked chin here, an elbow placement there. They were learning. Some, like Therese, were sucking up every physical technique I could throw at her. Some, like Tonya, were beginning to seriously connect the dots, but even those like Jennifer and Pauletta, who thought they knew nothing, were light-years past the place they had been two months ago.

I walked the circle again. Everyone now had their favorite. Six of them liked the little-finger. It didn't surprise me. It was a small move, a woman's move, one for which no judge or police officer or spouse would ever blame or fear them if they had to use it against the bogeyman.

After fifteen minutes, we were all sitting again.

"We'll finish with an item from the list. The last page. Yell fire, not help or rape. Studies have shown that bystanders, neighbors, are far more willing to call for help if they don't think there's malice involved. Fire is a natural disaster. They won't feel as though they're 'interfering' in a domestic dispute if you yell for them to call nine-one-one. Next: be specific. People in groups default to the lowest common denominator."

"More math!" Nina said, and they all groaned.

When I was ten, Mrs. Russell, the equivalent of my fourth-grade teacher, had marched to the blackboard and written, in very large letters, *The square on the hypotenuse equals the sum of the opposite squares,* then put the chalk back on the lip of the blackboard and waited. No one said anything. After about two minutes of silence, an eternity in the world of ten-year-olds, she said, "Does anyone know what that means?" We were used to Mrs. Russell being kindly and approachable, adapting her explanations to the meanest understanding, but that day she was terrifying. Perhaps she'd had a hard day, perhaps she'd been inspired by some new teaching theory to try an experiment. None of us dared say anything. "Your job," she said, "is to find out what that means."

I had responded by writing the sentence carefully in my blue-lined note-

book, *The square on the hypotenuse* . . . and then staring at it, as though by focusing my mind I could get beneath the atoms of the paper surface—I had recently encountered the notion of atoms—and swim lusciously in the flow of
understanding beneath. But all that eventuated was a headache.

In retrospect, it was clear that Mrs. Russell had wanted to shock us into a
state of inquiry, to lead us to the idea of looking things up: to open a diction-
ary, look up *hypotenuse,* ask her what "sum of" meant, something, anything,
but to just begin, to demonstrate that one of us had a particle of scholar in our
blood, that her life had not been a total waste.

Mrs. Russell had been disappointed that day.

"Crowds," I said. "Think of soccer hooligans, religious mobs, people gawp-
ing at car accidents. No one does anything. Why?"

Therese folded her arms. She never liked it when I pointed out unpleasant
human traits.

"Groups of people need leaders. It's a human response; most of us immediately want someone else to take responsibility, particularly in a new or
frightening situation. So if you ever get knocked to the ground, or are in a car
accident, and a crowd gathers and stares at you moon-faced, you're going to
have to direct them. You don't say, 'Someone, get help,' you say, 'You—yes,
you—in the red shirt, call nine-one-one, and you, in the blue shoes—yes,
ma'am, you with the barrette—please bring me a blanket.' You pick specific
people and give them specific tasks. You'll find that once the crowd stirs to help,
others will work out what to do on their own initiative. But don't discount that
initial inertia."

"You're saying treat them like children?" Kim said. "Jimmie, carry those
dishes to the sink; Junie, wipe the table. Like that?"

"Yes."

"That I can do," she said.

For the first time this week, nods all round. "Good. What else? Nothing?" We
had five minutes left. "Stand up. We'll work a bit more with joint locks." They
got up one by one. I realized it was warm. I went to the air-conditioning unit
jammed high in the outside wall and thumped the plug. The fan started to turn
reluctantly. "Joint locks are most—"

"The thing on the list I don't understand," Sandra said, still sitting, "is the
one that says, 'If they abuse you, make them stop.'"

Everyone turned to listen.

"And you say, 'There is always a choice of some kind, always.' Are you saying anyone who gets hurt is making a choice, that it's our fault?"

The air-conditioning now burst into a slow clatter that quickened as the motor warmed.

" 'If someone abuses you, make them stop' is the heart of self-defense." Hypotenuse, square, sum. They weren't going to get it in one gulp. "Let's break it down."

Suze sighed out loud.

"First of all, by 'someone' I mean anyone, everyone: parent, child, friend, relative, spouse, partner, boss, priest, police officer, stranger, casual acquaintance, member of Congress, the queen. Everyone. Anyone. Abuse means the trespassing on our basic rights as human beings. Make them stop means to leave, tell them to stop, or fight. Whichever is the most efficient."

"Are we talking basic assertiveness-training stuff here?" Nina said, crossing her legs so that her right foot rested sole up on her left thigh. I was always surprised by her hip flexibility. She moved so stiffly in other ways. "You know, you have the right to your own feeling and moods, you have the right to make mistakes, you have the right to change your mind. Blah, blah, blah."

"Yes." Assertiveness training. I'd have to look that up. "Anyone else familiar with it?"

Therese, Tonya, and Katherine nodded. Suze made a noise like a horse clearing its nose, and Christie said, "I've never even heard of it."

Nina laughed. "It's a second-wave thing, honey. Your momma might know. Or maybe your grandmomma. There are seven basics." She looked at me. I gestured for her to continue. "The three I already said, plus you have the right to say no without explaining, you have the right to go where you want—when, with whom, and wearing whatever—you want. You have the right to refuse responsibility for others—unless it's your child, of course—and we have the right to act without the approval of others. That last one is tricky. It'll screw you every time, least until you hit fifty." She sounded cheerful about it.

"Much of this is tied together," I said. "For example, one, having the right to wear what you want, even just a thong and stilettos, and go wherever you want, whenever you want, such as a roadside bar at one in the morning, and, two, having the right to make mistakes."

Half the class laughed.

"Think of it this way," I said to the other half. "If a richly dressed man walks through a high-crime area late at night with his wallet sticking out of his pocket, is he to blame if he is mugged?"

"Oh," said Jennifer, "I get it, I get it."

"The woman in the thong and the man with the wallet would be stupid, making a grave error in judgment, but still the ultimate wrongdoer would be the perpetrator. If you make a mistake—with the clothes or the wallet—it doesn't mean you asked for it. Or deserve it. You have the right to make the perpetrator stop if they attempt to abuse you."

Sandra was sitting very still, very erect. "But sometimes the other person is bigger and faster and stronger."

"Yes."

"So sometimes we don't have a choice."

"No. We always have a choice of some kind, just not always the choices we would like."

Her smile was light, whipped cream over old and bitter coffee. "The 'die whimpering or with your head held high' kind of choice?"

"Usually there are lots of branches on the decision tree before you get to that point."

"But not always."

I studied her. This was the Sandra who wanted to break from her cage and run wild and free across the moonlit meadow—but knew, as she knew the sun rose in the east and set in the west, that a hunter would rise from the brush and shoot her.

"No," I said, "not always."

TEN

AT EIGHT-THIRTY THE NEXT MORNING I WAS SITTING AT THE BEVELED-GLASS DINING table in my suite, before a brand-new laptop. It was downloading Corning's entire desktop. I'd gone online with the brand-new, empty machine and input her user name and password at the Carbonite website, and answered her security question. It had taken me five minutes on the Web to find out she had attended Lincoln High School.

Once I'd downloaded the software, I hit restore files, and now the hard drive was chattering. The download-in-progress bar read 73 percent. By the time I finished my breakfast, I'd be able to peruse the whole at my leisure.

I finished the last of my grapefruit and started on the spicy sausage, leaning back as I chewed, staring at the dirty grey sky—like foam on boiling lentils, rent here and there by the wind and gaping bright blue. The download bar read 89 percent complete. I poured myself tea.

As I was sipping, wondering what Kick's early appointment was, Anton Finkel called.

"Not too early?" he said. His voice was thin with speakerphone echo.

"Yes," I said. Ninety percent complete.

"What? Hello? Did you hear what she said, Stan?"

"I'm here," I said. I closed the laptop. "What can I do for you?"

"First of all I'd like to apologize for getting distracted yesterday—"

"Not a problem."

"I was—"

"Not a problem." The window flickered on the edge of my vision. Rain. "Did you get your safety-equipment issues sorted?"

"We did, indeed," said Finkel, sounding jovial and beefy, utterly unlike his personal physical presence. This was how he wanted to be regarded, I realized: one of the boys, worldly, in charge. He was still talking, ". . . matter, easily resolved. But you don't want to involve yourself in our petty details. I am calling"—I wondered what had happened to *we*—"to assure you that from now on there will be no interruptions in our lease-payment schedule."

"I see."

"Excellent," Finkel said. "Though I did want to raise the matter of your . . . generosity so far."

"Go on."

"It was most kind of you to step in on the medical payments front. I'm sure all the crew appreciate it."

"I sincerely hope the crew knows nothing of it."

"Of course, of course. Confidentiality. I understand. However, I was wondering how you'd feel about putting things on a more formal footing."

I didn't say anything. Rusen cleared his throat.

"It's a worthwhile project," he said. "You've seen the script."

"I haven't read it."

"Oh. Well, you've seen how hard everyone is working."

"Yes."

"Then you understand, Ms. Torvingen," Finkel again, "when I say this is a once-in-a-lifetime opportunity to make a real difference."

"Is that right?"

"Anton, let me talk. Ms. Torvingen, Aud, you've been a great help. As much in the giving advice and just listening and being patient as anything, and we really appreciate that. But we've come to a . . . to a fork in the road, a time of decision, which . . . Boy, I don't know how to say this but to just say it. We've burned through our cash. We've taken every measure imaginable, and some I couldn't have imagined four weeks ago, and we still have a few crucial scenes and a boatload of post-production. I believe in this project. I think you understand what we're trying to do. I believe we can do it, if we have fresh investment. I've heard that you might be in a position to help us out. Now, I wouldn't want to lie to you, investment in the movie business is risky, but, well, this could be a good thing for everybody."

"So you're saying you would like me to write you a check so that you can be sure to pay me my rent on time."

Silence. "Yes, I guess. It sure sounds silly when you put it that way. I'm so sorry if we offended you in any way, and of course—"

"I'll take it under advisement."

". . . top priority as our landlord. You'll what?"

"I'll think about it." The sun slid out again, making the rain-spattered window glitter and sparkle. I began to see a fairground: painted horses and Ferris wheels . . . I blinked it away. "Meanwhile, I've been meaning to talk to you about security for the set. That security guard. You should fire him."

"I'm not sure—"

"I'll find someone more suitable." Sticking a pin in the yellow pages would probably yield a better candidate. I thought of the man who had followed me the other day. "Fire him. I'll have someone there this afternoon. And, Rusen."

"Yes?"

"Your lease depends on talking to OSHA. So talk to them. Before you do, ensure that the paperwork of the young employee we discussed the other day is in order." I didn't want to remind Finkel of his dead son through discussion of the living one. "Four o'clock is good for me." And maybe Kick would be there. I thought about calling her, but decided to wait. She'd said she'd call me.

I put the phone down and reopened the laptop. Download complete. I now had a mirror of Corning's desktop.

Follow the money. I opened her password file in one window, and then scanned her browser bookmarks. There it was, Capital One Visa. I smiled, and scrolled through her passwords. Under COVisa was Richbitch and covisaword001. I entered the information and logged in to her account.

It was a platinum card linked to frequent-flyer miles. She used it for everything, from buying lattes to paying for dry cleaning to her parking. And there, front and center, was a payment, dated yesterday, to Hilton Hotels. I opened a search box. There were Hiltons in Bellevue and by the airport. Immediately following the hotel payment was one for Tiffany's, in Bell Square. Easy. Corning was at the Bellevue Hilton.

In another day or so she would be nicely fear-marinated.

I minimized the Visa account window, then searched for and opened her correspondence files. I found myself humming. This was a rich vein: offers to owners of property adjacent to mine. Letters to and from her attorney about loans and collateral and some complicated tax maneuver. Nothing to or from Bingley. With luck, that wouldn't matter.

There was too much here to absorb in one session.

I leaned back in my chair again and pondered the question of security for the warehouse.

I had spotted the man trailing me on the seventeenth. I maximized the Visa account window and searched debits between the fourteenth and twentieth. Most of them were easy enough to identify: QFC, a wine merchant, a drugstore, an M.D., Chevron . . . There were three I couldn't initially place: Leith, Bankersen, and Heshowitz; Turtledove; and Sandewski's. Then I recognized the first as the law office I had called when looking for the identities of JB and ETH. Turtledove sounded like a place that sold flowers and chocolates.

I dragged out the white pages and leafed through the end section, found Sandewski's. Dialed.

"Erotic Bakery," a pleasant female voice said.

After a moment I said, "Is this Sandewski's?"

"Yes. Sandewski's Erotic Bakery. Do you want to place an order?"

"No. Thank you."

An erotic bakery? I had an unpleasant image of Corning opening wide to bite a pink, phallus-shaped cake. The imagination is like a plasma screen: pictures burn in too easily.

I tried to think of pink elephants, which led to worse pictures.

I leafed forward a few pages. *Turtledove, D. H. and P. T., Discreet. Direct. Determined. Est. 1991.* They were in Fremont, less than a mile from Hardy's offices.

IT WAS a storefront place. Tasteful grey carpet; comfy chairs; potted plant; Formica countertop, which, not coincidentally, was chest height: too high for most people to vault over easily.

A lean, relaxed-looking man in his early forties looked up when I walked in. He knew me instantly. He stood, then carefully, consciously shrugged the tension from his shoulders.

"Turtledove," I said. "D. H. or P. T.?"

"D. H.," he said. "Deverell. Philippa is my wife."

"You know who I am."

"Yes."

His hair was very dark brown, trimmed in a close, stylish cut and stippled with grey around the temples. I couldn't see his hands but from his stance he was simply waiting. His shirt was a deep plum linen. "I have a job for you. If you're available. May I step into your office to discuss it?"

"You understand I can't divulge information about a former client?"

Former. "I understand."

"Okay." He stepped to the counter, unlatched something, lifted the top, and motioned me through. The inner face of the partition was quilted. I nodded at it. "Personal protection?"

"Kevlar. Enough to stop anything that leaves the muzzle under a thousand feet per second. Not proof against gas, earthquakes, biological agents, or anything more than a handgun."

"Every little bit," I said. We nodded approvingly at each other.

GARY WAS once again hovering by the door. His shirt shone distractingly white and stiff. Obviously I was getting too used to the Seattle Eddie Bauer/REI dress code. His lips were bright red from biting at them. He ushered me into Corning's office, where he had coffee waiting, with a bottle of iced water for good measure, a brand-new yellow legal pad, and three different pens laid out carefully in the middle of the desk. He hesitated, unsure at which side to sit.

I took the customer side. Looking scared but determined, he took the other.

"I need you to negotiate some deals for me."

Now he looked terrified, but he gamely picked up a pen, the red one, and nodded.

"The federal government will soon be selling the plot of land adjacent to mine. Assuming that in the few days she's been out of the office the deals she was negotiating with the owners of the two plots north of mine have not closed, I want to buy those, quietly, from the owners." I had no idea what I'd do with it. I just wanted to make sure no one else could destroy it while I decided.

"But that's . . . We're talking two, two and a half million dollars at least."

"Double it and you'll still be off the mark." At least according to Corning's correspondence. "I'll authorize up to eight million. Are you up to it?"

He nodded and wrote *$8,000,000* carefully in red ink on the pad. His flush was now a waxy pallor.

"A tip," I said. He looked up. His eyes were the same soft brown as those of the security guard who probably had been fired by now. "If we're going to do business, you'll need to learn a shorthand way to write 'million.'"

He stared at the rows of naughts. Just as the waxy look began to go pink again, as he began to understand what his percentage of eight million might look like, I said, "Of course, as you're not fully qualified, I think a reduced commission is in order. Say forty percent of the customary amount. And we'll have to work more closely than usual with a reputable real estate lawyer. Your usual attorney is Leith, Bankersen, and Heshowitz, yes? When we're finished here, get me the direct line of whichever partner Corning usually deals with." Madison Leith. "I assume that you're free the rest of the week, and available for appointments?" He nodded so violently that I thought his teeth would fly out.

We talked it over for a while. Corning's data was useful but it would take time to go through it, and it was no substitute for personal knowledge. I didn't know the right palms to grease for a project this size, what was customary. "I want you to set up the kind of lunches, or dinners, or drinks Corning would have organized."

"Breakfasts and lunches, mostly. I can do that."

"And, let's see, yes, set up something with Bingley."

"The zoning board staffer?"

"The very one."

"May I ask in reference to what?"

I smiled. "He's been a bad boy. I'm going to have a little chat."

"He's . . . ? Oh. Did Ms. Corning make improper, did she—"

"Bribe him? I believe so."

He looked fascinated and unwell at the same time. This was heady stuff.

"Just tell him I have a delicate matter to discuss. Be brisk, impersonal. We have no proof, and I don't want him scared." If I got Corning's testimony, I wouldn't need Bingley's, but there was no harm pursuing the matter from every angle until I was sure.

We talked about money.

"If you can show a guarantee of a secured investment already in place for the financing," he said, "it might give you the winning hand."

"I don't need financing."

"But . . ." He stared harder at his red naughts.

"What's the customary escrow arrangement?"

"Earnest money is anywhere from five percent to twenty percent, depending. On, hmmn, eight million, that would be, say, point eight million in bank guarantees, with, say, eighty thousand in actual money."

Actual money. It was hard to say whether he meant it to sound exotic or déclassé. "Feel free to tell them they would get their point eight in actual money if we sign the deal within ten days. And the balance, in cash or equivalents, on closing." Laurence would just have to figure it out.

Gary was paling again.

"I'm going to leave you to think things over. In an hour or so I want you to call me and tell me honestly whether you think you can do this. If you can't, I want you to suggest someone you'd like to work with, and I'll make sure you get a nice consideration for all your help. It'll be good experience and no one will think any less of you."

"I can do it."

"Take some time."

"No. I can. I think. I mean, I can. Definitely. If I can work with an attorney. With Ms. Corning I set up all the preliminary arrangements, and sat in on a lot of meetings." He blushed again. His capillaries were certainly getting a workout. "The hard part will be, well, it'll be having people take me seriously. I'm young, you see."

I nodded gravely.

"So I'll need lots of proof of your intent, and ability to do as you promise."

"And what do you think is the best way to do that?"

"Well"—he doodled in the margin—"you could transfer a hunk of cash into the bank Ms. Corning usually uses. Set up an account. All those guys know each other. They'll make phone calls. Gossip."

"All right," I said. "Set up an appointment for me with the right person at that bank, and pick another bank, too, that you think would be good."

"Which one?"

"I don't know the banks in Seattle. That's why I'm asking you."

It started to dawn on him that to earn his commission meant making decisions, taking responsibility, running risk. I stood. I wanted to think about happier things than risk. "Think it over. Make those appointments. Call me. Oh, and, Gary, where would I go to buy a wedding present? A nice wedding present."

"Nordstrom," he said. "I'll give you directions."

NORDSTROM STRETCHED along Pine Street between Fifth and Sixth Avenues. It was huge. Inside the door, I paused. Shoes, handbags, scarves. I identified the elevators and stairwells. The center of the store was a vast, atrium-like space, lit from above, designed for customers to float down from floor to floor. The Gift Gallery was on the fourth floor.

I wandered around the blown glass, the pottery, the tasteful metal wall sculpture and wondered what one bought for a mother and new stepfather. Something for their official residence? I didn't know where they were spending their time, or what their rooms might look like. Cartoons on the wall? Sixteenth-century Dutch oils? French furniture in the aesthetic style? Julia would have known what to buy. I had no idea whether Kick would.

I paused by a tapestry cushion. The colors were luxuriant: gold and crimson and moss, sapphire and ruby. A young woman in flawless makeup, her hands clasped carefully in front of her, nodded and smiled warmly at me, but was smart enough to wait for me to raise my eyebrows before approaching.

We discussed the philosophy of wedding presents. "Something timeless," she said, and I was about to sigh at the platitude, when she smiled again. "An object that will last at least as long as a lifetime, and look as beautiful in ninety years as it does today." Nothing fashionable, she said. Nothing perishable. "Perhaps if you give me some information about the couple you're buying for, and your budget?"

"It's for my mother." Whom I had no idea how to describe in two sentences or less. "And there is no budget."

She nodded, as though that were usual, and suggested that she might know just the thing, if I would follow her?

Just the thing turned out to be a beautiful, fat-bellied incised black-on-black San Ildefonso bowl by Maria Martinez. Early twentieth century. It was valuable, and breakable, but she took it out of the glass case and handed it to me without apparent hesitation. It was heavy and cold and very smooth. I wrapped both hands around it, and hefted it.

It was simple, almost plain, but fascinating in the way all good art is. Casual elegance. And, as she might say, black goes with everything.

"I'll take it," I said.

Carefully boxed bowl under one arm, I floated down the escalator and got off at the ground floor. I walked through the jewelry department and amused myself by trying to spot security.

In Seattle, very few people wore gold or pearls, and there were no padded shoulders or wingtips. Bizarre behavior was not necessarily a sign of mental illness. Security personnel probably had recurring nightmares about apprehending a suspected shoplifter with an awful haircut, cheap glasses, and dorky lunch-stained clothes only to find out he was a software billionaire.

In the end, she was easy to spot: neither young, like the two teenage girls giggling and trying on costume jewelry near the Sixth and Pine entrance, nor rushed, like the thirtysomething women selecting hose on their lunch hour. She was wearing a tasteful hunter green jacket and a red slash of lipstick, and despite the early lunch hour rush, managed never to stand next to a customer or meet anyone's eye.

My attention was caught by a four-strand pearl choker lying fat and snug around a dark blue velvet form. Julia had loved that particular shade of blue. Before I could stop myself, I imagined the pearls around Julia's neck, imagined fastening it there, the way the strands would move as she breathed. I rested my hand on the counter, thought I saw her face reflected next to mine in the glass, only it was a curiously two-dimensional image, and colorless. A dream, a memory.

"Ma'am? Can I help you?" A middle-aged man, smelling of cologne.

I shook my head, then changed my mind. "Do you have something similar in black pearls?"

He thought he did. He produced a key with a flourish and moved to the display case on the opposite side, but as he started to open it, I heard Kick saying, *Where the hell would I ever go to wear pearls?* "No," I said. "Don't bother. Another time."

It was a pity. The bluish-grey of black pearls would heighten the mysterious soft blue-grey of Kick's eyes. And her finely muscled neck would—

The floor rippled. With a grinding crack, the mirrored pillar by my head splintered. That, I thought, is not normal. Glass rained down in slow motion, glittering like fairy dust, or the ray of sunlight piercing a forest dell in some fantasy painting.

I put my box on the counter. Everything tilted sideways and people began flying about, like the snowflakes in a shaken snow globe. Well, I thought, I hope the bowl is well packed. Somewhere in the distance, a roar grew. Herds of bison? A train? And then I got it.

"Earthquake!" I bellowed. "Everyone out on the street." I grabbed the man behind the counter under his tailored armpits and lifted him bodily over the counter and away from the glass.

And then everything was silent and still, and a woman in a green jacket was standing too close, and there was no glass on the floor, no crack in the column.

I turned and surveyed the store. Everyone was staring at me. In the shoe department a man with one shoe on and one shoe off had grabbed his toddler and pushed her behind him protectively.

"Ma'am," the green-jacketed woman said.

My boxed bowl stood exactly where I'd put it. The jewelry clerk was white-faced and swallowing over and over. His tie was askew.

"Ma'am," Green Jacket said again. "Are you ill?"

"I'm not sure," I said. It was quiet enough to hear the teenagers in the lingerie department giggle. They were giggling at me.

"Perhaps you would like to come with me, someplace quiet, and sit for a moment."

She put her hand on my arm. I considered it. The skin between her wrist and knuckles crinkled, just beginning to get crepey. Late forties, then. Not old enough for there to be much danger of her bones being brittle from osteoporosis. A swift wrist lock wouldn't hurt her. There again, she was only doing her job. I remembered the sound of breaking bone just three weeks ago, and I hesitated. "A glass of water would be nice," I said.

"Very good. I'll have someone bring your purchase."

After two or three steps, she let go of my arm, but she kept very close. In the elevator, we stared at each other in the reflective chrome.

The office was quiet. Some people spoke. I spoke back. Everyone was very calm. "Medication," I said. "A momentary confusion." Which, in its way, was true. I apologized for any distress I might have caused. Someone brought me a paper cup of icy water. They assured me they were only concerned for my well-being. I thanked them. They insisted on calling me a taxi and then escorting me to it. The car would be perfectly safe in the parking garage, they said.

I got into the taxi, gave the driver directions. Outside the Fairmont I found I didn't want to be inside, several stories up. It might not have been a real earthquake but I still felt safer closer to the ground. I told him to wait, took the box to Bernard and asked him to send it up to my room.

I got back in the cab.

"Take me to a park."

"Looks like it might rain."

"I don't care."

"You're the boss." He pulled into traffic. "Volunteer Park. That's the place. There's a conservatory, too, in case of that rain. And there's a museum. Asian Art Museum."

"Fine," I said, wondering why that sounded so familiar.

I leaned back, took out my phone. Dialed.

Eric answered on the first ring. "Are hallucinogenic flashbacks to be expected?" I asked him.

"They are certainly within the realm of possibility."

"How can I avoid them?"

"Flashbacks are often triggered by stress. Physiological or emotional: extreme temperature, for example, or worry. Even low blood sugar. Lack of sleep, or grief. Excessive stimulus. Extraordinary physical effort. Take your pick, really. Have you had an episode?"

I ignored that. "So I could have one of these anytime?"

"No. We don't really understand how it works, but they're rare. My guess is that you're unlikely to have another. Of course, I would have said it was unlikely you'd have one in the first place." Pause. "I don't feel as though I'm being very reassuring."

"No. Is there any treatment?"

"Lead a perfectly regulated, boring existence." Silence. "Aud, what happened?"

"I thought there was an earthquake. In Nordstrom."

"Ah." Silence. "I'm sorry. Is there anything you need?"

"Thank you, no."

Another silence. Then, "You understand that, although I don't have a license to practice, I still regard our discussion as carrying the weight of doctor-patient privilege."

"Thank you. But I don't mind if you tell my mother. Unless you think she'd worry."

"She's your mother."

OUTSIDE THE museum a banner announced the new exhibit of Chinese furniture. Petra and Mike, I remembered. I wondered if they'd gone.

WE LOOKED at the Ming high-yoke-back chair and the docent shook his head again. "The owner paid almost a quarter million dollars for that one chair alone, and that was eighteen years ago. Rare as all get-out. I don't know of any others in this neck of the woods. Not of *huanghuali*. Elm, or some other soft wood, maybe."

But no softwood could ever look like this, even one lavished with care and the patina of fifteen generations of reverent handling. Its dense golden wood was simple but sensuous, with an S-shaped splat and indented yoke-back, and delicate curved arms that flowed like wooden streams. Simple, organic, precise. The joinery was seamless, yet the mortise-and-tenon construction meant it could be dismantled and reassembled without using pins or glue. It was solid and stable and undeniably real. It had the visual balance and functional elegance of a Japanese sword. I wanted it.

"It looks strong."

"Yes," he said. "As sound today as when it was made."

I nodded, and squatted, and wanted to run my fingertips along the yoke-back. It would be silky, and cool to the touch. I imagined stroking the inside curve of the left arm. Not an ounce of wood wasted. The rear legs were longer and thinner than Kick's spine, and arched as gracefully as she did when I touched her.

It had been made before Shakespeare wrote *Hamlet,* before Newton watched apples thump to the ground outside his childhood home. Its crafters had not had the benefits of modern steel blades or precision measuring tools, yet I would pick this chair above a warehouse full of Wiram furniture without thinking. This chair wasn't about thinking. It wasn't even about doing. It was about being, absolutely itself.

The bowl and the chair were simple and beautiful, form and function wholly aligned. They could be nothing other than themselves. Who was I?

What was my function? Who was I if I couldn't trust my own senses? The body knows, I'd told my self-defense class. But sometimes the body was wrong. I began to understand the awful, confused world my students must live in.

I walked through the park for an hour. There were very few people about; the wind was gusting, and every now and again rain rattled the foliage overhead. I felt some of that almost-ecstatic delight in the ordinary that the drugged coffee had induced: rain sparkled on the bole of an apple tree and I paused to look, and noted the screw-type distribution of leaves around its stem, which ensured each leaf got as much sunlight as possible. I picked a rain-flecked daisy. It had thirteen petals. She loves me. I picked another: thirty-four. She loves me not. Another. Twenty-one. She loves me. All numbers in the Fibonacci series. Nature didn't need to measure. Even its improvisations were orderly and graceful.

I was wet. It was a little after three o'clock. I called another cab and headed back to the Nordstrom parking lot.

KICK'S VAN wasn't in the lot, but the big rolling doors were open, and I saw Dornan just inside the entrance, wearing a bright yellow construction hat, handing up a pipe to a rigger on the growing scaffold.

I was surprised by how glad I was to see him.

"Dornan!"

He handed up his piece of pipe and pulled off his gloves. "Well, hello to you, too, Torvingen." He looked quite unlike himself in his yellow hat. "Things here are progressing, as you see. Kick's not around, as I expect you know, but doubtless you're here to see Floozy and the Winkle."

Floozy and the Winkle. I wondered if everyone called them that except me. I wondered if everyone knew they had asked me to invest. I would have to read that script at some point.

"I have a few minutes," I said. I wished he would take that hat off. "How about you? Due for a break? I've just seen a chair."

"Chairs again, is it?"

"I'll buy you a cup of coffee if you take that hat off."

He did, and we went in search of a café. In the end, we settled for Americanos to go from an espresso stand a mile from the warehouse, and talked and sipped as we walked. The air was cool and rainy, the coffee hot and tasty. He talked about building the scaffolding, how bloody awkward steel piping was when you were wearing huge, great gloves, and how he'd wrenched his wrist once already and dropped a steel connector on his left foot.

I saw an earthquake, I wanted to say, but it already felt as though it had never happened. Which of course it hadn't.

"That's a most peculiar expression."

"Um," I said, and found I couldn't talk about it. Maybe I'd be able to talk to Kick, but I didn't know where she was. "So, how's everybody?"

"Everybody is just fine."

"I suppose there's not much call for Kick to be on set at the moment if no one is eating her food."

"You know, Torvingen, when I first met you, I never knew what you were thinking, but there have been times lately when I can practically see the thoughts form on your face. It doesn't seem natural and I'm not entirely sure I like it. I am sure, however, that I find your unwillingness to simply ask the question wholly tedious."

We waited for a light.

"If you have a question, or something on your mind, say it. Just open your mouth and let the words roll out. It's not so very hard."

Where is Kick? How come you always know where she is and I don't? Why isn't she here so I can hold her and bury my face in her hair and know it's real? I tried to imagine the words rolling out as bright and sturdy as toy trucks, immune to all misunderstanding.

The lights changed and we started to cross.

"It is hard," I said.

"Do it anyway."

I put one foot in front of the other. Trucks roared by, rain hissed. It would be easier to talk to someone I could hold.

"Usually, if people want you to know where they are, they tell you," I said.

After a moment he said, "Is that a question?"

"Yes. I don't . . . I want to talk to Kick and I don't know where she is. She didn't tell me. I just, I wonder why she didn't volunteer the information."

"She's not a mind-reader, Torvingen. Besides, sometimes people like to be asked. It shows you're interested."

"Not that you're being nosy?"

"She's a grown woman. If she wants you to back off, she can say so." He shook his head. "Christ, you're as bad as each other."

"So . . . I should just ask?"

"Yes! Yes. A thousand times, yes. Look." He stopped and turned to face me, but a truck thundered past close to the curb and threw up a curtain of muddy puddle water, drowning whatever he had been about to say. He sighed and wiped the lid of his go-cup with his T-shirt, and changed his mind about saying whatever it was. "This is a sorry excuse for a summer." We walked for a while in silence under a scudding sky. "Now," he said, "what's this about a chair?"

I told him about the chair, and the trees, and by the time we got to the warehouse, I still hadn't told him about Nordstrom, or teaching my mother to punch, about Corning or Ed Tom Hardy, about my plan to buy more land, about much of anything, because all of a sudden I had no faith in my ability to integrate any of it, to plan and execute. I couldn't be sure I was making the right decisions. I couldn't even trust what I saw.

When we were halfway across the parking lot, his phone rang. He fished it out of his pocket and waved me on before answering. *Jonie,* I told myself, *some problem with the coffeehouses,* as a maroon Subaru Forester pulled into the parking lot and Deverell Turtledove and a woman who looked a bit like Green Jacket got out: his wife, Philippa. Dornan had turned his back to me, so I said hello to the Turtledoves and led them to Finkel and Rusen's trailer.

When I stepped back down into the parking lot two hours later holding legal paperwork, I found the sky bright blue, the air washed clean and now fat with warmth. Several cars were gone from the lot. Dornan was gone, too. I lifted my face to the sun. I considered calling him, but decided against it. Perhaps I would go to the dojo. Perhaps I should call Kick's house.

My phone rang, but it was Gary, with an appointment for tomorrow morning at a downtown bank. I thanked him and folded the phone. Walked to my car, threw the paperwork on the backseat. My phone rang again as I got in the car, and this time it was Kick.

"Want to come over?" she said. "I'll grill us something. We can watch the sun set over Troy."

———————

SHE SAT cross-legged on the back patio next to a tiny Hibachi grill, tending tuna, and vegetables in foil, and sipping a bottle of Stella Artois.

I lay with my head on her lap. She had showered just before I arrived, and in the early-evening sun her damp hair smelled sharply of fennel shampoo. Her bare legs were warm, and her tank top had been sheared off just below the breasts. If I looked straight up, I could see the shadowed swell. Her stomach touched my hair every time she breathed.

When I had arrived, she had smiled, and kissed me, and busied herself with starting the coals and preparing the food, but although she chopped and marinated and tasted with every appearance of engagement, it was clear that most of her attention was focused on some interior plane.

I didn't mind. We could talk later. For now it was enough to feel her skin on mine, to sit inside her smell. I enjoyed the scrape of aluminum foil as she turned the vegetables, the warmth of the sun on my face. Every now and again, the early-evening breeze shook a few of the afternoon's raindrops from the ancient cherry tree and they hissed on the coals.

Two cats appeared, one black, the other a tawny puffball, and sat silently by the fence.

"Meet El Jefe Don Gato and Der Floofenmeister," she said, the first time she'd spoken in ten minutes.

The cats turned their gaze, laserlike, in my direction, then returned their focus to the sizzling fish. The black one was wearing a blue-and-red collar with a blue tag. I read it upside down. "According to his tag, his name is Sylvester."

"Well, that's what the neighbors call him, and seeing as he's theirs, I can't stop them."

He did look like a don riding about his hacienda, thin and aristocratic, greying but formidable. I squinted. "The other one's tag says Blondie."

She made a sound of disgust and adjusted the vent at the base of the grill.

The cats looked at me again, and back at the fish. "Are they expecting a handout?"

"They won't like the lemon marinade." She lifted the boning knife from the Pyrex dish she'd brought the fish out in, and pushed the dish over the concrete to the cats. The black one leaned forward a millimeter and blinked as though someone had flicked him on the nose, just like Dornan when descriptions of gore got too graphic. He sneezed, turned, and walked away to the fence, leapt up and disappeared over the other side. The fluffy one gave Kick a disappointed look, and ambled off towards the bottom of the garden. It looked as though she were wearing puffy pantaloons.

More rain dropped from the cherry overhead. I raised myself up on one elbow and reached for one of the many twigs littering the patio directly beneath the tree. No buds. It had been dead awhile before it fell. I pondered phyllotactic ratios.

"I went to the Asian Art Museum today." She nodded that she was listening. "I saw a chair. It was simple, made five hundred years ago of hardwood, but it was beautiful. Perfect. Perfect the way a circle is, or a flower, or a river. Flawless. I found myself thinking about proportion, and grace, and beauty, and then I saw it all around me." I held up the twig. "The ratio of how these stems grow is perfectly uniform, twig after twig."

She was silent for a while. "Perfection is important to you, isn't it?"

"It's pleasing. And orderly. It works. I like things that work." Except, of course, I wasn't working one hundred percent. But if I told her about the flashback it would only serve to remind her that the drugs had been delivered through her coffee, and then we'd talk about Corning. I didn't want to do that, and, judging from her behavior, she had enough on her mind.

"So if something isn't perfect, you throw it away?"

I sat up. She was studying me, but, again, I got the impression a vast part of her was about some interior business. "It depends. Yes, if it's meant to be a functional object. I've never seen the point of keeping something that doesn't work. May as well get rid of it."

She said nothing, and her face was still, and then she shrugged abruptly. "Well, now it's time to get rid of that twig, and eat."

We sat on the step that led down to the lawn, warm plates balanced on bare legs. The fish was succulent, the roasted pepper and mushrooms luscious. A Steller's jay swooped into the bay hedge at the bottom of the lawn and sang something rude. Its feathers were radioactive blue. Nordstrom was a million miles away.

The sun hung low at our backs, a hairbreadth from sinking behind the house and leaving the garden in shade. A dragonfly like a three-inch titanium helicopter zoomed in and out of the light, skimming the sky of mosquitoes. I put my arm around her waist, and she leaned against me briefly, then went back to eating. I finished my food one-handed.

"That twig," I said. "It was dead."

"They usually are when they fall off."

"Yes. But there are a lot of them. And not just twigs. A few fair-sized branches. And that whole limb, the one that hangs over the dining room extension, is dying."

"So?"

"The tree is diseased."

She slugged back the rest of her beer. "She's beautiful."

She? "Well, yes. But that's not the point."

"Who says? She's old, yes, and bits of her aren't doing as well as they used to, but so what? She's been a beautiful cherry tree for nearly a hundred years. She's still a beautiful cherry tree."

"No cherries for a year or more, though, I imagine."

"When women get old and stop producing babies, do you think they should be hacked off at the knees and thrown in a pit?" I stared. Her eyes were inimical, hard, as they had been that first time, when she had thought I was attacking Rusen. Then they glimmered with tears and she turned away and wiped at them with her fist. "Shit."

"Kick . . ." I reviewed the conversation in my head. "I'm sorry. About the cherries."

"Oh, for Christ's sake, it's not about the fucking cherries!"

"What—" But she stood up and cut me off.

"I'm getting more beer. Want some?"

She was gone for more than five minutes. I stood and stretched and wandered about the garden. A bush juddered to itself and a cat yowled. I sat on one of the brick steps that divided the upper lawn from the lower. The sun was going down. The side of Queen Anne began to twinkle.

She came out with her beer and sat next to me and laid her head on my shoulder. I put my arm around her.

I cleared my throat. "Kick."

"Give me a few minutes, okay?"

"All right."

I kissed her bare shoulder—very slightly salty. I should have bought her those pearls.

"What did you do today?" she said eventually. "Just tell me about your day. Distract me."

She didn't mean, *Tell me about the bad things that happened.* "I talked to Floo—to Rusen and Finkel. They want me to invest in the production."

"And will you?"

"You've done a lot of film. What do you think of it as an investment?"

"Realistically, it's hopeless."

"But?"

"But now the asshole director is gone, Rusen is doing an incredible job. I've seen some of the rough edit, and some of his ideas for the new finale. I wouldn't have believed it possible."

"But?"

"But, okay, here's the thing. As a movie, it won't ever be a success, but it could go to DVD or maybe even to get a contract from a network. It will get people's attention. And then they'll hire the people who helped them make this one. And I'll have a success to put on my résumé. You don't have a clue what I'm talking about, do you?"

"No."

"Hollywood people, and TV is as much Hollywood as the movies are, are incredibly superstitious. They have no idea what makes a hit, so they hire on the magic-bullet basis. They look at your résumé—whether you're the best boy or grip or second AD or caterer or set dresser, it doesn't matter; if they see a flop sitting there, it's a like a big cow patty stinking up the dining room. They want to get rid of you. You'll taint their project. But if they see you've been part of a box office hit, they'll take you. You have the golden aura: you've been associated with success. So, *Feral,* the *Feral* we're shooting now, won't ever be released, but it could get turned into a real project, which will go on my résumé, and Steve Jursen's—he's out of the hospital by the way, did you know?—and Joel Pedersen's, and five years from now we'll all have more work than we know what to do with, and Hippoworks will move to swanky new digs in Century City, and hire a receptionist with a boob job." She blew a mournful tune on her beer bottle. "If they get the cash for post, and if the big finale works."

"It might not?"

"They don't have a stunt coordinator."

"You could do it."

"I'm a cook," she said.

Years ago, I'd met a girl called Cutter, a fourteen-year-old living on the street, jamming her veins with heroin to stop the nightmares about what Daddy used to do to her. Once she got used to me, she would talk about all her plans for One Day, and beam at me, a blindingly sweet smile from such a thin, scabbed face, but if I ever asked how she was really doing, whether there was anything I could to do help, she'd slam the shutters and get ready to run. Then there had been Sandra. I had learnt that, whatever Dornan said, there were times to talk in gradually diminishing circles.

"Troy," I said, and nodded at the twinkling hill. "Have you ever been to that part of the world?"

"Yep. Thrown myself off cliffs into the Aegean, into the Black Sea, dived in the reefs off Belize and Australia, driven a car that plunged into the Bosporus. Did I tell you my first few real gigs were as a stunt diver?"

I nodded. She hadn't, but the clerk at Hollywood Video had. I stroked her hair. "Ever been to Mycenae?"

"Nope."

"The Lion Gate is still there. It's massive, but brutal. No grace, no subtlety, just massive. And in the center is a huge beehive. Not a beehive, exactly, but a tomb that looked like a hut made of stones, empty inside. Part of the mighty Mycenaean civilization. And it's nothing but crude lumps of stone stacked up like a beehive. I know it was the Bronze Age but I was expecting . . . more."

"Orators in white chitons, people declaiming in iambic trimeter?"

"Something like that."

"What do you expect from a yahoo like Agamemnon?" But she stroked my arm, leaned down and kissed it, kissing away my old disappointment, reassuring me that there was more that was good in life than bad.

After a moment the quality of her stroking changed, and I could tell she was no longer really aware of me, that she was back in whatever place she'd been half the evening.

The stroking, paused, resumed. Her muscles firmed. She lifted her head.

"Yesterday," she said. "After the Duwamish park, when I had to leave, it was because I had an—Shit." Something thumped into the concrete behind me. She jumped up. "Jefe! Drop it. Drop it right now!"

It was the black cat, weighed down by a huge rat in its mouth. He dropped the rat at Kick's feet and looked pleased. The rat lay on its side, panting.

"Oh, God," she said. "Oh, God. Is it hurt?"

The rat jumped to its feet and made a dash for the gap under the fence. Jefe pounced, seized it, threw it in the air, caught it, shook it, brought it back. Dropped it again in front of Kick. How much simpler life would be if we could act like cats: just drop our trophy at the beloved's feet.

"Oh, God. Aud, get him away. The cat. Get the cat away. Get him away."

I picked Jefe up, carried him to the fence, and dropped him over.

"Don't," I said, when Kick bent to the rat. "It will bite." It could have rabies.

"It's hurt. Look. It's not moving."

Its chest was heaving, its heart beating so hard its ribs shook, but from the hips down it didn't move.

"Do something," she said.

I walked back to the grill, picked up the boning knife.

"Do something," she said again. Then she saw the knife. "What are you doing?"

"You might not want to watch."

"What are you doing?"

"Step back a little, please. Thank you." I knelt, put the tip of the knife in the soft place at the base of its tiny skull, and pushed, once. The thin blade slid past the brief resistance of skin and through the spinal cord. The body convulsed, then went still.

"You killed it."

"Its back was broken."

"We could have done something."

"No. Its back was broken."

"So, what, that's it? It doesn't work perfectly anymore, so throw it away, like an ugly, broken toy?"

She wasn't making any sense to me. Was this still about the cherry tree? Except the cherry tree hadn't been about the cherry tree.

"What were you going to say, earlier?" But she didn't hear me; she was looking at the bloody knife in my hand. I walked to the grass and stabbed the turf a couple of times. Kick watched me. When I put the knife in the Pyrex dish and walked back to the rat, she backed up again.

I picked the rat up by its tail. If I threw it into the bushes at the bottom of the garden, it would be gone by morning. But Kick, I knew, would object.

She watched silently while I unfolded the aluminum foil she had used to cover the fish, laid the rat on it, and folded it into a neat package. "Where do you keep your garbage bags?"

"I'll get one."

It took her a minute. I saw she'd got herself another beer, too. I put the foil packet in the garbage bag, tied a knot in the top, and dumped it in the rubbish bin by the fence. Jefe was sitting there, washing his face.

"I need to wash my hands," I said.

"Yes," Kick said. "You go do that. And take your—take the knife, too." She stepped aside so I could go through the door. She didn't touch me as I passed.

When I got back into the garden, she was covering the grill, one handed, beer in the other. When she was done, she tilted back her head and drank the bottle dry. She stared at it, half turned as though to get another, then changed her mind. "I have to get out, go somewhere."

I stood. I wasn't sure whether she wanted to get out or to get away from me. "Are you all right?"

Her laughter was like the spill of mercury from a broken thermometer: slippery and fascinating and one small step from toxic. "Am I perfect as a circle? Oh, no, no, I don't think I am. I'm definitely flawed."

"I meant, are you all right to drive?"

"Not being perfect doesn't make me incapable."

"You've already had three beers." And it was clear she would be having more. "I'll drive you, if you like."

"Fine. You do that." She turned her shoulders from me, though not her hips. Pushing me away, begging me to stay. I'd seen the dynamic before with people who had been sexually abused, a twisty self-hatred: Love me, but if you do I'll find you contemptible because I don't deserve love. There's something inside me that is wrong and bad and you shouldn't touch it.

"The grill's still hot," I said.

"It'll be fine." She put her hand on the gate. "If you want to drive, do it now." In the car she found a rock station and turned the music into a wall.

KICK DIRECTED me to a bar in Ballard's old town. I pulled up outside. NO FOOD, it said on the door, and MUST SHOW ID. I left the engine running but turned off the music. She unfastened her seat belt but didn't get out.

"Will you be all right?"

"Are you offering to hold my hand?"

"I don't understand," I said. "What's wrong?"

"I don't have a fucking drink," she said, and got out and walked inside without a backward glance.

HER GATE squeaked. The hinges needed oiling. The coals were cooling. Nevertheless, I carried the grill to the middle of the concrete patio, made sure the lid was secure and the vents fully open to speed the heat loss.

Overhead, the cherry tree creaked, and creaked again. One more storm and the whole thing would come down.

THE SUITE was cold; the maid had left the air-conditioning on high. I opened the windows the three inches they allowed and tore off my clothes, which smelled of grill smoke and Kick. I started a bath, running it very hot, and faxed Finkel and Rusen's legal paperwork to Bette for review. I sat on the arm of the sofa and balanced the Corning-mirrored laptop on my knees, scrolling idly through lists of file names. I had the Corning-to-Bingley-to-ETH connection, now I needed to trace the other way, Corning to whoever had drugged me. Nothing obvious so far.

I put the laptop aside, checked the bath water. Dried my hands, scrolled some more. There. Something. I scrolled back. Nothing. I rubbed my eyes. Too tired. Too irritated. I put the laptop down. I'd have a bath. Order some coffee. Look again.

I climbed into the deep bath and lowered myself slowly. The bath was warm and my muscles perfectly limp. I drowsed.

Luz stood looking at Kick, who had her arms around the cherry tree. "Will you kiss it better?" she said, in her fast Mexican Spanish. "And then can we have a Big Mac?"

I jerked awake. Big Mac.

I walked dripping to the laptop, wiped my hands on the sofa, picked up the laptop.

There. A folder called Big Mac. I opened it. A record of payments to "Mackie," three so far. I dropped the laptop on the sofa, went into the bedroom for my own. Pulled up the employment data Rusen had sent me days ago.

Studied the attached thumbnail photo. Found the information supplied by James I. Mackie. Twenty-two, supposedly, a graduate of Western Washington, Bellingham. A recent graduate, therefore no work references for Rusen to check, but he had checked with WWU; someone called James I. Mackie had graduated with honors in French.

The Mackie I had met did not strike me as the studying kind.

Still naked, I dialed Turtledove and left a message.

"Take a look at Mackie. A pseudonym. I'll forward his picture and employment records. Pull the WWU transcript and photo of James I. Mackie, class of '06, and if it doesn't match the one I send you, run mine past your sources in local law enforcement." I realized I was telling him how to do his job. "Call me first thing tomorrow."

I got myself a towel, dried off, dressed in clean clothes, ordered coffee. I had just opened Corning's Visa account when my phone rang. I picked it up. Dornan.

"Yes?"

". . . a rat." Then something else, smothered by a blast of music. He was in a bar.

"What?"

". . . your contribution today was to kill a rat."

"Are you with Kick?"

Noise.

"I said, Are you with—"

". . . have to kill it?"

"What? Dornan, the rat was dead already."

". . . upset. Today of all days."

"And what day is that?"

". . . very hard day . . ." More noise. Then, "Peg's going to sing? Joel, Joel, look, Peg's going to sing."

Peg? Joel? Singing?

". . . hard to understand . . . All you had to do was talk to her about her day—"

No one had asked me about my day. My day of earthquakes that weren't there, and twisty, incoherent speeches about cherry trees and perfection.

". . ."

"Dornan, I can't hear a word you're saying. Keep Kick safe for me. Dornan. Dornan?"

"..."

I thumbed the phone off. I stared at the screen, not seeing the data.

I considered driving back to the bar, decided against it. Clearly, she was surrounded by friends. Equally clearly, I had not been invited.

I focused on the list of debits. Two more from Bellevue. Corning was still at the Hilton.

Turtledove had good working relationships with Seattle PD and the King County sheriff's department; it was impossible to stay in business for fifteen years as a PI without them. By morning I would know, one way or another, about Mackie. Then I would talk to him, get the information I needed to give me leverage with Corning. Then I'd pay her a visit. Then we would go to Mindy Leptke. Then I'd get Kick's reputation back.

The coffee came. I poured, cradled the cup between my hands. I wondered if Kick had drunk herself insensible. I wondered what she was so afraid of.

I thought about the cherry tree. Luz. Kiss it better. I couldn't kiss better whatever was bothering Kick, at least until she told me what it was. But I could take care of that tree. I could make that better.

THE AZALEA BLOOMS WERE DELICATELY TINGED WITH BROWN, AND SOMETIMES, NOW, in the late afternoon, storms would boil out of nowhere and flash and throw water on everything and blow transformers in a writhe of light—turquoise, magenta, lime—similar to the titanium earrings that had been popular when I was a child. It had been on a night like this, with spring singing in my bones, that I'd met Julia. We hadn't exchanged a word. The next day she came to the police gym. After the rookies left we faced each other in *chi sao,* knees bent and wrists touching. As we circled, her toes gripped automatically at the mat. Narrow feet, I remembered, aristocratic, and golden, already toasted to biscuit by judicious exposure to sunlight.

Almost a year later, I stared at ten pairs of feet in the Crystal Gaze basement. Therese's feet, soles up in full lotus, were strong but brutalized—those of an ex–ballet dancer. Christie had peasant feet, blunt and solid and healthy, nails cut square and pink-and-white clean, utterly un-gothlike. Kim's toenails were painted metallic blue, the same color as her fingernails. Suze's left foot had a massive bruise on the instep; Pauletta's were close to the color of old tea, her ankles delicate.

Sandra's feet were a complete surprise. They were lovely: smooth, unhurt, and clearly cherished. Part of me had expected her to treat her feet with indifference, for perhaps the toes to have been broken and reset many times, for there to be evidence of cuts from broken glass. They reminded me of something, someone, and I was surprised by a strong, sudden urge to pat her on the leg and tell her everything would be all right.

Katherine and Jennifer were both hiding their feet, Katherine by tucking them under her and Jennifer by draping them with her hands.

I stood and gestured for everyone to do likewise. "Some people find working in bare feet makes them feel as vulnerable as working naked."

"I'm not getting naked for anyone," Nina said.

"Another reason to be grateful today," Pauletta said.

They were starting early with the banter. "Why do you suppose having naked feet makes us feel so vulnerable?"

"Is this one of those call-and-response, we're-not-going-anywhere-'til-you-get-an-answer things?" Pauletta said.

"No," I said, surprised. "I hoped one of you would know."

Silence. Today, I didn't mind. Today, I felt as whippy and light as a sapling.

"Today we're going to learn about falling. And then throwing."

I ignored the ripple of unease.

"Culturally, Americans are taught that being down in any way is shameful, inferior: something to be avoided at all costs. The older we get, the more we absorb this message. It becomes more and more important to stay on our feet: stand your ground, find your feet, stand tall. It's likely that we become more scared of falling as we grow for two simple reasons: the ground seems farther away, and we heal less easily.

"We're taught that once we're down, we'll never get up again, that we'll be defenseless. It's not true. There's a whole martial art dedicated to floor techniques. Jujitsu is built on defending yourself from the ground."

"Show us that, then," Suze said.

"All right." I gestured everyone but Suze away from the mats and lay down on my back in the middle, knees pointing at the ceiling and feet flat to the floor. "Attack me."

"How?"

"Any way you like."

She tried to run around my feet for my head. I swiveled on the mat. She ran the other way. I swiveled again. She lost patience and came straight at my feet, which I lifted into kicking position. She backed away.

"What if there's two of them?" Jennifer said.

What if they have flamethrowers? What if they're driving tanks? "Let's find out. You step into the circle and attack my head."

She stepped a cautious six inches towards me and Suze, predictably, took the opportunity to rush me.

I waited until Suze was close, swept her feet from under her with one leg, swiveled a hundred eighty degrees, and held my feet menacingly at Jennifer. She backed away, hands up.

Suze leapt to her feet. From the way she was shaking out her right hand, she'd landed on her arm.

"Before I can teach you how to do that, you have to learn to fall first." I rocked back and did a totally unnecessary kip-up. The perils of spring. It was fine to feel the sap rising, but not to act that way in a class full of beginners. I took a slow, meditative breath.

"The first step in thinking about falling is to regard it as something you're actively doing, something you're controlling rather than something that's being done to you. You're the subject, not the object."

"The hammer, not the nail," Tonya said.

"Yes. As with all things, we begin with breath. Relax. In, slowly, slowly, through the nose, out through the mouth. In. And out. In. Out." They fell into the rhythm faster than they had in previous weeks. Several of them—Tonya, Christie, Therese—automatically dropped their shoulders and lowered their chins. I felt an unfamiliar blossom and swell of . . . something. Pride. "Keep breathing. Nice and slow. All the falls I'm going to teach you have been designed specifically for hard surfaces. I've practiced them all. Some of them I've used out on the street. They do work. Trust them."

Trust me.

"Some key points about falling: The first thing is to keep your chin tucked in. This makes your spine the right shape and stops your head from snapping back onto the floor. There are seven points to remember." It had worked well enough for striking. "One, breathe. Two, tuck your chin. Three, when you go down, aim to make contact with the ground with the fleshy muscular parts of your body, not bone: shoulder muscle here, or the pad of fat on your hip. Four, spread the impact over as large an area as possible." A couple of frowns. "Falling safely is about understanding weight distribution. Spreading out the area of contact makes for less damage. Five, don't roll on your neck. Six, when you practice falling, get up again quickly. If ever you're knocked over unexpectedly, you'll be used to bouncing back. Seven, relax, be fluid. If you're going down, go willingly. Make the ground your ally. You can use it, as you would a wall if you were pinned against it. The ground is not your enemy."

Therese raised her eyebrows: The ground is not your enemy?

"Partner up. Stand about arm's length apart, in a line. We're going to begin gently." I caught Suze's eye. "Gently. Remember the earlier list: Bend your knees. Keep your knees over your foot. Have your feet about hips'-width apart. Have one foot in front of the other." Jennifer opened her mouth. "No, it doesn't matter which." I tended to stand with my left foot forward; most right-handed people did. "Move your hips in a small circle so your weight shifts. Your center of gravity is about two inches below your belly button. You want that point to move parallel to the floor. Like this." I stood wide and easy, left foot forward and circled my pelvis slightly. Nina hummed "Time Warp," from *The Rocky Horror Picture Show.*

I motioned Suze aside and took her place facing Christie. "Partners, you're going to step forward—one step only—and as you breathe out, put your palms on your partner's shoulders and push, like so." I stepped forward and pushed Christie so that she swayed slightly. "When you feel yourself moving backwards, go with it. Christie, you push me."

Christie stepped in, pushed—she even remembered to breathe out—and I slid my right foot back a further eighteen inches.

"Note how I simply widened my base. Your turn."

They pushed each other.

Sandra, instead of gliding back, turned in and to the side, a flinch built of a thousand blows. I adjusted her body as she moved.

I went down the line, pushing, letting them push me, so they could feel how to melt backwards from the thrust, reminding them of chins, knees, shoulders.

I motioned Sandra aside. "Now we're going to step up the force a little." I nodded for Therese to push me. She did, both hands firm on my shoulders and body behind the thrust. I moved back—right leg, then left leg—and had to rein in the automatic diagonal step, turn, and throw that would have put Therese on her back. I breathed. In and out. It was good to feel the living moment between two bodies, to feel the feedback, play with some of the strength. I smiled. "Good." I gestured for Therese to ready herself. I pushed, a solid thrust. Therese stepped smoothly. "Very good. Now you try. Imagine you're a train just sliding back on a rail in a straight line. Easy."

Except Suze wasn't finding it easy.

"It's not a fight," I said. I reached out slowly and put my hands on her biceps and triceps. "Breathe." I shook her, very gently, until her arms unlocked and she stopped tilting her torso forward, stopped resisting. "Good. Now step back." I guided her. "And again. And again." I guided her more quickly, and again, until she was walking smoothly backwards. I brought her back to the line and motioned Christie in to push Suze. "Good. Balance isn't about never going down, it's about free movement, self-determined movement."

She let Christie push her. And again, and started to get it right.

I clapped for attention. "Watch." I stood straight, and in one movement tucked my chin, raised my arms out before me, squatted with a gushing out-breath, and toppled onto my back, turtle-like, rocking. I reversed the movement and stood. "It's not hard. We'll begin with squats."

At first it was as though they had never squatted in their lives, but after three or four tries, muscle memory took over.

"Next time you go down, stay there. Arms out. Chins tucked. Squat as deeply as possible. Get your backside as close to the mat as you can." I squatted opposite Therese and pushed her very gently so that she tipped over backwards. She rocked. I tipped Suze, who went over like a rolling puppy. She laughed as she bounced back up. I tipped Christie, and Tonya, then Katherine, who went down with a thump, straightened out with fright, and bumped her head on the mat. "Keep your chin tucked. Feel the difference? Good." Pauletta. Kim. Nina. Sandra watched me as I squatted opposite her. "Chin in." She tucked, and her eyes unlocked from mine. I found myself reluctant to touch her, but did anyway. I pushed. She went over as though committing herself to the deep, a giving-over of her whole self. It made me want to wipe my hands on the carpet. I moved quickly to Jennifer, who went over with a thin gasp and found herself amazed to have survived.

"And again, only this time you let yourself fall backwards without me touch-ing you." They did that, some more readily than others, but once they'd all done it at least three times, I had them stand. "Now we're going to put it to-gether, all of us at the same time. Breathe in, chins tucked. Arms out. Breathe out, and squat, and over backwards." Neither Katherine nor Jennifer went over. I pretended I hadn't noticed. "And up. And breathe in, chins in, arms out, squat and breathe out, and back." Jennifer went over. Katherine swayed. "And up again."

And again, and down Katherine went. And again, and again, until none of them was hesitating.

"Sit up, please."

Most of them were grinning. I was, too.

They seemed to have forgotten how vulnerable they had felt about their naked feet.

"Anyone dizzy?"

"Bit," Katherine said.

"It's to be expected. Take a minute to breathe." I motioned them back, so they scrambled off the mat, then I did an easy forward shoulder roll and back to my feet. I did it again, backwards, and again, forwards, on the other shoulder.

"Show-off," Nina said.

"Yes," I said, and grinned.

"I can't do that," Jennifer said.

"We'll start slowly. Watch." This time I squatted. "I know you can do this." They smiled. I reached forward and down with my left hand and then under my right knee, almost a scooping motion, until my left forearm lay along the ground. I touched the palm of my right hand to the mat directly in front of me, between my left elbow and my knees. "Now I tuck my head and turn it so that I'm looking back under my right armpit. Then I bend and bend and bend until I can't stay on my feet any longer." And over I went, in what as a child we had called a tipply overtail. "We'll do it one at a time. Make a line. Jennifer, you first."

She looked panic-stricken but I ignored it.

"Squat. Left arm here, right hand here, tuck, look back under—no, as far as you can, I want you to be able to see the wall behind you. Good. Keep your head tucked and your abdominal muscles tight. Just curl up and let me push you. Over you go," and I pushed her backside lightly and she went over like a ball of wool. "Off to the back of the line. Next."

We got all the way through the line—Suze, Sandra, Tonya, Christie—without serious trouble, but then, to my surprise, Nina balked.

"I'm old," she said. "What about osteoporosis?"

"All the more reason to learn to fall properly. You won't spend your old age terrified of icy pavement and polished tile. Squat."

"But . . ."

"Squat. Left arm here. Right hand here. Tuck your chin. Breathe. In and out. Can you see the wall behind you?"

Pauletta said, "She's so old and decrepit she probably can't see it without her trifocals anyhow."

Nina practically shoved her head under her armpit and I pushed her over. "Whoa!" she said, and shot to her feet, and realized she was in one piece. "Son of a bitch! I want to go again."

And so we all went again. At the beginning of the third round I had them squat not so deep, and the fourth less deeply still. "Faster," I said. "And this time push off from that front leg." And they rolled merrily. "Now a volunteer to get on all fours at the front of the mat."

Both Suze and Christie stepped forward.

"Two of you, then. All right." I got them to crunch down next to each other, like cars lined up for Evel Knievel, and then I dived over them in a roll, smooth and soundless, and faced them. "To go over an obstacle, all you have to do is push off hard. Anyone want to try?"

Suze stood up. "I can do that."

"Suze, remember all the . . ."

She just hurled herself over Christie and described an arc big enough to have overflown a Volkswagen. She landed a little harder than necessary but it was a sound, safe, sturdy roll.

"*Whoo!* That's a rush!"

Some of them were white-faced and tentative, some sweaty and boisterous, but one by one they threw themselves over one another and emerged unscathed. The tang of adrenaline rose through the room like mist and the air conditioner labored to hold back the building heat. I couldn't believe how well they were doing. I'd expected at least two of them to refuse. I began to feel responsible for their brilliance.

While they were eager and brave I showed them how to step back and tuck a leg behind them and roll back over their shoulder towards an impact they couldn't see coming. I showed them how to slap as they went down, to spread the impact and to boost the backward roll. I showed them how to come to their feet bent-kneed and ready.

Then I had them stand easy and breathe until the hectic light in their eyes began to die.

"Now sit." Time to reintroduce the real world. "How did you feel working in bare feet?"

"Okay. I guess," Christie said. Katherine surreptitiously slid her feet out of sight.

"Good. It's how we'll work from now on. The vast majority of attacks on women happen in the home. How many of you usually wear shoes in the bedroom or bathroom or even the kitchen? If something happens when you're at home, you can't say, Hold on a minute while I put on my steel-toed boots. You have to be prepared to respond at any time, to any situation: when you're in the bath, on the toilet, in the kitchen. That means not feeling vulnerable. And that means sometimes practicing things that feel silly or uncomfortable or just plain ridiculous—so that when and if something unexpected happens, you can respond without thinking. It means thinking about situations that you don't want to think about.

"Lie down. Imagine you're in bed. You're alone. A noise has woken you. What do you do?"

"Take my Louisville Slugger and go find the bastard," Suze said.

"Can you reach out and find it in the dark?"

"It's under the bed."

"Can you reach down and grab it with your eyes closed?"

"Sure."

"No clutter under there?"

"Well, maybe."

"Do you sleep naked?"

"Yeah. So what?"

"When you have your bat, are you all right with facing an intruder naked?"

"Well, I'd put on a shirt, maybe."

"Do you keep a shirt right by the bed, in a familiar place, folded in just such a way that you can pull it on in the dark and without thinking?"

She shook her head.

"So you wake naked, and the first thing you think is, Where's my bat? Then you think, Where's my shirt? And then you start to sweat because you're thinking too hard, and you start to worry. By this time next week I want you to be able to tell me that if the power was cut in your house you could be at your bedroom door with your T-shirt on and your bat in your hand in less than three seconds. Or you can tell me you don't need the bat or you don't need clothes."

"Do you sleep naked?" Sandra.

"I do."

"Do you have a bat?"

"I don't." I'd never swung a baseball bat in my life. Cricket, yes, and hockey, and rounders, and lacrosse.

I realized I was smiling to myself, remembering the scents of meadow grass turning to straw in the summer sun, and shook myself free of the memories.

"So by next week: ready in three seconds." Everyone was half sitting up. "Lie down again. So you've just woken in the dark. You're alone. What do you do. Kim?"

"I'm never alone. My kids are always there."

"In the same room?"

"No."

"So what do you do?"

"Go check on them."

"Do you get dressed?"

"I have a robe on the back of the door."

"Always in the same place?"

"Always."

"And can you cross your room in the dark without tripping over something?"

"Done it a hundred times when they were infants. Besides, I could always put the light on."

"You could."

"But I shouldn't?"

"Up to you. If you leave it off, you have an advantage: you keep your night vision, and if you've memorized where everything in your house is, an intruder won't be able to find their way around as easily as you."

"Okay."

"So you put on your robe, you check your kids. Then what?"

"I dunno. Depends."

I smiled. Gold star. "On what?"

"Well . . ." She put her hands behind her head. "I guess I could go check the rest of the house."

"And leave your kids sleeping and alone upstairs?"

"It's not upstairs. All one level."

"At one end?" She nodded. "Then your job by this time next week: figure out the most efficient way to sweep your house, outwards from where your kids are, to keep yourself between them and harm. Assuming that's your top priority."

"Of course it is!"

"Right, then. And you should also think about what you'd say to your kids if you had to wake them and tell them there's someone in the house." All the mothers on the floor looked sick. Luz, what would I tell Luz? I made a note to spend some time thinking about the children issue. "Tonya, what's on your bedside table?"

"A clock—"

"What kind?"

"Too small to beat someone on the head with."

"Could you throw it?"

"I . . . Well, I guess I could."

"What else?"

"Books, usually. And a pen or two."

"Good for stabbing at the throat or eye," I said. "But could you reach out in the dark and find them, precisely?"

"I guess so, yes."

"Excellent. What else?"

She looked faintly embarrassed. "Usually three, four mugs of half-drunk tea. I take it to bed and then I fall asleep, and when I get up in the morning I'm too much in a hurry to—"

"Could you find those?"

"Not sure."

"Practice."

"I could throw them?"

"Yes. Cold liquid is a shock to the system, especially if it's unexpected. But imagine you've just woken up and you're lying there. You're not sure if you've heard anything or not. What would you do?"

"Shout out."

"Why?"

"Let whoever it is know I'm awake."

"Good. It's your house. If this is an intruder situation, you don't need to be quiet. Unless you know it's a professional assassin armed and ready to shoot, which I'm assuming is unlikely. Though, frankly, so is the likelihood of being attacked by a stranger. It's more often someone you know."

Their eyes glazed; it was enough, for now, to have introduced the topic.

"If you think there's someone in the house who might mean you harm, get off the bed. Mattresses are bad places to get pinned down. Get up and shout that you know they're there, that you've called the police, and that you want them to leave. Shout out to them where all the doors are. Tell them you won't come between them and an exit—that you just want them to leave. You always want an intruder or potential attacker to leave rather than have to fight you to escape. The point is to survive, not to win. When you've shouted, you should call the police. Call nine-one-one. Stay calm. Stay on the line. If anyone comes for you, don't hesitate to use whatever force you need to stop them from abusing you. It's your house."

"So you should always know where the phone is."

"Yes. You should have nine-one-one and a neighbor's number on speed dial. You might even consider calling nine-one-one on your land line and your neighbor on your cell." Because in Atlanta 911 was variable. Sometimes you got put on hold. Sometimes the dispatcher got things wrong. Sometimes they didn't think women in danger were a priority. "You should also know where the cutoff valve for your water mains is, and for the gas; you should know where your circuit box is, where your spare keys are, where your fully stocked first-aid kit is. If you need to know, it's likely you'll need to know in a hurry. Find out now. Be prepared. It doesn't do any harm."

I paused.

"In our very first class I asked you to consider what you might be willing to do in various circumstances. I think you now have a better idea of what that means. However, we haven't discussed what happens afterwards. What happens if you do defend yourself and you do hurt someone."

Sandra was looking at her fingernails as though she'd never seen them before, but if she'd been a cat, her ears would have been pointing at me.

"The law might seem designed to protect those in need of protection, but occasionally defendants find it works more to protect the status quo. Officers of the court don't much care for women who hurt people if for one minute a case can be made that you didn't have to. So always be prepared to make a case. You're allowed to use reasonable force if someone attacks or threatens to attack you. There's usually a little more leeway if someone intrudes into your home. You have to show that the threat of attack is credible. Many judges and juries will not be kindly disposed towards anyone who seriously hurts a male, white middle-class citizen and can't show bruises, or have no witnesses to testify to a knife or gun. I will deny saying this if anyone ever tries to quote me, but I've been a police officer and, frankly, there have been times when I wished the defendant had been willing to help the laws of evidence along a little."

Jennifer frowned. "What do you mean?"

"She means make shit up," Pauletta said, and looked at me.

"If you have to. Nine times out of ten, if you follow the guidelines I've given you, you won't have to. Just document what actually happened. But be prepared. Who is your best friend? Would she or he be willing to back you up in court? Do you have your friend's phone number on speed dial?"

"I couldn't lie to a police officer," Jennifer said, shocked.

Pauletta said something under her breath.

"What?"

"I said, you'll probably never have to. You shouldn't worry about it."

"What do you mean?"

Tonya looked at the carpet, Pauletta glanced at Kim, who flicked her nails and shrugged, and Suze snorted. Nina smiled kindly. "Honey, I think what she probably means is that you're the kind of person the police will always treat nice. A lot of us are. Nice clothes, wedding ring, good job, white skin."

"I don't see—"

I had a sudden appalling vision of Jennifer's face, or Tonya's, or Katherine's, streaked with dirt and tears, and the flash of police lights, and her saying, *No, no, Officer, he didn't have a gun; no, he didn't have a knife; yes, I did date him, but only once, about a year ago. What's that got to do with anything?* And the looks of contempt from everyone around her as she was led away; the officer's big hand on her head as she was bundled into the car; staring bewildered at the plastic restraints on her wrists. *But he said he would hurt me. And I only hit him in the throat the way she taught us.*

"Some of you are less likely to have trouble than others, yes, but the law tends to come down very heavily on women who hurt men. If you can afford it, keep the number of your lawyer on your cell phone." Sandra put her feet together and scrunched her toes into the carpet, and suddenly I knew what they reminded me of: Luz's feet. Young, untrammeled. The feet of a child who needed someone to protect her.

"What if we don't have a lawyer?" Christie said. "What do we do?"

"Call me," I said. It just came out.

ELEVEN

THE NOISE OF THE CHAINSAWS RIPPING THROUGH THE BRANCHES ON THE CHERRY TREE made my head ache. Wherever Kick was, her headache would be worse. The tree surgeon, Guttersen, and his son, Ben, lopped off the first few smaller branches of the limb overhanging Kick's dining room extension. They fell onto the concrete with a dry rustle. And then the rustling turned to thumps as the small branches gave way to medium-sized ones.

"Yo!" Guttersen let his saw stutter into silence and Ben followed suit, and Guttersen waved at the man in the truck standing by the huge winch. With an industrial beeping, the arm and canvas sling swung ponderously over the garage to the tree. Guttersen and Ben strapped and wrapped the right-hand limb. Guttersen checked his work, nodded me and Ben back, then yanked his saw to life. The teeth tore through most of the foot and a half in two minutes. He signaled the winch operator. The engine note changed up a gear and the cable tightened. Guttersen cut through the last few inches. With a creak, the sling sagged slightly, and then the limb rose majestically and was swung over the garage and into the bed of the truck.

Guttersen put his hands on his hips and grinned. He looked at me. "Sweet work."

I nodded.

"Just in time, though, eh?" He pointed with his saw. Where the limb had been sheared away, the wood was dark inside, rotten to the core. "Could have come down anytime. Bye, bye, garage, maybe even the side of the house. The whole tree needs to come down. Could fall on the neighbor's house. On the neighbor. Big liability."

I pondered. "How long would it take?"

"Another thirty, forty minutes."

I didn't know where Kick was. My head hurt. I looked at the lopsided tree. Rotten to the core. Dangerous. Big liability.

"Go ahead." As soon as I said it, my stomach rolled. I would have said it was a hangover, but last night I hadn't had even two beers.

Guttersen started on the left-hand limb. Ben took his chainsaw into the bed of the truck and carved the severed right-hand limb as though it were a roll of butter.

I wandered down to the bottom of the garden. On the other side of the fence, the fluffy cat hunched under a raspberry bush, ears flat. "No rats," I told her.

I sat on the grass. It was dry and prickly. Up close, I could see how much moss there was in the turf; although summer had barely begun, it was already greener than the grass. I had always thought Seattle was like Ireland, eternally soft and damp and green.

The sky was mostly blue, with a few aggressively cheerful little white clouds. A breeze came from the south, gentle, but strong enough to keep the smell of furious engines downwind. I turned my face to the sun and closed my eyes, and breathed in the scents of sun-dried earth and burgeoning berries.

The chainsaws stopped. I opened my eyes.

"Ma'am?" Guttersen said. I stood, but he wasn't talking to me.

"I said, what the fuck are you doing to my tree?"

Kick was wearing a plain white T-shirt that fit at the shoulders but was tight around the breasts. A man's. Dornan's. Last night's cut-off T was probably in the grocery bag she clutched in her left hand. Twined among the diesel smell was that of old smoke and stale beer.

She saw me as I crossed the lawn.

"Is this your doing?" She was very pale.

"Ma'am?" Guttersen said again.

"Well?" Kick said.

"It's rotten," I said.

She was even paler around the eyes. "You can't do this."

"It's rotten," I said again, but my stomach rolled again. "It's dangerous. Tell her," I said to Guttersen.

"This isn't your tree?" he said to me.

"You're fucking dangerous," Kick said. "How dare you do this to my tree? Look at it."

We all looked at it. There was nothing left but six feet of trunk.

The truck rumbled to silence. Ben jumped down from the back. "Dad?"

"Secure what's in the truck," Guttersen said. Ben turned to obey. Guttersen put down his chainsaw, took off his gloves and tucked them in his belt, and wiped both palms down his jeans. "Now," he said to Kick, "it looks like there's been some miscommunication here. Are you the owner?"

"Yes."

"Would you like me to take the rest of this tree down?"

"No."

"All right, then." He pulled a card, bent at one corner, from his back pocket. "There's my phone and e-mail. If you change your mind, let me know. If you don't, well, I understand how you might be pissed, seeing as I didn't check that this lady was the owner, and didn't get any paperwork, and I apologize, I just . . ." He couldn't find a way to end his sentence. "I apologize," he said again, and held out his hand. Kick shook it. Such small hands.

"It's not you I blame," she said, and Guttersen was wise enough to simply pick up his saw and leave. Thirty seconds later, the truck ground its gears and eased out of the drive. She turned to me. "I don't want to hear anything you have to say. Not a thing. Not one word. I want you to leave. And if you send me flowers I will kill you. Do you even know what you've done?"

I paused, one hand on the gate, not sure if I was supposed to answer that or not. Not, I decided, and left her there, still holding her grocery bag.

TURTLEDOVE CALLED me just as the Fairmont parking valet drove off with my car.

"Mackie's real name is Jim Eddard. He has a string of juvenile arrests, everything from vandalism to petty dealing and minor assault. The last arresting officer thinks he was also involved in an arson eighteen months ago, but there wasn't enough evidence to charge him."

"Where are you?"

"I'm on the set. He's not here."

"Do you have an address?"

"We have two possibles."

"Is Finkel Junior there?"

"Who?"

"Bri. Mackie's young friend." I'd hung tags on both of them.

"One moment." After a twenty-second pause he said, "He's here."

"Then stay there. Keep your eye on him. If Mackie comes in, watch him. If you have to choose, go with Mackie. I'll be there as soon as I can. Less than twenty minutes. Meanwhile, start going through all the employee records."

"Philippa started on that as soon as we saw Eddard's sheet."

"If you need to use staff for the record scrutiny, hire a couple of people."

"We should be okay."

"Good." I shivered. It was cool in the shadow of the hotel. "For now, let's not bother Finkel and Rusen or anyone else on set with this."

"Of course."

I folded the phone and waited for the car valet to come back.

"HELLO, BRI," I said.

He straightened from the box of metal scaffolding connectors. "Hi?" He had a spray of pimples on one side of his mouth.

"I can't find Mackie." Or Peg, or Joel, or Dornan. "Do you know when he'll be in?"

"He said he'd be here before lunch?" He twitched, as though he really wanted to get back to his box but knew it wasn't polite.

It was close to noon now. "What time's lunch, do you think?"

"About now. Or twelve-thirty?"

I nodded. Turtledove was watching from the door. I held up my wrist, made a half-dial motion, waited until he nodded he understood, then turned back to Bri, who smiled uncertainly. "Do you know who I am?"

His nod was jerky, too.

"Then you know I was one of the people you poisoned."

He smiled wider and he locked eyes with me. Like a puppy that thumps its tail and cringes at the same time. "I didn't."

"Yes, you did. You and Mackie."

"No."

"Yes. You were at the coffee urn just before I drank. Mackie was laughing." I was certain now. Adolescents love to hero-worship.

Something of my certainty must have penetrated his adolescent dimness. Like a lot of teens, he was unpracticed in the subtleties of lying. He couldn't equivocate. He flipped, suddenly eager to please.

"It was supposed to be a joke! Mackie said it would be funny."

"Was it?"

He didn't know whether he was supposed to nod or shake his head.

Mackie could be here any minute. I needed to shortcut this process. "Are you hungry, Bri, or thirsty? No? Because I am. Let's go sit down out of the way, have a little chat." He followed me, sneakers squeaking on the concrete floor, to the craft-services table, where dozens of plastic-wrapped bottles of water were lined up with military precision, along with packets of crisps and pretzels. Rusen, or Joel. Kick wouldn't organize things that way, nor would Dornan. I put them from my mind.

I pulled a bottle from its plastic and sat on the other side of the table, gestured for Bri to join me. He twisted his head to and fro.

"Mackie's not here. Your father isn't here. Even if he were, he couldn't save you. Maybe he wouldn't want to. You're sixteen, Bri, not twelve. You know what Mackie's like."

"No." But he did.

"Sit." He sat. He didn't know what else to do. "You know that it's not smart to put drugs in anyone's food or coffee. What did you think would happen?"

He stared at the floor. It was tempting to force him to respond, but I didn't know how long we had.

"But it was all Mackie's idea, right?"

He muttered something.

"I can't hear you."

"Yes."

"All right. Tell me what else was his idea."

"What do you mean?" He looked up at me from behind his flopping hair. I had lost count of the number of adolescent suspects who had given me that look, thinking maybe that now they'd admitted something, maybe they could skate a little.

"Let's just do this, Brian. Tell me about the film, and the lights, and the lab, and the drugs. Let's start at the beginning."

"My dad won't let you do anything to me. Mackie says I'm too young to be prosecuted."

"Maybe not." He was of an age to be legally responsible for his actions, but knowing that would only discourage him from admitting guilt. "But I could tell Mackie you told me everything, because I know a lot of the details, even though I don't have proof, and he won't care about the fine print. He'll just beat you into the dirt." I flexed my hands: *If he doesn't, I will.* "And he'll turn on you in a second. So here's your chance to tell your story and score some points. Tell me. From the beginning."

He was sixteen, and not bright. I would give him a minute or so to work out where his best interests lay.

He took forty seconds. "The film stock? He said he'd buy me a beer if I swapped it out for some other film? And, y'know, it wasn't like it would hurt anyone or anything. I mean, it's just film. Right?" I nodded. "Right. And it's not like my dad is broke or anything. So I said okay."

"How did you do it without anyone seeing?"

"Oh, man, it was so easy. I didn't have to swap the film, Mackie doesn't know anything. I just changed the exposures. Like, thirty seconds' work."

"Pretty good, wasting thirty thousand dollars in half a minute. What does that work out to an hour?" He was getting uncertain again, which would just waste time. I gave him my best smile. "So you're pretty smart. Smarter than Mackie, I'll bet. The drugs were your idea?"

"Nah, they were his. He was like, We can get them so totally fucked up! and I'm like, Okay, all right, so he goes, I'll get the stuff and we'll, like, do it right now. So I said okay."

"So he had the drugs with him, even before you discussed it."

He thought about it. "I guess."

"So when did you do it?"

"You were there. That night. We just dumped the baggie in the pot. You were macking on the craft-services girl, and she was, like, ignoring you so hard she wouldn't have noticed if I took a dump in the food. So I held up the lid and Mackie shook out the baggie into the coffee, and then stirred it with a wrench."

"A wrench?"

"We didn't have a spoon. Anyhow, someone would have noticed if one of us had been carrying a spoon, he said."

Mackie wasn't nearly as dumb as Brian. I looked at my watch. "So what do you think I should do with you?"

"Do?"

Perhaps there was no such thing as consequences in the world of almost-Hollywood high school parties. But it wasn't my job to teach him morals. "I'll just let your father deal with it."

Now he panicked. "My father?"

"He'll decide about the police. But you won't be working here anymore."

"But I don't go back to school for three months."

"Not my problem." I waited until I caught Turtledove's eye, and gestured him over. "Do as you're told for the next few minutes."

I stood, and he tried to stand, too, but I pressed him back into the seat without effort. His face went slack; he still didn't really grasp what was happening. It was tempting to punch him until he understood; I was grateful when Turtledove came up.

"Watch him. I have to talk to Rusen. If Mackie comes in, don't let him leave."

I drank my water, threw the bottle in the trash on the way out to the trailer. I knocked and went in. Rusen and Finkel looked up. "Rusen? A word?" and didn't give him time to consider, but stepped outside again.

He joined me.

"Bri Junior and Mackie are the ones who have been sabotaging things."

"Bri? Mackie? Are you sure?"

"Yes. The drugs, the film stock, everything. Bri has admitted as much. Mackie, real name Eddard, was the leader, of course. I haven't talked to him yet."

"But Bri's just—"

I needed him to pay attention. "Do you still want me to invest?"

"Well, sure."

"Then listen. Turtledove is going to babysit Bri. You keep Finkel in the trailer, away from his son, until I'm finished with Mackie. Do you understand?"

He understood.

I stood by the scaffolding for a while. It was more than thirty feet high. Carpenters were banging busily nearby. I recognized one of them; he'd been talking to Steve Jursen the day I arrived. Perhaps he didn't like coffee.

Turtledove and Bri were not in the line-of-sight of anyone walking into the warehouse. There were no obvious weapons lying about, no crew whose stance would scream "Take me hostage!" if things went bad. I went out into the lot and sat in my car.

Mackie's car turned out to be an unremarkable Toyota, old, but not too shabby or too bright. He got out, slung his leather jacket over his left shoulder, and headed for the warehouse.

I shimmed his door open, released the hood, lifted the distributor cap, removed the rotor, closed it up again. Hummed to myself as I followed him in.

He was admiring the scaffolding, nodding at the carpenters, his wide-spaced eyes clear and friendly: matching the appearance of his prey, a small-predator trick. Either he spent more money on tailoring than I did, or he was unarmed.

He was alert. He turned when I was ten feet from him, one foot carefully positioned in front of the other.

"Don't run, Jim. I'd have to knock you down." He dropped his shoulders in an appearance of instant relaxation. I smiled. "Or run if you like. Knocking you down might give me an appetite for lunch."

"Why should I run?" His voice was as whippy as a steel antenna. He probably thought he was a good actor.

"Why do people usually?" I shrugged. "Come and sit and tell me everything."

"Make me."

"All right."

"Nah, nah, just kidding." Rueful smile. The it's-a-fair-cop routine. Casual glance this way and that to see if there were any uniforms at the exit. "What do you want to know?"

"Oh, I already know. I just need verbal confirmation of when Corning hired you and how much she paid."

That rattled him: I knew. I smiled, allowed myself the indulgence of imagining how I'd take him down if it came to that.

He made a show of swinging his jacket off his shoulder, fiddling with the zip, slinging it back onto his other shoulder. It hung there as easily as it had on the other side. Ambidextrous. That would make it more fun. I wouldn't want to leave bruises, though: it would shock Finkel and Rusen and, by extension, Kick.

"And what do I get?"

"What would you suggest?"

"Immunity."

"No."

"Then I've got nothing to say."

"Your choice." I got out my phone, let him watch me dial 411, press TALK. His shoulders relaxed a little more, but the weight moved to his back foot. Clearly he wouldn't be expecting a foot sweep. "Yes," I said to the operator, "Seattle police, nonemergency. Yes, please. Thank—" He bolted.

He got to his car before I did, but that was because I wasn't trying. He leapt into the driver's seat. He gave me the finger and slid the key home without slamming the door. He turned the ignition. Nothing happened.

I hummed to myself as I pulled him out and kneed him on the sciatic nerve hard enough to collapse the leg.

"Get up."

"You've broken it!"

"No. But I could if you like. Get up. Sit." He dragged himself into the driver's seat and rubbed at his leg.

"I can't feel it."

"There won't even be a bruise." I was really tired of people whining today. "Now, tell me about Corning."

He wasn't scared, and if he was angry he didn't show it, but he knew a no-win situation when he saw it. He talked.

Corning, he said, had given him five thousand dollars, with a promise of double that when he was done. "But if I'd known it'd take so long, I'd have asked for more."

The five thousand was a lie. She'd given him three installments of two thousand dollars. "What did she ask you to do?"

"If you don't know, then why are we having this talk?"

"I know what you did. I want to know what she asked you to do."

"Wasn't specific. Make them leave, she said. Make them go broke."

"Why?"

"Don't know. Don't care." Another young man who liked breaking things for no particular reason. Maybe a horrible childhood was to blame, or some genetic glitch. It really didn't matter; he was twenty-two, and he saw no reason to change a life with which he was perfectly satisfied.

"Did she give you the drugs?"

"Karenna?" He laughed, and it struck me that Corning had a penchant for young men: Gary and Mackie and probably Johnson Bingley. Big Mac.

"When and how did you meet her?"

He shrugged. But it didn't really matter. I had the date of the first payment.

"Come with me," I said, and motioned for him to stand.

"My leg."

"You'll just have to limp."

Inside the warehouse, people glanced at each other as he limped in ahead of me. "You got any duct tape?" I asked an electrician. He passed a roll to the carpenter, who passed it to me without a word.

I walked Mackie to the food-services table, where it looked as though Bri had been crying. Turtledove seemed interested in his nails. "Yo," Mackie said to Bri. "Fucking pussy."

I made him kneel and put his hands behind his back. I put his jacket on the table, and taped his hands and feet together, then lifted him onto a chair. I taped him to that. No more hammering. The crew stared openly.

"One more question. When were you going to claim the rest of the money from Corning?"

He shrugged, though not as elegantly now that he was bound. "When the job was done."

"How were you going to get in touch?"

"Her cell phone."

I went through his jacket, found his cell phone, slipped it into my pocket. "Hey!"

He seemed genuinely outraged that I was taking his fifty-dollar phone. I could have taken his sight, or his life. I just looked at him. Something deep in his eyes squirmed like a sea mollusk under pressure. I went through his wallet, but there was nothing interesting. I dropped the jacket on the table.

I said to the listening crew, "This man that you know as Mackie is really Jim Eddard. He and Bri spoiled the footage and drugged the coffee. If that pisses you off, feel free to let them know." To Turtledove: "Don't let either of them move."

NO POLICE, Finkel and Rusen decided.

"That's not wise," I said.

"It would be too hard on the boy," Rusen said. "His brother has just died."

This wasn't about how Bri felt. But I hesitated. What did I feel? What did I want? One called the police to ensure protection, punishment, or revenge. I didn't need protection from a sixteen-year-old boy. Punishment was only useful when it triggered remorse, or acted as a deterrent. Revenge, as George Orwell pointed out, is the product of helplessness. I wasn't helpless, though I had been for a few days, thanks to Bri and his friend. Perhaps if I'd understood a few months ago how it felt to be helpless, I could have explained to my students that having power meant not needing vengeance. Perhaps things would have turned out differently.

"Fine," I said. "But I don't want to see either of them on my property again."

"But Bri is just a boy. I'm sure he wouldn't—"

"He already has. Several misdemeanors and at least one felony. He would be tried as an adult. He might well go to prison." It didn't really matter. Turtledove would keep them off the set if I said so, and I'd be gone in a week, back to Atlanta, after which I wouldn't care.

I went out to the parking lot to call Kick. She didn't answer. I waited for the beep. "It was Bri and Mackie who drugged the coffee. I have verbal confessions. They've been banned from the set. Finkel and Rusen don't want to prosecute, but there's nothing stopping you from doing so." Though there wouldn't be much point bringing suit against Mackie, because he had no money, and if she sued Bri, his father would make sure she never worked in the industry again. I hesitated, wondering if I should remind her to drink lots of water, wishing I could take back the morning and do it again, unsure what I'd do differently. The tree was rotten. It had had to come down. "I wanted you to know."

The interior of the Audi was hot, aromatic with the new-car volatiles drawn out by the sun. I tossed Mackie's phone into the glove compartment, then was tempted to curl up in the backseat and drowse like a cat, reset my day, but my phone rang.

"Aud?" My mother sounded tentative. "I have just had a most interesting conversation with Eric, who had just spoken to your friend, Hugh."

"Hugh?"

"Matthew. Matthew Dornan." I opened the car door and got out, leaned against the Audi's hood. "Aud? Are you there?"

"I'm here." Hugh? I couldn't remember anyone ever calling him that before.

"It seems you have upset your friend. Your other friend."

"It seems you always blame me when things go wrong."

Silence. "So," she said. "Your friend. She is upset with you?"

"Yes."

"And was it something you did?"

I sighed. "Yes."

"Are you are sorry for it?"

"Yes."

"But she didn't accept your apology?"

Silence.

"Aud."

"I don't want to talk about it."

"Then say nothing while I talk. Your last friend died. I didn't meet her. This friend—"

"She's not my friend. I'm not even sure we like each other."

"No?" I said nothing. "Tell me what happened."

"I did her a favor."

"What kind of favor?"

"One she didn't want."

"Eric is very keen on a paperback writer called Heinlein, whose books almost all have spaceships on the cover. He is dead now, I believe. But Eric is fond of a quote from one of these books: 'In an argument with your spouse, if you discover you are right, apologize immediately.'"

"I don't know if I am right."

"All the more reason."

"I'll think about it."

"Good. And when you have apologized, I'd like you to bring her to dinner. We're leaving very soon."

"I know."

"Well, then," she said in her it's-all-settled voice, the one she used with recalcitrant parties in a negotiation, then rang off before I could muster an argument—which was another favorite trick.

I was still staring at my phone when Dornan arrived in a taxi. He paid the driver, got out—a little more slowly than usual—ran his hand through his hair, and saw me. He turned his head slightly, like someone approaching an unpleasant task.

We stood silently for a moment. He looked sweaty. It could have been a hangover. It could have been because it was hot.

"So, Hugh. You called my mother."

"Someone had to do something."

"Someone could simply tell me what is going on."

"No," he said. "No. You can't ask me. I can't— She made me promise."

"So you do know what it is."

"No. Or, yes, I knew she was going to find out yesterday what the—" He blinked, shook his head. "You have to ask her."

"I did."

"Ask again."

A gull flew overhead. "I dreamt of Luz last night. And Kick's tree."

"She loved that tree."

"Yes." I watched the gull, wheeling round and round. "I shouldn't have done it, should I?"

"What do you think?"

I tried not to think about how my stomach had rolled when she came home, clutching her carrier bag.

"Aud . . ." He wiped his upper lip. "Try to figure it out." He headed for the warehouse door.

It was definitely hot.

I sweated lightly as I dialed. "Kick? It's Aud. I was wrong. I'm sorry. I'm coming to your house to tell you in person. I'm sorry."

I called Gary. "Reschedule my appointment with Bingley for tomorrow. Make it afternoon."

"But he's already nervous. He might—"

"Just do it."

LESSON 11

THE BASEMENT, WHEN I ARRIVED, HAD SMELLED OF PATCHOULI AND INCENSE AND strange women. I had turned on the sluggish air-conditioning unit and propped open the door, and my students had arrived carrying their own smells, but the room was still heavy with alien scents. I felt displaced. Perhaps it was just strange to be back in Atlanta after a weekend in Arkansas with Luz and the Carpenters. Her tenth birthday. Everything there had smelled of children and red clover and pine needles.

We had warmed up, and practiced falling again, and now they were sitting, waiting.

"Today's subject is children." I looked at Suze. "Even if you don't have kids, you probably have younger siblings, or nephews and nieces. You might have a frail elderly relative. You might be out—or in—one night with a friend or roommate. A lot of what I'll teach today applies in those situations. Also, of course, you never know when you might end up with children in your care unexpectedly. Children are not like adults. They don't think the way we do or know what we know." Sometimes this was good, sometimes bad.

Very briefly, after being pulled off the streets and before the police commissioner had been pressured to remove my badge altogether, I'd been assigned to visit local schools and talk about safety. Some of the things they had been taught astounded me.

"What do you currently teach your children about safety?" I said.

"Don't talk to strangers." Kim said. Some nods.

"What's appropriate in terms of touching," Therese said. More nods.

"All right. Let's go back to that first one. What's a stranger?"

"How do you mean?" Kim said.

"I've asked roomsful of children to describe or draw a stranger and they come up with a remarkably similar picture. A man, usually with dark facial hair, wearing dark clothes, and often a hat."

They came up, in fact, with the classic mugshot caricature of a rapist, whose race varied with both the socioeconomic status and race of the child. Women taught their children to be afraid of what the news had taught them to fear.

"More children are harmed by people they know—teachers, pastors, club leaders, relatives—than by those they don't. The same is true for women. According to the *Journal of the American Medical Association,* the leading cause of injury for women aged fifteen to forty-four is domestic violence. It's not the stranger who poses the danger."

"You're a poet and didn't know it," Nina said.

"Don't," I said. "No more jokes. Not today." I surveyed them, one by one. "Do I have your attention?"

Nods.

"The best way to protect your children is to protect yourself. In homes where domestic violence occurs, children are abused one hundred and fifty times more often than the national average."

No one said anything.

"Like your children, you need to know when something is wrong. Like your children, you need to believe you have the right to defend yourself. Self-defense is about self-worth, self-esteem, self-love. Self. We are worth fighting for."

I watched Sandra, remembering my last conversation, years ago, with Diane, at Arkady House, a women's shelter. I'd asked her why so many of these women didn't do the sensible thing and prosecute. She had said, "These women are grown-ups. They know what they need. If a woman comes in here all beat to shit and I say, 'Honey, you need medical attention, you need to leave that man right now,' and she says, 'Well, Diane, what I really need is a pair of shoes for my youngest,' I give her a pair of shoes. You know why? Because maybe her youngest doesn't have any shoes, because that's how her husband controls them. And if the kid can't walk out, then they can't leave. So if she says what she needs is shoes, then what she gets is shoes. If she says nothing, then maybe it's because she needs to, or maybe she's still lying to herself. Don't make her talk to you if she doesn't want to. If she's lying to herself, she'll only lie to you. No one can change that woman's life but her. Don't try to do it for her. Down that path lies madness and despair."

Madness and despair. She could have been talking about Sandra.

". . . want to teach my kids to be scared of everyone," Kim was saying. "Even their uncles, their daddy. I won't."

"No argument," I said. "Teaching children more fear isn't useful. They should be taught instead to understand what's acceptable, and from whom. They should understand who they are: where their sovereignty lies, if you like, just as you've started to learn in the last few weeks. They should learn that if someone abuses them, make them stop. They should learn that it's not smart to hand out information that may make you vulnerable. But what does that mean with regard to a ten-year-old?"

I thought of Luz, the ten-year-old I knew best: her avarice, her covetousness, particularly when it came to good leather and precious metals, her occasionally unfathomable combination of cynicism and naïveté, suspicion and trust. Ten-year-olds, in many ways, were far more capable of looking after themselves than teenage girls because they had not yet fully learnt the social imperative of fitting in, of being submissive.

"Here's what I would talk to children about. I would tell them to never answer the phone and tell someone they were alone in the house. I would explain that they must never open the door without the chain being fastened, even if they're expecting Santa or the Tooth Fairy. I would suggest that they never, ever get into a car with someone you hadn't expressly told them they should go with. It doesn't matter whether they recognize this person or not. I would tell them that if ever they were frightened to be in a room, any room, even with a relative, it's okay to run from that room and come and find you. I'd make sure they had a phone with your own phone number on speed-dial."

"Not cheap," Katherine said.

"Kroger has those pay-as-you-go kind, three for forty bucks," Kim said, in a *What planet are you from?* tone. "My kids bust theirs all the time. Carlotta even flushed hers down the john last week. You just give them another. Cheap compared to a kid's life."

"About touching," I said, "you'll have to work out the wording for yourself." No doubt there were as many coy euphemisms as southern women.

"Telling them don't let anyone touch you where your bathing suit covers works pretty good," Kim said, and this time the *what planet* tone was meant for me.

All the mothers nodded.

I wondered if Luz knew this. Of course she did. Didn't she?

"Or if anything creeps them out, they should just yell," Nina said. "Kids like yelling. Dan did that, my sister's youngest. He's eleven. His coach got him in the locker room one day and Dan yelled and another teacher came running, and they called his mom, only they couldn't get ahold of her, so they called me, and when I had him in the car, taking him home, I asked him what had made him yell, and he said, 'He was a bony-faced creepazoid! He creeped me out!' And then he wanted to know if we could go to McDonald's."

"And they should run," Kim said.

"Yes, but where?" Therese said. "You don't want them running from the frying pan to the fire."

"Walk the 'hood," Pauletta said. "I did that with my nephews and nieces when they were staying after that big storm down in the Carolinas. I showed them the routes from home to school, and school to safe places. I introduced them around to the good folks and warned them about the bad."

I thought of all those times I had moved: Oslo to London to Oslo to Yorkshire to London. I couldn't remember my mother showing me the safe places. There again, I had assumed everywhere was safe. I had assumed the world would protect me.

I remembered the kittens.

During my first few years in uniform, my partner, Frank, and I got called in to deal with a lot of bodies. More than our fair share. It became a joke in the department: a citizen calls in something suspicious and it was always Frank and I who ended up being closest and discovering the body. One winter, during a cold snap, we answered a call from an old man's neighbors who had not seen him for two or three days. Newspapers were piling up. We broke down the door. He had died on his bed. He must have been dying slowly for two days, because although the apartment was cold, he was still warm. At some point, his cat had crawled onto the bed and given birth to five kittens. She was a skinny thing, nothing but bone; she probably had not eaten for three or four days. But when we burst in, she stood over those kittens and arched and hissed, ready to take on the world. Frank left, said he'd find a box to carry them all to the cat-rescue place. And while he was gone, the coroner's deputy arrived and told me to move the cat so he could get at the body. I refused, told him that Frank was going to get a box. I said we would wait: what difference did five minutes make? But the coroner's deputy thought his time was too valuable to wait, and he reached to pick up the cat. She opened his hand from his wrist bone to the base of his thumb. The blood had been shocking, as were the frantic, blind wiggling of the kittens trying to find the nipples that were gone, and the wide-eyed, pointed-whiskered mother cat who was ready to die.

I blocked his access to the bed after that, and eventually he went away. It turned out that he was the brother of a city councillor, and that day was the start of my troubles with the department. But I didn't know that then. He left and I sat on the floor, and watched as she settled down again and gave the kittens her teats, and tried to understand. It made no sense. It wasn't logical. She must have known that if she tried to defend those tiny things against something human-sized, she'd die. And she did it anyway. Why?

I didn't understand until last year, when I met Julia. And suddenly it was clear. I would protect her with my body against an army—I would drink fire to keep her safe.

And now there was Luz.

". . . know all the commonsense stuff," Kim was saying. "What about the other stuff, that no one talks about?" I blinked. "Like what do you do when some . . . some creep tries to use your kids against you? What if they try to snatch your kid while you're there? What if they try to grab you both? What do we do?"

They were looking at me.

"It depends." I forced myself to be here, now. "Give me an example."

"I'm walking with my youngest, Carlotta, across the parking lot. Two guys come at us."

"How old is Carlotta?"

"Five."

I thought of the terror of trying to protect a five-year-old, the terror of the five-year-old; words wouldn't be much use at that age. "In an open, unprotected space get into that instinctive, favorite position, the one that works for you." She assumed it now: left leg back, right leg forward. "Get Carlotta to wrap both arms tight around your back leg, your left leg. That way you know where she is at all times, and she's behind you, and no one can snatch her without your noticing, and, as a bonus, she's helping to anchor you. Children like to help."

I hadn't known that until late last year when, as I sat in the Carpenters' Arkansas bathroom, bruised and uncertain, Luz had offered to kiss it all better.

"For grown children, or another adult, you hold hands. Try it now. Hold hands." Sandra was reluctant to take Therese's, but did. "Christie and Suze, swap sides. You want to keep your strong hand free." Christie, left-handed, on the left, Suze on the right. "If you're touching, you always know where your partner is. You can't get separated. You can do the fire technique, just charge, or you can stand your ground."

I held my hand out to an imaginary partner.

"If I need to kick on uneven ground, she can act as a counterbalance." I mimed leaning. "And vice versa. You protect her as she helps you. You help each other."

T W E L V E

"I tried to reschedule Bingley, but he's out sick."

"All right."

"Except, well, he's not."

"Oh?" I pulled over. The car threw a long shadow before me. I considered running the air-conditioning. It was very hot.

"Not that his assistant exactly said that. It was more a tone."

"A tone?"

"You know. The assistant tone. The one you use when your boss is blowing chunks in the can and you say her conference call isn't winding up on schedule."

Blowing chunks. "Then call Turtledove. Have Bingley tracked down and questioned. Turtledove will know what to ask."

"Would you like those other appointments moved to the afternoon also?"

Other appointments. Banks, attorneys. "Yes. Thank you."

THERE WASN'T a single parking space on Kick's street. I parked in the lot at Tully's and walked the three blocks south.

The sky was as red as a forge; the sun seemed to compact the air as it sank. The heat had gone to Wallingford's head: the neighborhood was a seething sea of urban humanity. People paused as they swung open the pub door, white teeth flashing and muscles sliding with unconscious animal health under elastic, sun-browned skin; many of the women seemed to be wearing flowing white muslin trousers and brief halter tops in intense colors. I could have been in Persepolis or Babylon or King Herod's palace. Only the occasional Birken-stocked foot reassured me this was Seattle.

My pulse was as heavy as a mallet as I walked down Myrtle. The sky deepened from orange and cherry to hints of wine, and edged into dusk; the air glimmered around the edges. The voices of two adolescent boys sharing a cigarette as they walked up the other side of the road seemed gilded, hemmed with dream. Their smoke smelled of incense.

Kick's front door was open and the screen door unlatched. Music, bone-hard rock, a woman's voice, poured into the street, stopped abruptly. Then new music, a male voice: sharp cymbal work, insistent bass.

"Hello?" I rapped on the doorjamb. Nothing. "Hello?" Come in, the open door implied. I eased the screen open. "Hello?"

I took off my shoes. I don't know why. The oak floor was smooth and hard under my feet, not quite cool. I didn't recognize the music, but I liked it. My pulse rate began to edge up, but not from anxiety. From something else, as a child's does when she is playing an enormously exciting game. Hide and seek.

The singer sang of dancing beneath a cherry tree.

"Hello," I said again, and walked into the kitchen.

Kick was at the stove, a cutting board piled with stir-fry vegetables in perfect heaps by her hand. Orange carrots, enamel red peppers, spring onions greener than pine leaves. Garlic and ginger hissed and sizzled in hot oil. She was throwing the frying vegetables in a perfect arc from her wok, catching them neatly, throwing them again, in time to the music. Her hips moved, side to side, then a figure-eight weave, and her feet stepped this way and that, just a shade behind the beat, deliberate and sure. Salomé in the kitchen.

She looked dense with life. Full and secret.

"Kick," I said, from six feet away, and she turned, and I saw her as though through a crystal-lensed scope, every grain and pore of her skin, every eyelash follicle at full magnification. I made some sound, low and hoarse, that neither of us heard, and reached out to brush a strand of oak hair from her forehead, but she moved, too, and my thumb plumped against the furrow between her brows, and the world split neatly into two, as lakes do, one layer warm and bright and light, moving easily over the older, denser, colder depths.

Kick spoke to me in two different languages. Her words, her lack of words, said, I don't know if I forgive you, I don't know why you're here, I don't know if I want to talk to you. But the rest of her body, her smell, her full lips and open hips, the music she'd chosen, was saying something altogether different, and saying it very clearly. I hung, poised, between two worlds, knowing I had to choose and that one kind of mistake would cost more than the other.

Pheromones are scentless. Their molecules slide past our conscious notice and snick home on the waiting receptor sites in the nasal epithelium, triggering a cascade of information. The body knows.

When an ovulating woman offers herself to you, she's the choicest morsel on the planet. Her nipples are already sharp, her labia already swollen, her spine already undulating. Her skin is damp and she pants. If you touch the center of her forehead with your thumb she isn't thinking about her head—she isn't thinking at all, she's imagining, believing, willing your hand to lift and turn and curve, cup the back of her head. She's living in a reality where the hand will have no choice but to slide down that soft, flexing muscle valley of the spine to the flare of strong hips, where the other hand joins the first to hold both hip bones, immobilize them against the side of the counter, so that you can touch the base of her throat gently with your lips and she will whimper and writhe and let the muscles in her legs go, but she won't fall, because you have her.

She'll be feeling this as though it's already happening, knowing absolutely that it will, because every cell is alive and crying out, Fill me, love me, cherish me, be tender, but, oh God, be sure. She wants you to want her. And when her pupils expand like that, as though you have dropped black ink into a saucer of cool blue water, and her head tips just a little, as though she's gone blind or has had a terrible shock or maybe just too much to drink, to her she is crying in a great voice, Fuck me, right here, right now against the kitchen counter, because I want you wrist-deep inside me. I hunger, I burn, I need.

It doesn't matter if you are tired, or unsure, if your stomach is hard with dread at not being forgiven. If you allow yourself one moment's distraction— a microsecond's break in eye contact, a slight shift in weight—she knows, and that knowledge is a punch in the gut. She will back up a step and search your face, and you'll try to recover but she'll know, and she'll feel embarrassed—a fool or a whore—at offering so blatantly what you're not interested in, and her fine sense of being queen of the world will shiver and break like a glass shield hit by a mace, and fall around her in dust. Oh, it will still sparkle, because sex is magic, but she will be standing there naked, and you will be a monster, and the next time she feels her womb quiver and clench she'll hesitate, which will confuse you, even on a day when there is no dread, no uncertainty, and that singing sureness between you will dissolve and very slowly begin to sicken and die.

The body knows. I listened to the deep message—but carefully, because at some point the deep message also must be a conscious message. Active, not just passive, agreement. I took her hand and guided the wok back down to the gas burner. Yes, her body still said, yes. I turned off the gas, but slowly, and now she reached for me. I pushed the chopping board to one side, lifted her onto the counter, and slid my hand beneath her waistband.

She was hot and swollen and I held her close, her face against my neck and she groaned. The singer pleaded to his baby to not sing yet, but before the track was over she kissed me in triumph, slid off the counter, pulled her trousers the rest of the way off, planted her feet on the floor and her palms on the top of the stove, laughed that shimmery glad laugh, and said, "More."

After a while, I remembered that the door was open, but I didn't care.

And a while after that, when I was lying on the floor smiling at the ceiling, she finished cooking the stirfry, and we ate it, properly clothed, at the dining room table. The windows were open but there was no breeze.

"That song you were playing when I got here—"

"Salomé."

"Interesting words."

She looked puzzled, then stared up at the ceiling as people do when they rerun lyrics or conversations in their head, and laughed. "All that stuff about dancing beneath the cherry tree. Poor Aud. Did you think I'd chosen it especially?"

"The subconscious can play interesting games." I put my fork down, took a breath. "I am sorry about your tree. It was wrong of me."

"It pissed me off so much, that beautiful tree. Baobab the Bold."

"Baobab?"

"Better than Fred."

It was a tree. But this time I kept my mouth shut.

"She was beautiful. Oh, I knew she was going to have to come down, but she was my tree. My tree, my decision."

"I was trying to help. I really am sorry."

"You weren't yesterday. You stood there like you were glad you were cutting down something pretty in my garden, like you wished it was me they were cutting up with a saw. I thought maybe you were trying to hurt me because I'd, well, because of my behavior the night before."

"The subconscious can play interesting games," I said again.

"Yes. And I'm sorry for mine, too."

We nodded at each other, and held hands, and let our palms talk to each other. They seemed to be better at it than our brains. Her hand was cool. I lifted it, kissed her fingertips. The garlic and ginger made the mucous membrane of my inner lips tingle pleasantly.

"I'm glad you hadn't been cutting chilis."

"What?"

"Nothing."

"I don't . . . Are you blushing?"

"No. It's hot in here. I'm flushing. It's different."

"If you say so," but she was grinning, and I didn't care, because I wanted to make her grin every day. So unlike last night's twisted, self-hating smile. My hand faltered in its conversation.

She felt it, and understood, and her breathing ratcheted up as the tension between us rose. It was like stepping into a static electricity field. The hairs on my forearms lifted. My scalp tightened.

"Kick." I cradled her hand between both of mine. "Help me understand what happened last night."

"Oh, I drank too much." I waited. She sighed. "You talked about perfection. It— I didn't like that."

"No."

"I'm not perfect."

"No one is." She didn't say anything. I stroked the soft, thin skin over the tendons on the back of her hand.

"I'm like the tree." Now I was thoroughly confused. She pulled her hand free. "Don't you get it?"

"No."

"I'm sick."

When I was fifteen I had gone running along the beach in Whitby. It had been a sunny March day after more than two weeks of rain and fog, and I was warm and happy. In a moment of sheer joy I'd stripped off my jeans and dived headfirst into a breaker—and thought I had dived into a wall. The near-freezing water paralyzed my chest muscles and cut off my oxygen as effectively as a sheet of glass sliding through my neck. I thrashed in the churning breakers, but no one noticed. Last year, I had been shot and had to dive into a glacier lake to escape the gunman. I had understood, this time, about freezing water, thought I had been prepared, but the cold still stopped my breath.

"Are you dying?"

"What? No, of course not."

When that first flood of air hits your lungs again, nothing matters but the rush of oxygen. It doesn't matter if the air is smutty with smoke, or stinging with rain; it only matters that you'll live. I stared at my plate, at the jewel-like vegetables, and savored the tangy aftertaste of lime, the bite of garlic, the hiss of ginger on my tongue. Dead people couldn't do that. I looked at her. "Good. Don't die. I need you."

Her eyes filmed. One tear spilled down her right cheek. I ran the back of my finger up her skin and caught it.

"Is it cancer?"

She shook her head.

"Then what?"

She scrubbed at her cheeks with the back of her free hand. "Something. I don't know. I had an appointment." I nodded. "An MRI, but the pictures weren't very clear, my doctor says. But it's something."

"When will they know?"

"He's getting another doctor to read it tomorrow. Or the day after."

"You should get it done now."

"I don't think there's a rush."

"But you don't know. You said yourself. You should get it done today. He ought to—" I shut up. Her hand had gone passive in mine and she was studying it impersonally, as though already separating herself from her body, from life, from our conversation. "If it's a question of money . . ." She drifted farther away. "What kind of doctor?"

"Neurologist."

"And they're sure it's not your hip? Those pins?"

"They took the pins out more than a year ago." She smiled gently. "Couldn't have had an MRI otherwise."

A neurologist. None of it made sense. She looked so good, so alive. Her skin was firm, her muscles dense, her eyes bright. "You're so strong."

"Most of the time."

I didn't know what to say.

"What do you know about my accident?"

"That it was a miracle you survived."

"I didn't make any mistakes."

"No."

"I didn't make any mistakes," she said again. She lifted her hand, studied it, flexed it, held it out, palm up, a few inches from the table, as though it were the top of a cliff a hundred feet from the sea. "Everything was perfect: setup, departure point, landing area, wind, temperature, light, cameras. I felt good. The rehearsal had been clean and easy. It was going to be beautiful. I knew it. I felt it. I jumped. I ran and bent, and my muscles compressed like a spring before it flies loose, and I leapt, and the muscles in my right leg just . . . The spring just broke. There was nothing there." Her hand rose and turned and fell slowly, inevitably to the table, palm down. "Nothing there."

I picked it up. "You are here. Your hand is here. Right here. I'm here."

"Yes," she said. "But for how long?" She stood, and patted my cheek, as she would a child's, and filled the kettle.

BY SEVEN O'CLOCK the temperature in the house had climbed to eighty degrees. Kick turned pale, and when she talked, she slurred very slightly, and I said, What's the matter? and she said, I'm hot.

I ran a cool bath and laved her with water until her skin began to pebble and her waxy pallor warmed back to gold.

A neurologist. Heat reduced conductivity, and the central nervous system was one electrical system. Increase heat, reduce signal.

"Kick, why don't you have air-conditioning?"

"Because people in Seattle don't. Why spend ten thousand dollars for a system you'd only use ten times a year?"

"It's just money."

"Just money I don't have."

"I do."

"I know."

I couldn't find a fan, so she stayed in the bath while I opened all the windows. I checked the weather forecast for tomorrow: cooler in the morning, hot again from the late afternoon.

By nine o'clock cool air was moving in blocks through the house. I lay awake a long time, coming up with cooling strategies if she couldn't move, or couldn't breathe.

IT WAS eight o'clock when I woke. She was sitting on the side of the bed, stroking my head with cool hands, staring into the middle distance, lovely and strong and fine as a Chinese chair.

I wasn't conscious of moving, but her hands must have felt some message from my body, and she blinked and looked at me, and smiled.

She smoothed the hair back from my forehead. "When you're a bit more awake I want to ask you a favor."

"I'm awake."

"What are you doing this afternoon?"

"Nothing I can't postpone or bring forward to this morning."

"My five-year-old nephew is coming over around two o'clock. His mom is supposed to be picking him up again around four, but she's not always great with timekeeping, and I have a message that they want me to go in for another scan at four-thirty."

"I'll come with you."

"No. It's nothing. Just an hour or so. And Maureen should be here to pick him up before I leave. But I want you to be here to watch him for me in case she's late. Will you do that?"

"A five-year-old? Couldn't you just tell Maureen you have a—" Of course. She hadn't told Maureen anything about this. "Yes," I said. "I'd be happy to."

I CALLED Turtledove from the car before I set off and left a message. He called me back when I was on the bridge over Lake Union. I couldn't pull over. "Make it fast." Traffic was light, but anyone who thought it was possible to talk and pay attention to the road at the same time was a fool.

"Bingley's in Oaxaca."

"He ran?"

"For a while. It's a last-minute package deal. He's back in six days."

Six days. I'd be on my way back to Atlanta by then.

"If you want to spend the money we could bring him back."

"No. Leave it."

I rang off. Then I was off the bridge. I pulled over and called Gary. "This afternoon's appointments with the banks and Finkel and Rusen's attorney—see if you can bring them forward to this morning. I have to be done by one-thirty." To babysit.

"On it," he said.

He called back as I was giving my keys to the Fairmont valet. "Ten-thirty, Nguyen the banker. Eleven-fifteen, a preliminary meeting with Brooks-Page, the representative of Contalmis, the company that owns one of those Duwamish lots you want. Twelve noon, Clinch, another banker. No response as yet from the attorneys or their principals." He sounded pleased and terrified.

"Keep trying."

"Okay. I've e-mailed your schedule, and a packet of relevant information is being faxed to your hotel as we speak."

I could get used to having an assistant.

The fax was waiting when I got to my room, along with one from Bette, together with a cover note in her huge scrawl. *Here's the revised Hippoworks contract. What were they thinking?? They got money, you got bubkes. Thanks to me, you now have some control. Buy me mojitos when you return.* I sighed. I didn't want control. I just wanted to help Kick.

I showered and changed. Checked my e-mail. My schedule, as Gary had promised, and an e-mail from Laurence. *Money's there, everything you asked for, but I hope you know what the hell you're doing.*

I had a few minutes to search the Web for neurological signs and symptoms. A seemingly endless list, from acid maltase deficiency to Zellweger syndrome. I tried again. Leg weakness and MRI. A much smaller list. Brain or spine tumor—but she'd said it wasn't cancer. Parkinson's and multiple sclerosis. Guillain-Barré and Huntington's disease. Brown-Sequard and ALS. Still too many, and all of them frightening.

While I changed my clothes and tried to think about something else, my brain, in orderly fashion, began to construct a hierarchy of disease. The best diagnosis would be a discrete, benign, operable spine tumor. Two hours under the knife and everything fixed. The worst would be ALS, or maybe Huntington's—a complete dismantling of self not unlike Alzheimer's. Guillain-Barré was a mixed choice; it generally killed you within nine months or went away on its own.

I had known her only two weeks. I had known Julia six weeks before she died. With Julia, I'd had no warning. And no choice.

THE NEPHEW'S name was David. "Not Dave," he said through his tiny milk teeth, "David." It reminded me of meeting Luz for the first time, though she had been nine, and she hadn't been clutching a moose backpack stuffed with a Nerf gun—he called it his Pop Shotz Pistol—and three G-rated DVDs.

"Jesus," Kick said after we'd settled him down in front of the TV with the first one and were making a late lunch in the kitchen, "what is it with these movies? Why does the parent fish or lion or deer always get brutalized in the first few minutes while the fishlet or cub or fawn watches? Jesus. And why does his mother think I need audiovisual aids to keep my nephew entertained for a couple of hours?" I didn't say anything. It wasn't the films she was tense about. "Look, can you watch him while I finish this?"

I left her to it and settled down with David in front of the TV, which was showing brightly colored fish.

I looked at David's gun. It looked as though it worked by squeezing the butt and forcing the Nerf missiles, which were spongy quarrels with suction-cup tips, out of the muzzle with air pressure.

I swapped the gun to my other hand. It was nicely designed, one quarrel already in the barrel and three slotted into a kind of cartridge underneath. It fit my palm well. There was even a sight midway down.

"Do you want to play with it?" he said.

"I don't want to disturb your film." He looked blank. "The movie."

"I've seen it before," he said in that world-weary way children have. "Three times yesterday. Go on, shoot it."

I pointed at the fireplace and squeezed. The arrow shot out with a satisfying *phhtt* and stuck briefly to the painted brick. I slotted another arrow and squeezed. Again, it clung for a microsecond before dropping to the hearth.

"Does it help if you lick the ends?"

"No," he said, "but if you shoot at a window or something, it sometimes sticks."

I got up and went to the other side of the room, and shot at the window. The arrow stuck on the glass.

"Yes!" he said, and we grinned at each other. The arrow fell off. "Try that big booger. You have to stick it on the outside, not the inside."

The big booger was a torpedo-sized missile slung beneath the arrows. It had a hole in its tail that fitted over the muzzle, rather than into the barrel.

"You gotta aim it up," he said. "It flies different."

A child who appreciated ballistics. It had never occurred to me to wonder if Luz would. I aimed the length of the room and it went sailing majestically into the coat tree, a good yard to the left of where I'd aimed. He jumped up and scrambled to get it. "My turn."

I gave him the gun.

"Okay," he said. "Come and watch this."

Gun in his right hand and remote in his left, he squinted carefully down the barrel and squeezed the butt and pressed PAUSE at the same time. The arrow stuck, right on the frozen fish's tail fin. "Huh," he said. "A flesh wound. Tails don't count, only a tap in the hat."

A tap in the hat. Where did a five-year-old pick up the language of hired killers? School? What was Luz learning that I didn't know about?

"Now watch me off the TV with this big booger." He carefully fitted the torpedo. He missed on his first try, but not by much. "Oh, yeah. You can laugh, but I'll get you. You better start squealing for mercy, 'cause I'm gonna get you."

This time he knelt and aimed with both hands.

"Die, sucker!" The missile bounced cleanly off the center of the screen. "Oh, yeah. Oh, yeah. It's dead. Never coming back."

Kick walked in with a tray. "Time for soup," she said.

While David watched the rest of the fish film, Kick and I cleared away the dishes. "I'll try to be as quick as I can," she said. "If he gets cranky, there's ice cream, and don't forget he has those other two movies."

"Right."

She smiled, but it was distracted, harried. "Just don't try to parent him, okay? He hasn't had any of that from his mom and dad. It'll just confuse him. I have to go. Are you sure you'll be all right?"

"Absolutely," I said. I held her, palm against her spine. I imagined a neat, rubbery little tumor, like a latex robin's egg, that would just pop out when you opened the skin.

I **WAS LYING** on the floor and David was asleep on the sofa when she got home. Gauze and medical tape flashed white in the crook of her left arm.

"Christ," she said, crossing immediately to the sofa. "Is he dead? What did you do to him?"

I sat up. "Nothing. He's asleep." She looked down at David dubiously. He had his thumb in his mouth. I put my arm around her waist. She leaned into me and her muscles softened little by little. She felt warm.

I stroked the side of her arm. "Blood draw?"

"IV for the MRI. Some kind of contrast thing."

"Big Band-Aid."

"They had to try twice."

A blue Mini screeched to a halt outside the house—on the side of the street where no one was supposed to park—and the driver honked and left the motor running. Like a dog who recognizes the sound of his master's footsteps, David stirred.

Kick picked him up. "Mom's here," she said, but he was still floppy, asleep with his eyes open. She turned to me. "Where's his stuff?"

I picked up his backpack and held it out.

The horn honked again. "Bring it. You can meet the family."

But all I saw of Maureen was an artificially bouncy river of strawberry blond hair and bangles flashing on her right wrist as she leaned over and shoved open the passenger door. All I heard was a "Yeah, hi," to Kick's introductions, and "Just put him in his seat, Kick, for Chrissakes. I'm late." It was Kick who snapped the seat belt buckles and kissed David on the cheek, and Maureen was revving the engine even before Kick slammed the door.

THE PUB was air-conditioned. The darts were the kind they always keep behind the bar: cheap aluminium barrels coated with a faux brass finish, plastic shafts, plastic flights. I threw a one, a five, and then, finally, a twenty. I pulled them out, chalked up my sad score, and handed the darts to Kick.

"Inferior darts," I said.

She just smiled and walloped in a twenty, a triple twenty, and triple nineteen. It wasn't a fluke. She'd already beaten me soundly in our first game. "One hundred and thirty-seven," she said in a sweet voice. "Mark it up." I did. It left her with thirty-two, the perfect closing position.

I threw again, and managed a respectable score of sixty-one.

She took two darts to finish: a sixteen and double eight. "Should have done it with one," she said, "but, like you said, they're inferior darts."

We took our beer to a table.

"So," she said, "you survived trial by nephew."

I nodded.

"Sorry I was so late. But Christ, when I came in and saw him lying so still on the couch . . . He's never slept at my house before. How did you do that?"

"I took him into the garden for some good, clean, healthy fun in the fresh air and sunshine." She gave me a look. "All right: we shot at each other with the Nerf gun. Moving targets." We'd also shot at squirrels, but she didn't need to know that. We'd missed, anyway.

We sipped the rich, nutty beer. Fuller's Extra Special Bitter, served in imperial pints.

"Was it a problem with the scan that made you late?"

"Just the IV. I have pathetic veins." She shrugged. "Hopefully it'll be worth it. They said the gadolinium will . . . They said . . ." She stared into space. The tips of her fingers, where they wrapped around her glass, were pale. "They said the gadolinium would make the lesions show up more clearly. Lesions. Christ."

Two tables away, three women and a man burst out laughing at the end of some joke. "Drink some beer," I said. She did. I did. "They think you have lesions?"

"Brown-Sequard syndrome."

Which was a set of symptoms, not a diagnosis: weakness or paralysis on one side of the body, numbness on the other, caused by a spinal lesion. But the spinal lesion could be the result of a tumor, or MS, or trauma, or infection with something like TB. Had she had a cough recently? Or smelled oranges in the middle of the night, or newly mown grass, or heard music? Did her arm ever get weak? How was her vision? I opened my mouth, then shut it, and tried to imagine how she felt. "Do you want to talk about this?"

"No."

I nodded. "All right. Just tell me when you're due to get your results."

"Tomorrow. I have to go back to Northwest. Eleven o'clock."

The patient was always the last to know. By now, half a dozen people would already have seen the results. Some radiologist would have shoved the film up under the steel clip at the top of the light panel and given it a preliminary read, would have looked at the pictures of the delicate sheathing on her spine, the thin image-slices of her brain, and would be sitting at home eating a Reuben sandwich and saying to their sweetie, *Saw a sad case today, hon. She's only twenty-eight*... They would have sent the information to her doctors, where it would be printed and read by nurses, then handed off to receptionists and neatly filed.

"All right," I said.

"I just . . . Today I want to talk about ordinary things, and drink beer, and pretend there's nothing wrong. Because after tomorrow I'll know, and there won't be any more pretend."

"Tomorrow, then." If I knew who her doctor was, I could break in, read the results for myself. Or rip it from the Northwest Hospital's servers.

Four men came in and sat at the table between us and the joke-telling group. Business clothes, or at least shirt and ties. Their voices were very loud. I looked at my watch. "How's the food here?"

"Pub food. Burger and fries. Club sandwich. It's okay."

We ordered. She had the garden burger and cole slaw. I had fish and chips. Ordinary things.

"So, the scaffolding's about done," she said.

"Good." The chips were almost English: fried in lard, and soft. They tasted good when doused with vinegar. "How big is it?"

"Forty-two feet."

"And I imagine someone's going to have to jump from that."

"Bernard."

"Is he up to it?"

She sighed. "No. He doesn't understand the camera. He can't act. He's afraid, which is dangerous for everybody, and he can't fall. Pass the salt, please."

She applied salt and rearranged her burger for a minute, obviously working up to something.

"Falling isn't like any other kind of stunt work. To fall, you have to understand the ground. You have to embrace not being on your feet." She pushed her fries around. "Listen to me. I'm probably not even making sense."

"You're making perfect sense."

She hesitated, and then went on in a rush, "It's about letting go. It might sound crazy, but it's a kind of acceptance. A being right there and a not being there. Christ, no, that's not right, that makes it sound like a fortune cookie. Wait a minute. Let me think."

This time it was the pepper shaker, followed by ketchup. Her eyebrows went up and down, the muscles to either side of her mouth tensed and relaxed, tensed and relaxed, as they moved in tandem with her interior monologue. "It's much more than the possibility of being hurt. It might have started out that way, when our ancestors were swinging from trees, but it's become this whole moral metaphor. A fall from grace. Pride before a fall. Feeling good means you're up, bad means you're down."

"Lucifer's fall."

"Exactly. It's the most basic prohibition of all: Do not fall. It's drummed into us. We're not as scared of the landing as we are the falling. Think about it. A fall from thirty feet can kill you just as dead as one from a hundred feet, but fewer stunters will do a hundred feet because it just feels more scary—and that's because it takes longer to fall."

She dipped a fry in her tartare sauce. Munched it. Dipped another.

"When you're preparing for one of those falls you have to know the physics and the math, the geometry and architecture of the thing. And you have to think all the way down, but in a way you have to not think."

"It sounds a bit like martial arts."

"Does it? Well, anyhow, before, I planned and I calculated and I imagined forces and angles and safeties and redundancies, but I never really thought I'd ever get into trouble. I was as confident of landing well and walking away as I was of walking to the fridge for a beer without tripping. You need that confidence. You can't afford to lose it."

I nodded.

"There are two kinds of people, those who thrive in acute-stress, high-input situations, and those who don't. Bernard doesn't. When I jump, when I step out of the plane or dive off the cliff, there's this kind of internal flash, and I can feel my heart slow for a second or two. It slows down, and I focus like a machine.

No, that's not right. Like a laser, maybe, except I feel so alive. And I don't make mistakes. The more stress I feel, the more my concentration improves."

Her gaze was unfocused, her food forgotten.

"I don't know anything like it. It's like being God for a few seconds, except it can feel like hours. Everything looks and sounds, I don't know, different, like it's outlined in crystal."

"Like being washed clean."

Her eyes focused on me. "Yes. How do you know?"

"It's happened to me." Now it was my turn to hesitate. I wasn't used to talking about this. "It's like dancing, like being a hummingbird among elephants, like having all your joints lubricated and everything suddenly tuned to perfect pitch. Even the light changes. I call it the blue place."

We stared at each other.

"It's the limbic system," I said. "It changes the way our neurons work."

She was nodding. "It changes everything. It changes the whole brain network."

All of us see the world in images. We tell a kind of instant story about every moment. But when fear triggers the amygdala, it releases neurotransmitters; the hypothalamus dumps adrenaline. They change the rate at which we form and process those images: we form them faster and then we connect them together more richly and widely. Meanwhile, all that adrenaline is opening the arteries and speeding the heart rate, changing the physical machine up to top gear. We don't just feel smarter, stronger, and faster; we are.

It was getting more crowded. I signaled a passing server for another round. After it came, we sipped for a minute. I moved my glass around on the beer mat, sometimes centering it on the Fuller's logo, sometimes fitting it to the corner. "It's funny how the mind can interpret the same signals in different ways. That adrenaline arousal—elevated heart rate, breathing, galvanic skin response—can be felt as fear, or sex, or excitement. It's all in the mind."

"I tried to tell that to Bernard: just grin like Rusen and tell yourself, boy howdy, this is fun! and eventually you'll believe it. But he doesn't get it."

"No."

We shook our heads, like two old soldiers drinking at the veterans' hall and despairing of the youth of today. "But let's get back to arousal," she said, and grinned. "My flash, your blue place. I did some reading. Psychology books call it *flow*. They talk about losing awareness of your surroundings, about being swept up in the tide—not exactly surrender, but a kind of letting go."

"When you can do nothing, what can you do?"

She frowned.

"A Zen thing," I said.

"But it's not doing nothing. Is it?"

"Not for me." And when, two years ago, your muscles failed you on the drop, what did you do about that? Why have you waited so long?

"Right. What was I talking about? Oh. Those books. Flow. So, anyhow, flow leads to the gestalt thing, and physical fabulousness, but also disinhibition." She drank more beer and grinned again, but it wasn't the twisty grin I'd seen two nights ago. This was the otter, diving in and out of the water for pure joy. "In other words, there's a reason those po-faced puritans of every stripe hate it when people take risks or have fun. You jump off a bridge with a bungee cord around your ankles, or go dancing, or surf that rip, and the next thing you know your body is not only giving you the arousal message, it's telling you there's no reason not to have sex."

"Bodies are smart."

"Yeah." She clinked my glass with hers. "You know that fall metaphor? I sometimes wonder if the Adam and Eve thing, getting kicked out of the garden of Eden, is a species memory of coming down from the safety of the trees, of losing paradise in order to walk upright and grub about on the forest floor."

There wasn't a single bone in her neck and shoulders that was too big or too small, not a single muscle that should have been more or less developed. She was perfectly proportioned, slight and exceptionally strong and beautiful. "I don't want any more to drink," I said. "Come back with me. Have coffee in my suite."

"Your air-conditioned suite."

"Stay the night."

The night was hot and airless but intensely alive. In un-air-conditioned Seattle people sat on their porches, by windows. On the two-block walk to my car we passed through miniature seas of music, laughter, wafts of marijuana smoke.

Kick talked about falling. The difference between a controlled, green-screen studio shot, with backgrounds inserted digitally later, and a live shot. "You can fall a hundred twenty feet from a specially built platform that's perfectly dry and level, and even the airflow is controlled. Falling off a real building from sixty feet is three times as dangerous. There's always the risk of a distraction—a traffic accident on the next block, a sudden rainstorm or gust of wind—and then there's all the bits of building that stick out that you have to compensate for, flagpoles and ledges and pipes, and the way wind moves over a solid surface."

She talked hard and fast, waving her arms for emphasis. "And, oh, I just had a thought. About safety and risk, and falling and beginnings. About stunts and film and human story. A grand theory of everything, or at least a reason you could make a case for film being the ultimate narrative medium . . . the most basic thrill narrative of all. The ultimate high-stakes story. We care about what happens. It has a beginning, middle, and end, and it's all or nothing. The stumble, the fall, the landing. You either walk away or you don't. Success or failure." She talked faster but walked even more slowly. "It's turning the clock back to a million years ago, when Junior fell out of the tree and the whole troop watched, banana half-chewed, to see if she caught herself in time or broke her back in the dirt."

The closer we came to her house and my car, the slower she walked, until we stood at the bottom of her steps and she was still talking, and her eyes shone a strange electric blue under the sodium street lamp, and I realized she was trying to give me it all, tell me everything she knew about falling, because maybe this time tomorrow it would no longer be true, or at least no longer her truth.

For a moment she seemed to bend and glimmer. I said, "You're not coming back to the hotel, are you?"

Her arms sank to her sides. "No."

I knew the answer to my next question, too. "Would you like me to stay at your house?" Halos sprang out around the street lamps. "I could come with you to the doctor's tomorrow."

"No. Thank you, but no. It's— This is mine."

The halos fractured. "Will you call me?"

"Yes." She reached out and touched my cheek with the back of her hand and when she lifted it, her skin gleamed.

"I mean, will you please call me as soon as you know anything? And call me if you change your mind. Call me for anything, anytime."

"Yes."

"And stay cool, remember the bathtub. And that fan Dornan bought for you. If you can't find it—"

"Aud."

"—I could probably find a twenty-four-hour—"

"Aud." Again she reached out and brushed my cheek, then the other. "It's all right."

I caught her wet hand and kissed it. "It's not." How could it be.

I enfolded her, cradled her head against my collarbone, felt her hips sharp against mine and her ribs, sheathed in taut muscle, bending like bone bows in and out, in and out, and I wanted to howl and hurl myself against the world, to lay my body down to keep her safe. I breathed the Kick-skin, fennel-shampoo, and beer scent of her, then squeezed and let her go.

I WALKED DOWNHILL. It wasn't the way to my car but it was easier. After about a mile, I was at Gas Works Park, but I didn't want the comfort of night-breathing greenery and the confusion of natural and industrial. I turned right. In another half a mile, I was walking along the ship canal in Fremont. I turned right again where the Highway 99 bridge ran over the water, walking under its blank shadow, seeking the place where its soaring impossibility met the dirt.

On 36th Street I tracked the trail of used condoms and dirty syringes, of empty potato chip bags and, oddly, a child's wooly winter cap, to the armpit of Fremont.

Hunched in the concrete crease was a troll, holding a VW Beetle in its left hand. I stopped. Breathed. It was still there.

I approached cautiously. The VW was real. Life-size. The troll was made of concrete. It had long hair and wild eyes. There was a sign, saying something about a sculpture competition, but it was so defaced with graffiti that I couldn't read it.

The troll always wins, I'd said to Julia in Norway, and I had been right. There was always someone, something, bigger and faster and stronger. Always.

MY SUITE was silent and cool, as still as a burial chamber undisturbed for a hundred years.

I dialed Rusen.

"Yes?" He sounded distracted and grown-up. The Avid's hard drive was chattering in the background.

"It's Aud Torvingen. Before I sign the agreement, I have some questions about crew insurance and employee status."

"Boy, okay."

"Kick Kuiper." Silence. "Rusen?"

"Um?"

"Rusen, turn your chair around so you're facing away from the screens. Turn your chair around."

A long, floaty sigh and chair creak. "That thing sure is hard to resist."

"Yes. Kick Kuiper. What's her employee status specifically as it relates to health insurance?"

"Hold on one second." Tap, tap, tap. "Okey-doke. Well, it looks like she was hired as a contractor, so no insurance. At least—"

"Change it."

"That's not legal. But—"

"Change it."

"Wait up, just hold on now. What I'm trying to tell you is that I might not have to." I waited. "I offered her the job of stunt coordinator earlier today."

"Stunt coordinator."

"She's more than qualified. Tell you the truth, I have no clue why she's working in craft services to begin—"

"Did she accept?"

"Well, now, she hasn't exactly accepted yet, no."

"What did she say?"

"Here's the thing. She's been out a couple days. I had to leave a message on her machine this evening . . ." When we were in the pub, talking about the blue place and falling, about flow and otherness, about being larger than life, brilliant with it, on top of the world. ". . . in particular?"

"I'm sorry?"

"I said, is there any reason in particular this is coming up now?"

"Just sign her up as stunt coordinator from the time you left her the message. I want her on the company's insurance."

"I guess I could stretch a point that far. For Kick. It's not really wrong, when you think about it, I mean, I have offered her—"

"Thank you. Please see to the paperwork before you get lost in editing again."

"Boy, that's a good thought. That thing sure is—"

"Rusen. Good night."

The phone felt big and bulky in my hands but I didn't want to put it down. I imagined dialing Dornan, waking him up, his creased voice saying, *What on earth is it that won't keep until tomorrow, Torvingen?* And what would I say?

I called Leptke and left a message. "Be available tomorrow. Tell your counsel. I'll have your proof before midday."

Then I e-mailed Laurence instructions and the information necessary to wire funds to my Seattle bank. I also asked him to make sure someone at that bank had a cashier's check waiting for me so that I could finalize the Hippoworks deal.

I called room service for some tea. Tomorrow I would deal with Corning. I saw myself tracking Corning to her hotel, backing her into a corner, flexing my hands perhaps, so that she bolted and I chased her, and brought her down like a lion with a young impala. I would take her throat, just hard enough to suffocate her slowly, and as her eyes rolled back, I'd rip out her soft insides. Her right leg would kick once. If I closed my eyes I could feel her skin under my hands, feel her pulse flutter and still, taste her fear. She would never be able to hurt Kick or anybody else again.

It wouldn't make any difference. At eleven o'clock tomorrow, it, whatever it was, was coming to get Kick and I wouldn't be there.

LESSON 12

THEY HAD MY PHONE NUMBER, A LITTLE PIECE OF MY LIFE, AND STILL THEY UNDERSTOOD almost nothing of what I knew of the world. They were peering at it through a keyhole: I wanted them to open the door.

"The important thing to remember," I said as they obediently lowered themselves to the floor and rolled onto their stomachs, looking scared, "is that there's a kind of joy to all this."

"Joy?" Pauletta said, sitting up again. "Excuse me, but are you insane? You get off on imagining someone's about to pin you face-first in the dirt?"

"The mat's quite clean," I said. "Perhaps that's not what you meant. Except it is, in a way. Lie down again. All of you, lie down. Facedown, arms at your sides." I sat cross-legged so that I wouldn't loom over them. "Those of you on the mats, can you smell that sharp scent? It's vinegar. I wipe the mats down with it after every lesson. It's a natural disinfectant. Feel the mat, how it pushes back at your hips, how you have to turn your head to one side to breathe comfortably, how that pulls at the muscles that attach to your jaw, that run down your neck, that connect to your arms. Feel it. Feel yourself, your body, your bone and muscle, the blood singing in your veins. Breathe deep. Feel your lungs expand, how your spine lifts another inch from the floor. Imagine your rib cage, what it holds and protects: your lungs, your heart, your spleen, all those blood vessels. It's a fortress—very, very strong. Feel your knees, delicate and strong and indispensable. It's all yours, every inch. Even when it feels bad, if you get a bruise, a graze, a cut, a break, a puncture, a sprain, it feels good because it's yours. You are it, and it is you. Enjoy it at all times. Enjoy using it. Enjoy defending it."

Someone had forgotten to wear underarm deodorant today. I tasted it, the tang of fatty apocrine sweat, full of much larger, more complicated molecules than the simple $C_2H_4O_2$ of vinegar. It was faint, and it was healthy, clean sweat on a clean body wearing clean clothes, but unusual in Atlanta, where almost everyone equated any kind of body odor with filth and wrongness, where people liked to pretend the body didn't exist.

"This is your body. Yours. No one but you has the responsibility to keep it, to keep yourself, whole. If someone pins you to the ground, what will you do?"

The underarm scent grew, perhaps, slightly stronger.

"So you're facedown. The first thing you do is protect your throat, and neck, and your breathing. Turn your face forward again. Stretch the crown of your head towards the wall in front of you. That will stop your neck bending the wrong way, it will pull your chin down."

"It puts my nose on the floor," said Tonya.

"Bring your arms under your body. That will make it harder for an attacker to grab hold of them. But keep them bent, elbows down by your ribs, hands up between your breasts. If you can, while keeping your upper arms close to your body, bring your hands up, like this." I made the international sign for *vulva:* palms out, tips of index fingers and of thumbs touching. "Keep your elbows in. Put your hands in front of your face. Put your face in the gap. If your attacker starts banging your head on the ground, it will afford you some protection."

This time the strengthened body odor was definite.

"Everyone, sit up." They did. I looked from set face to pale face to lightly sweating face. Katherine had carpet fluff stuck to her lip gloss. "Pick a partner." Katherine turned to Tonya, Pauletta to Nina, Christie to Suze; Sandra didn't look at Therese, but Therese understood it was her job to be Sandra's partner, and sat a little closer; Kim looked at Jennifer and sighed—though, to her credit, silently. "You're going to learn this together. You're helping each other learn. When you play the attacker, remember that your partner is a grown woman and needs to know the truth; she needs to know that you won't let go immediately to make her feel better. She needs to know that in a real situation the techniques she learnt here will work. When you play the one being attacked, try not to panic. This is a controlled situation; you're safe. We'll begin with lying facedown and your attacker on top of you because that's the worst position to be caught in. You'll learn how to get away from that and then you'll know you can do anything. A volunteer."

No one.

"Therese." She had been the most confident tumbler last week. "Come here and pin me. Everyone, move back a little." I stretched out, facedown, put my face in its protected gap. "Sit on my back. Pin my wrists to the floor." She sat on me, but carefully. I doubted she weighed less than 120 pounds, but she was keeping about half that on her feet, taking the strain on her quads. "No. Sit on me. The point is to pin me so I can't move." She did. "Now pin my wrists. Hard." She leaned into it. Her hands were cold and slightly damp. "Think you can roll out all right if I throw you over my head?" I felt movement. "Are you nodding or shaking your head?"

"Yes, I can roll." She sounded grim.

"All right. Like a Band-Aid. One rip and you're off. Ready?" And I breathed out with a *whoosh,* shot my hands forward, and bucked her off. There was no crash, and she stood about the same time I did, so I assumed she'd landed well.

"Whoa," said Suze.

"Ready to go again?" I asked Therese, and she nodded, though she wasn't grinning, which surprised me. The first time I'd been thrown and had landed well enough not to get hurt, my exhilaration had been fierce, burning brightly enough that I could have thrown back my head, opened my mouth, and lit the sky. I would never understand these women.

I turned to the rest of the class. "This time it'll be slow motion, so you can see for yourselves how easy it is."

Therese perched back on top of me.

"What would an attacker be expecting from me in this position?"

"Panic," and "Struggle like crazy," Nina and Tonya said at the same time.

"And what would you do in a panic?"

"Curl up like a bug," said Nina.

"Why?"

"Because I'd be panicking," she said with obvious patience.

"And why would you, Tonya, struggle? What's the ultimate point?"

"To get him as far from me as I could. Protect myself," she said.

"Nina?"

She nodded. "Get him off of me."

"Pin me," I said to Therese. She did. Her hands were less cold and damp. Perhaps relief and lessening of stress were her version of exaltation. "Now look at her balance. Where's her weight?"

"On your wrists," Jennifer said.

"Yes. She's leaning forward, thinking that what I'll do is pull in like a bug, to protect myself. Or thrash about, to get her off me, away from me, somehow. The last thing an attacker will be anticipating is any kind of move that pulls them towards us, or that appears to spread us flatter to the ground and therefore make us more vulnerable. So that's exactly what we do. It also happens to work to pull them further off balance. Watch."

Instead of the untrained, instinctive move to pull my hands down to protect my belly or breasts and groin, I exhaled and slid them smoothly forward along the mat, wrists first: Spider-Man shooting web at the wall. Therese started to topple forward.

"Now if that's all I did, she'd just fall on me." I turned my face slightly and said to Therese, "Get off for a moment, please." She did. I got back into my initial position. "What I do is tighten my abdominal muscles and jerk my knees up underneath me"—I showed them in slow motion, pulling into a tight mushroom, then down again, then bunching again—"and I shoot my hands forward at the same time as bucking." I showed them. "Now watch while I do it at full speed." I nodded to Therese.

Even though she was expecting it, she went over. This time she smiled as she came up, a small smile but definite.

I smiled back. "You want to throw me this time?"

"You weigh a lot more than I do."

"True. But it will work." Using exactly this technique, on a gravel road in Arkansas last year, I'd thrown a man weighing close to two hundred fifty pounds.

"All right."

She lay down like a woman going to her execution. I sat on her sacrum. "Remember to protect your face." She did. I pinned her wrists firmly. I could see her pulse thumping madly in her carotid arteries and felt her rib cage swell and shrink, swell and shrink. Then she stilled, and with a cry of despair and rage, she threw me off. She threw me far harder than necessary and I flew seven or eight feet.

The class clapped and Pauletta whistled and stamped. As I rolled to my feet, Therese sat up, looking pleased.

"Man, you practically sent her into orbit," Pauletta said to her.

"You can't do that from a mattress," Sandra said.

"You can," I said. "It's more difficult, yes, but possible."

"Well, I couldn't."

"Perhaps you haven't, yet, but you could."

"I can't. I'm speaking from experience."

"Yes," I said. "But that was before you had me to teach you."

She glared at me. "And an attacker wouldn't pin you like that, anyway."

"All attackers are different," I said. "But I'll be happy to show you a way around any pin. What would you like to try?"

"I want you to tell me what to do when they break down your bedroom door and grab you from behind around the throat with their forearm and pin your arms to your body with their other arm and then push you facedown into the bed so you're suffocating and while your hands are trapped by your own body they pin you down with one hand on the back of your neck and you can't breathe, can't think, and then they have their whole body weight and they have a hand free. Can you picture that?"

"It's very clear."

"Tell me how to get out of it."

"Think of first principles."

They all stared at me. First principles when in their heads they were all about to be anally raped in their own beds?

"First principle: make sure you can breathe. You have time to think, you can keep your head clear enough to think, if you can breathe. Christie"—she seemed to be the least inherently frightened person in the class, perhaps it was a generational thing, "lie facedown on the mat, please." She did. I sat on top of her. She started to push her hands into the face-protection position. I'd taught her that. She'd absorbed it as naturally as limestone does water. "Very good," I said, "but let's pretend for a minute that your arms are trapped down underneath you. Good. Thank you." I brushed her hair gently out of the way so that I wouldn't trap it and put my hand on the back of her neck. So small. I felt the sixth vertebra under the web between my thumb and index finger. I knew three different ways to displace it, to sever her spinal cord, to snuff her life between one breath and the next. "If I started to press here, her face would go into the mattress." I looked at Sandra. "Yes?"

She nodded.

"And your attacker would probably be expecting you to try and lift your head to breathe, yes?"

Again I waited until she nodded.

"So you would do the unexpected. The opposite of lift. What would that be?"

"Tuck," Nina said. "Chin down, try get your forehead to the matt, mattress, and make an air pocket."

"Good. Do that, Christie." And my bright swelling of pride at Christie's bravery was tinged now with streaks of anger at Sandra. "Now, Sandra, tell me what you're afraid of in this situation."

She shrugged.

"Are you afraid your attacker will strangle you to death? Tickle you until you're crazy? Sing Barry Manilow? No? Then what?"

"What do you think?" Now she was angry, too.

"I have several guesses, but tell me exactly, specifically."

"Rape," she said, and something in her voice, some solidity in tone, reminded me of con artists I had met who looked you in the eye and spoke firmly, and I knew she was lying, or at least not telling the whole truth. She was less afraid of rape, something that had probably happened to her dozens of times, than of . . . what? I found I didn't care enough to force the issue.

Rape was what everyone else was frightened of, so that's what I would address.

"All right. So if you're tucking and bending your spine to protect your breathing, it means you're also reaching down with your hands. Christie, try that please—just bend and reach down. Reaching down means two things. You'll have extra leverage—you can use your arms as well as your legs to push against the mattress—and you can reach down far enough to protect your anus and vagina. Christie, can you reach down as far as between your legs?"

"Yes," she said, surprised.

"But he'll just push the hand away," Sandra said.

"All right." I leaned back and reached down. "But see how that shifts my weight? You could find some leverage now."

"Not if he's breaking your fingers. You won't be thinking about leverage if you're in pain."

I knew then, as surely as though I'd just watched video, how it would be for her when her spouse started to beat her. She would probably never think of leverage; she would probably not think at all. Maybe she had the first dozen times it happened but now, as with so many people who are habitually abused, she would simply relax when it began because at that instant she could stop waiting, she could stop worrying what form it would take, this time; it would begin, and she would know. It would be a strange kind of relief.

Most of the class were not habitually abused and I addressed them. "For most people, being in this kind of situation usually leads to a huge gush of adrenaline. We've talked about this before. You'll either panic or your automatic pilot takes over. Either way, it's unlikely you'll be thinking or feeling much at this point. You'll be doing, probably unconsciously. You'll be focused, as both Tonya and Nina have said, on making your attacker stop, get off, get away from you any way you can. Once you commit to that, once you begin, you'll do almost anything to see it through. He might break one or more of your fingers, yes, but you'll feel his weight move. You'll be on that like lightning—"

"Well, *you* might," Sandra said.

"Yes," I said. "I would. Christie, I'm leaning back now, to get at your hands, so what can you do?"

"I don't know. I can't see which way you're tilting."

"Backwards," Suze said.

"Sshh. Christie, you won't have anyone to see for you. Feel it, feel where my weight is, which way I'm leaning, feel how easy it would be to tip me one way or another, or to hit me with something."

"But you've got my hands!" she said. I waited. "Oh." And she kicked up and back with her heels and thumped between my tipping shoulder blades, and as I twisted to grab her ankles, she yanked her hands from between her legs and, weight on her knees and palms, hurled herself backwards and literally sat on me.

"Oh, my God," she said, leaping up, mortified. "Did I hurt you?"

"You could have. How would you, right now, if you wanted to?"

"Kick," Katherine said.

"Elbow!" "Knee in the face." "Stomp her like a snake until she doesn't move anymore!"

Christie froze.

"Use them all. I've fallen back, on my hands, so if you kick at my face or neck, I can't grab and trap your leg. Pretend to kick. In slow motion." She did—a tentative *mai-geri* to the chin. I pretended to topple sideways. "Now another kick—slow, slow, make it slow—to my face, then, while I'm choking on my blood, you prepare and deliver an axe kick: spine, preferably, or rib cage. Then you run, leave the house, and call nine-one-one."

"And your lawyer," Pauletta said.

"And your lawyer," I said. "And don't clean away any blood on you. Don't change your clothes, even if they're torn or soiled. Make sure the first thing you mention is not how you learnt to do this in a self-defense class. Now"—before they could think too hard about any of it—"let's practice. Find your partner. Try the double-hand pin first. Good. Make sure you're spread out, that you won't be throwing your partner into someone else." I said that particularly to Suze, who tended to forget that others might mind having a body hurled in their direction.

We ran through the double-hand pin, then the one-handed strangle. They were tentative at first, then began to toss each other about as children would.

"With both, remember what should come next. Think of your bedroom: when they're down, what can you hit them with easily? Where's your clock? Your potted plant? Your baseball bat? Where's your phone, so you can take it with you when you run? Good. That's good, Kim, very good," as she sank her nails into Jennifer's hands in slow motion.

This was more like it. Even Sandra was mechanically following the plan. Katherine and Tonya were—

Tonya's nose blossomed red and she shrieked and clapped both hands to her face.

"Sit up, put your head back." Wail. The whole room focused. Blood in the room. "Tonya. Sit up. Put your head back."

"Oh, God," Katherine said, "oh, God, I'm sorry. I just—"

"Tonya, move your hand." I spoke slowly and very clearly. "Move your hand. Tonya, please, move your hand so I can see." The initial spill of blood from her nose was already slowing. Her eyes were wide with pain and panic. Everyone in the room was poised to run, as though blood would make the sharks come.

"I'm so sorry," Katherine was still saying, "I didn't—"

I tapped the back of one of Tonya's wrists, then deliberately put both hands behind my back so she knew I wouldn't be touching her face, and she moved her hands just enough for me to peer at her nose. "It's not broken. You'll be fine. The blood's already slowing. You're fine. Nice deep breaths. Katherine, are you hurt? No? Good, then I want you and Therese and Kim to help me. Therese, I want you to get me a hot, caffeinated drink with sugar. Kim, your job is to find ice and a soft cloth. Katherine, bring me something to clean the mat before it stains." Cleaning. Before it stained. Yes. She nodded, followed Therese and Kim like a zombie through the door. "The rest of you, do some stretching, and when you've done that, we'll take it in turns to hit the bag."

I waited until they'd started their unwilling stretching, then sat by Tonya.

"At least you're wearing a black T-shirt," I said. "When the ice comes, put it on your face."

"It'll hurt," Sandra said matter-of-factly, and squatted down on the mat. "But it'll keep the swelling down. If you take two ibuprofen every four or five hours for a couple of days, you won't even be able to tell anyone hit you."

Therese came back with a double mocha latte.

"I don't drink coffee," Tonya said in a shaky voice.

"You do now. Caffeine and sugar will help with the shock. It will make you feel better. Sip, good. And another. And why aren't you all hitting that bag?" They went back to punching. "Ah, here's the ice."

After another minute, her shakes began to subside. I helped her up and moved her to the bench.

"Drink more coffee, keep the ice on your face, and if you're feeling all right in ten minutes, I'll drive you home."

"Let me do it," Katherine said.

"You can clean the mat," I said, nodding at the cloth in her hand.

"I'll sit with her," Sandra said. I nodded, and moved to supervise the punching of the bag, which wasn't all it could have been.

After another five minutes, Katherine gathered Tonya's things and they made their way to the door. Everyone watched them leave.

"All right," I said when the door closed behind them. "Excitement's over. Let's get back to pins. This time on your backs with a one-handed strangle."

They moved like old women, newly aware that they could be hurt. Even Suze was tentative when she put her hand around Christie's throat.

I kept my tone brisk. "What did we learn about strangles? Tuck your chin— protect your throat. Breathe, if you can." Slight movement as the supine women tucked their chins. I pretended not to notice. "Distract. And where there's a joint, there's a weakness. Watch."

I lay down and gestured Therese over. She smiled politely and climbed on top of me and laid her left hand lightly on my throat. I tucked my chin and said, in that deep, exaggerated voice it's impossible to avoid when stretching one's vocal folds, "I have so many choices here it's almost embarrassing. Suggestions?"

"Hey," Christie said, "it's like— Get off me a sec," she said to Suze, who obeyed.

"That was easy," I said. No one laughed, though Nina smiled. I sighed internally; after the blood, we were back at square one. "Saying, Get off me is always worth trying. You never know. So, Christie, you were saying?" She looked blank. "What is it like?"

"Oh. Like last week, the week before I mean, with the one-handed strangle against the wall. You could twist and bash her elbow, or bring her face into the mat like it was a wall, or, well, shit, anything."

"Exactly."

I showed them. How I could put my left foot flat on the mat and use that to leverage the same twist into the slam of forearm on inside elbow. How to pull myself down and yank Therese's face into the mat as though it were a wall. The swing and whole-arm pin of the opposite twist with my right foot on the mat. And they wouldn't do any of it. They had seen blood and they were afraid: that swinging elbow might connect to a nose, that moving fingernail might graze a cornea, that wrist or shoulder or knuckle might get dislocated.

"Up," I said. "Everybody up. Let's get back to the bag. I want to see combinations: fist, elbow, knee, one after the other."

The bag couldn't bruise. The bag couldn't look at you reproachfully if you slipped a little and banged the wrong place. The bag wouldn't remind you of thin skin and red blood. Even so, they were tentative. "Shout," I said. "Blam. Kapow. Whap. This is an attacker who is trying to hurt you. Why should you put up with that? Defend yourselves."

Not much difference.

"They are coming after your children." The thumps got meatier. "You are not going to let them hurt you, or your family—not you, not your sister, not your mother, not your children. You. It's up to you. No one else. Come on. Hit it!"

"It's just a bag," Nina said.

And that was the problem.

THIRTEEN

BELLEVUE WAS MORE OF A GENERIC SUBURB THAN A CITY. THE SAME MIDSIZED OFFICE buildings of white concrete and green glass; the smooth six-lane blacktop; the uncrusted, still wet-looking red brick of libraries and schools. Bland, moneyed, characterless. Ideal for Corning, the kind of woman who thought running away made the problem vanish.

In my mind's eye I saw Kick's brilliant white smile, the white in the crook of her elbow, her white knuckles as she said, *Lesions. Christ. God.*

I checked my phone again. 8:08. No messages.

At almost every stop light, I imagined the fall of her oak hair, her delight as she expounded her theory of everything, her laugh like sun shimmering on water. I began to cut in and out of morning traffic.

Amateur, she said in my head.

The hotel was efficient and faceless and could have been in Atlanta. I walked through the lobby. No quiet corners. I went back to the car, retrieved Mackie's cell phone. Texted a message to Corning's phone: need money now, meet me in parking garage, by elevator, level P2.

Underground parking garages, like the interior of submarines, are malevolent in their ugliness and lack of human comfort, in their machine-oil smell, their lack of natural light, their sense of confinement. I parked on the lowest tier, and walked to the elevator.

I waited twenty minutes. Then the elevator light dinged, and Corning stepped out.

"Good morning," I said.

She dropped her purse and backed up against the cinder-block wall. I picked it up, weighed it, remembering another woman and another bag, opened it, looked inside, checked to make sure there were no obvious weapons in hidden compartments, and gave it back.

She hadn't been sleeping well, clearly. And possibly someone had cut out her tongue.

I pondered that. You would need to hold the tongue with gauze, otherwise it would slip from your grip. I tried to remember if there was any bone at the base of the soft tissue. The tendons might prove difficult, if one were to use a small blade.

But I needed her willing and able to talk.

"You have an appointment with a reporter at the *Seattle Times*. Her name is Mindy Leptke. You will tell her everything about your land scheme, and she will quote you as an anonymous source." She stared at me, mute. "Do you understand?"

She held her purse in front of her stomach with both hands.

"Do you understand?" Nod. "I won't prosecute on three conditions: One, cooperate fully. Two, agree to pay one hundred thousand dollars to Hippoworks. Three, allow your real estate license to lapse in the state of Washington."

Run, I thought, *squeal*. Give me an excuse.

"But it must be full cooperation: every name, every meeting. Your statement will be recorded. Leptke will keep one copy, I'll have the other."

She blinked like a semaphore.

"You will pay your hotel bill, and return with me to Seattle. You will arrange for a certified check for one hundred thousand dollars as soon as the banks open. We will go to the *Times* offices."

She kneaded her bag. It had a blackish smear across the left side where it had fallen on the tire-striped concrete. "I don't have a hundred thousand dollars."

That was true. But her condo was worth many times that.

"Sell your condo."

"But it takes time, it—"

"You know a lot of people in the real estate business. Someone will be happy, as a personal favor to you, to give you fifty cents on the dollar in exchange for expediency."

"I don't understand why you're doing this to me."

"Because it's more polite than tearing you limb from limb in a parking lot. But I could do it that way if you'd prefer."

9:42. I SAT with Corning in the *Times* reception area. Every time I moved slightly, the cashier's check rustled in my breast pocket.

I PULLED INTO the warehouse parking lot. My phone said 10:58. I turned the ring volume up.

Dornan was sitting on one of the old couches by the craft-services table, leaning forward and talking to Peg and Joel. His hair was sticking up in a tuft and he wore a white T-shirt with a cartoon palm tree on the front.

He stood as soon as he saw me.

"Why aren't you with her?"

"She wouldn't let me," I said.

I expected him to demand how, exactly, she'd stopped me when I outweighed her by thirty pounds and topped her by five inches, but his arms half lifted, twitched as he began to hold them out to me, then thought better of it, and returned to his side. "I'm sorry," he said. "This must be . . . You must be having all sorts of bad memories."

I nodded.

"But this is— She's not dying, Aud. Remember that."

So fragile, like that thin sheet of canvas in the gallery daubed with pigment, and something was hacking holes in it. *Lesions. Christ.*

"She is not," he said again. "It'll be nothing. Well, not nothing, but you'll see."

I looked at my phone. 11:06. I wanted to shake it to make sure it was still working.

"You'll see," he said again.

I stared at him. "You think you know what this is, don't you?"

"I . . . No, no. I don't want to say. It's just speculation, and we'll know soon enough."

He ran his hand through his hair, and tugged on it. "What time is it?"

"Eleven-oh-eight." He nodded. Perhaps he was imagining, like me, Kick sitting alone in a cold waiting room. "Do you know what doctor she's seeing?"

He shook his head, ran his hand through his hair again, tugged.

Standing here wouldn't get anything done. "If she calls"—if she calls you first, if she doesn't call me at all—"I'll be with Rusen and Finkel." He nodded vaguely, raised his hand to his hair. "And, Dornan, try not to snatch yourself bald."

He dredged up a smile.

11:10. No reply to my knock at the editing trailer. 11:11. My knock on the other trailer was answered promptly.

The trailer was very neat, which meant Rusen was being obsessive again. Their office chairs were next to each other, in front of a screen full of spread-sheets. A lot of the figures were in red. Finkel folded his glasses and put them in his top pocket. His eyes, too, were rimmed in red.

Rusen, tie knotted more tightly than usual, fussed with finding me a chair. Finkel chatted about the wonderful weather, his jovial voice at odds with his haggard face.

"That medical-insurance issue you raised is dealt with," Rusen said. "Effective midnight yesterday."

"Thank you. How are preparations coming along for the final scenes?"

"Wonderful," Finkel said.

"A little tricky," Rusen said.

I waited.

"We're in trouble. We need more film stock, the film processor wants us to cover our expenses so far, the equipment rental place says we owe them a pre-mium for the overage on camera and rolling stock lease, the city just sent the electricity bill, which is twice what we'd budgeted, mainly because of the air-conditioning, and now we have a lawsuit on our hands."

"A lawsuit." Petty problems. 11:18. How long did doctor's appointments usually take?

"One of the grips had a flashback at home and acted crazy enough to scare his wife. She's suing us for the resulting emotional distress."

Flashback. "Did he hurt her?"

"Hurt her?" He seemed surprised. "No. According to the papers filed, he and his wife were having a barbecue for friends, and his wife was opening a can of beans when he starts saying, *God's brains are spilled.* Anyhoo, their barbecue was ruined."

"It's a pure nuisance suit," Finkel said. "We'd sue her right back, but we couldn't cover the attorneys' fees."

I took Corning's check from my pocket and slid it across the table to Finkel. "This will help."

He opened it, studied it judiciously for a moment, then took out his glasses, fitted them to his nose, and looked again. He turned the check over, and back, then passed it with a frown to Rusen.

Rusen looked at the check, looked at me, looked at the check again. "Is it real?"

I nodded. "Payment from the person behind all your troubles in the last month or so. Appeasement. I said we wouldn't sue her."

"You've got no right to make that decision for this company," Finkel said.

I looked at him for a moment. "I do. As of ten-thirty last night, when I signed the papers. Here's my investment." I slid another check to Rusen. This one was much bigger. "If you disagree, tear up the check."

Rusen covered it protectively with his hands.

In addition to the frown, Finkel's chin now jutted forward two or three inches. It would be very easy to break it. Rusen beamed at him determinedly. "Boy howdy, this is like a miracle."

"Yes," Finkel said, unwillingly.

"It'll make all the difference," Rusen said. "I'd been storyboarding, but then, with the money troubles, I shelved those plans, and was trying to come up with a less expensive way to do things, you know, maybe some smoke, and a big noise off camera, then pan back to people lying on the ground, that kind of thing. And I was worrying about insurance for that, too, since our stunt coordinator left, and Kick hasn't signed on officially yet, and even the use of firecrackers requires permission from the fire department. But, cripes, this changes everything."

11:23. This changes everything.

DORNAN AND I sat on a bench in the little park overlooking the Duwamish. My phone was between us. 12:14.

"Well, now," Dornan said. "This is lovely."

The air was bright and lively, friendly, and it was possible to fool yourself into believing the world was a harmless place.

"She should be done by now," I said. "Shouldn't she?"

"I really don't know, Torvingen."

I closed my eyes, and let a purplish afterimage of the river twist behind my lids. When it faded, I opened my eyes again. 12:17. "I'm going to drive to her house. You want to come?"

"I do not. She said she'd call when she had news. She'll call when she's ready. It might be hard for her to talk about."

"That's assuming it's bad news."

But we both knew it would be bad, just not what kind of bad: brutal and clear as an executioner's axe, or the death of a thousand cuts. How do you tell someone that kind of news?

"Oh," I said, and flipped open my phone and dialed the Fairmont. Yes, the front desk told me, I did indeed have a voice-mail message. Would I like to access my voice mail now?

I would.

It was Kick. She sounded breezy and offhand. "It's me. It's MS. They're pretty sure. So there you have it." Click. "To repeat the message, press one. To erase the message, press two."

I pressed one.

"It's me. It's MS. They're pretty sure. So there you have it." Click. "It's me. It's MS. They're pretty sure. So there you have it." Click. "It's me. It's MS. They're—" 12:22. I closed the phone. The river kept flowing, the sun kept shining. The bench was warm under my thighs.

Dornan was watching me, terribly alert.

"She left me a message," I said. A message. "They think it's MS."

He sighed, the way a zip-lock bag does when you squeeze out the excess air. His shoulders lifted, then sagged. "Where are the lesions?"

"What?"

"Are the lesions on her brain as well as spine?"

"Lesions? How on earth do I know? It was a bloody message."

A bumblebee droned stupidly over a spill of yellow flowers sprouting at the base of the bench supports. A message.

His hands lay still in his lap, no longer tugging at his hair.

"You guessed, didn't you?"

He sighed again. "There was this man who used to come into the Little Five Points coffee shop. We talked about it sometimes. He didn't like the heat. That's what I noticed first. And his crutches. I always used to turn the AC up a notch when he sat down with his coffee."

"Used to come in. What happened to him?"

"John. He joked about it once, how you could never predict what was going to happen to someone with MS. 'It gets worse,' he said. 'You can't tell how someone's doing, really. They fight, and they seem okay and full of hope, and then one day, they just don't show up anymore and you know they've lost the battle, that they're stuck in a motorized bed somewhere, surrounded by strangers.' One day he didn't show up anymore."

"Did he have good medical care?"

"I imagine so."

"Was he on any of the experimental drugs?"

"He was a customer. He came in one day with crutches. A year later he was in a scooter. Two years later he didn't come in anymore. All right? That's all I know."

The bee came back. I listened to its deep, round soothing sound, and wondered what had happened to that fly in Kick's house.

I DROVE TOWARDS Kick's house but as I crossed the Fremont Bridge a seaplane flew low, west to east, and suddenly I had to know where it was going.

I swung off the bridge and along 36th, driving faster than I should. I still lost it. But I followed another plane. I dropped down to 34th, swung right along the water.

Over Lake Union, a seaplane overhead dipped one wing and turned sharply, then evened into a shallow approach and came in to land. Water planed up and out from its fat pontoons the way it would under the webbed feet of a landing duck.

Hope. Maybe it was like falling. If you felt the physiological effects, and called it exhilaration, not terror, then it was exhilaration. What did hope feel like?

I pulled over and called Kick. After four rings, the machine clicked on. "It's me. I got your message. Thank you. I'm standing by Lake Union, wondering if you've ever taken one of those tourist seaplane rides. It looks as though there are three different-sized planes, one is—"

"Hello?" She sounded wary but curious.

"Hey," I said. "How are you?"

"Well, you know, I have MS."

"Yes," I said, matching her light tone. "I heard that." Silence.

"So what's this about seaplanes?"

SHE MET me at the terminal on Westlake. She jumped from her van as lithe and strong as an acrobat. Vitality sang under her skin, shone in her breeze-whipped hair, flowed like a poem with the pump of muscle as she slid her door shut. Beautiful. She even looked as though she'd slept well, better than I had. The only sign of shock was a barely perceptible pause between my conversation and hers, as though the signal were being routed through some intergalactic worm-hole for processing. She seemed to have walled up the whole diagnosis, en-cysted it somewhere deep inside, to be dealt with later. She smiled cheerfully as she swung herself up into the plane.

The smell of fuel was overwhelming to begin with. The noise was over-whelming for the entire flight; we wore earplugs, and I still felt crushed by the din. Once we were two hundred feet up, I didn't care.

We were the only passengers on a seven-seater Beaver. We held hands across the aisle, to begin with, but as soon as I realized that meant we would be look-ing at different things through our separate, tiny portholes, I unbuckled and took the seat behind her. There were no headrests, so I could put my chin on the back of her seat and lay my cheek against hers as we gazed at the water.

The plane stayed almost entirely over water: north over Lake Union to Gas Works Park, then east across two bridges—one was up; toylike cars formed a shiny tail to north and south—to another bay, the university to the north, the green swath of arboretum to the south. East some more, and the water abruptly paled to an almost royal blue, and we were in a steep turn south, fly-ing low over a floating bridge. Down, along beautiful coastline; west, directly over the city—the Space Needle seemed close enough to touch; a jag south again, down the Duwamish—I tapped Kick's shoulder and pointed to Kellogg Island and the tiny patch of park. She nodded, and reached up and back. I kissed her hand.

West over West Seattle, then a great curving arc around Alki, and the deep, deep blue of Elliott Bay. From above, the orange cranes looked nothing like brontosaurus.

From up here, everything seemed very clean and tidy and contained, easy to deal with, easy to understand. Beautiful, delicate, precious. The messy details were hidden, the power and angular geometry of humanity's controlling stamp clear. If we could bend the landscape, surely we could find a way to defeat some autoimmune molecule gone awry?

We flew over the familiar four-chimney building of one of Seattle's bigger biotech companies. Kick's head turned to watch it diminish behind us.

Clouds were streaming up from the southwest. The plane bumped a little as it cut over Queen Anne Hill—no fires over Troy in the early afternoon—over Fremont and its troll, Wallingford and Kick's house, and turned sharply to come south over the northeastern horn of Lake Union.

The pilot turned slightly and made an up-and-down hand shape: bumpy landing ahead. We both nodded and smiled: risk, the spice of life. I left my cheek by hers—soft and dry as a well-handled cotton sheet—all the way down.

The pilot taxied to the dock and turned off the rotor. The silence was shattering. "So," she said, "want to come back to my place and look at MRIs?"

WE SPREAD them out on the dining room table and I held them up one by one to the light while Kick commented.

"That's my favorite," she said. "My eyes look just like pickled eggs."

They did: enormous, bulging white orbs starting from a delicate grey skull. I could see the folds of her brain, the bone of nose and cheek, even a line of ligament.

"The lesion—or plaque, as Dr. Whittle insisted on calling it—is that tiny little fleck of greyish white there. No, there. See?"

I peered at the stiff, plastic film. "No."

"Give it to me. There. I think. Or maybe there. Hmmn. Do you know where the parietal lobe is?"

"No."

"Well, that's where Whittle said it was. The left parietal lobe. If it was a lesion—sorry—plaque at all. He said he wasn't really sure, it was so small."

"All right."

"The parietal is where you store your nouns: chair, hat, cat, mat. So if I forget your name, you know why. Just kidding. Now this one"—she sorted through the slippery pile, pulled one from the bottom—"this one's where the real action is."

Looking at her spinal MRI was like looking at something left hanging from a tree after the vultures have been at it: bones, stripped bare, hanging in a knobby, gristly curve in the middle of nothing. I was suddenly, viscerally glad they didn't do these things in color.

"This, apparently, is the thoracic spine. And there, that big white splotch, on the left side of the spinal cord, is what's causing the trouble."

"You sound as though there's no doubt."

"Multiple sclerosis means, basically, many scleroses, or plaques, scar tissue, on the fatty myelin sheath of brain and spinal cord. Identification of two definite plaques are required to fulfill the multiple part of the criterion." Her voice was impersonal but her eyes began to dart back and forth.

"Kick."

"There's no such diagnosis as mono sclerosis. Whittle will only swear to one plaque, that one on my thoracic spine. Which of course is the main trunk line of the power cable system in the body."

"Kick—"

"No. Let me say it. Think of the spinal cord as a power cable. Imagine the myelin sheathing as insulation. Imagine the plaque as this place where something has stripped away the insulation. Signal can't get through as strongly. It leaks off. There's a basic neural deficit. You send a signal and it doesn't get through, or it gets through scrambled and you get paresthesia, dyesthesia, weakness. Sometimes plaques heal themselves. Sometimes they get worse, and the underlying axons die. Then you are, to put it technically, fucked. Permanent paralysis. No one knows what causes it."

She paused, and if it weren't for her eyes, back and forth, back and forth, I could have imagined her at a spotlit lectern, with overheads.

"Mostly it's believed to be an autoimmune disease, the immune system in overdrive and attacking itself. Some, of course, think just the opposite, that it's an insufficiency. Everyone agrees that the course of the disease is variable. Sometimes very mild, sometimes leading to premature death. The neural deficit can appear in cognitive thinking, in the autonomic nervous system—which means breathing and heart regulation, digestion, and other basic functions—or it could mean not seeing so well sometimes, or being dizzy, or getting weird tingles down your spine."

Stop it, I wanted to say, just stop it.

"So there you have it. MS in a nutshell. That's what I've got: some disease that no one knows the cause of, and that they don't know how to fix. One that might not affect me much at all, or might kill me, or reduce me to a drooling idiot. Though Whittle was kind enough to tell me he thought I had the kind that, quote, wouldn't make me stupid, unquote. Would you like a cup of tea?"

Tea? It took me a moment to change gears. "Yes. Please." I didn't, but she clearly needed something to do with her hands. "So what happens now?"

"We wait and see what develops."

Develop: grow, change, increase in size. While she filled the kettle and got out tea bags, I stacked the MRIs, and wondered if she'd discussed drugs. We could get to that later. First I wanted to talk to Eric about his contacts in the biotech industry. There might be treatments her neurologist didn't know about. I concentrated on aligning the slippery plastic sheets.

"So," she said cheerily, "how was your day?"

"My day." I found I could remember nothing except bright numerals on my phone. 12:22.

She rinsed cups. "You look tired."

"Not much sleep." Maybe she thought I'd been out carousing till all hours, untroubled by the upcoming diagnosis of a woman I'd known barely two weeks. "I spoke to Corning. The woman behind all the set trouble."

"Corning?" She paused, one hand on the fridge door, one holding milk. "Right. Why didn't you say?"

Hi, honey, I have MS. Do you really, how interesting, I had an interesting day, too, I found some woman you don't even know.

She was staring vaguely at the milk in her hand. "What'll happen to her?"

"She's spilling her guts to the district attorney."

I wasn't sure she'd heard. She seemed utterly focused on pouring milk into her cup.

"I also went to the set. They have money now, but I think Rusen is getting anxious about this stunt finale."

She turned the cups so that both handles faced out at the same angle.

"He told me he'd offered you the coordinator job."

She poured tea with great concentration.

"Have you talked to him?"

"Um? Oh. No."

"They'll be able to afford to pay you now."

"Yes. If I decide it's what I want."

"But it's what you do."

She put the pot down carefully, and turned. "I'm a cook."

"Yes, and a very good one."

"Don't patronize me."

"I'm not patronizing. You're very good. You know that."

"But? Being a really good cook just isn't good enough for you?"

What? "I don't understand. You're a stunt—"

"Was. Was a stunt performer. Past tense. I'm not anymore. It doesn't matter what I used to do. What I do now is cook. It's who I am. Face it. Look at me. Face it. I have. I'm just a crippled diseased has-been who can't even make a career out of cooking things. And now . . . And now . . ."

I stood.

"Don't touch me."

I put my arms at my side.

"You put him up to offering it to me, didn't you?"

"No. I didn't need to." If she would just let me touch her arm, her hand, her hair, I could think, put the words together in a way that made sense. "It's going to be all right."

"No, it's not." She was very pale. "This thing is inside me like a stain. It's all different now."

I took a deep breath, in and out. I sat down again, because if I didn't she would bolt. "It's not different." I held out my hand, unthreatening, like a rancher squatting, hand out, sugar cubes on his palm. "Give me your hand." She took a reluctant step forward. "Please."

She slid her warm, small hand into mine. I felt that familiar electric flood, saw the answering looseness in her shoulders, the way she nearly tipped back her head.

"See?" I held her hand very gently. "Not everything has changed. There is still this."

She folded onto the floor and began to cry.

I held her with one arm, and stroked her hair, her shoulder blades, her arms, her hair again, kissed the top of her head, kissed her ear. Held her, held her, held her.

After a minute, she lifted her face. "Do you really want tea?"

"No."

"Good." She rested her cheek against my chest. After another minute I slid down to be next to her on the floor.

"Tell me what you need."

"I need to do this by myself."

"All right."

"I mean it. Don't meddle. Don't push me. On anything."

"What will you do first?"

"I have to tell my parents."

"When?"

"Tonight."

"Will you want to talk afterwards?" Surely it was all right to say that?

"I don't know. They're in Anacortes. I might stay over. I'll call you tomorrow. Or you'll see me."

IT WAS after six o'clock and the park by Elliott Bay was empty of tourists. The air was salty enough to lick. My mother and I walked over the undulating grass and I told her about the grass that grew in the pocket park near my warehouse, about how I'd told Kick I was sorry, about going up in a plane, about taking Corning to see Leptke and how easy it had been to get Corning to talk.

"Once she started, she fell in love with the story of her own cleverness. I left them cooking up a way for Leptke to be able to name her as a source. They're going to go talk to the DA about immunity from prosecution in exchange for full cooperation on council staff corruption." Eight hours ago. It seemed like a decade, something dimly remembered and unimportant. But it was important. She had ruined Kick's new career before it got properly started.

We walked on a path for a while.

"And did your— did Kick talk to the reporter?"

"I don't think it's top of her list at the moment." Plus, she didn't know about it.

In the distance, out of sight, someone began playing a flamenco guitar.

"You don't sound very happy."

"Corning will lose her condo, and her license, yes, and you might argue that her hundred thousand is already making a difference to the people she hurt most, that it will help them pay their bills, help them keep their jobs, allow for the possibility of success, but, Mor, it's just money."

"And money isn't justice."

"No." Dancing and vomiting in Pioneer Square. Bellowing about earthquakes in Nordstrom. The graphite sheen under Kick's eyes and the molecules chewing at her spine. Stress was the worst thing for MS. Corning had contributed directly to that.

We walked on. The guitar player came into view: an elderly woman. I dropped ten dollars in her guitar case.

"You seem to have stopped losing weight, at least."

"Yes. I've found— Kick showed me some things I could eat."

"Kick. Will she have dinner with us?"

"It's not her top priority at the moment."

"I see."

I doubted it. "She's sick."

"We can postpone, until . . ." Her step faltered, as though she had tripped over an invisible crack in the pavement. "Ah, I see. Is it very bad?"

"It's multiple sclerosis."

"I'm so very sorry."

"She hasn't died."

"No."

"And she won't die. No, Mor, listen. Please. MS isn't like that." And I poured out the conflicting opinions and research I'd read on the Web, and what Kick's doctor had said. She listened without comment.

When I'd finished, she said, "And she is well currently?"

"She gets a little tired. And when it's hot she sometimes limps a little, but not always. But she looks . . . You can't tell. She's strong." Very strong. "She only found out today. She is . . ." I wasn't sure how to describe her offhand cheeriness, followed by her weeping. "She's in shock, I think. As you can imagine."

"Yes."

"I wanted to be with her tonight but she's with her family. Telling them." Right now. Explaining, probably, how she wasn't going to die. Or probably wasn't.

"What will you do?"

"I don't know."

We followed the path to the water's concrete-bound edge. "The light is extraordinary, don't you think?" she said.

It was. To the west, the view could have been one from a north European coast, all heather tones: a deep blue sound with hints of slate in the shadows between waves, lacy whitecaps, low islands in the distance, their outlines softened by the low clouds, which were layered, moving in two distinct directions, the way I imagined two armies might, streaming past each other, heedless, in an effort to regroup. I was reminded of the Western Roman emperors: blank-eyed, massive, calm, carved to inhuman size from white marble. The view east from Kick's window would be more like that of the exotic Eastern Empire: crimson, rose gold, molten brass, the air twinkling with dust rising from the drying dirt, burning to umber. The clouds, too, would be different, gauzy and light, like a bundle of harem silks sliced through with a cheese wire and draped over Queen Anne where the windows would be glinting like the gilded dome and minarets of Hagia Sophia.

Hadrian had built his wall at the westernmost tip of his empire, and turned his face inward, and the Roman Empire had begun to die. In the east, Justinian, at Theodora's urging, had faced his enemies, kept expanding. The Roman Empire of the west had merged imperceptibly into the barbarism of the Germanic tribes in the fifth century. Byzantium had continued until the Turks crushed it in the fifteenth.

". . . glad," my mother was saying. "Atlanta must be very beautiful for you to want to leave this place."

THEY ALL STARED SILENTLY AT THE MATTRESS PROPPED AGAINST THE FAR WALL. IT was a brand-new double which I planned to donate to Arkady House when the classes were over.

"Here is a handout covering some of the topics we've talked about in the last couple of weeks, and one or two other things that might prove useful." It was a retread of my previous list, grouped into related headings: information you should never hand out to a stranger, ways to protect yourself at home, and so on. At the top, in big, bold font were phone numbers of Bette's new associate, who would be eager to represent any of them in an emergency, Arkady House, the Georgia Domestic Violence Coalition, emergency hotline numbers, and the phone numbers of three hospital emergency rooms. Perhaps these numbers would displace mine in their minds and speed-dials. I'd also copied from a website a checklist of items one should assemble before leaving a violent domestic partner: passport, birth certificate, checkbook, medical records, children's records, etc.

Most of them flipped through the sheaf with one eye on the mattress. Sandra ignored the mattress completely and examined the checklist one item at a time. I studied her. She seemed to have gained weight.

"Put the lists away now." They all turned to their various bags and backpacks and Tonya flinched as Suze swung her bag quickly from the bench about a foot from Tonya's head.

The nose looked fine to me, but clearly she was gun-shy. They all were. Time to discuss the elephant in the living room.

"Tonya, how's your nose?"

"Okay. I guess."

"It looks good, no swelling. Does it hurt?"

"Not especially."

"Any problems with breathing? Odd nerve sensation?"

"No. It's cool."

"Good." I let them consider that for a moment. "So how did it feel, to get hurt?"

"Painful." She made a careful face and everyone smiled in sympathy.

"Do you feel more vulnerable?"

"I guess. More jumpy anyhow."

"More scared, deep down, or less?"

"I don't know." She thought about it. "Both, maybe. I mean, I sure wouldn't want anyone to hit my nose again anytime soon. But the notion of being hit somewhere else is less scary than it was. Kind of. I mean, it hurt, but it, like you said, it gets better. It's just a . . . a . . . It's not the end of the world."

"Or your good looks," Nina said.

The smiles were rueful, and I understood that Nina's remark wasn't entirely a joke. For them looks mattered as much as permanent disability.

"But what's it like?" Jennifer said. "To get whomped like that?"

"And, Katherine," I said, "what was it like to do the, ah, whomping, even though it was accidental?"

"Awful," she said. "I felt sick."

"So did I," Tonya said.

I let them sit with it. It was an inescapable fact: getting hurt hurts. Several of them stared desperately at the floor. Perhaps I would donate a large sum to Crystal Gaze so that future classes could at least stare at a nicer carpet.

"Omelets," I said.

"Oh, no," Pauletta said. "Please tell me you're not going to give us that crap about breaking eggs."

"Crap. I see." Cliché, possibly—but I didn't know how else to describe it. Which annoyed me. "Tell me, then, how you make an omelet."

Silence. Nina cleared her throat. "Egg beaters?"

Despite my irritation I almost smiled. "Someone broke those eggs."

"Yes, but not me."

"Those eggs get broken. Yes or no?" I looked around the group. "Yes or no?"

Reluctant nods.

"To learn to walk, you have to fall down. To make an omelet you break eggs. To defend yourself from physical attack, someone gets hurt. Yes or no?"

More nods, one or two *Yeses*.

"Nothing is free. Nothing is magic. You get out what you put in. Risk and reward. Suze, help me move the mattress to the other wall." We lifted it away and there lay ten gourd-sized piñatas. I picked up the nearest, crimson painted with gold donkeys and stars, and shook it in their direction. "That rattle is a single poker chip. On it is a number that corresponds to an item on this list." I pulled a piece of paper from my pocket. "On this list are ten items. A day at Gleam, the day spa. Dinner for two at the Horseradish Grill. Hundred-and-fifty-dollar gift certificates from places like Saks and Tiffany's and Teuscher. Mostly luxuries, but not all." I'd included certificates from Chevron and Kroger. "You give me the chip, I give you the corresponding gift certificate. The only rule is that you have to use a naked body weapon to break the piñata open."

"Won't that hurt?"

"It might," I said. "You won't know until you try."

"And they're just piñatas, right?" Pauletta said.

"Plain old papier-mâché. I broke one myself yesterday." And that had been so satisfying I'd broken another two and had to buy more.

"Did it hurt?" Jennifer asked again.

"Only one way to find out. Would you like to go first?" I tossed her the piñata ball. She dropped it. It didn't break.

She picked it up tentatively and shook it. "Don't people usually break these things with sticks?"

"Usually. There again, they're usually blindfolded, too."

"It should hang from something."

"If you like." I pulled a piece of string from my other pocket, glad I'd spent the time combing the city for the kind of piñata with two little holes at the top for string instead of the cheap kind with the hook.

"Well, how else do I hit it?"

"Entirely up to you."

She cradled it in her arm and patted it as though it were a puppy that might have rabies. "It's hard."

I nodded.

"It will hurt if I hit it."

In reply I pinned the list to the door with the thumbtack already pushed into the wood. "Take a look and see if you think it's worth it."

Nina was already looking at the list, with Christie standing by her shoulder. "Jimmy Choo!" she said. "If you don't break that ball, I will."

But Jennifer was hugging it possessively.

"Think of all your body weapons," I said.

"Give me that," Nina said.

"No," Jennifer said. "But you could hold it for me, so I can hit it." She gave it to Nina.

"If you hold mine for me next."

"Think of—"

"Not like that," Jennifer said, completely ignoring me. "In front of you."

"—the room. Think of—"

"Like this?" Nina said, holding it against her stomach.

"Okay."

They weren't listening. I shrugged. They couldn't do themselves too much damage. There were no corners, no rough edges, no dangerous metal hooks to tear skin.

They'd formed a circle with Nina and Jennifer at the center, just like children at a birthday party. Nina snugged the piñata more firmly against her belly and set her back foot to prepare for the punch. Ready to take one for Jimmy Choo. Jennifer began to breathe and bounce around on her toes like a boxer.

"Hurt it," Suze said.

"Kill it." Kim.

I wished I'd thought of bribery weeks ago.

And with a thin, gull-like cry, Jennifer hit the piñata with her fist. Nothing happened.

"Love tap," Pauletta said. "Get closer. Kill it."

Jennifer set her chin and hit again, harder. "Ow!" She shook her hand.

"Think Jimmy," said Nina.

"Ow," Jennifer said again, but absently, and stepped in close and hit it again, and it buckled. "Ha!" Whack. "Ow!" This time she scowled.

"Oooh, now she's pissed," said Pauletta, and Jennifer was.

"Ow!" This time it was more accusation than complaint, and she threw a series of unscientific, uncoordinated, but totally committed punches, and she screeched like a herring gull fighting with a crow. The piñata crumpled and she seized it from Nina and shook it until the chip fell out. She snatched up the glittery disk. "Four!"

"Number four," Christie said from the list on the door. "That's wine.com."

"Champagne!" Jennifer said, then looked at her reddened knuckles.

"Worth it?" I asked.

"Totally!"

Nina picked up a green-and-blue piñata and tossed it to Jennifer. "My turn."

The rest of the class closed around them, like punters at a cockfight. Three minutes and scraped knuckles later she had the caviar. "I'll trade with whoever gets the shoes," she said with a satisfied smile.

"No way," said Kim, "those shoes are mine. Me next."

"What about your nails?" Tonya said.

"Shoot." Kim stared at them a minute. "Anyone got any clippers?"

"Wait," I said. "Think. What other body weapons do you have?"

"Elbow," said Christie.

For the inexperienced, elbows were difficult to use accurately, and even a beginner could generate enough power to break a nose or a cheekbone.

"We'll hang this one," I said, and produced the string again. Soon the piñata was hanging from the bag frame, swinging gently.

"Kick it," Suze said suddenly.

"Knee-high or lower," I said.

"No, seriously. Give me one of those."

"Which?" Christie said.

Christie tossed her the orange piñata. Suze caught it, and without pause threw it in the air, and on the way down, just before it hit the floor, she kicked it as though going for a forty-yard goal. It burst in a spectacular shower and a yellow chip tumbled slowly, inevitably to lie faceup on the carpet. Number six. Jimmy Choo.

"Give me one," Therese said. Christie obliged, and Therese put it against the baseboard, and with one kick, broke it to smithereens. "Number one," she called to Christie, who said, "Chevron," and Therese shook her head, and Kim yanked her ball from the string, put it against the wall, and kicked it to pieces. Number eight: Barnes and Noble.

Katherine grabbed a blue-and-yellow ball and put it on the floor. "Hey, Fred," she said. "Die, you son of a bitch." In the startled silence she said, "Axe kick to the head," with the air of a pool shark naming her pocket, and delivered an executioner's blow.

Sandra named someone called George and knelt by it and destroyed it with successive hammer blows with the meaty parts of her fists. Tonya called it Ma'am Yes Ma'am, and had Christie hold it against the wall at chest height, where she burst its spleen with her elbow. Pauletta yelled, "Watch this," and put hers on the carpet in the middle of the circle. When everyone was watching, she sat on it violently, crushing it. She jumped up, face dark and eyes flashing. "How's that?" she said. "Who's sitting on whose face now, you fuck?"

I decided not to reinforce the "naked" part of the body weapon rule.

They started to bargain over the chips.

"Anger," I said, and waited. Gradually they turned to look at me. "What is it? Why is it?" Blank, though this time no one looked at the carpet. "How does it feel?"

"Good," Pauletta said. "Man, it feels good. Kind of clean."

Nina nodded. "Naughty but nice."

Lots of nods, some smiles. "But in the real world it feels wrong," Therese said. "Losing my temper feels childish, like a two-year-old screaming in the supermarket until it gets what it wants."

"Is feeling angry the same as losing your temper?"

"Hmmn," she said.

"Anger, like fear, is an emotion, not an action. It's a particularly strong emotion and, again, like fear, releases adrenaline. It won't just go away because we want it to. What makes you angry?"

"Idiots," said Suze.

"Oh, yep," Nina said. "And when my husband leaves the cap off the toothpaste. Nearly thirty years he's been doing it."

"When people cut in line," Tonya said. "I really hate that."

"Little things and big things, then. And they can vary from day to day. What makes a person angry today might just make us shake our heads tomorrow. But if you do get angry you can't 'rise above it' because it's a hormonal thing. It has to be acknowledged, even if just to ourselves. It's best, if possible, to alter the situation so that we're not being made angry anymore, and it's good to do something with the adrenaline charge if you can, to use it in some way, because it makes you feel better."

"You mean like telling the person you're mad at that you're mad?" Christie said.

"Maybe. It depends. Would you find that hard?"

She nodded.

"Anyone else?" Many nods. Suze shook her head. Sandra didn't commit one way or the other. "In every culture I've come across, from Oslo to Yorkshire to Istanbul to New York, women are disapproved of for showing anger; it's not feminine, not desirable. And women have been trained for so many years to never, ever get angry that they think if they let themselves slip just a little, just once, it will be a crack in the dam, that the dam will break and unleash a torrent of inappropriate, uncontrolled rage. In specific situations, a lot of people think that if they get angry, they'll provoke a violent response. Women, in short, have been trained to believe that they're not allowed to be angry."

"Trained," Katherine said loudly. "You're always talking about training, like we're dogs or something."

"It's not polite to raise your voice," I said, and she immediately hunched and blushed. Suze frowned. "Don't frown," I said to her, "you'll get wrinkles."

Silence.

"Basically, much of what we women hear about anger implies that showing anger means we're not 'real women.' Or, conversely, because we're women, our anger isn't real, it's not to be taken seriously. Our anger, we're told from day one, is either laughable or disgusting. Effectively, we're trained to fear and resent our own anger."

They looked at each other.

"All of you," I said. "All trained. Women are not innately good and kind and wise. We're trained to be that way. It can be a serious obstacle to getting what we want and need. We're conditioned. An attacker sometimes has to merely invoke that conditioning and it's as effective as a leash and muzzle."

"Damn," Nina said.

"It's a little like escaping a bad cult. You have to be active in your deprogramming. The first part of what I'd like you to do between now and next week is listen to your body. Learn what makes you angry. Big or small. Don't judge, for now, whether your anger is reasonable or rational. Anger, for the simple fact that it's an emotion, is never rational or reasonable. Understandable, yes, but not a rational process. Don't worry about it. Just learn how you work inside. And then, when you get angry, admit it to yourself, and do something about it."

"Like what?"

"Depends. The first thing must be to find a way to use the adrenaline created by anger. What do you usually do when you get angry? For example, I like to hit things—such as the punch bag. I also like to break wood for kindling."

"I kick the soccer ball extra hard," Suze said. "Or throw the softball."

"Slam doors." Christie.

"I walk extra fast." Tonya. And then they were off: kneading bread, stabbing the dirt with a trowel extra hard, singing "real loud," strangling a towel, punching a pillow, peeling a lot of vegetables, and, Kim's, my favorite, "hitting the wall in the garage with an old tennis racket."

"And how does that make you feel?"

"Better." "Cleaner and calmer." "More in control."

I nodded. "Control comes from having choice, bleeding off the pressure on a regular basis, so you're not seething all the time. Then, when something makes you angry, you can choose whether or not—and how—to respond."

Physically venting also meant they would get used to it, and be able to produce a response more quickly in an emergency. It was all a matter of use.

"It's good for your breathing and coordination, too. And the next time you're strangling a towel"—a nod for Sandra—"or punching that pillow"—Pauletta—"I want you to really feel the emotions, the physical sensations—the speeded-up heart, the breathing, the rising strength."

Some nods.

"I want you to feel it, and remember it. Remember it so clearly that you can recall it in the middle of the night, if necessary, or while you're brushing your teeth in the morning—and while you're brushing your teeth one morning, recall very specifically three strikes or joint locks or throws that you think you do well."

I held up three fingers.

"Three things. That's all. A kick, a knuckle strike, and a pinkie wrench. Or an elbow strike and two kicks. Or two throws and a punch. It doesn't matter. Three."

I motioned Christie over to hold the bag.

"So I might pick a back fist"—I lunged and unfurled a whipping right fist into the right temple of my imaginary opponent—"then an elbow strike"—the back fist had brought me close enough for a flat, hard drive into the solar plexus—"and then a kick to the knee."

Christie staggered at the last blow. I could feel the energy boiling in my bones.

"Rehearse the anger feelings, the adrenaline, and rehearse the strikes in your head. Rehearse them as you're driving, as you're preparing dinner, as you get dressed. Enjoy the sensation. Just three things. Over and over."

I scanned the faces around me.

"Anger isn't a bad thing. It's just a feeling. Learn it. Understand it. Feel it—and then start matching that feeling to your three strikes—your punch, your kick, your hold release, whatever. Then start matching the strikes with possible attacks. Imagine someone pinning you to the wall, or jumping you from behind, or touching you on MARTA. Tie the imagination to the anger to the adrenaline to the strength to the strike. Over and over."

More nods. Some of them, I could see—a shifting of the feet, an increased pulse at the neck—were imagining as I spoke.

"Yes. That trowel in the dirt is a sword-hand to the neck. The towel is your attacker's throat. The soccer ball is a knee. The tennis racket is a sword-arm to the groin. Imagine the combination blows—the fist, the kick, the strangle. Or the throw, the kick, the knee. Imagine what you will shout as you strike out or throw. One word is best: *no,* or *blam,* or *die,* or *fuck.* It doesn't matter. Pick one, practice it. If you can, practice it as loudly as you can. If you can't, run through it in your heads. Play with it. Play with the scary thing. But play hard, play clearly, and play a lot. I want you ready by this time next week, because I have a treat for you."

"Why does the word *treat* from you make me nervous?" Nina said. "What do we get next week?

I smiled. "A real live boy."

F O U R T E E N

WHILE THE EARLY-MORNING GYM PATRONS EBBED AND FLOWED AROUND ME, I FOCUSED on the blue punch bag. Feet first: snap kick and roundhouse, back kick and crescent kick; heel, instep, side and ball of the foot. Then knees, both with the bag hanging free and pulling it to me as I thrust. Elbows next. Ram the nose into the brain, crush the top of the spine where it joins the skull, burst the kidneys, crush the larynx, break the ribs. Forwards, backwards, uppercut and side strike. Left and right. With elbows you have to be close, close enough to kiss.

I stripped off my outer shirt and wiped my face and hands.

Hands gave you a little more distance. Fists first. The whipping, snake strike of the back fist, the driving *gyaku zuki,* the snapping *oy zuki.* The palm strike. Sword-hand and knife-hand. Fingertips like sharpened pistons.

Then mixing it up. Heel, move in, elbow, knee, move out, back fist, in again for punch. Combinations and repetitions, whirling and standing, changing up and changing down, until I ran with sweat and the late-rising patrons exchanged sidelong looks.

I finished with a right back-fist, left punch, right elbow combination, and stepped back. Now I could eat breakfast.

I had been in the gym for an hour and twenty minutes. When I got back to my room, I had five messages. I put them on speakerphone and stripped my sweats as I listened.

The first was Bette. "I talked to the newspaper people yesterday. They agreed: no mention of you or your mother, no mention of Brian Finkel, Jr." Then Rusen, "Boy, this is great! The energy sure is back. You wouldn't think it would make such a difference. Finkel is beaming and rubbing his hands. Oh, and if you should see Kick, if she isn't wearing shades and being famous, could you tell her, please, that we need to hear from her about that job?" Gary: ". . . reminder of our lunch appointment at twelve-fifteen." Edward Thomas Hardy: "I see you smoked the snake out of the weeds. Do I want to know how you got her to talk? Thanks for keeping my name low profile. I owe you. I'll see if I can't help out with your future real estate and zoning needs, as far as the law allows, of course." My mother: "I hope your friend is feeling better. I hope she's pleased with the article."

Leptke had promised me a heads-up.

I called down to the front desk and asked them to put a copy of today's *Seattle Times* outside the door. The shower was hot and hard.

Don't meddle. Don't push me. I mean it. Maybe they didn't get the *Times* in Anacortes. Maybe she wouldn't see it as pushing.

I toweled off, dressed, and took the still-folded paper down to the terrace restaurant, where I ordered breakfast. Tea, pan-fried trout, grapefruit.

It was the front page of the B section: a long, crisp publicity still of Kick, from *Drop*, in a fire-opal formfitting suit, falling through nothing, arms wide and eyes closed, smile beatific, hair streaming behind her like a war banner, skin peach with dawn.

The server who brought me tea looked at the picture as she poured more ice water.

"Oh," she said. "Excuse me." Then, unable to help herself, "It's just such a beautiful picture. She looks like she's worshipping. Your food will be right out."

I read the opening paragraph, a breathless repeat of "the terrible night of May 14, when the unsuspecting crew on Seattle's latest hope for indie glory, *Feral* (see page 4), found their worst nightmares coming true, and brave Victoria 'Kick' Kuiper, already pluckily reimagining her life after personal tragedy— *cont'd p. 3 . . .*"

Worship. Yes.

I turned to page three.

Despite the first paragraph and heavy reliance on journalistic cliché, it did the job. It cataloged clearly Corning's "ill-fated scheme" to bankrupt the production by finger-pointing to regulatory agencies, detailing how "pranks" had escalated to poisoning and the admission of seventeen people to Harborview with "life-threatening symptoms." The consequences for the innocent caterer, trying so hard to drag herself back onto the film map, this time with food instead of falling. Then the real meat of the matter, as far as Leptke was concerned: the ease with which the zoning process could be manipulated if you had enough money. There were brief definitions of OSHA and EPA, and sidebars on the Seattle independent film industry, the committee structure of the City Council, and a B-article on the human face of ruthless business manipulation—complete with a black-and-white head shot of Steve Jursen, the carpenter. I was mentioned only in passing as "the concerned out-of-town landlord" and Corning and Bri Jr. not at all. Mackie was there, though, under his legal name, Jim Eddard, labeled a "person of interest." Which meant the police did not yet have him. Johnson Bingley was named, too ("though unavailable for comment, due to being out of the country"), and there were quotes from Edward Thomas Hardy ("respected Seattle council member running for reelection") and the local prosecutor who promised, as they always do, "a swift and thorough investigation."

Bri's family had money. Hardy had clout. Corning had struck a deal. Mackie, aka Jim Eddard, had been left holding the bag. Money isn't justice.

I traced Kick's smile. It was the exact size of my little fingertip.

THE DRIVE to the set was as smooth as caramel; the sky was hidden by polished, nacreous cloud, and as I took the curve on the viaduct alongside Elliott Bay, I felt as though I were moving into the heart of a chambered nautilus.

The set hummed the way it had on Sîan Branwell's last day of filming. Carpenters and painters swarmed around the scaffolding. The air rang with hammering and stank of paint. I heard the hiss and froth of the espresso machine as soon as I walked in, and my heart beat with dread and joy, but it was Dornan behind the counter. He saw me, and nodded, and focused his entire concentration on a quad grande latte and then a mocha spin for John and Andrea, the props people I had overheard that first day. They gave me sidelong glances ("the concerned, out-of-town landlord") but said nothing until Dornan handed them their coffee with a flourish and they beetled off.

"Busy," I said. I wonder what their—my—burn rate was now.

"Extra money means extra crew. And not only can we afford decent food, people know it's safe to eat. Kick's rehired her assistant, but she can't make it in until the afternoon, she said. So for now it's coffee and premade sandwiches, and I'm it."

"Where's Anacortes?"

"Ah," he said. "That's where she's hiding?"

"She's not hiding."

"No? Well, if you say so. Now, I know you're not drinking milk, but have you tried soy?"

"No."

"Let's try it now, then. A nice soy latte."

I watched him fuss with spigots. "Why do you think she's hiding?"

"I imagine many things frighten her at the moment. No doubt she'll get over it. And in answer to your question, I believe Anacortes is somewhere north, on the sound. Lovely views. Her parents, by all accounts, are not poor."

"They're not?"

"Not even remotely."

"She said her father was 'in trucking.'"

"And so he is. He's the COO of a giant truck-making corporation. Here you go." He handed me a paper cup. "Sorry it's paper. There's been a run on coffee this morning, and no time to wash cups."

Drawn in the foam on top was a lopsided flower. Imperfect. Vulnerable. Ephemeral. "What's she hiding from?"

He poured himself coffee from the urn and added two shots of espresso. "How long have you known her?"

"You know exactly how long."

"That's right. You barely know her, and she barely knows you. And she's just been diagnosed with an incurable disease. If I were her, I'd be thinking you might cut and run. Most people would."

Over by the scaffolding, one of the carpenters dropped a hammer and began to swear. Someone else was laughing.

"You never met my wife," he said.

Deirdre, who had died at twenty-two of leukemia. He never liked to use the names of the dead.

"Illness isn't like the movies. It's not like *Love Story*. It's not all off-screen treatments, or pale faces filmed through a Vaselined lens. It's not crisp white sheets and brave smiles and poignant, self-sacrificing farewells. It's messy and

hard. Physically and emotionally." He paused. "We'd known each other eighteen months, been married for six. I don't know if, I don't know if I would have, if she'd found out when I first met her, if— It might have been too hard."

His eyes were hazed with memory, the way I imagined the blue glass of a doll's eyes might look if had been left too long on the floor of an abandoned nursery, light streaming pitilessly through bare windows until the cheap glass clouded and cracked. Had he seen Kick's illness right from the beginning and decided it was too hard?

"Are you going to drink that?" he said at last.

I put the coffee down. "I have to go."

"Of course you do."

"I have an investment to protect. There are lot of things to sort out. That article, for example, will make things worse, if anything, with OSHA and EPA." With the violations a matter of very public record, the caseworkers' superiors would start asking public questions. I should have been able to give them a heads-up before it appeared. I should have been able to give Kick a heads-up. *Don't push me. I'm a cook.*

"Invite them."

I looked at him.

"The regulatory bigwigs. Everyone loves the movies. They'll be putty in your hands."

"That's . . ."

"An excellent idea. I do have them sometimes. Yes. Now go."

Outside, I was surprised to find it was raining.

ED THOMAS HARDY'S office looked just the same, though this time the window was sheathed in fine silver droplets.

His shirtsleeves were rolled up and his tie loose, a pen in his hand. The epitome of a man of the people.

"As of half an hour ago, I have contracts for both of the private land parcels adjacent to mine," I said. "The third, the federal land, might take a little longer."

He nodded. "What do you know about federal, regional, and local tax incentives?"

"Nothing."

"Well, I know a lot. And as well as owing you for your, ah, discretion, I know of several ways you could make a lot of people rich."

"Profit isn't my motive."

"You've said that before. What do you want the land for, then?"

I imagined my land along the Duwamish, the river dimpled with rain. I saw a woman, sitting on a bench.

"What does the city need?"

"The city?" He gestured at the window. "Which city? The business city, the working people's city, the city of coyotes and eagles and sword ferns?"

The woman had a fading black eye.

"Profit might not be your motive, but let's pretend it is. Otherwise the people who can help or hinder you in this won't trust you. So, what do you want to do with this land?"

The woman with the black eyes sat on the bench, watching a heron, and seeing the bird pluck its shining dinner from the river and take off into the grey sky hardened the amorphous hope under her breastbone to a burning point.

In Atlanta, I had taught ten women. Only one had been Sandra. I could do better next time.

"A foundation," I said. "Classes. A park, a library."

"Maybe some low-cost housing?"

"Explain."

"Form a corporation—"

"I am a corporation."

"Make a new one. Call it something attractive and well meaning, something stolid and impressive, that sounds semiofficial, like CharterMae Trust or Foundry House or—"

"You've thought about this before."

He nodded. "I've thought about this a lot. There's an ocean of money out there, washing from pocket to pocket. I'd like to see some of it get used. But to get it, you have to give something. Tax credits." He looked pleased with himself.

"I'm none the wiser."

"Private developers build affordable rental housing if they get tax breaks. The federal government alone hands out more than five billion dollars a

year in credits to anyone who will keep rents low for fifteen to forty years, and rent to tenants who earn no more than sixty percent of the city's median income. The state administers those credits. I know all the people down in Olympia."

I waited.

"So what you do is build the housing, then sell the tax credits to syndicators, who bundle them and sell them to investors looking to offset their own taxes. Then you take that money from the sale, and use it maintain your building. You mix luxury and affordable on an eighty-twenty ratio and you can sell tax-exempt bonds. You'll make lots of money."

"I don't need to make lots of money."

"The more you make, the more you'll have to spread around to other people. And the ones you'll be making the money off of are the rich people."

"It sounds too good to be true. Why haven't you already done this?"

"You need a lot of money to start with."

"And you'd be willing to help shepherd this through the local regulatory process?"

"For a say in some of the community benefit."

"It sounds . . . tangled."

"That's the price, sometimes."

It would be Bette and Laurence who would work out the details. ETH would handle the work. I thought of those herons.

I need to do this myself, Kick had said. Not all women could. "My lawyer will call you." I would also have to donate to his campaign. He couldn't help me if he was no longer in office.

KICK CALLED just as I stepped into the rain.

"I'm back," she said. "What's left of my tree fell down."

"Ah." I stood very still while pedestrians parted grumpily around me and rain ran down the back of my neck.

"I'm wet, I hate my mother, and the tree . . . The goddamn tree. Probably the rain. It's tipped right over and lying all over my yard. And El Jefe . . . Stupid cat."

"Are you all right?"

"Of course I'm all right. I wasn't here."

"Is the cat all right?"

"He's hurt."

"Is it bad?"

"He can't sit down. And he's complaining. But he's eating and he lets me stroke him. It's probably not even broken."

"So it's . . . his leg?" I didn't know why we were talking about a cat that wasn't even hers. I started walking along the sidewalk.

"His tail. It's sort of bent. Hold on." A strange ripping sound rasped in my ear. "That was him purring into the phone."

"Oh."

"So, anyway, I thought that I'd take him to the vet, and while I was gone you could finish what you started with the tree."

"You want me to . . . Kick, have you seen the paper?"

"Yeah. So are you coming, or what?"

"Yes."

"Great. Gotta get to the vet." Click.

I folded my phone and waited in bemusement for a light. I wouldn't have been surprised to see the traffic pole flash magenta and turquoise, or burst into a chorus of "Louie, Louie." The rain began to ease. By the time I'd crossed the road, it had stopped.

SHE OPENED the cardboard carrier and the old black cat stalked off, looking rumpled and annoyed, but fit. She straightened, closed the door of her van.

"Subluxation of the tail," she said. "Good as new in two days. Whose is the truck?"

"A rental. Like the chainsaw. I bought the gloves." I shut up before I said anything else foolish.

She looked at the sawn chunks of trunk stacked by the gate and then at the growing patch of blue sky above the dining room extension. "If it had come down a week ago it would have crushed half the house." She stepped closer. Damp earth, sawn wood, the rich, sharp scent of Kick. I took off the gloves, dropped them on a stump, and held out my arms.

Later, in her bed, she eased herself into the curve of my arm. I stroked her hair and her back, and wondered under which knob of vertebra, exactly, the lesion lay. The skin and muscle felt the same.

"How did it go with your parents?"

"I hate my mother." Perhaps she was aiming for a light tone, but the attempt was ruined by a deep undertow of hurt and puzzlement. "I told them. My mother . . . my mother's a drama queen who thinks she's Lady Pragmatism. 'Right,' she said. 'Well, the family will have to organize twenty-four-hour care.' I said, 'What are you talking about?' She looked at me kindly, like I was a three-year-old, and said, very slowly, 'For when you're paralyzed, honey. Who else is going to help you?'"

I thought of my mother's reaction, and she'd never even met Kick.

"It was like she *wanted* me to be helpless so she could feel important. It was all about her. I know it was probably a shock but, Christ, paralyzed. So I looked at Pop, hoping for a bit of reason, and you know what he said?"

I shook my head.

"He said that, hell, he was sure it was all some big mistake. His little girl couldn't have a disease like that. I should just see. I should just wait. Everything would be A-okay. I didn't know whether to puke, scream, or bury an axe in his head."

"So what did you do?"

"I laughed, and said I wanted a glass of water, and Mom jumped up and said she'd get it, and I had to practically arm-wrestle her to the sofa. I'm not a fucking cripple yet, I said. Except I didn't say 'fucking.' And then I went into the kitchen and cried. And then I came back and told them I was just fine, and that for their information I'd just accepted a job as stunt coordinator on a series pilot, and thanks very much for their pity and denial, but I didn't need an ounce of help from them. And now I have to find a way to tell Maureen and my brothers."

My brain jumped to three different places at once. She'd accepted the job.

"I don't think I can face telling them right now. Ted's in the Seychelles, anyhow."

"The stunt rigger?"

"No. That's John. He's in Arizona. Ted's an accountant. But Maureen's right here."

"Yes." Maureen, who would look blank, then say something kind and caring, such as, "I really need to get my nails done soon." I took Kick's hand—the nail beds were pink, the nail white—and kissed her fingers, one by one.

"So, like I said, I hate my family." Rain pattered on the skylight. "This weather," she said.

She had taken the job. I thought of her jumping, face peach with dawn. "So. You saw the paper."

"Yep."

"What did you think?"

"Always hated that picture."

"Seriously, what—"

"*Shush.* I'm trying to tell you. Seriously. The way my parents treated me, more Crip than Kick, I saw I've been doing that to myself. Cutting myself down to size before anyone else could do it."

"Protecting yourself."

"Making myself small."

"So you told Rusen you'd accept his offer."

"Yep. I knocked on his door and went in and announced importantly that, 'Hey, I'll coordinate your stunt,' and he nodded and said, 'Boy howdy, that's great, can you deal with the fire department permit situation today?' I felt crushed—drums should have rolled or lightning cracked or something equally portentous: Kick steps up to herself." She sighed, and the long, sough-ing breath had a crack in it, and the crack widened and wobbled and grew and became, to my surprise, soft laughter, which, in its turn, grew sturdy and bright.

She laughed until she was as red in the face as a newborn, and as helpless, and kicked her feet. I held her tight enough to snap someone whose muscles weren't as dense and resilient as rubber bands, and she squeezed back and swung me onto my back and pinned my hands to the mattress, and I laughed and flipped her over in turn, and she tried to turn me back the other way, and then we were on our sides, matched muscle to muscle and bone to bone, strong and fine and taut, mouth to mouth, belly to belly, eye to eye. We breathed each other's breath, sucking the warm expelled air deep into alveoli and bronchiole; oxygen that had been in her blood dissolved in mine, fed my cells, moved the hand that curved over her bottom and between her legs, pulled her against me, gentle, inevitable, as slow as the turning of the world.

Later, she lay with her head on my thigh and her back against my ribs. I laid a hand on her rib cage and felt it rise and fall, rise and fall.

"Is it really this simple?" Her cage of bone and cartilage buzzed slightly un-der my palm as she talked. "Believe in yourself?"

"It's like self-defense. You have to refuse to be trespassed against. You have to refuse to believe what people want you to believe. It helps if someone shows you a few simple things, but mainly you have to be willing to simply do it."

"But what if some giant grabs some little old lady—"

"It doesn't matter how small you are or how big they are. I can teach any reasonably able woman to render an attacker unconscious inside twelve seconds, if she's willing. If she's not willing, nothing will make a difference."

"Twelve seconds. How long would it take you to teach someone like me how to do that?"

"You're more than reasonably able. And you're smart. Five or six hours, total."

She rolled onto her back. "Kick Kuiper, killing machine." She smiled. "Okay."

"Okay?"

"You can teach me. But you have to let me teach you something in return."

"What did you have in mind?"

"Whatever you like. How to fall."

"I know how to fall."

"When someone throws you, maybe, when there's no choice. But what about willingly, deliberately letting go?" She reached for her clothes. "Your truck has a tow bar, right? You want to go for a drive?"

I DROVE. She directed me north, along wet surface streets. Traffic was light and the air as sweet as the steam that comes off a cake just pulled from the oven. I kept to a sedate pace.

She approved. "I get so tired of people trying to impress me by weaving in and out of traffic as though they were riding a motorcycle."

There was a motorcycle at the triple-sized storage unit. There were two. "This one," she said, slapping a Suzuki's metallic green tank, "is my off-road machine. Custom shocks. This one here is for high-speed freeway chases. But what we've come for today is my Model Seventy air bag, some crash pads, couple mini-tramps, and the air ram. The trailer's in the next unit."

THE LOT was quiet. Lights showed in the editing trailer, but the second one was dark. The warehouse door was closed. A young, alert-looking man in a rust-colored jacket nodded at us pleasantly, bid us a fine evening, and asked to see ID. A small name badge on his left lapel said he was Janski, of Turtledove Security. We obliged. He clearly recognized both our names, but nonetheless checked his list before smiling and stepping aside.

"How have things been?" I asked him while Kick held her card against the lock.

"Quiet."

The door thunked and clicked open. It was cold. My skin tightened and my stomach tensed, but there was nothing obviously wrong. I considered, then made a mental note to talk to Turtledove about changing the locks, or the access code, whichever was best. We went in.

The standby lighting, pale and cool, made the set alien and vast. The islands of light had a greenish cast and seemed to ripple. The unseen roof loomed. Kick and I stood there, listening to the quiet.

"Cue creepy music," she said.

Air moved on my cheek when it shouldn't have; the tips of my fingers prickled.

"Hello, Earth to Aud."

I listened hard. Nothing. My mind playing tricks again. "Yes. Sorry. I'll find the lights."

I pushed the levers up, and light blazed from every corner. "Oh," I said. A five-story office building stood at the north end of the set in front of an enormous green screen—which still rippled lazily from the swing of air we'd let into the building.

"Yeah. I thought you'd think it was pretty cool."

We unloaded the air bag and mats and other equipment, and Kick settled down to begin her methodical check for wear or damage.

The new building was the scaffolding, now clothed in a painted facade, which completely obscured the front and reached four feet around the sides. How had they done it so fast? I touched a window. Plywood. A ledge. Carved polystyrene. I walked around the back, shook an exposed metal cross-brace. Very sturdy. There were scaffolding steps bolted neatly up the inside.

"So, what do you think?"

"Impressive. How high did you say it was?"

"Forty-two feet, four inches."

"Looks bigger."

"Well, it's supposed to. Want to go up and take a look?"

The steps were narrow and steep, but they didn't move an inch as I climbed. The platform was painted wood, and there was none of that uneven surface or slight shifting I was used to in temporary construction.

"It all feels extremely solid."

"It has to be," she said. "Look down." It was like looking over the edge of a four- or five-story house. "That floor is concrete. My bag is only twelve feet square, about the size of two of those judo mats end to end."

The mats looked like fingerprints. Tiny.

"And if you don't hit the center, you'll go flying off into the wall or a camera. The most important thing for a safe diving stunt is a safe takeoff. When you're thinking about how far out you have to jump, exactly, and you're doing it on cue, you don't need to be worrying about an uneven or unstable takeoff point. Come down, I want to show you the bag. If you're going to learn, you should know your equipment.

"Now," she said, at the bottom, "this is a Model Seventy, which means that it's rated for falls up to seventy feet. Fifteen feet wide, twenty feet long, six and half feet high when inflated—which takes fifteen minutes or more, and every time someone lands on it, you have to inflate it again. See these flaps on the side? They act as valves. When you land, air squeezes out of them. Otherwise you'd just bounce off and get flung into the wall."

I looked up at the tower, down at the air bag.

"You're going to teach me to jump off that thing?"

"We'll start with something smaller. Remember that fifteen-footer from the beginning of the shoot?"

I nodded. That wouldn't be a problem. "Those valves. I imagine that means you can't have two people jumping at the same time."

"Right. Even if there was room for both in the sweet spot, which there isn't, whoever landed a split second behind the first would have no air cushion and, boom." She slapped her hands together, and the side door slammed open.

It was Rusen, grinning, glasses and teeth glinting. He waved a piece of paper. "She's coming back!"

"Great," said Kick. "Who?"

"Well, jeezy petes. Sian Branwell, who else? I just got an e-mail confirming it. I saw that truck in the lot and thought, Well, who would be here at this time of night? Janski said it was you, and, boy, am I glad you showed up. We need to get to work on this right away."

"Good evening, Stan," I said, stepping into his line of sight. "How are you?" He looked confused. "Never mind. Branwell's coming back, how long for?"

"Just a day. But that'll—"

"When?"

"Day after Memorial Day." He turned to Kick, head bobbing this way and that in an agony of anxiousness. "That's just four days."

"No problem," she said.

"Really?"

"Really."

"Oh." He peered doubtfully at his e-mail. Then he smiled again. "This is going to make all the difference. It's a knockout stunt, but not having to shoot around Sîan's absence will . . . Boy howdy." He looked at me. "Has she shown you the new storyboards?"

"Not yet."

"They're exciting." To Kick: "You should show her."

"I was working my way up to—"

"We could look at them now," he said, and if she had been wearing something with sleeves, he would have plucked at them like a seven-year-old begging his mother to please, please come and see his spaceship made of cardboard boxes.

WE TALKED about it on the drive back. The stunt Kick and Rusen had dreamt up was to be a climactic battle between the fox woman and her corporate nemesis on top of a burning five-story building, with the winner throwing the loser to a slow-motion fiery death. Kick had talked knowledgeably about green screens, footage of a modest flame shot in the parking lot, fire department regulations, safety rigging, forced perspective, digital overlay, backlights, fill lights, key lights, and setups. The technical jargon lost me occasionally, but she seemed convinced they could make it look realistic. The scene hinged on getting a good, long shot of the falling body in front of the tower, and convincing close-ups of Branwell struggling with her opponent at the top of the same tower.

"I just hope she's a quick study. She's only going to have a couple of hours to rehearse."

"And you're not worried about the fall?"

"Not with Buddy on board. He's a real pro."

"Buddy," I said.

"We go way back. He coordinated on *Tantalus.*"

"Buddy is going to do the jump," I said. She nodded slowly, the way people do when they don't take their eyes off you because they expect a fight. "Can we afford him?"

"He's doing it as a favor to me. Scale. He'll come in and do that jump on the first take, and then I won't have anything to do until Branwell gets here on Tuesday. This way I get time. Lots of lovely time. I could even take two or three days' break. Get back Monday to oversee last-minute details. It would be cheap at five times the price. Besides, there just isn't anyone else available at short notice to do this."

"There's you."

"I have MS."

"But you're fit right now."

"Am I?" She gave me a measuring look. "Besides, no one would insure me."

"I could."

She laughed. "You don't know what you're saying." She peered at me. "You really don't, do you? You'd have to underwrite the whole production."

"Yes."

"Do you have any idea how much you'd have to guarantee?"

"I've looked at the books. Given two or three days to liquidate some securities, I could cover the whole thing."

"This production is costing six million," she said gently, trying not to burst my bubble.

"More than seven, with my current investment."

"And you could raise that in three days."

"It's less than ten percent of my net worth."

The words hung between us.

We drove in silence. Halfway across the ship canal bridge she said, "You're ten miles over the speed limit."

I slowed down. Cool night air flowed between us instead of words. I slowed down further.

"Now you're fifteen miles under the speed limit."

"Stay the night in my suite," I said.

"It's not warm tonight."

"It's not about that."

"What is it about, then?"

"It's a hotel, but tonight it's the closest thing I have to a home to share."

She thought about it for a while. "Okay."

I drove east along North 34th. "Do you need anything?"

"If I can borrow some of your underwear tomorrow, no."

I turned north up Stone Way, west on 38th, and headed south again and back across the bridge. I drove at the speed limit, paid attention to my rearview mirror, changed down in orderly procession through the truck's gears at traffic lights.

We were silent as I pulled into the hotel courtyard. We got out. I handed the keys to the valet, who seemed momentarily nonplussed to be given charge of a pickup full of sawn-up cherry tree.

Kick was standing with her arms wrapped around her ribs. I had an idea.

"Would you like a new table?"

"A table?"

I patted the wood in the truck. "I want to make something for you. Something to remember your tree by. Your dining table is cherry."

"Is it?"

"Come with me."

Two doormen, one for each handle of the double entry, swung the doors open with a flourish. Kick's chin went down.

Bernard was behind his desk in the upstairs lobby. "Ms. Torvingen."

"Bernard." Kick was staring at me, and then him, and then me again. "Do you know of any woodworkers in town? I have some cherrywood that I'd like stored until my next visit."

"As a matter of fact, I do." He smiled, as though this were a request he dealt with every day, and gave me the name of a cooperative, "With a charming sales outlet," in Pioneer Square. He wrote it all down. I folded the paper, put it in my pocket, thanked him, and said good night.

"Next visit?" Kick said as we waited for the elevator.

I was scheduled to leave a couple of days after my mother. I didn't say anything.

"So. You said you'd make it. The table or whatever. Or did you mean you'd get some minion to cause it to happen?"

"I would make it," I said. "With these hands." I held them out to her. The elevator dinged.

We rode in silence up to my floor.

The suite was quiet and still. The thermostat read seventy-two degrees. It felt colder. Kick looked around without a word.

"I'll order us coffee," I said. "Unless you'd prefer something else."

"Coffee's fine."

"Make yourself at home."

From the bedroom phone I ordered a pot of French roast, good and strong, with cream and sugar in case she liked it.

Back in the sitting room, Kick was prowling about. She had taken her shoes off. "Your bathroom doesn't have a tub."

"The guest bathroom doesn't."

"A guest bathroom," she said, and ignored the sofa to sit on the striped-silk chair. She pulled her knees under her chin and wrapped her arms around her shins. "How much does this place cost a night?"

I sat on the sofa and wished she was next to me. "I don't know."

"You don't know."

Silence. "Would you like some music?"

"Sure."

I took Barber out of the player and slotted the jewel case neatly back next to Brahms. From farther down the row, I slid out Sweet Honey in the Rock. Their a capella voices filled the suite with bravery.

A man tapped on the door and announced he was room service.

For once, I wished they hadn't done such a good job. The whole presentation shrieked of money: silver tray draped in creamy linen, gleaming coffeepot and creamer and sugar bowl. The cups were white Wedgwood. A yellow rose so fresh it still had dew on the leaves graced the corner, next to a plate of fresh brownies dusted with powdered sugar and a beaded carafe of ice water.

Kick's expression got more and more distant as the server laid everything on the table, one piece at a time, without a chink or rattle. I signed the chit and hung the Do Not Disturb sign on the door.

I sat down again on my too-big sofa.

"So. This is how you live."

"I don't normally live in a hotel."

"That's right," she said. "You live in Atlanta."

In a pause between tracks, the ice cubes in the water carafe shifted audibly. I put my hand on the coffeepot. "Black or with cream?"

"Black."

I poured, sniffed the aromatic steam that curled up from the transparent bone china: smells of Africa and licorice and sun on teak.

She wrapped her arms even more tightly around her shins.

"What is it?"

"You terrify me."

"What?"

"You terrify me," she said distinctly.

It was like being harpooned.

"I didn't mind that article. I told myself it was okay. It was okay. It is. But it frightens me that you can do that kind of thing anytime you want. You could buy half this city. You can take care of me. You can give me everything I ever wanted, everything I need, everything I might ever have dreamed of but might otherwise be unable to have, now. Because of . . ." She let go with one arm long enough to gesture at her body, the spine with its bright white lesions. "You offer me a way to have everything, to give up fighting. To just . . . give it up, give in, go gracefully into that good night. And the frightening thing is, I want to go. I want to never have to lift another finger, never have to worry about money again in my life, but then who would I be?"

"You'd be Kick."

"No. Because who is Kick? I am what I *do*. And if it's all done for me, what's left?"

"I don't understand."

"I know. And it's tempting to let you do it, anyway. But I can't, because I don't know what the hell I'm doing anymore, who I am."

"You are Kick."

"I was Kick. Before."

I put the cup down, stood, and lifted the coffee table up and set it to one side out of the way. She watched me. I knelt at her feet. "You are Kick." I bent and kissed her bare instep. "I know your skin." I leaned forward, so that my cheek rested on her feet and each of my palms were flat on her hips. "I know the shape of your muscle, the heft of your bone." I lifted my head. Her eyes met mine. I came to my knees and leaned in and kissed the corner of her mouth. "I know your mouth." I ran my hand over her hair, down the side of her neck. Her pulse beat hard. "I know your pulse." I kissed the other corner. Her lips opened. "I know your breath." A light, almost-not-there kiss, like kissing a butterfly's wings. "I know your scent. I know you. I always will."

LESSON 14

OUTSIDE CRYSTAL GAZE, I UNLOADED THE LAST OF THE HEAVY PADDING. DORNAN watched and tugged at his hair.

"And you swear you won't be hitting me?"

"Won't touch you."

"It's just for your ladies?"

"Yes. Now take this to the main-floor bathroom and"—a pale green Beetle convertible swept into the parking lot. Therese—"get changed. Go now, Dornan. Come into the room at exactly six-ten."

"Ten past, yes, yes, now, you're sure—"

Therese got out, she was waving something at me. She was clearly agitated.

I picked up the pile of padding, dumped it in Dornan's arms. "Go." I turned to Therese.

"I am so glad I can get a word with you," she said. "I need you to listen to this." She waved her phone again.

"What is it?"

"A message. From Sandra. Listen." She hit a key, listened, then another, handed me the phone.

A woman's voice, a whisper, as though she were hiding in a cupboard. " 'Moreover the Lord saith, Because the daughters of Zion are haughty, and walk with stretched-forth necks and wanton eyes, walking and mincing as they do, and making a tinkling with their feet: Therefore the Lord . . .' " She paused and spat softly, as people do when clearing their mouth of blood. " 'Therefore the Lord will smite with a scab the crown of the head of the daughters of Zion and the Lord will discover their secret parts.' " Another pause. Musing. " 'Discover their secret parts.' "

I turned off the phone, handed it back to Therese.

"When did you get the message?"

"Last night."

"What did you do?"

"I wasn't sure what to do. She didn't ask for my help, I didn't know . . ."

I waited.

"I called nine-one-one."

"And what did you say?"

"I gave Sandra's address."

"She gave it to you?"

Therese nodded, kept nodding as she realized what a coincidence of timing that was. "I gave her address and said they should get an ambulance there."

"And then what happened?"

"I don't know. I was up all night thinking and thinking about it. This morning there was nothing on the news. Nothing anywhere."

There never was, unless someone died.

"Did I do the right thing?"

"It never does any harm to call nine-one-one. They would have sent police as well as an ambulance. If Sandra was hurt, she would have got help. If she was in danger, she would have been protected."

Another car pulled into the lot, a battered Civic. Tonya: tense, ready.

"You didn't call Sandra?"

"She didn't give me her phone number. I don't even know her last name."

"I see." I didn't. But another car was arriving. Time to go in.

SEVEN MINUTES later, the basement air smelled singed, like an iron skillet heated too long on the stove: partly someone's overuse of hair spray—odd, the way some people prepared—and partly adrenaline sweat. Sandra was the last to arrive. Her left arm was strapped close in a black sling. When she dropped her purse on the bench and turned, the new bruise along her collarbone was momentarily visible. Her face was expertly made up. No one said anything, but the taste in the air intensified to gunmetal and cordite.

Therese dithered, unsure whether to talk to Sandra, whether she should acknowledge the phone call, admit she had called 911.

I didn't wait for her to make up her mind.

"In"—I glanced at the clock—"nine minutes, my friend Dornan will come in. He will be wearing body armor and padding. He will attack you impartially, without malice, one by one. We will decide on the order before he arrives. You will hit him with everything you've got. You can't hurt him. Even his joints will be specially braced. He will keep attacking you until he signals that he's sustained what would be a knockout or structurally disabling blow if he weren't padded. He will signal this by patting his head with his hand—or slapping the mat with his foot or hand if his head is unreachable." If, for example, it's rolled off into the corner of the room and is being smashed like a piñata. "I'll repeat all this before we begin."

Jennifer's face was glaucous and glistening. Good. That fear would translate nicely to the kind of adrenaline I—they—would need.

"This is the order in which he'll attack: Tonya, Suze, Sandra, Nina, Pauletta, Jennifer, Therese, Katherine, Kim, Christie. You know everything you need to know about knocking a man down. Dornan is in his early thirties and reasonably fit, average height, and a little below average weight—until you add in the sixty pounds of padding. Sandra, tell me about your injury. Will you be all right for this exercise?"

"It's just bruises."

"Were you X-rayed?"

"No. But it's an injury I'm familiar with. Soft-tissue injury. Muscles, not ligaments. And it's been documented."

Documented. Was that a reference to the ambulance? She seemed almost supernaturally calm. *Because the daughters of Zion are haughty . . .* She had reached the place some people find before they die. I doubted she could do much to harm anyone in this class with me watching, but she could hurt herself, which would distract everyone. I considered. If it were only bruises, being attacked would be painful but probably wouldn't pose a danger of serious damage. I'd tell Dornan to grab her around the waist. I nodded, and continued with the task at hand.

"Dornan will attack you as you walk. He will attack you from the side or the front or the back. For the purposes of this scenario, you should assume he wants to drag you somewhere such as his car or yours, that he wants to hurt you. This is not a situation in which to talk. You fight. Questions?"

"What's he dragging us off for?"

"Whatever is the worst thing you can imagine, but you will not stop in order to elicit this information. Ideally you will render him unconscious or otherwise incapable of pursuing you. Think of your best moves, the ones you've rehearsed this last week: your kicks or your throws or your punches. There is no reason, given your training, that you couldn't half kill an attacker in under twelve seconds."

Now they were all pale. Lots of glances at the clock. Six minutes.

"Remember everything we've learnt about fear. The most important thing is to breathe. What is the most important thing?"

"To breathe," Christie said.

"Good. Please stand. Sandra, take off your sling. Line up along the mat, in the order in which you will be attacked."

Some reluctant shuffling. Some stress clumsiness and bumping. One startling high-pitched giggle from Katherine.

"Raise your arms. Take a deep breath. Stretch up, stretch that spine." Spinal muscles were always the ones that got wrenched, and Sandra, at least, hadn't had time to warm up. I watched her carefully. Her left arm went up as smoothly as the right. Pain is just a message. "Breathe out as you lower your arms. Raise and breathe in. And now we'll squat and breathe out, hard. And up and in. And down." Therese and Tonya both went backwards. "Good. Yes. Why not. We'll do some rolling. And up and in, and down and out and over. And up. Good. Yes." Much less pale now. Though still some glances at the clock. Five minutes. "Breathe. Down and out, loudly please, loudly, and over, and up." Down and out and over and up, and down and out and over and up. I could see good steady carotid pulses. Too steady in some cases. I needed them pumped. "Down." Down they went. I thought of the Haka, a traditional Maori war chant designed to provoke and intimidate the enemy while pumping up the chanters. *It is death, it is death, it is life, it is life. . . .* "This time, when you go down, use your voice. Shout whatever you've been imagining all week in your anger scenario. And up, and fill those lungs, and down!"

"Die!" bellowed Suze, and I caught two or three halfhearted no's and a weak *blam* from Nina.

I laughed. Suddenly it was all quite ridiculous. "Apart from Suze, you may as well be asking them in for tea. We have four minutes to get you ready. So once more, with feeling. Up. Breathe. Long and slow, long and slow, and this time when you go down, I want to hear you. And *down.*"

I went down with them and bellowed. "*Hoo!* And up. And again. *Hoo!*" More noise now. Suze was enjoying herself. Christie began to cut loose.

Three minutes.

"Stand tall. You are about to be attacked. You're about to defend yourself as though your life depends upon it. I want you awake. I want you ready. Yes, you've just come from work or picking up your children. Yes, this is a basement room with bad carpet. Yes, essentially you're safe. But if you can do this now, you can do it anywhere. Anywhere. So this is a real test. Feel your pulse beat. Feel your breath. Feel how solid, how strong you are. Remember that no one has the right to hurt you, no one. Who has the right to hurt you?"

"No one," Suze said.

"I can't hear you."

"No one!" barked Tonya.

"That's right. On the count of three, everybody: Who can hurt you? One, two—"

"No one!"

"Who?"

"No one!"

One minute. "With me, now." I lifted my hands. Clap-clap, stamp; clap-clap, stamp: the opening beat of Queen's anthem, "We Will Rock You." "With me." Clap-clap, stamp. Clap-clap, *stamp.* Clap-clap, *stamp.* They all picked it up. You'd have to be dead to be impervious to that rhythm. Clap-clap, *stamp.* Clap-clap, *stamp.* Now they were lifting their arms with the stamping.

The air-conditioning began to grind. It added another layer to the rhythm. Thirty seconds.

Clap-clap, *stamp.* Clap-clap, *stamp.* The concrete floor trembled. "Face front!" Clap-clap, *stamp.* The line was straight, facing the door, an army focused on a weak and contemptible foe. Clap-clap, *stamp.*

The door opened.

Dornan lumbered in. He moved slowly, deliberately—the only way he could—and the rhythmic breathing along the line matched his steps exactly: harsh breathing, protect-the-homeworld breathing.

His helmet was huge, padded inside and out, with protective plates welded on the front, back, and sides, and themselves padded; triangular eye holes covered with Perspex, a mouth grille, ear grilles—a big metal pumpkin head. He wore a quilted suit covered with body armor and then more padding. Special braces at wrist, elbow, and knee made him move awkwardly. I'd sprayed parts of it silver to look even more otherworldly and menacing.

He stopped at the far edge of the mat, as I'd asked him to, and swiveled his head this way and that. No doubt he was simply trying to see through the triangular eye holes, but it was a particularly machinelike and alien movement.

I felt—or at least imagined I could—the women on either side of me draw together like a muscle: organic, flexible, strong.

I stepped out of line, surveyed them, nodded, and said, "Tonya. You will walk along the center of the mat. When he attacks you, fight back. Do not stop until he touches his head or until I tell you otherwise." I gestured her forward.

Her legs shook. The air-conditioning shut off abruptly. She walked with very small steps to the left-hand edge of the mat. Dornan had strict instructions not to attack anyone until she began to walk across the mat. As she passed me I realized she was whispering something to herself that might have been "No one, no one." At the edge of the mat she stopped, and turned, and hesitated.

I looked her full in the eye. "No one," I said, and gave her an encouraging nod, and she took that first step. Dornan simply stood there. She took another. Tiny steps. "No one," I said, and raised my eyebrows at her.

"No one," she said tremulously. "No—"

Dornan moved.

"—*one.*" It was a shriek.

She flailed at him, he lowered his head slightly and stood while her first three blows—they couldn't really be described as punches—bounced harmlessly from his chest and shoulder.

The class tightened, groaned and gasped.

I tuned my voice to cut through the noise. "Put him down: throat, knee, eye."

She was so far down the tunnel of the Adrenaline Now that I wasn't sure she would hear me or even see anything. Dornan lifted his arms and stepped forward again to engulf her but with a shriek she threw herself at him: double-fist slam to the chest and then, astonishingly, a head butt right over his nose, *wham,* and over he went.

"Finish him," Suze yelled.

Tonya dropped to one knee and drew her hand back. I saw the supported finger a second before she launched a knuckle strike at his throat that would have put an unpadded attacker in the hospital, if not the morgue.

Dornan patted his helmet but no one noticed. Tonya threw back her head and ululated, tears streaming down her face. The room exploded with hoots and screams and cheers. "Next!" I said, and while Suze gradually realized that was her, I helped Dornan to his feet. He managed a wink before resuming his place at the edge of the mat.

"You are going to die, you fuck," Suze said. Her face was pale and she had both fists up. Everyone cheered. "Totally die. Come and get it!"

"Suze, you have to walk on the mat."

"What?"

"On the mat. He won't attack you until you walk."

"Right. Okay." She didn't move.

"Just take a step."

She looked unsure.

"Kill him, Suze." "Yeah!" "You can do it."

"No one," Nina said. "No one!"

Suze took one step. Another. Her shoulders tightened. Dornan just stood there.

"Walk," I said, implacable.

She ran, and Dornan ran, and they both went down, and Suze went berserk: her knees, her elbows, her feet, her fists pumping like wild things. Somewhere in that blind rain of blows, something must have hit something vital because Dornan patted his helmet decisively and rolled away.

Suze stood up and blinked. I went to her and said, "Good, that's good."

"Yes," she said.

"You can stand with the others now. You did well. Stand with the others." Dornan was already up and in position, the class was clapping. I stood by him a moment. "Avoid the next one's shoulder if you can." He nodded. I returned to my place. "Next," I said. "Sandra."

The class started to call out encouragement but she smiled and strolled to her edge of the mat as smooth and cool as a cup of cream and the yells clotted and died. In the silence she looked at Dornan, nodded, and stepped onto the mat. He didn't make her wait.

She jumped to one side and with eerie precision kicked his left knee out from under him. He went down like a stunt horse in a cavalry charge. I could have sworn I saw a hint of a smile on her face in her split-second pause, but then she fell to her knees, raised both hands as though to God, and slammed two elbows down on his spine. Axe kicks are a more efficient use of power, but without body armor, even those blows might have paralyzed Dornan. He patted his helmet. She stood, looked down, then deliberately balanced and gathered herself.

"Sandra!" I shouted, just in time to spoil her aim slightly, and the axe kick she'd aimed for exactly the same spinal target missed and hit his ribs instead. "Dornan, move away. Move away." He didn't move. "Sandra." She turned. She was definitely smiling. "Sandra, it's done. Over."

"Over," she repeated.

Dornan stirred. She turned back.

"Sandra, it's done. You did it."

"Done." She watched Dornan pull himself into a ball, and then uncurl and haul himself to his feet.

Light glinted off the Perspex eye protection. I couldn't see past it. I moved to one side, stepped closer. His eyes were a little wider than usual but didn't seem panicky. I raised my eyebrows. He nodded, I nodded back. I had no idea what I would have done if his courage had failed him, or the padding.

"Next. Nina."

Dornan was getting wilier, or perhaps Nina had been shaken by Sandra's performance, but he managed to get his arms around her waist and lift her from the mat for a moment, "No," she shouted. "No, no, no, no," and struggled, futilely, until Pauletta yelled, "Three-year-old, three-year-old," and "No!" Nina said, with ragged gravitas, and made herself a dead weight until he sagged and she could get her feet on the ground and shove backwards with all her strength. They both went down, after which the usual panic blows followed in a hail of no, no, no's and at some point he slapped out.

The rite of passage continued. One by one they stepped up, lashed out, and were led off the mat in a triumphant daze: Pauletta, who laughed maniacally through the whole thing; Jennifer, who cried before she'd even begun; Therese, who dispatched the lumbering Dornan with a neatly executed elbow to the side of the head, followed by a foot sweep, followed by a stamp on his knee: disabling, but not lethal. Katherine, of course, began and ended with kicks, and Kim was the only one who used a palm strike—which clearly took Dornan off guard. Christie, though, was the best of all. She let herself be grabbed by the shoulders, then simply fell backwards and hurled him over her head. He was patting his helmet before she even stood up. She stood up grinning. She knew she'd done well. She knew they all had.

Brief silence, then pandemonium: shrieking, laughing, more tears, hugs. On the other side of the room, Dornan lumbered to the bench, started to sit down, and changed his mind. He tugged at his helmet. I wandered over.

"All right?" I said.

He got the helmet off and held it under his arm, like a fencer. He breathed for a moment. "You owe me, but you know that." Then he grinned. "Though it is nice to make so many women happy. If I'd known that all it took to worm my way into a woman's heart was to let her beat the shit out of me, my early life would have been very different. Help me with all this nonsense." As soon as his gloves were unstrapped, he yanked them off and tucked his hair behind his ears.

"That kick to your ribs didn't hurt?"

"It's nothing," he said, then straightened suddenly, got a twinkle in his eye, and his brogue thickened, "nothing in service of helping these lovely ladies."

They had regained their awareness of the room beyond their own triumph and had noticed that the evil space alien was a not-unattractive male.

"Oh, my goodness," said Jennifer. "Are you all right?"

"Perfectly fine. In the peak of health."

"Bet we scared you, hey?" Nina said.

"Absolutely. Terrifying."

"Did we hurt you?" Therese wanted to know.

"My pride, possibly. I had no idea ladies could be so fearsome." Brilliant smiles all around. "You astonished me."

"We had a good teacher," Christie said.

"Indeed?" Dornan gave me a wink, as if to say he saw I was glowing under a bit of flattery as much as anyone else in the room. "Oh, indeed. Yes."

"And we really didn't hurt you?" Kim seemed a little disappointed.

"I'd have to get out of all this padding to find out."

"Did you like that palm strike I gave you?" she said.

"Blinded and surprised me," Dornan said, though if I'd had to bet it would be to the effect that he couldn't remember one blow from another. "Took me completely off guard."

"And my knuckle strike?" Tonya said.

"Ah, now that I remember very clearly. Like a bolt from heaven. My life quite passed before my eyes."

He was troweling it on. Any minute they'd realize that. "No doubt Dornan would really appreciate the opportunity to get out of that extremely uncomfortable suit."

"Oh, my, yes indeed." "Oh, you poor thing." "We mustn't keep you." Good southern women, they said all the right things while still managing to look crushed: they had not yet had the chance to refight their battles.

"But no doubt he'd be willing to rejoin us for a debriefing?"

"No doubt, ladies, no doubt."

It would give me the chance to debrief them properly, after which Dornan could twinkle at them and make them feel mighty. They'd done well. They deserved every ounce of their triumph. Meanwhile, though, it wouldn't do any harm to lead them through another round at the punch bag, refining what they'd learnt in the heat of their personal battle.

FIFTEEN

ON SET, KICK WAS ENTIRELY PROFESSIONAL AND IMPERSONAL. "THE FIRST STEP IS TO visually inspect the air bag, both before and after inflation." I wondered if I hid my feelings so well when I was teaching.

She lifted this piece and that of the deflated bag, talking about the sensitivity of the plastic to temperature change and how it must always, always be checked. "One stunter died a few years back when they flew his air bag out to Portugal in an unpressurized cargo bay. The cold, high altitude changed the physical properties of the material and the vents didn't hold. Dead as a stone."

Then the compressor thudded for fifteen minutes and we walked solemnly around the Model Seventy once again. She moved smoothly.

"Now we test it from the tower. It'll test the camera orientation, too."

Again, there were three cameras. One to the side, one on top, one directly behind the bag to focus on the falling object as it fell. Once they were set up to Rusen's satisfaction, she borrowed one of the props manager's clothing dummies, carried it to the top of the tower. Then she came back down, handed me a very heavy grocery bag, and said, "Follow me." Climbing the scaffolding steps with the bag made me aware of the pull of humerus from shoulder socket, the compression of cartilage in my knee and ankle joints, the smooth lubrication of synovial fluid around my hips. We are such delicate machines.

It was surprisingly crowded at the top with the two camera operators. Everyone but me was wearing a headset. I nodded. They nodded back.

Kick took several sets of ankle and wrist weights from the bags and wrapped them around the dummy's limbs and waist. Some of them had been carefully sewn together to be long enough. Then she cinched me into a harness, standing close to check the fit—the impersonal touch was disorienting—clipped a line to the D-ring at my waist, jerked it to be sure, then did the same for herself. I eased one strap, tightened another.

We picked up the dummy, carried it to the edge of the platform.

"Clear," she said conversationally, then, for the benefit of people on the set without earphones, she shouted, "Stand clear below." Then she turned to me. "Follow my swing. Let go at the top, don't try to push it." She waited for my nod, and we began to swing. "On three. One"—swing—"two"—swing—"three"—release, and the dummy sailed up and out in a rapidly climbing curve, seemed to pause, then plummeted in an almost straight line to the bag, which hissed and sagged and caught the dummy safely in the center of its sweet spot. Whistles and general applause from below—I saw the flash of Dornan's grin.

"Of course a body, a person, falls differently," she said, and unhooked her safety line. "With an active leap and flailing arms it's more of an overhand, egglike curve. It takes a little longer, and it's easier for the camera operators to follow."

"Do they know that?" They seemed barely out of film school. We unbuckled our harnesses. I resisted the urge to help her.

"They will when Buddy gets here."

We climbed down, a lot easier without the weights, and started the compressors pumping the bag full again.

"Sandwiches?" Dornan called from the craft-services table. He gave the impression of wearing an apron, though he wasn't.

"Later," Kick said.

We sat cross-legged on the floor while we waited. She looked around, at the quietly humming set. "We're pretty much set. Buddy'll want to test the bag himself, but essentially we're good to go."

"I thought you said most serious stunters had their own bags and own air-bag people."

"I used to be Buddy's air-bag woman. He coordinated on *Tantalus*. He trusts my bag work. He'll walk in here, we'll get it in one take. Two at most, then I'm free for a couple of days. I can take care of . . . things." Maureen. Her brothers.

The air compressor clicked off, and on, and off again.

At eye level, the bag looked huge. She reached out and patted it. It shivered like a big square jellyfish.

"Buddy's not here," I said.

"He will be."

"Yes," I said. We admired the bag some more. "Is it calling to you?"

"Yes."

"Insurance aside, would you be up to it?"

She snorted. "It's only forty-two feet."

"It occurs to me that you don't need insurance to jump if it's just for fun."

She looked at the bag some more.

"And the cameras could probably do with the practice. Save Buddy having to do two takes." She didn't say anything. "How long's it been?"

"Long time."

"You—"

"Hush," she said. "Stop there. Stop. Give me a minute." She uncrossed her legs and leaned back on her hands, tipping her head to take the measure of the fake office building. She folded over her legs, chest touching knees, stretching out her hamstrings, breathing easily. She straightened, looked at the tower again, began to fold back, then jumped to her feet so fast I didn't see the transition. She seemed different, burlier. "Roland!" One of the cameramen poked his head cautiously over the lip of the tower. "Live rehearsal!"

There was a moment's silence, in which several crew stopped mid-hammer or mid-yammer, then Roland said, "You want us to load?"

"Film for three cameras? You and whose fucking checkbook? Rehearsal," I said.

Einstein once called quantum entanglement—when the quantum states of two objects have to be described in reference to each other even though the individual objects are spatially separated—"spooky action at a distance." He believed that it was impossible to use this entanglement to transmit information. Einstein had never been on a film set. I didn't see anyone leave the building to go get Finkel or Rusen, I didn't see anyone pick up a phone, but by the time Kick got to the top of the tower, they were both there, watching.

I stood twenty feet from the bag, two feet behind the camera dolly, in direct line-of-sight to the tower. She would look as though she were falling right at me. Dornan stood a little to my left. He looked worried.

She came to the lip of the platform, in safety harness and headset, stood wide-legged for a moment, then sat, feet dangling. She adjusted her headset, appeared to be saying something. The camera operator squinted and made some adjustment. Rusen came over, they conferred. Rusen took the operator's headset a moment, looked up at the figure on the tower, said something, listened, nodded, said something else, grinned, and gave the headset back.

"Okey dokey," he said loudly. "Everybody, keep still. Try not to make any sudden moves or loud noises."

You can't distract her now, I thought. She sees nothing, hears nothing but what is to come.

And she did that trick again, stood so fast I didn't see her get up, and her headset was gone, and she was unbuckling her harness, and it was like watching a quarter horse, stripped of its tack, roll in the dust and stand and remember what it meant to be alive. She stood motionless, and I knew her nostrils would be flared, her heart thumping like a kettle drum, that she would be testing the air for unexpected currents, rocking imperceptibly on her feet, feeling the delicate articulations of the talus, the anklebone: the ends of the tibia and fibula, the heel bone, the rays of the metatarsals. So much work for one bone, sliding back and forward on its springy ligament. Less delicate, in comparison, than a horse's paten.

She was already going to that place, the heart-stopping moment when the world pauses, then resumes as a crystal dream. She was like the horse running, running around the corral, getting up speed before heading towards the fence, gathering itself, listening to its own rhythm, nothing but the heart, nothing but the blood, nothing but the breath. Bit and bridle forgotten, iron shoes now weightless, ribs working like bellows and arteries wide open.

She stepped back, and all I could see was the top of her head, and it moved slightly, as though she had nodded to herself, and then she ran, and leapt, up and out, and—

"Oh!" everyone moaned, as she faltered, then crumpled as though shot, and fell like a dead thing.

Gravity seemed to triple for a moment, then adrenaline burned through my system and kicked me into hyperdrive. Kick fell in slow motion. Sound fell away. I started to draw breath before leaping—to do what, I don't know—when my automatic processing of images caught up with my brain and I realized she was smiling. And then she thumped neatly into the exact center of the bag, and swung herself to the ground like a pro. Her grin was big enough to split the world.

Noise swelled around me: applause. She bowed, laughed.

Dornan was there, patting her on the back, saying, "Jesus, God in heaven," and Rusen pumped her hand like a maniac. I stayed where I was. My muscles trembled with unspent power.

Then she was standing in front of me.

"Well?"

Her skin looked perfectly elastic, blooming and alive. I touched her cheek. "You were good," I said. "I believed it. I thought you were going to die."

"Yep," she said. "Pretty much perfect."

"And you used to do that every day?"

"Only higher." She grinned. "Still want to learn? When Buddy's done the jump I'll pack away the Model Seventy and we'll get out that old Forty and give it a try. Hey," she said, as Dornan ambled over with two cups. He gave one to her, held another out to me.

"I remembered no cream," he said. "But I put sugar in it. You looked as though you could do with it."

I accepted the cup.

"I can also recommend the sandwiches," he said. "Tuna or jerk chicken."

Kick sipped at her paper cup. It smelled strange. She saw my look. "Red tea. Don't need caffeine after that. But I could eat. Aud?" I shook my head. She nodded, then gave me a one-armed hug. She squeezed hard, then kissed me. "I'm glad you were here."

She headed back to the air bag, swaggering slightly. Dornan said, "She's different, isn't she, when she jumps."

"Yes." Hearty and careless, unfragile, unneeding. "I think I'll take my coffee outside. Join me?"

We sat outside on the hood of my car and watched clouds sweep in two different directions, as though the sky were being torn apart.

IF KICK was a quarter horse, Buddy was an old steer, sinewy and rawboned, grazed on arid land all his life. His skin was leathery and tightly stretched, and when he shook hands with the crew, I saw a scar twisting up his left forearm like a brand. He walked around the air bag with Kick and listened attentively as she talked about the testing and her own fall. His limbs were lanky, and next to Kick he seemed uncoordinated, but there was a kinship, a live-free-or-die lift of the head, a risk-calculating twist of the mouth. I looked at him, nodding and listening, unbuttoning the cheap flannel shirt, looking over the harness Kick handed him, and understood they shared a world I couldn't. I wondered if her stunt rigger brother looked like that.

I left them talking to Rusen and the camera operators.

Finkel was in his trailer. "That was some jump of Kuiper's," he said. "We should've been rolling for that, saved the cost of this Buddy guy."

"Mmmn," I said. Had Kick not told anyone about her diagnosis apart from me and Dornan? I sat down. "We need to talk about OSHA and EPA. And Sîan Branwell's PR value. Let me see her contract."

We were both on the phone an hour later when Rusen came in, glowing. "We got it!" he said. "In one— Oh, sorry." He made a production out of putting his finger to his lips and sitting with conspicuous quietness in a chair in the corner while Finkel and I wound up our calls.

We finished at about the same time. I nodded to Finkel and he crossed two more names off an already heavily striped list.

"What's that?" Rusen said.

Finkel handed him the list. "We're inviting everyone and his goddamn dog to the set on Tuesday to hang with Sîan Branwell. Well, not with her, exactly, just around her. See her from a distance. Watch a real movie being made."

"Dornan's idea," I said. "The regional manager from OSHA is bringing her two children. The woman from EPA might come with her mother. Apparently her mother is a big fan."

"Are we allowed to do that?" Rusen said to Finkel, who nodded to me.

"We all agreed that this in no way affects the official business of their respective offices," I said. "That the public good must be considered, we must be shown no undue favoritism, and so on. What it will do is ease the pressure these higher-ups might have brought to bear on the case officers handling our paperwork because of the newspaper article. Now we'll go back to waiting our turn in the queue; it will take time to get to us. And time is all we need." And without Corning paying Mackie to call in every single violation, we would be in only one queue. "Also, the fire department has agreed to expedite the pyrotechnic permit, and the reporter who wrote that *Times* piece will show up with a photographer."

"What do we have in the way of publicity stills?" Finkel said.

Rusen looked blank.

"Maybe we could strike a side deal with the photographer," Finkel said. "So, Stan, I'm sorry, you had some news?"

"We got the shot. The fall. Perfect. All three cameras the first time. They're already packing away that huge bag thing. We're in good shape. Great shape. I was thinking it might be good to give folks a break."

"It is a holiday weekend," I said. "And we could cut some checks."

"Bad idea," said Finkel. "You give these people a couple days off and who knows if they'll come back, 'specially if they have money burning a hole in their pockets. You know what these creative types are like."

I wondered how Rusen and Finkel had met and started working together; they seemed to be from different continuums.

"What is there still to do?" I asked Rusen.

"On set? Not a lot. Rigging the pyrotechnics, which Kick says is eight hours' work, max, even including testing. The rest has to wait for Sîan on Tuesday. We could give them Saturday and Sunday, get everyone back first thing Monday, and still have a pretty good margin for error."

"And off set?"

"Editing."

"Lining up product placement," Finkel said.

"But you don't need the crew for that," I said. "And they've been working hard, and you've some money in the bank."

"We sure do. Boy, Anton, I really think we should do it."

THE CLOUDS had slowed from scudding to drifting. One layer, moving from the southwest, looked like an indigo veil. Kick's van was gone. I'd helped her and Buddy wrestle the Model Seventy into the back. She and Buddy would drive it back to the storage unit.

"And then we'll maybe go out for a beer . . ."

I imagined them at a rickety table in a smoky bar, with beer and shooters, pausing in their conversation for a moment to watch some pretty woman walk by before going back to agreeing that all directors were assholes who didn't know nothing about nothing.

". . . and then I have to spend a couple of days breaking the news to the rest of the family." On her own.

"**AUD,**" Eric said in surprise when he answered the phone. "Your mother was just about to call you. We were hoping you could have dinner with us tonight."

"Yes. Yes, that would be fine."

Pause. "Are you all right?"

"Yes."

"No more . . . episodes?"

"I'm fine."

"Taste?"

"About the same. Perhaps a little better."

"Good. That's good. I spoke to my colleague the other day and he admits that they're no nearer to determining a couple of the mystery ingredients. His guess is that it came from some illegal basement lab. It's astonishing just how— Hold on one moment." Muffled conversation. "Your mother would like a word. We'll see you tonight?"

"Yes."

"Aud, are you all right?"

"I'm fine."

"You called Eric's phone. Did you have a medical question?"

"I did. I wanted his opinion on MS research. But it can wait until we have dinner. He didn't say where."

"Rover's. Eight o'clock. A special occasion. My negotiations are over. One last dinner together, and then we leave tomorrow."

ROVER'S WAS the kind of place that provoked conversations about love and art and philosophy, so while it was clear from my mother's particularly erect spine that she wanted to talk about something specific, we kept to small talk over the first of our eight-course *grand menu dégustation:* an egg, lightly scrambled with lime crème fraîche, returned to its shell and topped with white sturgeon caviar. The tiny beads were dark olive and tasted nutty, perfect over the creamy egg.

"Were the negotiations satisfactory?"

"They were very useful. However, it became clear that the needs of the software company and the Norwegian government were very different, and would remain so, so I concluded the talks."

"You don't seem too dismayed," I said.

"In any circumstances, it would be hard to be dismayed while drinking this marvelous Pauillac."

I sipped the 1990 Haut-Batailley. It bloomed in my mouth like an origami rose, structured, geometric, and precise. "Your attitude to negotiations wasn't always so relaxed. Was it?"

She sat up straighter. "When I was young it was all about winning, about making the other do what I wanted. But sometime in the last ten years . . . Well, I changed." She didn't look at Eric, but I got the impression their feet were touching under the table. "Now instead of charging at people, sword drawn, I find it much more enjoyable and productive to run alongside them, learn their stride and rhythm, whether or not we could run together in the long term. In the course of my discussions with the software company, I found that our basic philosophies were radically different, and although I could have found a way to negotiate an agreement, it would have been temporary and unsatisfactory to everyone. The government would have ended up wasting years of various departments' time trying to enforce an openness that the company simply wasn't capable of offering. My recommendation will be that all contracts be terminated and the state move to adoption of open source code. In the long term, it will save time and money."

After the egg came oxtail soup, which reminded me of the lentil-and-chicken-liver soup I'd eaten with Dornan.

"In the long term, one needs true partnership for a relationship to endure. Common interests, common goals, common expectations."

It was clearly a prepared statement, a preamble to her main point.

"Your little girl, Luz. You would risk a great deal on her behalf."

"I would."

"You might even risk sacrificing her goodwill in the short term in order to discuss the prospects for her long-term happiness."

"I'm prepared, Mor. Just speak."

"This is very difficult."

Eric leaned forward. "Your friend has recently been diagnosed—"

"Her name is Kick."

"Kick has recently been diagnosed with multiple sclerosis."

"Yes."

"It is a very unpredictable disease."

"Yes, it is."

"What do you know of it?"

I put my spoon down and looked directly at my mother. "Perhaps you should tell me what it is you think I should know."

"Like any mother, I am only concerned for my daughter's happiness."

"I am happy."

"Yes, but for how long?"

"How long will you and Eric be happy?"

"I don't know," she said, and now I was certain they were touching feet beneath the table. "But neither of us has an incurable disease. I . . . please, Aud, I feel the need to speak."

I could take one last sip of the lovely wine, remove my napkin, drop it on the table, say good-bye, and walk away. But there were tears in my mother's eyes. She was not managing me, not negotiating. She was pleading.

". . . know that you've heard my concerns. And after that, no matter what you choose, you are my daughter, and I love you. I will respect your choices."

"Good. Because they're my choices. And MS might be incurable, but it's treatable." Silence. "Wouldn't you agree? Eric?"

Eric looked troubled. "The efficacy of most treatments is as variable as the disease course."

"There's a lot of research. You should know that. You've been working with those biotech companies."

"Research is . . . well, I wouldn't say this to anyone that wasn't family but, frankly, there are a lot of lies."

"I've read the studies. Someone at Kick's stage can be helped."

"The most optimistic information we have is that thirty or forty percent of people with the very early stages of MS can achieve a thirty or forty percent reduction in the deterioration of their disease."

After a long pause, I said, "That's not what I understood from my reading."

"That's not what the drug companies want you to understand. The drug companies want you to hope. Forty percent sounds wonderful—it sounds as though everyone who injects themselves with these rather far-ranging immunomodulators will get forty percent better, which is worth all the money, and the side effects, and the pain, and the inconvenience. But I wouldn't play those odds at a craps table."

"I didn't know you played craps."

My mother made a rare gesture of impatience. "Dice games are not the issue."

"Fine. What is the issue?"

"Money," Eric said. "Money and the lies and false hope it breeds. The pharmaceutical companies cast a rosy tint over their research pipeline and their products and their clinical trials. Consider this. All of the current recommended treatments for MS were developed under the orphan disease umbrella. It means there are tax advantages, government grants, and non-competition clauses. An orphan disease, strictly speaking, is one which fewer than two hundred thousand Americans suffer from. Most medical authorities would acknowledge that there are closer to half a million people in this country with MS. There is some evidence to support the opinion that there are very many more than that. Yet the drug companies have found their way around legislation. Preying on the hopes of ill people and their loved ones is easy in comparison."

"You have obviously spent a lot of time researching this. I appreciate your concern." I picked up my spoon.

"Aud, Kick's life may be measurably shorter than yours. She will need a lot of . . . help as the years progress."

"Not necessarily. There are people who, ten years after diagnosis, are absolutely no worse than they were before."

"And those people are unlikely to get worse. Yes," Eric said. "All true, but—"

"But are you prepared to wait ten years to see?" my mother said. "Aud, she is ill. You will always be the strong one, the healthy one. Partnerships should be equal. You can protect her, yes, but shouldn't she also be able to protect you?"

Kick, protect me?

"It is more than likely that you will come to resent her because of that, and she you for being healthy."

I skimmed a spoonful of liquid from the surface of my soup. My hand was trembling. Interesting. I breathed gently. The trembling stilled. "It's already been pointed out to me that illness is not pretty, it's not romantic, it's not easy." My spoon jerked, and dumped congealing soup back in the bowl with an audible plop. The spoon slid under the warm liquid and one perfect globule shone on the white tablecloth. The same reddish brown as drying blood. "I understand what I'm doing."

"Do you? Illness can crush hope. It can crush intention . . ."

A server appeared with a fresh spoon, but I shook my head and gestured for him to take the bowl away.

". . . times when illness can be bigger and stronger than we are."

I focused on that perfect brown-red hemisphere on the white tablecloth. It was slowly sinking into the linen, spreading, losing its shape and focus.

"Aud?"

"There's always something," I said. "Unless we brick ourselves up in a box. There is no perfect security. You plan to the best of your ability, and then you improvise. Sooner or later there's always someone or something bigger or faster or stronger than you. You just do the best you can, and when you run into trouble, you get help."

My mother was studying me. In the subtle lighting, she seemed older than she was, and more powerful. "Is that what happened with your throat?" she said.

A fish knife lay by my right hand. I picked it up and turned it in my fingers, heavy and cool. It was silver, burnished with the tiny cuts of a thousand dish-washings. "I got my throat cut because I was tired, and careless, and afraid. Because I didn't understand that when you run into trouble, you get help. You ask your friends, and family, for their support."

Her eyes were aquamarine and fathomless.

"You are adult," she said. "We will leave the matter there. I trust your judgment. I ask only that you do judge and don't jump blindly. When you choose, you will have my absolute support." She didn't have to make extravagant vows. If I chose Kick, she would accept us without reservation and never remind me of this conversation by word or deed; she would close over it like the ocean over a swimmer's head. I remembered Julia on the fjord, saying, . . . *a land that doesn't know compromise . . . black or white, yes or no, on or off.* My mother's soul was still Norwegian, in a way that mine was not.

The next course was Dungeness crab with beets, two ingredients—like the lentils and cherry compote—I would never have dreamt of putting together, but that worked perfectly.

She and Eric were not looking at each other but I could tell that, in the way of some couples, they were intensely aware of each other's body language and were exchanging a private communication. I drank the last of my wine.

"In honor of our last night," Eric said, "I believe we should have something special from the wine list."

He consulted the sommelier, and between them they decided on a 1983 Château Margaux, which was brought up from the cellar with great ceremony. Eric gestured for me to taste.

I held the glass to the light. The wine was the color of an ancient garnet, something set long ago in a barbaric Anglo-Saxon brooch, acquiring depth and gravity through the ages. It unfurled in my mouth like a cloud.

"I think she likes it," Eric said, and the sommelier poured. "It will be hard to find wine like this in Oslo," he said sadly.

Servers, moving as soundlessly as though they were on oiled wheels, brought us a cèpes and game confit tartlet, topped with foie gras, which dissolved on my tongue. We ate with concentration, and sipped the Margaux, for several minutes.

"How is the wine?" our server asked.

"Lovely," my mother said.

I picked my last toasted hazelnut from the plate with my fingers and ate it. They were waiting to see where I'd take the conversation. "I've been contemplating buying an oil painting. I wonder what a Norwegian would think of it."

My mother raised her eyebrows, and her thought was as clear as sunlight.

"I know," I said, "but I haven't lived there for a very long time." They waited attentively. "It's a big painting, of a woman. She's . . . not fully clothed, exactly, but covered. But it's clearly from a particular tradition. It reeks of high art, the artist as savant, dedicated only to improving upon his talent at the expense of all else. No concession to the group. No acknowledgment of the Jante law." The almost fanatical Norwegian obsession with social and cultural equality.

A different server refilled our glasses. "How are you enjoying it?"

"Delicious," Eric said, and the server gave us all an approving nod before gliding away.

"It sounds fascinating," my mother said.

Our tartlet crumbs were replaced by lobster with white asparagus and perigord truffle, and yet another server took the opportunity to drift over and ask if we were enjoying the wine.

We drank in tiny sips. It lasted us through the lobster, the guinea fowl mousseline, the palate-cleansing spice-infused pinot sorbet, and finally the squab with chanterelles and caramelized turnip. It was beautiful food. I found myself longing for rough bread and homemade hummus, with cole slaw falling off all over the table and Kick smiling in satisfaction, knowing just what would please me. In my imagination I smiled back at her, then found I was smiling down at her, because she was in a wheelchair.

THE NEXT DAY, I didn't call Kick, I didn't call Dornan, I didn't call Rusen and Finkel. I left my phone at the hotel and walked to the gallery.

I CONTEMPLATED *Antique Dressing Table.* The woman was a study in contradiction. Clothed only in a thin silk robe and open to the gaze of the viewer, she remained inaccessible, enigmatic, hidden. Her expression was secretive. It conveyed a sense of someone leading a supremely autonomous inner life, yet— and I couldn't work out how the painter had made this so clear—she was vulnerable. Perhaps it was the eyes, focused far beyond the viewer, or the fact that there were no lines in her face. An innocent, or perhaps a victim past caring. It could have been her hands, one lying on top of the other in perfect repose, or complete resignation.

So flimsy, just daubs of oil on thin canvas.

This thing is inside me like a stain.

"Beautiful, isn't she," said the sales associate who had nodded earlier. "Would you like me to arrange a private viewing? I find that a few moments alone with the lighting just right can help a person make up her mind."

I WENT TO the dojo, where I worked until I sweated. I found myself working with Chuck, who flinched every time I laid hands on him.

I'm here. Yes, but for how long . . . those odds at a craps table . . .

If Chuck didn't relax, he might fall wrong, break his back or his neck. I began to feel horribly responsible.

. . . times when illness can be bigger and stronger than we are . . .

I threw Chuck too hard. I apologized. He shied at my voice.

I took a shower, and was just getting dressed when people started to arrive for another class.

There is no perfect security. There's always something. Always.

I put one of the communal *gis* on and went back out to the mat.

———

I **WALKED TO** Pioneer Square, consulted the piece of paper Bernard had given me the other night, the address of the woodworkers' collective.

In the square, I found myself staring at a twisted metal column.

"Pergola," said a homeless man with muddy green eyes and bright blue Gore-Tex jacket. "Fell down in the earthquake." He looked about forty, though he could have been a lot younger. "Spare a dollar?" But then his pupils dilated and he stepped back. "I know you. You're crazy. Stay away from me. You stay away."

A pioneer, one who hadn't wanted to dance.

"No, no, you keep your money."

There was a handwritten card on the door of the woodworkers' collective. *Back in an hour.* It was neatly printed, and hung exactly in the center of the glass, but it didn't say when the hour had begun or would end.

I could see a sideboard and a carved screen, and a dining table. I put my hands against the glass like blinkers, and squinted. Fine work. Better than anything I could do. But I could learn. It was a collective. I could talk to the artisans. I could buy the furniture and learn from them.

From one moment to the next, I couldn't breathe. My lungs just wouldn't work. The ground wasn't shaking, the air wasn't shimmering, there were no drugs in my system, but I couldn't breathe.

I bent at the waist, forced myself to count out five seconds as I breathed in, two as I paused, five as I breathed out, two as I paused. And again.

THE NEXT day was cool and rainy. I felt every minute of the work I had done in aikido. My muscles were sluggish with fatigue acids. I walked in the rain. I walked to a pier and watched the water. Kuroshio, the black current. I walked to the set. It was deserted, the door locked. I tried to remember what day it was. Sunday?

I'm here. Yes, but for how long?

THE SUITE was as cold and impersonal as a flatiron. I turned the AC off and sat on the bed. My joints and feet and head ached.

I started the shower, and the rush of water made me realize I was thirsty. I filled the tooth mug under the cold tap. I drank, filled, drank.

The shower was hot. I stood under it a long time. The water smelled of chlorine. I had not noticed that in Seattle before. Perhaps someone had added something to a reservoir. Perhaps my sense of smell was coming back.

I sat on the bed and dried myself carefully. Buckets rattled outside as the housekeeper cleaned something.

Something behind me kicked a bucket. No, a can. The can rattled and bounced down a cobbled alley. *I'm here*, it said, *right behind you.* And then all sound died, everything, even the sound of my heartbeat.

I woke on my back. The room was brilliant with sunshine. It had stopped raining. A housekeeper was banging and clanging in the hall. I felt as though I had a hangover.

I had another shower.

DORNAN ANSWERED on the third ring. "What did you mean," I said. "The other day. When you said you didn't live in Seattle?"

"Well, as you know, Torvingen, I live in Atlanta." Silence. "Are you quite well?"

"What did you mean?"

"Why do you ask, why now particularly?"

"I've been thinking. About things."

"Things, is it?" I didn't say anything. "And have you reached any conclusions?"

Yes. But for how long?

"I don't know," I said, and hung up.

THE SCENTS of sweat and mold and deodorant in the dojo's changing room were briefly overlain by that of fabric softener as I stripped the freshly laundered *gis* from their rain-wet bags and hung them on the rail. The next newcomer wouldn't have to wear clothes that stank of anyone else's sweat. I laid my new *gi* and *hakama*, the black-bloused trousers that *yudansha* are entitled to wear, on the bench.

I took off my clothes and folded them. I taped my left knee. I pulled on the *gi,* then the *hakama,* pulling ties tight, twisting this way then that, loosening, retying. They were stiff and harsh with newness, but despite this, and despite the fact that it had been a long time since I'd experienced the odd combination of tight belt, loose arms, and the swing of cloth around my calves, it felt deeply familiar.

When I went out onto the small mat in my *hakama* to warm up, Mike smiled, but nobody seemed surprised, and this time, when the bell rang, and we assumed *seiza* along the edge of the mat, I took the far left position, and after we bowed and sensei stood, it was me he gestured into the center to be *uke.*

"*Kokyu-dosa.*"

I stood opposite him, and took his left wrist in my right. It was a big wrist, flat and hard on top and bottom, with tiny dark brown hairs like wire sickles springing from around the wrist bone. As I gripped, he opened his fingers and I felt the massive tendons on each side expand and stretch my own fingers, opening them.

Kokyu-dosa, the blending exercise, is the most basic building block of aikido. It is gentle and fluid, and the *nage* does not have to worry about making sure that the *uke* falls well or protects his or her shoulder or wrist or elbow or hip; the *uke* doesn't fall at all. The best practitioners simply breathe, and step and turn and lift both hands before them as though carrying a lightly balanced tray of tea, and the *uke,* if she keeps hold of the *nage's* wrist, is twisted to one side and bent forward from the waist, forehead almost to the ground.

But there is beauty in even the simplest movements.

Sensei, Petra had told me, had been practicing aikido for twenty-five years, many hours a day. He was very, very good, but as I matched myself exactly to his strength and force, skin to skin, fascia to fascia, vein on vein, as I felt his wrist joint turn smoothly and his muscles relaxed and open, I understood that he was not great. He had never been hurt, never had his confidence taken away and had to refind it, never, since young adulthood, met anyone bigger, stronger, faster or better trained.

He couldn't teach me how to be the Aud who had never been drugged, who still had her sense of taste, who had never thought of letting someone else do the protecting: but, just as my mother was a woman who had lived twenty-five years longer than I, just as Dornan was a man with blue eyes who understood what friendship meant, he knew more aikido than I did; and I could learn.

It seemed to last for hours, but at some point it must have changed, because now he was the one wrapping his massive fingers around my wrist, heavy as a manacle, and I was the one imagining a pinpoint between my radius and ulna, leaving that point in exactly the same locus of three-dimensional space and pivoting everything else around it: keeping the same distance between that point and my center of gravity, two finger-widths beneath my navel, yet stepping forward, and turning and breathing out, and extending the imaginary tea tray. He was the one who bent down and to the side like a tin soldier slumping under a blowtorch. We changed hands, changed roles again, *uke* to *nage, nage* to *uke,* and soon my joints moved like frictionless electromagnetic bearings and my autonomic nervous system hummed like a transformer reaching capacity.

NINE O'CLOCK. The night was clear and I drove down the viaduct with the windows down, cool air sliding over my arms, tires hissing and splashing through standing puddles. In Atlanta the temperature would be about seventy-five degrees, and the air scented with jasmine and honeysuckle and laced with the creak and chir of crickets and tree frogs. There would be less atmospheric pollution, and the stars would be brighter and sharper. There would be less traffic.

Half the parking lot's sodium lamps were dead, and what remained painted the dark with brass. The right-hand side of the lot was crowded. The two Hippoworks trailers were lined up neatly, side by side, Kick's van next to them. The left-hand side of the lot was cordoned off and Janski stood in front of the cones, hyperalert, head swiveling this way and that, weight forward on his toes. I got out of the car. I could smell the metallic tang of adrenaline and testosterone.

"What happened?"

"Probably nothing, ma'am." He scanned the shadows.

"When?"

"An hour ago. I thought I saw someone approaching one of these gas lines."

"Gas."

"Propane, ma'am. For the stunt tomorrow."

My heart began to pump smoothly, powerfully.

"Just one person?"

"Hard to tell. They ran off when I challenged them."

"And you've searched the area?"

"Ma'am, Mr. Turtledove's inside, perhaps you'd like to speak to him about it."

I listened, sniffed. Nothing. I nodded to Janski and went in through the side door. Everything seemed to glow, as though specially lit. The lock looked different: newer, bigger.

Rusen, Finkel, Deverell, and Philippa were huddled in a knot about ten feet to the left of the door. They straightened when they saw me. "You've heard about our intruder," Finkel said.

I looked at Deverell. "Prowler," he said. "I tried to call. Janski thought he saw someone near the pipeline in the lot. He gave chase. He called me. He and I searched the immediate vicinity while Philippa and the stunt coordinator, Kuiper, checked the lines. Nothing damaged. No sign of the prowler."

"We used one of the production's portable arc lights to check the lines," Philippa said. "As far as is humanly possible, I can guarantee they haven't been disturbed."

There were no guarantees. *Beware,* my body said, but there was nothing.

"And the search?"

"Very close on the property itself," Deverell said. "Foot canvassing on a slightly wider perimeter, visual and audio beyond that."

Translation, they'd checked every window and door, turned over every garbage can and grate on my property, walked up and down the closer streets, and looked and listened. But *ware!* my back brain was shouting. *Ware!*

"I told them we should leave that light out there," Finkel said. "As a deterrent."

"No, sir," Philippa said. "Not unless you'll authorize more personnel. Remaining near the light renders night vision useless. We'd need more people to cover the perimeter."

"There's no budget for that."

I looked from Finkel to Rusen. "I was here yesterday. The place was deserted."

The conflicting messages—everything is safe, and beware—were making me jumpy.

"That's my fault," Rusen said, embarrassed. "I'd given everyone else the weekend off and it seemed wrong to make Jan stay. I told him to go home."

"Mr. Rusen suggested to Janski that he leave, so he did but, sensibly, he called me. I got here as soon as I could."

"How long?"

"No coverage for four hours. No signs of attempted ingress."

"The locks?"

He shook his head. "Not changed until this morning."

Four hours. Turtledove seemed about to say more, but I shook my head slightly, trying to think. "Stan, Anton, we'll need to talk later. The trailer? Thank you. Deverell, Philippa, walk with me."

When Finkel and Rusen were out of earshot, I said, "Where is Mackie—Eddard?"

"I don't know," Deverell said. "Nor do the police. The younger one, though, Finkel's son, has been back in New Jersey for two days."

"Find Mackie. Hire whoever you have to. Start now." Was that it? Something else? "I'm going to check with Kick about that gas line."

Behind the food counter, Kick had her hands on her hips and Dornan was looking mulish. ". . . asked me to run things tonight, so that's what I'm doing. You should rest while you can."

"I have too much to do." She wore jeans and a sleeveless, heathery-grey mock turtleneck. It must have been sunny in Anacortes; her skin was golden, her teeth and sclera very white.

"Then why are you pestering me? Look"—he held up his gloved hands—"I'm all hygienic." He picked up Kick's triangular knife. "The worst thing I can do is cut the sandwiches a bit crooked. Go. Take a break, for pity's sake. I've got things— Aud."

Kick swung round. "Where the hell have you been?"

"Here and there." Trying to decide.

"Why didn't you answer your phone?"

"I haven't been carrying it. Taking a leaf from your book."

Beneath the tan, there was a hint of the old graphite sheen under her eyes. Talking to the family had not gone well.

"My apologies for interrupting," I said to Dornan, "but I need to talk to Kick a moment about the prowler, and gas line safety."

"I've been over that," she said. "They're fine."

"Humor me."

"I would have humored you this weekend, if you'd bothered to answer your phone. Right now I'm pretty busy."

"I got the impression that Dornan has things covered. Dornan?"

"Yes," he said.

She had the grace to blush. "Oh, fine. We'll take a walk."

Outside, she paused in the dark and breathed the scent of damp earth and looked at the stars. "It stopped raining."

"Yes."

"Where did you go?"

"Nowhere. The lines. Are they truly safe?"

"Look, they aren't even connected to anything. It's just piping. The propane is safely under lock and key inside. I ran compressed air through the setup, twice, and there was no leakage. There's nothing wrong. Nothing happened. I'll run the same tests tomorrow, to be sure, as I would have done even without a prowler, but I'm telling you now, no one touched that pipe. And as part of my usual safety precautions there'll be a double cordon around the area, and the camera operators closest to the flames will wear Nomex. Even if the whole damn thing blew up, we'd be okay. We don't need much gas, and in the open air there won't be atmospheric buildup. I called you from Anacortes. I was going to suggest we go to Rainier for the weekend. Just you and me. Nowhere, you say. Why didn't you carry your phone?"

"I had some thinking to do."

"And what did you think about?"

Paintings. Odds at a craps table. Love as a bear trap. Doing the best you could, then improvising.

The world shimmered. No, I thought, not now.

"Aud?"

"It's nothing." Do you see that silver cloud? Do you hear the silence? Do you feel the distinctness of every molecule, all at once? No. It was another brain chemistry cascade. It wasn't real.

I shook my head. Neither of us moved to go back inside. Traffic sounds had drained away, sliding off into a bubble of silence. Even the trees were still. I could hear her breath.

"Is that real?" I said.

"Is . . ." She saw that I was listening, and tilted her head. "Wow. That silence. It's like a magical moment out of time and space. Wait." She listened some more. "Is that the river in our park? Let's go see."

"It's not safe."

She looked at me. "Listen. There's nothing. No one's out here. Are you all right?"

"I'm . . . not sure."

She touched my arm. "Come with me, then. We'll sit by the river."

It was too dark to cut through the line of trees so we walked up to Diagonal Way. It was half past nine on a holiday evening in an industrial zone. Perfectly natural for everything to be quiet and deserted, to look and feel like something from a post-apocalyptic film.

"Cue zombies," she said.

"You really want to go to the river?"

"Smell it," she said. "On a night like this it will be beautiful."

I nodded. "There's an old rail track we could follow once we're across the side street. I don't know what the light will be like but the footing will be level."

On the other side of the road, the Federal Center was silent and dark. The buildings appeared derelict. The wire fencing was torn here and there.

I crossed the side road. After a moment's hesitation, so did she; I realized that on her own she would have walked to the light and waited for it to change. We found the track. The night smelled of trees and river. My land, I thought, and, just like that, I felt good. Something inside me had settled. I wasn't sure what, yet, but something.

I smiled. "In some ways, you're more—"

The only warning was the skittering of a can the taller one kicked as they attacked. Everything slowed down. Two of them. I noted Kick's face, still and quiet, her relaxed shoulders. I saw the glint of something moving at my head, felt the wave front of air as a heavy body came at me.

This was a dream. Wasn't it?

I stood, irresolute, stupid, while one of the shapes threw Kick to the ground. Kick opened her mouth, but I didn't hear a scream.

Would she do that if this was a dream? I couldn't breathe. Something knocked me down. The dirt under my cheek felt real. I could hear my breath, now, and feel it. I breathed, long and deep. Something thudded on my thigh. I felt that. The body always knows.

"You asshole," Kick shrieked. "Leave her alone!"

Would you let her protect you?

Is that what was happening?

I kipped up. Something wasn't quite right with my left leg, but I ignored it. It was working well enough. Pain is just a message.

Two of them. One coming at me again, swinging something. *Kick*, I thought, and turned, and as easily as unscrewing a cap from a bottle I drew in the arm, twisted, and threw the attacker away. He and his crowbar landed on the concrete at the same time. They made different sounds.

Kick was half up, half down, shouting something, and this time the sound stretched and slowed, like whale song, and I stepped lightly to her side, and put my hands around that little waist and lifted her away, and laughed, and now the second attacker was behind me, and I pivoted and unfurled a back-fist strike, more to get the range, and then I was close enough for my favorite, which I gave him: a perfect elbow, driven hard and flat as a boar spear into his floating ribs. They broke like twigs. He went down with a querulous *oof?*

Scraping sound, hoarse breathing; the first attacker hauled himself like a zombie from the concrete, one arm swinging limp. His eyes were like pools of tar.

I dived into a roll and brought my trailing leg in a great arc, heel into his breastbone, and he went down.

Some drugs make their users impervious to pain—able to ignore the message. I picked up his crowbar. It was rough and pitted.

"You really should take better care of your tools," I said, and smashed his right kneecap. If you take out a support, the building can't stand. He started trying to sit up. I considered. Even a hopping zombie could do harm. I smashed the other knee.

I walked over to the second man.

"Kick," I said.

"Asshole!" she said, and kicked him again. "You asshole!" Her voice was shockingly loud.

"His ribs are broken. If you really want to hurt him, kick him there." That made her pause. "Step aside a moment."

It was Mackie. His eyes, too, were dark with drugs. "You," he said.

"Me."

"I knew you'd have to come. I knew they'd send for you."

He was lithe and capable, ambidextrous, and chemically removed from pain.

"There's some bits of broken wire over by the fence," I said to Kick. "Bring them, please." I turned back to Mackie. "The easiest thing, the most sensible, would be for me to break your spine, or crush your larynx, or smash your knees. Like his." I nodded back at his friend. "But she wouldn't like that. So your other choice is to lie still and be tied up."

Kick came back with a few bits of wire. I selected the two longest, unrusted pieces. "Turn on your stomach."

"I can't, my ribs." His lips were dark.

"Turn on your stomach."

The ribs crackled as he turned, and he groaned, but I doubted he could feel much. I sat on the back of his knees, facing his feet, and wired his ankles together. Then I sat on his thighs and wired his wrists. His breathing began to sound labored. "I wouldn't struggle too much when we're gone," I said. "Something's pierced your lung. Wait quietly for the police."

"You fucked me up."

"Yes." I thought of not being able to move, not being able to see, of doubting my own senses. He'd done that to me. "I'd do it again."

I threw the crowbar into the bushes and turned to Kick. She was real. "Shall we?"

We walked back to the set. I put my arm around her waist.

"So that's how you hit people," she said.

"Pretty much." For no reason, we both laughed, and then there was traffic again on Highway 99, and the world seemed almost ordinary.

"So, what were you going to say, before? When we'd just crossed the road?"

It seemed like a lifetime ago on a planet far, far away, a place where I wasn't sure and didn't know. Her waist under my arm was intensely alive. The body knows; I knew. "When you nearly walked up to the light, even though the road was deserted, I was thinking, in some ways you're more Scandinavian than I am." I had no idea whether she knew what I was talking about, but neither of us wanted to talk. She leaned into me as we walked and I adjusted my stride so we moved hip to hip. My left thigh hurt.

I still had my arm around her waist when we got to the warehouse. "Get Turtledove," I said to Janski. "And Rusen or Finkel."

"I'm not supposed to—"

"Get them now."

Kick and I stood forehead to forehead, breathing each other's scent. Someone cleared their throat. Deverell.

"I found Mackie, or rather he found me. Us." Rusen stepped out of the warehouse, blinking in the dark. "We hurt them. Two of them. Call the police," I said to Rusen. "Tell them they'll need an ambulance."

"You should tell them."

"Just tell them. Tell them we'll be . . ." I looked at Kick, who nodded. "We'll be at Kick's house if they need us. Persuade them not to need us for a while."

"What—"

"Just do it, Rusen."

He got out his phone. He looked at my leg. "You're hurt."

I looked at the rust mark on my trousers where the crowbar had thumped into my quadriceps. "It's nothing. Don't worry about it. Don't worry about anything. It'll be fine." It was all going to be fine.

SHE DIDN'T shake me awake, she simply held me tighter. "I'm here," she said. "It's a dream."

"It came up behind me in the alley," I said. "In the dark."

"It's a dream," she said.

"No," I said. "It's still there."

LESSON 15

I STEPPED OUT OF BOREALIS, DORNAN'S COFFEE SHOP, A LITTLE AFTER SUNSET. THE seventy-degree dusk smelled of blackened fish from the Bridgetown Grill and water, caught in magnolia blossom cups, evaporating after a long day in sunshine.

I had just told Dornan my news: my mother was getting married and wanted to see me. I didn't want her in Atlanta, in my life, but she was visiting Seattle. If Dornan wanted a working holiday in the land of coffee, I would cover flight and hotel.

I was fairly sure that the offer to pay would clinch the deal.

My phone rang. I recognized the number but couldn't place it. I answered.

"Hello."

"Aud?"

"Who is this?"

"Aud, this is Therese. Aud, it's . . . Oh, God. She's . . ." Shuddering breath. "Look"—suddenly brisker, almost impersonal, as though she had stepped out of the messy, hyperventilating body and become all frontal cortex—"I'm at Sandra's house. It's a terrible thing. I didn't know who to call. You have to come. There's blood everywhere. It's . . . There's blood."

IMAGINE A FULL cup of coffee. Imagine tripping over the rug and flinging it across your white wall and new pale green sofa. That's a lot of liquid—and a coffee mug is usually less than twelve ounces, less than a third of a liter. The average human body contains 5.6 liters of blood, fifteen or twenty times as much as that cup of coffee. And blood is brilliant red.

Sandra's house was a neat four-bedroom mock Tudor in one of the developments that had gone up fifteen years ago on the edge of Druid Hills, the kind of place where the kitchen should have been white and blond oak, with mediocre can lights in the ceiling, a tidy little breakfast nook, and children's pictures tacked brightly to the fridge with animal magnets.

Two of the ceiling lights at the far end of the kitchen, over the counter near the stove, had been hit with arterial blood spray. The end of the room dripped and glowed an eerie vampire-cavern red. Blood dripped onto the body below, thickly, silently, the drops absorbed by its clothes. A pool was spreading from its upper arm. Brachial artery. The boning knife was lying next to the gleaming, slow-moving pool. Henckel. Dishwasher safe.

The purple-green glisten of intestines protruded beneath it. Belly, too. Like a pig.

"Thank God, thank God," Therese said from the column by the dining room entrance. She clamped a hand on my left arm and tried to pull me into the dining room.

"Stop," I said, "stop. Don't move, not even an inch." I was reading the pool of blood on the floor, the smears and spatters, the little lake on the counter, already dripping off the edge, the streak along the kitchen wall to the dining room, sorting story lines, angles of arc, possibilities. "You mustn't move anymore," I said absently.

"But Sandra—"

"Can wait thirty seconds. If we're to save her, I need to think."

After a moment, I nodded. "Sandra," I said, "come here."

"She can't—"

"Therese, be quiet now. Get Sandra from the dining room, bring her here. Right now, Therese."

Sandra's skin was pale, paler than I'd ever seen it, but apart from the blood there were no marks on her face and hands that had not been there at the last class.

"His blood's still coming out!" Therese said. "He's alive. He's—"

"Not really," I said. No medical facility on earth could save this man: this was simple hydrostatic draining, not the vivid spurt of a pumping heart. His blood levels had already fallen below the crucial forty-percent level. Even without the gaping belly wound, he was dead. "Have you called the police?"

"No," Therese said. "No, I suppose I should. I just didn't . . ." She trailed off and looked at me.

She just didn't want it to be real.

"Where are the children?"

"I don't—"

"Sandra, where are the children?"

"Sunday school." She sounded quite composed.

"When will they be back?"

"At seven-twenty." It was a little after six now. One less thing to worry about.

"Your husband—"

"That's not my husband."

I breathed out slowly, deliberately. "This man on the floor is not your husband?"

"My husband is dead."

"Yes," I said. "He's dead, and we have to do something about that."

"That's not my husband," she said again. "That's George."

In. Out. "This man on the floor, with all the blood, is not your husband. He's someone called George."

"That's right."

"But you killed him."

"He's dead?"

"He is."

"Then, yes, I guess I did."

Therese was giving me urgent signals. "Sandra, you sit down again in the dining room for just a minute. Don't touch anything."

"I don't have to do what you say. I don't have to do what anyone says anymore."

"Just for the next five minutes. Five minutes."

She nodded and sat. I looked at Therese. "Please tell me you know what's going on."

"Her husband's been dead two years. That's George, her sister's husband."

"He's the one who beats her?"

"And more."

"Her brother-in-law."

She nodded.

"This is going to make it harder." I turned back to where Sandra was sitting patiently at the dining room table. Pale wood, ash. Never liked ash. Back to Therese. "She called you?"

Nod. "She said, 'You better come, I need you to be my friend.' I knew by the way she said it that it was something terrible, that she, that she meant . . ."

We both knew what she meant. I'd given them the idea: a good friend's number on your cell phone, help out the truth a little.

"Was anyone with you when you got the call?"

"No."

"Good." Back to Sandra. "Sandra, do you want to go to prison?"

"No."

"Then you're going to have to do exactly as I say, even though some of it will be unpleasant. Do you agree?"

"All right."

That was the closest I was going to come to informed consent. "Come here. Stop when you get to the edge of the carpet. Now, see the knife?" Nod. "I want you to take one step in, one careful step, and pick up the knife, then turn to the sink and rinse the knife." She moved like a sock puppet. "Good. Now give it to me."

She held it out. "You're wearing gloves!"

"Yes. Now where were you when he, when you slashed him?"

"Right here, by the sink, washing the knife."

Perfect. "Tell me what happened."

"He came in, said he didn't have long, that Betts thought he was stuck in traffic on I-20, that what the fuck had I done with the front hedge, he'd told me not to hire a yard boy, they always fuck up, then he pushed me against the sink, here"—she touched her midriff—"so I couldn't breathe and it was going to be like last week, last week when the children saw some of it, and I don't know, I'd been practicing, you see, the way you taught us, so I turned around and cut him, on his arm, and he looked all pissed, like he was going to hit me, so I slashed him again. He always made me keep the knives sharp. Nothing ticks a man off more than he should fumble at his meat like a goddamn pussy in front of his family, he used to say, he didn't keep food on the table and a roof over his wife's nephews and nieces to be treated . . ." Her eyes were dry. "Well, that won't be happening anymore."

"No. And then what?"

"And then . . ." She frowned. "I don't remember."

"You called Therese."

"Yes, yes, I guess I did."

That was her story, I couldn't see superficial evidence to contradict it, and there wasn't time to dig deeper.

"Stand here. Yes. Very good. Did George have any diseases?"

"Diseases?"

"HIV, syphilis, that kind of thing."

"No."

I nodded. "You'll want to make sure you get antibiotic and tetanus shots anyway." I hefted the knife. The edge glittered like a ruby scalpel under the weird light. Sharp, as she'd said. I laid it against her forehead and traced a thin line. Therese gasped. I ignored her. "You're right-handed, yes?" I asked Sandra.

"Right-handed. Yes."

"Put your left hand on the counter."

Blood was beginning to well from the slit on her forehead. She didn't seem to feel it. She did as she was told.

I took her little finger, imagined the fifth interpharyngeal joint, made sure I had it firmly, and then jerked. I felt the metacarpal snap cleanly.

She gasped. Blood ran in a thick sheet down her face.

"Therese, call nine-one-one. Tell them two people are badly hurt. That's all. Hurt. Blood everywhere. They'll want you to stay on the phone, but just pretend to panic and put the phone down. Go."

"But her hand, her face."

"Go."

Now Sandra's white skin was tinged with the grey of shock and her breathing was harsh. Exactly what I needed. A woman demonstrably in shock, covered in blood, hand swelling. Documented abuse. Clearly self-defense.

She swayed. "Don't faint, Sandra. Take this." I gave her the knife with her blood on it. "Touch it to George's arm, where you cut it before. You can tread in the blood, it's all right. Just try not to splash. Touch the blade to the cut in his arm if you can. Now, while you're bending down, put the knife in his hand. He's left-handed?" Therese was talking and crying on the phone: blood, hurt, hurry. Her voice shook and it sounded as though her nose was running. Shock was taking her, too. "Wrap his hand around the handle, get his prints on it. Now you take it again and drop it where it was on the floor earlier. No, no, leave it there. It's close enough. Now step out to the dining room. Yes, don't worry about the footprints." The blood was still draining, still spreading. It was going to cover a multitude of sins. "Sit down. No, don't faint. Don't faint."

Snuffling sound as Therese dropped the phone, replaced it on the cradle, wiped her face. Sunday, I thought. Sunday. They'd be here in less than five minutes.

"Therese. Stand here. No, it doesn't matter about the blood now. Listen. Sandra, here's what happened. He came in, just like last week, and pressed you against the sink, where you were washing the knife. You struggled because this was just like last week. Just like last week. He reached around, grabbed your hand, broke it, grabbed the knife. You were struggling even more. He cut your face. Dropped the knife. You picked it up, cut his arm, just the way you said, then cut him again. You were panicked, because this was just like last week, but worse. Then you called Therese. That's all you remember. Don't mention the self-defense class. Now, tell me what happened."

"Washing knife. Came in, like last week. Squashed me. Broke my hand getting knife. Cut my face. Like last week but worse, worse. Dropped the knife." She was beginning to gasp with shock and pain. Her face was a mask of blood. She looked like a woman who had just fought for her life. "Then called Therese. Then . . . I don't remember."

"That's fine. Therese, Sandra called you. You came straight here. You don't remember what you did, exactly, but at some point you called me. Later, they'll ask how you know Sandra, why she called you. Tell them you met at Crystal Gaze. Don't mention the self-defense class. They'll ask why you called me."

"Why did I call you?"

"You probably panicked."

"I did panic."

I nodded. "You knew I used to be police, you knew I'd know what to do. You met me at the bookshop, too."

"At the bookshop. When?"

"Don't worry about it. You won't be expected to remember any details in a situation like this." I studied her. She was sweating; she'd missed a bit of mucus by her mouth. The perfect picture of middle-class shock. "How are you?"

"I think I might vomit." I nodded. "You broke her hand. You just broke it. And you cut her face, like she was a . . . a piece of fish."

Sandra started to slide off the smooth wood of the dining room chair.

"Hold her up, please. I need to make a phone call."

I called Bette's new associate, who sounded bright as a new penny, despite the fact that it was both weekend and evening, gave her the address, told her to get here ASAP, and then scanned the room. The body was drained; the blood pool was no longer growing. It was already darkening slightly, congealing. The confused footprints and handprints of Therese and Sandra could be easily explained by the automatic movements of someone in shock.

The officers of APD Zone 5 were not fools. If they looked hard enough they'd see that some of the evidence didn't add up but at first glance there was enough plausible detail to hang a story on. Everyone knew Sandra was being abused. They themselves had been called out last week. And there was undeniable injury and shock of the victim.

I heard the first sirens in the distance.

I rinsed my gloves under the tap, shook them dry, then carefully stripped them off and put them in my pocket.

The kitchen lights had stopped dripping. Sandra's breathing was loud but even. Therese was murmuring something, stroking her hair. For one moment, Sandra's gaze caught mine, and her eyes flashed, and then they dropped.

In the current political climate no Atlanta DA would prosecute Sandra for defending herself, when she could prove she had reason to fear for her life, and when her attacker had clearly meant her harm. Why, it was even his own fault that the knife was so sharp.

The sirens were louder, and now the red kitchen gleamed with a more fiery red and flickers of blue.

She had done it very well: the children conveniently gone, her friend to back her up, me to provide the finishing, undeniable touches. I had shown her how, and I would even provide the lawyer. At least I had made sure it hurt.

SIXTEEN

THE DINING ROOM WAS ROUND AND TIGHT WITH SUNSHINE. THE STEAM FROM MY TEA appeared and disappeared in the bars of light and shadow. Kick was in her old silk robe, which kept slipping open. I wore her toweling one, which came barely to my knees.

She mused over the newspaper. I tilted my face to the sun and thought idly how pleasant it would be to sit here all day, warm and drowsy and thinking of nothing.

"Where are you?"

I blinked. "Thinking that warmed-up pizza and hot black tea make a surprisingly good breakfast."

"You want some more?"

"Yes." But I couldn't be bothered to move. I closed my eyes, opened them again when I heard her get up.

She fussed with paper towels and sprinkled water and pizza slices. I wondered what she'd make of my kitchen. I longed to see her in it.

"I've been thinking," I said.

"Mmmn?" She pushed buttons.

"About how well we know each other." The microwave started its hollow drone. She sat down. "You know what food I like but I'm not sure you really know me."

"Of course I know you. Food is everything." Her smile was affectionate. "No. Really. Sometimes I think I know you, know who you are deep down, better than you know yourself. You think efficiency is the key to your personality, but it's not. You're a sensualist, a hedonist of the first order. Look at the way you cradle that cup, the way you tilt your face to the sun like a flower."

"It's efficient. Absorbing heat means my body doesn't have to create its own."

"But it's also delicious."

The microwave beeped and I got up to attend to it.

"And see how you did that? Pushed the microwave door with precisely the amount of force needed to shut it? Not too hard, not too soft. The pressure of the hard plastic against your fingertips, the swing, the *thunk* as the catch engages, all without a micron of wasted effort."

"Erg," I said. "You meant erg, not micron."

"And the little pebble-like word, erg, feels better on your tongue than micron, so good you said it twice."

"Come with me," I said. "Come to Atlanta. Come see where I've been. See my life, see my house. Come sleep in my bed."

She was quiet for a long time. "I don't know," she said eventually, and now her face was remote and unhappy. "My life is here. The business, the climate, the people. My family. My doctors. I don't know."

We both stared at our pizza slices, the shriveled pepperoni, the wrinkled green pepper. She didn't know.

We went upstairs and showered and dressed in silence.

DORNAN POURED coffee for the crew, whistling through his teeth. "Well, I'm happy to see you this morning. Delighted that you didn't get yourself or Kick killed last night."

I nodded.

"You were a one-hour wonder here at the set. No one left until midnight. Isn't that right, John?" The wardrobe assistant waiting for his coffee nodded obediently. "I'm delighted, too, that you've—" He broke off, peered at me, and handed John a cup that was only half-full. "Go away," he said to John, and turned back to me. "Are you sure you weren't hurt?"

"I'm fine."

"Then what's the matter with you?"

"She doesn't know," I said. "After all this, she doesn't know. I asked—"

"Aud," someone said. I turned. Finkel, looking sleek and self-satisfied. "Allow me to introduce our star, Sîan Branwell."

Her smile was warm, her hand pressure brief but sincere, and her makeup flawless. I thanked her for being willing to fly back up for the day's filming. She thanked me for making sure she would now actually get paid, and laughed prettily. She was an actress.

"But we won't keep you," Finkel said. "If you need us, we'll be at the rehearsal stage."

The rehearsal stage: a corner of the floor where Kick had taped out an outline of an area the same size as the tower platform.

I turned back to Dornan. "I asked Kick—"

"Aud." This time it was Peg. "Our visitors are here. Did you know you have a great big smear on your pants?"

"Yes," I said. And a great big bruise under that. I fingered the rust, from the crowbar, mixed with dirt. I hadn't bothered to drive back to the hotel for clean clothes. None of the visitors were here to see me.

"We've got Pat Irenyenko, she's OSHA, and her daughter, Ekaterina, eleven. Irenyenko's the one with her arm in a sling. We've got Toni Merritt, she's EPA, and her mother, whose name I didn't catch but who's about a million years old. And we've got the reporter, Leptke, and a photographer called Cheney. I don't know if that's first or last. I told him no pictures that he hasn't cleared with you or Floo—Rusen and Finkel. Rusen's looking stressed. Joel, as usual, is fixated on what he can't do. Anyhow, I've already asked about tea and coffee." She looked at Dornan. "That's one macchiato, one breve, one chai tea, one green tea, and a swirkle."

"What in God's name is a swirkle?"

"No clue," she said cheerfully. I left them to it and headed for the main entrance.

Toni Merritt wore an Eddie Bauer business suit that had seen better days, and her mother's name was Margaret. I could see the genetic stamp on their narrow shoulders and strong chins. Irenyenko was considerably better dressed; there again, she was considerably higher up the food chain. I wondered if she'd even considered inviting Michael Zhao, the underling who actually did the work.

I was glad Peg had told me the daughter was eleven. Only a year older than Luz, but she looked more like a teenager than a child: rounder, almost womanly. She wore a bright green ribbon choker with a cameo around her neck. Cheney and Leptke stood apart from the others: the Fourth Estate, in all its impartial majesty.

I said hello, explained that we were very happy to have them. "Ms. Branwell is rehearsing at the moment, but perhaps later we can say hello. Meanwhile, let me give you a tour of the set."

I took them outside and showed them the gas lines and explained that the finale would be filmed in separate parts. I showed them the production office trailer, and spoke of the astonishing amount of paperwork that could overwhelm a production. We talked to Peg, to Joel, to the carpenters. "Wasn't it one of the carpenters who nearly died?" Leptke said. "Cheney, get a picture of these guys, would you?"

We spent two minutes posing and snapping. We were getting closer to the corner where Kick and Branwell were rehearsing. I could hear her clear voice, *Now, when you shove here, really show the effort. You're pushing this man from you, hard.*

Then it was on to the costume designer and props manager.

That's excellent. But move a little more from here, from the hips.

I hadn't taught her how to hit people. Perhaps she'd picked up pointers last night.

Okay, let's take five.

"I think we have a moment for a very brief introduction to Ms. Branwell," I said.

Branwell, lightly sheened with sweat—I turned back to Kathy and mouthed, "Tell Rusen to turn up the AC"—gave them the same gracious treatment she had given me. They basked. Kick spoke to them briefly, but no one but me had eyes for anyone other than Branwell, whom they crowded around.

Kick, outside the circle, looked tired. I wanted to pick her up, tuck her head against my shoulder, hold her while she fell asleep. I wanted to ask her when she might know. "Maybe we should forget the demonstration fall."

She shrugged. "It's only from the fifteen-foot platform. I'll get the Model Forty gassed up." And she walked away to do just that.

Getting the fans away from Branwell was like whipping hounds off a fox, but eventually I persuaded them that she had to get fitted for a safety line, and she escaped. In the background, the racket of an air compressor started.

"This is the scaffolding tower where later Ms. Branwell and the stunt actor will be staging the fight scene. As you can see, it's very economically designed, with the steps built right up the inside."

"Those tiny things are steps?" said Toni.

"Certainly. I'll check with the stunt coordinator, but perhaps we could go up and take a look at the platform."

"I think Mom and I will get that coffee now," Toni said.

"Cheney and I want to get more pictures." I remembered that Leptke hadn't even liked standing on her desk.

"Oh, I'm sure it would be so interesting," Pat Irenyenko said, "if only I could climb with this shoulder. But Kat will certainly want to go, won't you, darling?"

Kat looked as though it was the last thing in the world she wanted to do, but she was too young to know how to disagree with her mother.

"We can do something else, if you like," I said.

"Oh, no, she's dying to climb up," Irenyenko said. Mommy couldn't, and so darling daughter must.

"If you're sure?"

"Of course she's sure, aren't you, sweetie? She's not at all afraid of heights. And here's the nice stunt person. There's no reason my daughter can't go up there, is there? I mean, I'm sure it's a very safe structure." She leaned a little on the last phrase.

Kick knew as well as I did why these people were here, and what the right answer was. "If your daughter is fit and has a head for heights, and if she's accompanied by Ms. Torvingen, I have no objections." She turned to me. "When you get to the top, don't touch the rigging or headsets, and don't let her near the edge. Oh, and you'd better wear hats."

KAT WENT first, keeping both hands on the pipe railings, taking a rest every few steps. It was probably hard on her eleven-year-old quads. It certainly was on mine. I felt every flex and stretch of the crowbar-shaped bruise on my left thigh. It was just pain. Clenching and relaxing the muscle would flush away the miniature clots and speed healing.

"We can stop at any point," I said.

"My mom can't do this," she said in a determined voice. In her bright orange hard hat, her head looked very big.

"True."

"It's pretty high," she said, a few feet from the top. And then, "Oh," as her head emerged from the stairwell. She froze.

"Keep going, otherwise I can't get by. That's right. Keep holding on to that pipe, that handrail, right there."

She leaned to one side but didn't move a step farther away from the pipe. Her hand was white around the metal. Keeping her away from the edge wasn't going to be a problem.

"You don't have to look down, but if you look out, across that way, you can see Sîan talking to the director, Stan Rusen."

"The guy in the glasses?"

"That's the one."

She swapped hands carefully on the pipe. "They look pretty small from here." They did. "About the same size as the figures in a foosball table."

She giggled. The hand around the pipe rail wasn't as white. I imagined David up here, picking off the figures one by one with his Nerf gun. Luz would squat down, get on her belly, and inch to the edge. The set hummed. I had helped make all this possible.

It was a small sound, a flat *crack*, and I thought, *Oh*. I thought, *I should have asked Turtledove if we'd taken Mackie's swipe card. I should have asked Mackie what he did when no one was here.* But I knew, even before I smelled the distinctive, blue-smoke scent of dynamite, even before the platform dipped and swayed, exactly what he'd done.

With all the time in the world, I took Kat's left hand and put it next to the right on the pipe, lay flat on the platform, and pulled myself to the edge.

Everyone below was crouched in the startle reflex, except Kick, who was running to the soundstage. Behind me, Ekaterina started screaming, and a split second later, so did everyone else. I thought I caught a flash of blue as Dornan lifted his face to look up. The tower swayed again. I could still smell smoke.

Below, Kick ran back from the soundstage wearing a headset. She tapped it, and gestured at me. I took off my hard hat, pushed myself back from the edge, retrieved the headset from the neatly stacked gear by the top of the steps, and turned it on with a click.

"Here," I said. I went back to the edge.

"We've got fire," she said. "Hold." Click.

She looked so small from here. Unreal. She had grabbed someone by the shoulders, was shaking them, shouting, pointing. She grabbed another, pointed at something else. A ripple of purposeful movement started from Kick's nexus.

Click. "We've got fire on your tower."

Dornan was heading towards her. She made some gesture at him that he seemed to understand, because he stopped, turned around, and walked in a different direction.

She disappeared for a moment. I could hear her breath on the headset. "Steps are gone. Fire on the cladding is spreading."

No way down.

"Is that the girl screaming?"

"She's fine," I said.

Now Kick was breathing hard. When she reappeared I saw why. She and four hands were moving the Model Forty. While I watched she gestured for someone to take her place, and started talking fast to Dornan and one of the electricians.

I could smell the painted plywood burning, and the stink of melting polystyrene.

"You should get people out," I said.

Click. "Others can do that. I'm focused on getting you down."

Orderly groups were moving towards the door, including my tour group.

"Mom!" screamed Ekaterina. "Mom!"

A tiny foosball figure in a sling lifted its face. Another figure, in glasses, dragged her towards the door. A flash: the photographer. Perhaps I should wave.

Four people were ripping all the foam from the two old sofas by the craft table. Click. "The fire's moving too fast for ladders. Can you help the girl jump?"

"Yes."

"Mom! Mom!"

"Hold." Click.

Now she appeared to be directing one of the carpenters to strip polystyrene from a sheet of plywood. Someone stood by with a glue gun. By the craft table, Dornan and the electrician were throwing things out of cardboard boxes. She put her hand up, palm out, to the stagehands dragging the air bag. They stopped.

Click. "She's going to have go into the Model Forty. We're nearly three feet over the tolerance for this bag, but she's smaller than an adult. Hold."

I could feel the heat now and hear the lazy crackle of flame. The shrieking behind me climbed to the ultrasound range and disappeared.

"We've got the bag as close as we can until you give the word. When you give the word, we'll move it in, which will take us fifteen to twenty seconds, and then you're going to have ten seconds to get her down. Ten seconds. It's plastic. Any longer and the heat will distort the seams."

"Fine."

"On your word, then." Click.

I went to the girl. "Let go of the pipe and take my hand."

She was white around the eyes, white around the lips, white around the knuckles and the soft webbing between thumb and forefinger where she was clutching the pipe. Her carotid beat chaotically against her choker.

I walked to the edge of the platform. "Kick. The Model Forty will be at exactly the same position as the Seventy was the other day?"

"There'll be more smoke on that side."

"Yes."

"But that's what you want?"

"Yes."

"Then it will be." Click.

I set my feet a foot back from the edge, recalled my muscle memory of three days ago, the lift and fall. Reimagined the effort of swinging a dummy that didn't fight back, didn't panic, and weighed only sixty pounds. Remembered the way Kick had fallen. What did the girl weigh, ninety pounds? Thereabouts.

It was getting difficult to see. Thick smoke curled thickly up the front of the scaffolding and seeped between the planks of the platform.

"Go now, Kick."

"Say again?"

"Go now."

She didn't say, *But where's the girl?* She said, "It's a go." Click.

I crossed to the girl. Three seconds. We looked at each other. "You can keep your hands on the rail, but I want you to turn around and face the steps." Eight seconds. She didn't hear a word I said. I stepped behind her. "You're going to be safe. Relax if you can." She was rigid. "I'm just going to take off your choker."

The ribbon came free. I slid the cameo off and dropped it in my pocket. She didn't move. Couldn't move. Eleven seconds.

It was a strong ribbon. I strangled her with it.

The carotid arteries carry oxygen to the brain. Deprive the brain of that oxygen, and in less than five seconds it shuts down.

Ekaterina slumped and I scooped her up. A little less than ninety pounds. Four steps across the platform. Sixteen seconds.

Click. "In place," Kick said.

Smoke poured upwards like a waterfall in reverse. Right arm under her back, left under her knees. Shift. Right palm between her shoulder blades, left on her sacrum. Balance. Inhale. Set feet. Lift like a tray. Exhale and push, push my *ki*, push the girl, push her like a basketball, nothing but net, and she lofted up and out.

She came to in midair. Had time to open her mouth, and her shriek of "Mom!" was swallowed in the plump, oofing impact of body and bag.

Click. "Got her!"

I nodded. Coughed.

"Aud?"

I coughed again. "Here."

"We can't reuse the bag. We can't do ladders."

"Fire department?"

"There's no time. Will you trust me?"

"Yes."

It was hard to tell through the smoke, but seven or eight people were working frantically on something to the left of the platform.

"Before there were bags, stunters fell sixty, even seventy feet onto all kinds of crash pads. We've made one for you." She was very conversational.

"All right."

"The pros of the old equipment are that you don't have to land in the exact center. No bouncing off at an angle. The con is . . . well, there's no bouncing."

I coughed again. The planking under my feet was getting very hot.

"What we've got is cardboard boxes stuffed with paper cups, overlaid by a sheet of polystyrene with foam glued to it. It's about four feet deep, total, and seven feet on a side. You're going to have to land very, very well. Hold." Click. "We're in position now. Do you have visual?"

I peered through the smoke. "No."

"Hold." I saw vague movement, a flash of yellow. The yellow stayed still. "I've put a yellow blanket on the foam. Do you see that?"

"Yes. But not well."

"We're positioned the same distance out from the left of the platform as the bag was from the front. Do you understand?"

"Yes." I coughed again. The smoke waterfall was charcoal, with red flickers instead of white foam.

"If you land feetfirst, you'll drive bone into your abdominal cavity, or compress your spine, but you'd survive that long enough to get you to hospital. If you land on your head, you won't. Think of it as a dive into a swimming pool from a medium high board. Dive facedown and turn. Or fall backwards, or do a double-pike somersault, it doesn't matter, but remember how the body turns in forty feet. You're aiming to land as though it's a break-fall, on your back, spread the impact—"

"Kick."

". . . keep . . ."

"Kick."

"Listen." It was hard to tell if the crackle was in her voice or in the flames now shooting up the front of the platform. "When you fall from forty feet, it's different. You will turn whether you like it or not. Get a solid departure, that's important, and spot your landing. Think about your abs, your soaz muscles, your transverse laterals. Keep them tight. The most important thing you can do is keep your chin tucked in. Your head is heavy. It will want to fall first. Keep it tucked in. Some people would say, Put your hat back on, but this is your first time, you might fall better if you have the wind going past your ears, it might help you orient yourself."

"Kick."

"When you go through the fire, hold your breath. Don't breathe the flame. It's getting fierce."

"Kick."

"I'm done. Time to jump. And, Aud, I build a good landing. Accept the fall."

"Yes. I'm taking my headset off now."

I walked to the back of the platform, placed the headset carefully on the pile of equipment, and turned. Two long or three short running steps to the edge. Short, I decided. Keep the balance over my hips.

I closed my eyes, breathed through my nose, careful of smoke. I ran it through in my head. Push from my left foot, land on right and push, land on left and push, land on right and push up into the void. Jump high. Spot—lean forward and down to spot, turning and tucking right, twisting in midair as though from *kotegaeshi*, like a cat that falls from a high shelf, tighten belly muscles, double-arm slap, chin tucked.

I ran—step, step, step—I pushed.

I passed through the sheet of flame—it was like running my hand under a hot tap, brief, intense—and then, as I should have been leaning and spotting, I felt my body want to begin a great clenching, a stretching, a reaching back for the platform.

When you can do nothing, what can you do?

And I let go, and fell, smiling.

I landed in silence, and hands reached down, small hands, and pulled me up and I stood. She said something, but I was still falling.

Burning chunks of wood came down. A spark caught the edge of the blanket, and it went up with a soft whump. Then I could hear again. Lights flashed. Men in turnout coats. Someone threw a blanket over my shoulders. Kick's hand was still in mine.

After a jump cut I found myself outside, coughing, some fool shining a light in my eyes. I pushed the penlight away.

"I'm fine."

"Uh-huh," he said, and shone the light in my other eye.

"I'm fine."

"She's better than fine," Kick said.

"Is everyone all right? Dornan?"

"He's fine, everyone's fine." Her hand was in mine again.

"How come you're not wearing a blanket?"

"I don't have one eyebrow burnt off and a displaced rib."

"It doesn't hurt."

"It will." She was smiling, an otter playing in a smoky waterfall. My face ached. It seemed I was smiling, too.

Then there was a confusion of lights as another fire truck pulled into the lot and burly figures in coats jumped down. More lights, different. Cameras.

I pushed the blanket off. It was hot. Smoke reached a hundred yards into the bright blue sky. That wasn't going to look good on EPA paperwork.

Kick was there again. "Can you walk?"

"Yes."

"We have to move back, the whole place is going up. If you don't walk, they'll stuff you in an ambulance."

"Right."

I stood up. I felt remarkably steady. The ground was perfectly still and solid under my feet.

Six cameras were rolling. Three were network teams, three were ours. Rusen coughed, shouted something at me, flames leaping in miniature in his glasses, coughed again.

"Better than a bit of propane," Kick said. "You're insured, right?"

I laughed. She was right, it did hurt.

THE AIR-CONDITIONING UNIT APPEARED TO BE BROKEN. THE AIR IN THE BASEMENT FELT too big and humid for such a small space but I doubted we'd be doing much physical work today.

Sandra's hand was in a cast, her forehead hidden behind gauze. I was surprised she was there at all. She sat by herself at the end of the bench.

Violence very often acts as a social flocculant. When added to a community—individuals suspended in a liquid of custom and mores—it separates out the individuals. The common mix, the community, is threatened. The class had watched the splashy, television light, the microphone thrust in Sandra's face, the way she had stared impassively at the body bag on the gurney as it was wheeled into the ambulance without the lights, and the class had separated her out to protect their world, the one where violence happened to other people.

Therese stood with the others. She smiled and touched people on the arm as she talked, working hard to be one of them. Her connection with Sandra would not survive.

I studied them. They studied me back while pretending they were not, except Sandra, who stared openly. She had killed a man: why should she worry about minor infractions of the social code? I stared back.

I would never know exactly the extent of her premeditation. It didn't matter. It had been my decision to help her frame a guilty man. We are the sum of our decisions.

She looked away, and in profile, without blood covering the lines, I saw the difference: the plumpness, the softness, the change of skin texture around the eyes.

I turned my gaze to the others. Perhaps the sum of my decisions stared out at them. They dropped their eyes immediately. I nodded. To them I was like Sandra. They didn't want to meet my gaze in case something leapt from my eye to theirs and invaded their brain.

"Not looking at something never, in the history of the world, made it go away," I said. "So look at this."

Southern women can't stand silence. Eventually, Jennifer said, "How do you mean?"

"I mean face it. Engage. Ask questions. Think. Talk. Don't wish it away."

Uncomfortable silence again. "I still don't understand," Jennifer said.

"How do you all feel? You, Nina. You, Katherine. What do you think? Tonya, Suze, Pauletta. Anyone?"

It was like one of the early classes. *I don't think you know what you're getting yourself into.* If I had known, would I have done it?

"All right. Do you feel proud?"

"Proud?" Jennifer said.

"Proud: feeling pleasurable satisfaction over an act, possession, quality, or relationship by which one measures one's stature or self-worth. Feeling or showing justifiable self-respect."

"Why?" Nina said. "It wasn't us that did anything."

"Sandra couldn't have done what she did without this class. You worked together for nearly three months. You hyperventilated in fear together, you threw and let yourselves be thrown, you trusted each other enough to let yourselves be choked. You all learned together."

They cut glances at Sandra. I knew they were wondering: then was this our fault?

"The thing is, we can't judge another's actions. We can never, any of us, know the struggles someone else goes through. We might think we know, but we don't."

"I'm here," Sandra said. "Why not just ask?"

"Okay," Suze said.

Silence.

"I'm pregnant," Sandra said. "He'd hurt me before. I knew he'd do it again. My kids had seen me beaten over and over. When I found out I was having a baby, I thought, I just can't let him do that anymore. I couldn't, could I?"

"No," said Christie.

"I had to protect my baby."

"That's right," said Kim.

Their shoulders dropped a fraction, they turned slightly to face Sandra. The muscles around their eyes relaxed. I could have closed my eyes and known, just by the sound of their breath and the subtle change in their scent, that the group was re-forming, that Sandra was being conditionally reabsorbed. Protect the children, the old clarion call. I wasn't sure whom I disliked the most: Sandra for manipulating them, them for allowing it, or me for sitting witness.

"How far along are you?" Nina said. "Only I was wondering if that's why you signed up."

Sandra looked wary, but Nina plowed on, unaware of what she'd asked.

"I signed up because of what happened to my sister's youngest. Made me think. I went into a coffee shop in Smyrna, Borealis—anyone know it?"

"No way!" Pauletta said. "I saw the flyer in Borealis, too, only in Decatur."

"So why'd you sign up?" Nina said.

"Because some yahoo neighbor who'd been drinking thumped on my windshield one night and I thought he wanted to jack the car. Turned out he was just staggering around. Scared the crap out of me, though."

"I saw a flyer at college," Christie said.

"Which one?"

"Agnes Scott."

I wondered how it got there.

"Coffee shop," Tonya said.

"Me, too." "And me."

"E-mail," Suze said, "a friend. That's why I was late that first day. She was supposed to come along. She chickened out."

"I nearly chickened out," Katherine said. "That first day." I remembered the footsteps in the dust on the stairwell: down and then up and then down again. "I was so nervous."

"Yeah. I thought I'd get mashed in the face first thing," Tonya said.

"No, that was later," Katherine said, and everyone smiled.

"I think we were all afraid," Therese said to me. "But you taught us a lot."

All past tense.

Then they were all standing together, even Sandra—Suze helped her to her feet—facing me, smiling.

"Thank you," Therese said. She was holding something towards me.

They were happy, relieved, ready to reminisce: they were no longer scared because they were done. They'd finished their sixteen-week course and beaten up a padded man and frightened a bookstore clerk and looked a killer in the face, and now they were safe.

"It's a small token of our appreciation."

An envelope. I took it.

"It's a gift card."

A picture of azaleas. Bright and impersonal as a southern smile.

"We didn't know what you'd want, but then we thought, Well, everyone likes coffee."

"Or tea," Nina said.

"Right." They sounded anxious.

I forced a smile and opened it. A Starbucks gift card. The kind of gift one corporation might give another. Steel Magnolias, Inc., to Aliens from the North, LLC. But they had all signed it:

You taught me so much, Jennifer.

Now I will kick ass! Katherine.

My children are safe, Kim.

Aud, you rock! Suze.

Whether you know it or not, I think you've changed our lives a little, Therese.

Please, will you let me know if you give an advanced class? Tonya.

I want more, Christie.

With sincerest thanks, Sandra.

You scare the crap outta me, you really do, but in a good way, Pauletta.

I'll never know, but I hope she finds someone like you to learn from, Nina.

I ached for them. Most them would not be able to cling to their bubble world; one day someone, something, would burst it. I wished it could be different.

"Thank you," I said. "Be safe."

S E V E N T E E N

THERE WAS A RED DOT BY THE PAINTING. "WHAT DOES THIS MEAN?" I SAID TO THE SALES associate. But I knew.

"It's sold," she said.

"Sold."

"Yes. I'm sorry. You must be very disappointed. But there are several of his other pictures available."

"I want this one."

"I'm sorry, but it's no longer available."

HIPPOWORKS RENTED The Last Supper Club and invited all the cast and crew and dozens of industry insiders, local celebrities and hangers-on, and corporate sponsors.

The party had been going for three hours with some serious drinking, including bartender stunts involving flaming shots and leaping balls of flame that were probably illegal. I stayed in a corner. My eyebrow stung and my ribs ached and I didn't want anything to do with fire for a very long time.

"Hey," said someone with a bright red face and messy black hair. John. Wardrobe. "Hey, there's a rumor going round that you strangled that kid."

"Why would I do that?"

He looked puzzled. "I don't know," he said, and wandered off. Kick and Rusen and Finkel were surrounded by admirers at the other end of the club.

I took my beer upstairs, where I found a pool table. There was no one else around so I racked the balls and began potting them in order. The color and motion and geometry were soothing, and it was good to keep my muscles moving, work the stiffness out.

"Here's where you're hiding," Dornan said.

"I'm not hiding."

"No, of course not." He watched for a while as I stroked the balls into their pockets. He coughed once or twice. We'd all been doing that, particularly the ones who had left the warehouse last. "All packed for tomorrow? Oh, you should have had that one. No doubt it's your bandaged rib."

"No doubt."

"Would you find an actual game more interesting?"

"I might." I banged the eight ball in. "Help me set up."

He dug the balls obligingly from the top pockets and rolled them towards me. I racked them. He broke. For Dornan, it was a brilliant stroke: the cue ball actually hit the clustered balls at the other end of the table. It wasn't a legal break, because only one ball touched a cushion, but Dornan and I had long ago found that making him play strictly by the rules led to a great deal of frustration. He leaned on his cue. "Try not to pot all yours in one go."

I cracked in the two and the six. He sighed loudly.

"We should give you a handicap."

Handicap. I wondered how much longer we'd able to use that word in casual conversation.

"Kick's looking very pretty tonight."

"Yes," I said, squinting down the cue at the four, which was hiding behind the eight ball. I could do it if I banked off the left-hand cushion.

"Oh, nice shot. So why is she down there and you're hiding up here?"

I chalked my cue, walked around the table, leaned, measured, stroked in the five. "I'm not hiding," I said, lining up the next shot. "I'm waiting. I asked her a question. She hasn't answered me yet."

"Aud Torvingen, you are deeply stupid."

I missed my stroke, barely clipping the cue ball and sending it spinning in slow majesty into the corner pocket. He fished it out, polished it on his jeans, whistling, and put it three inches behind the eleven, in a direct line with the same corner pocket.

"Not a good idea," I said.

"And why is that?"

"Just look at it." He would pot the eleven ball, then without the skill to spin and bend the cue ball, would be trapped behind the eight ball and two of mine.

"It looks to be a perfectly reasonable position," he said, and potted his ball, and was sadly puzzled as to how to hit anything else. He walked around the table twice. "I see," he said. "I see now. You could have explained."

"It was obvious."

"Maybe to you." He pursed his lips. Walked around the table again. "So. Kick. You asked her to go to Atlanta, where the heat will make her ill and she knows nobody and there's no work for her. Why?"

"Because it's where I live."

"Is it?"

"Don't be gnomic. I didn't understand you the first time you said that and I don't understand you this time. I want her to come and see where I live. I've seen where she lives. One weekend, that's all I ask. It's not like it's forever."

"Ah." He nodded smugly to himself.

"What does that mean? Explain it to me. Stop. Stop walking around that table. Look, I understand the pool table. It's orderly. There are clear rules. It's obvious. But I don't understand what you're trying to tell me. Clearly there are rules about things that are just as obvious to you that I'm missing. About Kick."

"Not about Kick," he said gently. "About you. As you would say, it's perfectly obvious. You've been intending to come and live in Seattle since the first day you met her."

I stared at him. "I have?"

"Of course you have. It's as clear as day. It is to you, too, you simply haven't yet put it into words. I was hoping you'd figure it out for yourself, it's better that way, but, well, all right, here it is: Atlanta isn't your home. I'm not sure it ever was."

I heard the words, but they made no sense. "It's where I live. Where I used to work. People I know." You. "A whole system."

"Which is exactly what you've been building in Seattle, only better."

He was insane.

"You stopped talking about selling the warehouse almost as soon as you saw it. Ooh, you said, they need my help."

"Not anymore. It's all gone, nothing left but burnt timber," but even as I said it, at a deeper level I felt the words rolling magisterially towards their pockets, dropping one by one, making sense. For a moment my ribs seemed as though clamped in a vise. I couldn't breathe, but it was just a memory of standing outside the woodworkers' collective, thinking, *I'll get to know these people.*

"And you do know people. You know electricians and carpenters, movie producers and actors, private detectives and reporters, politicians and local government agencies, bankers and real estate agents, even a criminal or two, not to mention two police officers who won't forget your face in a hurry. You've found a dojo. Discovered parks and restaurants and pubs."

He coughed.

"Can I have a bit of that?" He borrowed my beer. "Ah, that's better. No, there's no question. You've made more of a life here in three weeks than you've done in five years in Atlanta. I only wonder that you've managed to hide from the obvious for so long. This place is ideal for a Norwegian who isn't really Norwegian anymore. It positively reeks of Scandinavia, all clean and shiny and Americanized, full of rules that people obey with a smile when it pleases them and break with a smile when it doesn't. Ideal for you."

I thought of the Jante law, and the painting. Of Gas Works Park, the little pocket park by the Duwamish, the land I'd bought. What hope felt like burning beneath the breastbone.

"For God's sake, there's even your own personal troll under the bridge. Do you understand now? Good. Now, return the favor, please, and show me how to beat you at this bloody game."

BACK DOWNSTAIRS I reclaimed my corner seat and settled in with a fresh beer. At the next table, Finkel was entertaining an industry journalist. ". . . stroke of luck. The warehouse and its contents—the sets, the props, the costumes—were a total write-off, but we'd more or less finished shooting anyhow. The beauty of it is we get reimbursed for all that stuff we had no more use for. The negatives were stored off-site and we had the foresight to back up the EDL twice a day. Not a frame was lost. And no one was hurt."

"What are you, chopped liver?" Kick slid into the chair next to me. "How's the face? I can hardly see any blisters."

She wore a cool, summery dress the color of the Caribbean, a necklace of green turquoise tubes, doubled casually into a choker, and her hair loose. Her bare shoulders gleamed.

". . . product placement for post-production has tripled," Finkel continued expansively, "and I have two studio meetings next week."

"The man's glee is unholy," she said. "But in a way this has worked out well. We're almost certain of some kind of deal now. It wouldn't surprise me to find he's cooking up a side deal for a Hallmark movie of the week about the Great Seattle Movie Drama."

"Not if I have anything to do with it. What's EDL?"

"Edit decision line."

Which left me none the wiser.

"Anyhow, I won't have any difficulty getting work for a while, coordinating or catering."

"So you'll be busy. You won't want to come to Atlanta. I fly back tomorrow."

Silence. "I'm sorry," she said at last. "I—"

"Don't say it. Just listen for a minute. I'm going back to Atlanta tomorrow. There are some things I have to sort out there. Some papers to sign. But it should all be done by the end of September or October. The movie season will be slowing down here, and it will be cooler by then, and I'm hoping you'll come out, just for a visit, just for a weekend. You could see how I live and work, the people I know, see my life. As it was. No, please, don't say anything yet."

I began to strip the label from my beer.

"You probably think I live in a giant house with servants. My house is about the same size as yours."

She looked skeptical.

"Maybe a little bigger. But not much. And I rebuilt it myself. With these hands. The point is, I'd like you to see. One weekend. And then I'll come back. I have some tables to build for you. And I'm setting up a foundation."

She watched me pick at the white underlayer left by the label. "What kind of foundation?"

"I don't know. For people who don't know how to fight back. Sometimes that will be street people, people who've given up hope, but sometimes it will be people who have been hopelessly civilized, to the point where they're powerless to fight back against convention. I've bought the land. It'll be a series of small buildings, set in peaceful grounds along the Duwamish. There'll be classrooms and offices, some low-cost housing. Offices. General admin for the foundation, of course. My offices—I can see that there would be a good business here in film security—and your offices. For your catering business, maybe, or your stunt work. Maybe even rehearsal space, and studio space, and teaching space for would-be stunters. And a garden, where we could grow things, things to attract wildlife, or things to cook in the cooking classes. I don't know. Something that makes people feel good while they're doing it. Maybe skills workshops, like carpentry. Opportunities for people to interact with their physical world. We spend so much time in our heads. And there would be classes on the basics of survival—not just self-defense but cooking, how to balance a checkbook, basic legal rights. Maybe we'll even have some law offices for idealistic young lawyers who want to help the community."

"That's all?" I wasn't sure, but I thought she was smiling.

"I have a lot of money. I want to use it. Money shouldn't frighten people. It's a tool. A very versatile one. Take, for example, your stunt work."

"Ex–stunt work."

"No." I started working on the label around the collar of the bottle. "We talked about that. I can form an insurance company whose primary client will be you and whichever production company you're working with. Maybe others, too. I've looked into it. Underwriters make a lot of money." All the more to feed back into the foundation.

She was silent; so still that her sea-colored dress didn't move. I couldn't even see her breathing.

"You'd accept money if you won the lottery, wouldn't you?"

"You bet."

"Even if it was me who gave you the winning ticket?"

"Well, yeah. I think. Sure."

"I could do that, you know, if that's the only way you'd accept my help. I could buy every single ticket for the Washington State Lottery, and give them to you. But it would be easier to just put ten million dollars in an account under your name. Yours forever, no matter what. It's just a tool. Don't be afraid of it. Of me. It would be yours, not mine. You could play with it, or spend it, or hoard it, or set it on fire. Whatever it would take for you to not be frightened of it, or me, anymore." I put down the bottle, collected all the strips of paper in a ball. "Or you could just earn what you earn and we could figure it out. That what's people who love each other do."

She reached for my beer.

"I do love you."

She drank. "You haven't forgotten that I'm ill."

"I haven't forgotten. You have MS. But you're fit now, as long as you stay cool, and maybe you'll be able to do stunt work for years. You also leap to conclusions without thinking, you give everything, even trees, their own name, you get weird and don't talk when you should." I looked at the oddly bald bottle in her hand. "And you steal my beer."

"What? You can spare me ten million but not half your beer?"

"Half wouldn't be a problem. You drank it all."

She looked at the bottle in surprise. "Huh." She put it down. "How do you know I wouldn't take all your money, too?"

"Because my lawyer, who looks like a lizard in pearls, would eat you for lunch. Besides, I trust you. I trust you with my life."

"You already did that."

"Yes." My blistered face hurt. I was smiling again. "And you saved me."

"You let me."

"Yes. I let you help. That's what people who love each other do. I helped Dornan last year. He just helped me."

She looked around.

"Upstairs. Over a game of pool."

"He plays pool?"

"After a fashion."

"I could probably beat you at pool." She tucked a strand of hair behind her golden ear.

"No, you couldn't."

"I beat you at darts."

"We're getting off the subject."

"You just hate being beaten."

"Call it one of my imperfections."

She laid her hand on mine. Small on large.

"Kick, I want to be able to send you flowers without you threatening to kill me. I want to oil the hinge on your gate and build you better railings. I want to sit with you in our park and watch herons catch their dinner, to ride with you in a limousine to the premiere of *Feral*. I want to find out who would win at pool. So stay here and sort through all your job offers, and pick a couple, and do the work, and maybe see your doctors, and understand the shape of things to come, and then come see me—just for the weekend, if you like—and see my life. See where I've been. The weather will be lovely. But come."

"Yes," she said. "Yes."

ALL THE way back to Atlanta I stared out of the window at the clouds.

"When will she come?" Dornan said.

"September."

"Did you buy the painting?"

"No."

Another hundred miles of cloud went by.

"So what will you be doing with yourself when we get back?"

"Flying to Arkansas to talk to Luz and the Carpenters about adoption."

"You've signed?"

"I've signed. Then I'll be organizing my foundation. You'll be helping."

"Me?"

"I need people I trust on the board. And people who know how to make money. I don't want it to be one of those institutions that just sucks money into a black hole. You'll have to fly back and forth, Seattle to Atlanta, but I'll pay for first class, of course."

"Of course," he said faintly, then rang for the cabin attendant. "I don't suppose you know how to make a kamikaze?" She didn't; they agreed on a nice glass of cabernet sauvignon.

"And you?" I said.

"Ah, well, I expect Jonie will greet me with the accounts all nicely balanced and the perfect cup of Americano. No one makes Americano like Jonie."

Maybe when I come home at night I want comfort and the smell of coffee and to feel safe. For the first time, I understood something about Dornan before he did.

"What?" he said.

I smiled.

First, this is a novel. I've taken a few minor liberties with Seattle and its institutions, icons, and landmarks for the sake of convenience.

Second, this is a novel. While I taught women's self-defense for five years in the U.K., and while all the statistics used in this book (from the 1985 Women Against Rape study, the U.S. Department of Justice, the *Journal of the American Medical Association*) are real, Aud is a fictional character. The way she teaches self-defense is particular and peculiar to her.

Third, this is a novel. My MS is not Kick's MS—MS, too, is particular and peculiar. However, Eric Loedessoel's opinion of immunomodulatory drugs is very similar to my own. I'd like to emphasize that this is merely an opinion; I'm not an M.D. and I don't pretend to be an authority on these things.

A note on self-defense: If you're looking for good, relatively current (written in the 1990s) nonfiction resources, an excellent place to begin is Gavin de Becker's *The Gift of Fear* (Dell). When I started out, in the 1980s, it was with two books: *Ask Any Woman: A London Inquiry into Rape and Sexual Assault,* by Ruth E. Hall (Falling Wall Press; visit womenagainstrape.net for more), and *Stand Your Ground: Self-Defence Guide for Women,* by Khaleghl Quinn (Pandora Press). Though the 1985 WAR study is more than twenty years old, the statistics have held up remarkably (and depressingly). I haven't read the Quinn book for a while; I remember it being a little touchy-feely in places, but it beats most of what I've seen in the last few years.

When it comes to recommending a self-defense class, I can speak only to Seattle. If you live here, check out Home Alive (homealive.org) or the Feminist Karate Union (feministkarateunion.org). If you live elsewhere, and know of a good class or instructor, drop me a line via my website (nicolagriffith.com) and I'll add the link to my Community Resources page.

ACKNOWLEDGMENTS

A handful of people made this a better book. Sean McDonald, my editor, was implacable. Shawna McCarthy, my agent, dealt cheerfully with the highs and lows. Therese Littleton (nothing like the Therese in the book) and Cindy Ward offered insights on an early draft. Kelley Eskridge, my partner, helped most of all; she always does.

A variety of written sources proved invaluable in terms of pointing out things I didn't know or clarifying things I did (or thought I did). For mirror neurons, I owe a great deal to Sharon Begley's *Wall Street Journal* science column; I applied her explanations rather literally. Much of the neat (or diabolical, depending) real estate tax info also came from *The Wall Street Journal* (Ray A. Smith's Property Report, June 1, 2006). A *House & Garden* article from about ten years ago, "Dealer's Choice: The King of Ming," by Amy Page, alerted me to Chinese furniture. Lawrence Weschler's intriguing *New Yorker* profile of Ed Weinberger was the basis for Aud's examination of the fictional Wiram exhibit in Atlanta. Some of Kick's theories about falling and story come from Garrett Soden's excellent *Falling* (Norton).

Mostly, though, I just made stuff up.

NICOLA GRIFFITH, the author of *Stay, The Blue Place, Slow River,* and *Ammonite,* has won the Nebula Award, the James Tiptree, Jr. Award, and multiple Lambda literary awards. She is also the coeditor of the Bending the Landscape anthology series. She was a women's self-defense instructor for many years, until she was diagnosed with multiple sclerosis in 1993. Born in England, Griffith now lives in Seattle with her partner, the writer Kelley Eskridge.